INVASION
POWERS LEGACY BOOK 4
STARR Z. DAVIES

CHARACTER ASSASSIN BOOKS

BOOKS BY STARR Z. DAVIES

Divica Stormborn Chronicles
Stormvalor
Stormveil
Stormcrown
Divica War of Two Crowns
Volume 1: Darkness Falls
Powers Series
Ordinary
Unique
(extra)ordinary
Superior
Powers Origins
Miller: Origin
Enid: Origin
Celeste: Origin
Powers Legacy
Powers Legacy: The Prequel
Desolation
Infiltration
Insurrection
Invasion
Fractured Empire Saga
Daughter of the Yellow Dragon
Lords of the Black Banner
Mother of the Blue Wolf
Empress of the Jade Realm
Prosperous Eternity
Stand-Alone Stories
Stones: A Steampunk Short Story

This book is dedicated to kindness, compassion, and understanding. In a world where we fear what we don't understand and shun what we don't agree with, be the light. In a world where you can be anything, be kind.

AUTHOR NOTE

T HOUGH YOU'VE MADE IT this far into the series, I still feel it behooves me to share a few trigger warnings with you. The book is darker and a touch more explicit than the others have been. So without further ado, here are the things you should be wary of:

- bloody violence (there is an invasion, after all)

- explicit language

- sexual situations

- mild torture

- same-sex couples/romance

- dry humor

- forced servitude (though considering how book 3 ended, this should be a given)

- lack of cliffhanger ending (sorry)

- religious topics (some from an agnostic POV)

- tons of water-based metaphors (only some of which are sexual)

Happy reading! I hope you cry.

CAST OF CHARACTERS

ELPIS

Paige Powers — Somatic Muscle Memory; Psionic Precognition/Dreaming (and more to come...)

Gavin Powers — Psionic Perfect Memory & Psychic Navigation; Naturalist Matter Manipulation, Mutation, Environment Creation, Electromancy (and more to come...)

Easton Sinclaire — Somatic Strongarm; Kingdom recruit

Harper — FlexVision; returned to Elpis

Doctor Adams — Healing Hands; returned to Elpis

Olivia — Tracker; died in the Battle of Old St. Louis

Ugene Powers — Powerless; Paige/Gavin's dad; current Minister of Elpis

Enid Powers — Environmental Creation; Paige/Gavin's mom

Aron — Visual Linking; data analyst & Gavin's co-worker

Tudor — Parabolic Hearing; Department of Security Specialist; Paige's ex

Higbee — Natural Mutation; Gavin's boss

Bianca Pond — Super Somatic; Department of Security Colonel; Paige/Gavin's adopted Aunt

Director Levi — Levitation; Director of Department of Security

Alex Miller — Electromancy; Paige/Gavin's adopted uncle

Councilwoman Howser — Telekinetic; councilor of Elpis

Director Perlberg — Psychometry; Director of Department of Science & Technology

Captain Wilson — Department of Security Captain

Mat, Carlos, Nate, Sam, Benny, Elly, First Sergent Camden — Specialist training team with Easton/Paige/Tudor

THE HAVEN

Drake — Silencer
Emil — Lie Detector
Minister Charles Garraty — Influencer; Senior Elder
Carmen — Matter Mutation; Resource Elder
Ally — Strongarm; Guardian Elder
Luke — Telepathy; Education Elder
Julia — Healing Hands; Medical Elder
April — Wind Dancer
Dani — Transmutation Conversion
Pippen — Powerless
Mrs. Garraty — Powerless
Ajax — Strongarm acolyte

THE KINGDOM

Alric Strong the Third — former king; deceased
Alric Strong the Fourth — former Crown Prince; deceased
Queen Elena Strong — Lie Detector; mother of Alric the Fourth, Bronwyn, Cypress, and Dominic
Lady Emry — Blood Cleansing; former king's consort; Zephyr's mother
Lord Baron Strong — Elemental Control; Admiral of Tides; brother of Alric the Third
Bronwyn Strong — Telepathy; princess; second-born child
King Cypress Strong — Item Tracing; third-born child; King of the Kingdom of Tides
Dominic Strong — Influencer; forth-born child; Keeper of Tides
Zephyr Strong — Power Negation; only child of Lady Emry; Captain of Tides
Lord Vincent Greene — Operator; oversees horse breeding and sales
Nat — Energy Absorption; friend to Zephyr and his First Mate

Commander Reginald — Queen Elena's royal guard
Ingrid, Mariah, Helen, & Maddy — Paige's maids/stylists
Officer Cante — Hematology; Zephyr's friend; Easton's trainer
Officer Ody — Scopic Vision; Zephyr's friend; Easton's trainer
Finrik — Operator; mainland recruit
Ian — Aurology; mainland recruit
Jeff — Stealth; fort guard

TRIBUTES

Alice — Environment Manipulation; mainlander
Bella Greene — Nature Manipulation; islander; Lord Greene's
daughter
Everly — Telekinesis; islander
Holly — Futuresight; mainlander; left behind her one true love
Ivy — Mimic; mainlander
January — Cellular Manipulation; mainlander
Layla — Psychic Navigation; mainlander
Maeve — Organic Mutation; islander; father operates farmlands on
the island
Nora — Hematology; islander; formerly engaged to Alric the
Fourth and close with the family
River — Shriek; mainlander
Summer — Sound Amplification; mainlander

1

GAVIN

THE GROUND BENEATH ME solidifies with each step, creating a path over the sunken forest ruins where the Haven once hid. Trees with exposed roots angle against one another like frightened people leaning together. The snow is mostly gone, only clinging to the areas where the ground gets the most shade. Everything else has been churned into mud thanks to hundreds of trapesing boots.

Somewhere behind me, someone organizes the surviving Havenites into search parties for resources. I hear hundreds of voices murmuring to one another or calling out orders, but nothing they say penetrates the wall my mind has created.

It's impossible for me to look any of them in the eye. I don't want to know how many died because of my actions. The Haven is gone. Collapsed beneath tons of rocks and dirt because of my anguish. The moment I heard Drake's screams of agony as the Elders burned him, I became a beast driven by wrath and emotion, with no understanding or logic. Anyone who was in my way I swallowed in the earth or burned with fire.

Grief and disgust rip into me with each step I take away from the survivors Emil managed to get out of the Haven before I lost control. Maybe I am Desolation. I certainly made quick work of destroying the Haven.

A lump swells in my throat, and I swallow hard to dislodge it. Tears burn my eyes, but I refuse to let them fall. I don't deserve the right to cry over what I've done.

The Elders had collected all my devout followers and forced them to their knees, methodically killing those who refused to accept that I am not who they believe.

Maybe the Elders were right, even if their methods of cleansing the Haven population were extremely twisted. I killed Elders, Havenites, Guardians, and acolytes. Mrs. Garraty died a horrible death as liquified Power stone raced through her blood at my command. *I* did that to her without hesitation. When Charles Garraty attempted to stab me with a knife, I turned him into stone. Then the massive head of an Idol statue crushed his stone form, grinding him into rubble.

I did that. All of it. I became something horrific.

I sniffle and swallow again, but the lump won't go away. It cuts off my breath. *How could I have done this?* I understand the Powers that did my dirty work, but not how I am even capable of such atrocities.

Yet here I am, walking over the mass grave of my making. Each step over the ruins is stiff. I'm in shock and I know it, but I can't seem to pull myself back from the edge of the abyss. This is wrong. All of it.

In the center of the sunken ruins, the ground rises to support me. Everything else falls away into the pit, creating a moat of mud and forest around me. In some places, the sinkhole is deep enough that one misstep could mean death for the unfortunate soul who stumbles into it.

It's gone. All of it.

My body won't allow me to take another step. I sink down, sitting on my heels, hanging my head while forcing myself to hold back tears. I have no right to cry, yet I could fill this earthen moat with my tears.

What am I?

Dad would hate what I've done. It reminds me too much of what happened in the Administration Building Courtyard the day of the revolt against the Directorate—how the Directorate Chief ordered the earth to open and swallow protesters whole. What I did is the same. I am no better than the evil that my dad worked so hard to purge from Elpis. He would be ashamed of me.

I'm ashamed of myself.

"Gavin?" Drake's gentle voice penetrates my despair.

Drake was dead. As dead as a person could be. I didn't just revive him from death. Somehow, I healed him. A few scars remain on his skin, but most of the signs of his death have been erased. I don't even know what I did, overcome with grief as I was. I brought him back yet can't bring myself to look at him. What will I see in his eyes? Revulsion? Anger? Pity? I'm not sure what's worse.

Shoes thump against a hollow wooden plank behind me. I don't know where the plank came from. I can't even glance back. Instead, I bury my face in my hands so Drake won't see my grief.

He says nothing when he reaches me. Drake sinks down beside me and pulls me into his arms. I want to pull away—I don't deserve his touch—but I lean against him. As if his touch were a hammer to my wall, the dam breaks. I cry for each person lost beneath us, for each life I took and each I couldn't save.

Just as he did on the boat months ago during our journey to the Haven, Drake says nothing. He simply hugs me close, offering silent support I don't deserve. I lose track of time, of the tears, of my sense of self.

At some point, a gentle rain falls. Despite the cold, Drake's warmth holds the chills at bay. When I have nothing left in me to cry, I close my eyes and allow the exhaustion to sweep over me, dozing in his arms.

A gentle prodding wakes me. I don't know how long I snoozed against him.

"Everyone is ready for you," Drake says softly as I pull back.

There is no pity, anger, or disgust in his eyes when I dare to steal a glance. But the compassion and adoration in his eyes is almost as bad because I don't deserve it.

Both of us are soaked. The rain gives his hair a sheen in the afternoon sunshine. His hands cradle my face.

"We don't blame the sun for burning our skin if we don't respect its power," he says. His thumb strokes my cheek.

My gaze flicks past him. Hundreds of Havenites crowd on the other side of a makeshift plank, watching. Waiting. But not with fear, as I would have expected. *They* should *fear me*. I can't place the emotion they all share as they watch me, but it makes me uncomfortable. I quickly avert my gaze toward the ground.

"Do you want to go home, Gavin?" he asks.

I nod stiffly.

Drake's hands slide down, taking mine as he rises. "Then let's go."

"We—" My voice cracks, then cuts out completely. It takes a few swallows to manage putting words together. "We need food. Resources. We don't have anything for all these people."

"We have enough for now." Drake pulls me up. "Emil, Ally, and Ajax organized foraging parties earlier. We know how to survive on little out here."

The moment I'm on my feet, Drake lets go of my hands and steps back. It takes me a moment to realize he is trying to keep some distance, so no one realizes what we are to one another—what we were. Does he still want me? That he might have changed his mind devastates my soul. If he rejects me, I will collapse in on myself like a dying star. And who knows how many others will go down with me, sucked into my black hole.

Drake studies me as we stand on our own little island. The Havenites remain on the other side of the earthen moat, watching us. Watching me. Whether Drake senses my worry about his feelings toward me, I can't be certain. But he edges closer, trembling. Is he scared of me, or of the people watching us?

"Nothing has changed for me, Gavin," Drake whispers. "I think you need to hear that."

I tremble as well, but not because I worry about how the people will react. The only reaction that matters to me is his.

Drake turns to walk the plank. I can't let him leave.

I need to tell him, to make sure he understands the depth of my need for him. If nothing has changed for him—*please let that be true!*—then I will no longer hide. The last time I took a chance similar to this had been with Liam years ago. He had harshly rejected me in front of everyone, then never spoke to me again. A week later, he had a steady girlfriend. Ever since, I've been terrified of taking this leap. But the fear of losing Drake broke something in me down in that temple.

Part of me worries how the Havenites will react. Will they condemn us? Will they second-guess their beliefs that our relationship is a sin, since they consider me their savior? The Elders burned Drake for this. But none of these people have the Power to stop us. They can either accept us or find their own way in the wild.

I won't let another day pass without him knowing how I feel. I can't.

"Wait." I snatch his hand and pull him toward me.

Gripping his hand tightly in my own, I slide my other hand to cradle the side of his face, then back along the nape of his neck. Drake tenses, and his gaze darts to the Havenites watching us.

"Gavin..." His voice is weak. He's nervous, and rightly so after what they did to him. But if anyone else dares to try touching Drake, I will grind them into dust.

"I love you," I say it loud enough for at least the closest Havenites to hear me.

Drake's lips part, but he says nothing. His hand shakes fiercely in mine, but he doesn't pull away. Taking that as a positive sign, I press my luck a little further. "I am completely in love with you," I say. My heart hammers wildly, not because of our audience, but because admitting all of this aloud puts everything between us on the line. "You are the colors of the cosmos, ebbing and flowing and beautiful...and always there." The words harken back to our conversation on the boat months ago. At the time, I had spoken of my love for my family. I need him to understand that he is part of that to me now.

Drake's dark eyes search mine. I hold my breath, waiting for some response. His tension is apparent in the muscles in his neck, and the way his grip on my hand tightens.

The Havenites murmur to one another as they watch us. Their feelings on this are unclear to me. I don't care. I only care how *he* feels about this.

"Gavin," he says, his voice cracking over my name. "I already told you..." He swallows. Will he reject me in front of everyone because of their beliefs? "I'm absolutely mad about you."

Relief floods through me. A burden lifts off my shoulders as our lips make contact. I don't care what any of the Havenites think. I won't keep Drake at arm's length to spare their feelings. If these people chose me as their Idol, they will learn to accept this as well. Bolstered by this reprieve, I deepen the kiss. Drake responds positively, though he still trembles in my arms.

When he pulls back, there is no shame or guilt in his eyes. They shine like stars, and it warms my insides.

Drake lifts our clasped hands. The bracelets slip along our wrists a fraction—bracelets he salvaged from a pre-Collapse shopping mall and later gave one to me. His is charred, but still in one piece. I brush my thumb over the wave medallion on his bracelet. The crest reminds me of the ebb and flow of the cosmos.

My own mountain medallion vibrates in response to the touch. Our fingers lace together. All around us, Havenites continue murmuring to one another, watching us. I can't tell their reactions, but it doesn't matter.

"*My love is and will always be yours,*" I say, reciting the inscriptions on the back of the face of each bracelet.

"*My love is and will always be yours,*" Drake whispers. His lips brush against mine again. Does he have any idea how much I needed this? His acceptance of me despite what I've done, his rock-solid support and affection, are the foundation of my fragile stability.

"Let's go home," he murmurs.

A sense of peace washes over me. Drake doesn't hate me or pity me for what I've done. He loves me despite it all. Knowing that he will stand by me even at my worst gives me the strength I didn't know I had or needed.

I nod. "Home."

Hand-in-hand, we cross the plank. Havenites stare at us as we enter their ranks, but no one says anything. Emil smirks slightly and gives a brief nod of approval. Ally stands close to him, but I can't tell what her curious expression means. Ajax puffs up with self-importance as he raises his chin, watching Drake and me. The reactions are mixed, but I can't tell what most of them mean.

I pause when I sense something else in the earth. A familiar electronic signal. The earth pushes it upward at my command, shifting around it until it rises to the surface.

I crouch and retrieve my Elpis radio.

Home, then I will go after my sister.

2

EASTON

A SOFT BREEZE BLOWS in through the blockhouse window, promising a transition to spring. We have been away from home all winter long. Hopefully, Doctor Adams and Harper made it back to Elpis with Gavin's data and news about the attack. I wasn't sure if we should expect some grand rescue mission—Paige is the Minister's daughter, after all—but when it didn't come, I can't say I was surprised. No doubt, Department of Security Director Levi stuck to the rules. Nothing can risk the security of Elpis.

I volunteered to come to the island so that Paige wouldn't have to face any of this alone...and on some convoluted idea that I could be a hero and rescue her out of this place. Foolish. I should have known better. I *did* know better. My emotions took control. Not only have I not once successfully managed a rescue attempt, but I've only seen Paige from a distance since we arrived—on the arm of a now-dead king. Failure is not something that I can accept.

My fingers dig into the brittle wooden frame of the open window, my gaze locked on the palace in the distance.

Two days have passed since the takeover. Taking control of the fort where we now reside had been far easier than any of us expected. Most of the soldiers who backed the usurper were around the palace, and those who stayed faithful to the queen and King Cypress joined her quickly.

Rumors spread like wildfire across the island by the morning after the attack. Zephyr and Baron had coordinated a hostile takeover by killing King Cypress and attempting to seize the throne. Then Zephyr betrayed Baron once they had control and killed his uncle. Prince Dominic stepped in and stopped Zephyr. All lies. All *very* convincing lies, too.

Only Nat and I had insisted that Zephyr was innocent. Princess Bronwyn had been hesitant to accept that Zephyr had been guilty of such treason as well. Probably because she knows what he and I were doing together. But Dominic had been so cleverly thorough at proving their guilt that I had a hard time refuting it, even when I knew it was a lie.

I sent men and women we trust—or that the Queen trusts, anyway—into the town to meet in private with people to rally their support for the Queen. It's been tedious and slow going. Dominic is doing something with the ships. Despite my warnings, the Queen's commander wants more information before taking action. I think we are taking too long. I've seen massive carriages going from the palace into town, assumingly to the docks. We need to investigate them.

Yesterday, Dominic requested his mother and sister be "returned safely to him", implying that we were holding them in the fort against their will.

Today, Dominic's envoy slogs along the road toward the fort walls—just as Queen Elena predicted he would do. No doubt she and Bronwyn are somewhere below, scrambling to prepare for his arrival and the inevitable confrontation. It's the first time we'll speak directly to Dominic since the takeover.

I watch the slow procession, trying to convince myself that I'm not scared, but Dominic is horrifyingly conniving. Who knows what he will do?

When Dominic's royal carriage passes out of sight of my window, I pull away and make my way to the north gate. My nerves hum with anxious energy beneath my skin, ignorant of the spring chill in the air. *I'm not scared of him.*

Our soldiers hustle into tight formations around the gate. A few of them glance at me as I stroll past. Many of these men—some little more than boys—have been in training for service here far longer than I have. My rise to command in the Capital has set some of the older soldiers against me, but it isn't anything I'm not used to already. Elpis Specialist training was highly competitive.

Queen Elena stands in the arching gate with half a dozen guards at her back and Princess Bronwyn at her side. Commander Reginald waits on her other side. The man is in his late thirties and stacked like a Somatic Strongarm despite his Naturalist Creation Power. I met him just after the attack on the palace. Commander Reginald has worked as the queen's personal guard for nearly as long as she has worn the crown, melting into the background unless needed.

I hope he isn't needed today.

Reginald's gaze darts to me as I step up beside the princess. He doesn't hate me, but he doesn't like me, either.

No one says a word as we wait for Dominic's carriage to stop at the end of the sidewalk leading to the gate. The driver hops down and swiftly moves to open the door, lowering the steps all the way to the ground.

Bronwyn clenches her hands in front of her, trying to look demure and calm, but her agitation only enhances my own. I want to take her hand and reassure her, but don't dare touch her right now. She wouldn't thank me. Nor am I sure if she would want me to touch her. The princess is all silken and demure on the outside, but there is steel in her veins.

My gaze sweeps the envoy, calculating the guard Dominic has brought with him to the fort. A dozen men surround the carriage. Another dozen men are mounted and leading the way. Behind the carriage, nearly fifty troops form ranks. The sheer number of guards Dominic has brought with him almost makes me laugh. He's worried.

I've trained here long enough to know that every one of those troops has a carefully honed Power at their disposal. If a fight breaks out, it will be a matter of Powers, not weapons. Still, I wrap my hand around the sword attached to my hip. Months of training have improved my sword-fighting skills, bolstered by my Strongarm Power. Dismemberment is an easy feat with the sword.

Hopefully, it won't come to that, but I will protect the princess and queen with every weapon I possess.

A man I've never seen before with dark hair and razor-sharp eyes steps out of Dominic's carriage first. He must be at least as old as the Queen, if not older. The sight of him makes everyone in line tense. They know who he is, even if I don't, which I assume makes him the infamous Lord Vincent Greene. Bronwyn informed me Vincent is what they call an Operator, but we in Elpis would call an Influencer. And he's very skilled with his control ability. Something happened between the princess and Vincent at some point, but she clammed up and wouldn't tell me more. I didn't push.

The moment Vincent is out, he pauses beside the carriage door and offers his hand. A young woman in an elaborate gown steps out, her skirt gathered in her hand. Her brown hair is poised perfectly on her head in silken waves. Were it not for her fancy clothes, she would appear very ordinary and unassuming. The sight of the girl makes Bronwyn gasp. I can only assume this is Bella. Bronwyn's reaction makes me tighten my grip on my sword.

Bella steps aside, head held high, and waits for the final arrival.

The young man who emerges is all hard lines and angular features—just like the Queen. His sapphire eyes sweep our line. The sight of him stiffens my muscles. *It's him. It's definitely him.* I've seen those eyes in my nightmares for weeks. *I'm not scared of him.*

To his credit, Dominic puts on one hell of an act. If I didn't know better—and I *absolutely* do—I would buy the soft expression, the youthful hope.

As the Greenes take position at either of Dominic's shoulders and they march toward us along the avenue of flags that stretch the gap, Dominic's gaze settles on me. The corner of his mouth twitches upward in a wicked smirk. It only lasts for a moment before he dismisses me, but the recognition is clear. Did anyone else notice?

I swallow and raise my chin in open defiance. *I'm not scared of him.*

"Mother, Wyn, I'm relieved to see the two of you unharmed," Dominic says as he and his shadows march closer. His voice bleeds innocence. *This guy is good.* "I was worried when you didn't return to the palace."

Are they buying this act? I glance at the princess from the corner of my eye. She studies her brother but is nowhere near as skilled as Dominic is at hiding her emotions. Confusion and hope and sorrow war with one another for dominance on her face.

"We've heard some distressing rumors," Queen Elena says. "And I wasn't sure it was safe to return."

"About Zephyr and Baron?" Dominic's voice catches like the fake betrayal of his brother and uncle truly hurt him. He shakes his head, a stiff motion of disbelief. "It was a shock, but with the help of

Lord Greene and Bella, I overtook Zephyr. But not before he…killed Baron."

I clench my jaw so tight my teeth grind together. The leather-wrapped hilt of my sword creaks under my tightening grip and I have to force myself to loosen the hold before I break it. There's no way in hell Zephyr killed Baron.

Dominic continues speaking with his mother, but as I watch him, I can't stop thinking about how he stood behind the physician who surgically removed my eye. The empty socket burns, creating a micro-headache that I know will turn unbearable if I don't get a hold of myself. The ice in his voice that day makes my heart race now as I listen to the soothing, melodic register of his tone.

I've caught the princess's gaze. I can hear her voice in my head, pressing past the haunting memory of Dominic's voice that horrible day. At first, her voice is distant, like a far-off bell. But as our gazes lock, her gentle tone clarifies as if she were whispering in my ear.

"Easton, take a breath. Calm yourself. We are okay. You are okay." Her honey-colored eyes search my one good eye.

"Lies," I think, hoping she can hear my thoughts. *"Princess, he is playing everyone. He wants you to believe he isn't capable of any wrongdoing, but he is. Please. See it."*

She squints at me for a moment, then her lips part in terror. Her gaze darts to her mother as her stunning face pales horribly.

Her brother is a monster. Now she knows it. She read my mind. She knows what he did to me. My gut churns at the realization that I've just bared the darkest part of my soul to her. Worse is the agony that she will look at me differently now. She will know I'm broken and see my weakest points. I don't like exposing weakness to anyone.

Lost in my own thoughts, my own worry, I hadn't even noticed the Queen embracing her son. And Dominic hugs her back like a boy desperate for his mother's reassurance.

"She is falling for it, Princess," I think. *"Help her."*

"Zephyr is alive then?" the Queen asks.

"For now," Dominic admits. He pulls away and casts his eyes at the ground as if ashamed. "I don't know what else to do. I need you."

Queen Elena strokes Dominic's face affectionately. "Okay. We will sort this out, Dominic."

I nudge the princess gently, and she gets the hint instantly.

I hear her call to her mother in my mind. *"Mother, no! We can't go back there."* Bronwyn glances at Dominic, anger in her eyes. "Dominic, tell her what you've done."

His face crumples. "What are you talking about, Wyn?"

"Torturing Easton."

I do my best not to react, to remain stoic as the princess bluntly throws the horrible truth in Dominic's face.

"Who?" He honestly looks confused. "You mean Paige's friend?" He looks at me then, as if noticing me there for the first time. "I didn't do that to him."

"Dom!" Bronwyn steps toward him. I want to stop her before something horrible happens. My instincts are screaming caution.

"He's telling the truth, Bronwyn," the Queen says, studying her son.

How can she tell? I groan inwardly. Lie Detector. She should know the truth... *Except he didn't lie.* The physician did it, not him.

"You're right, Dominic," Queen Elena says. "You shouldn't deal with this alone. I should have come back to you immediately."

What?

I throw a look of utter shock at the Queen. Is she falling for Dominic's lies? Is Vincent manipulating her? Or is she making a different play?

I want to move, to speak, to tell all of them the horrible truth about this monster before us, but I can't move a muscle. All this strength and it's worthless. *What is happening to me?*

My lips part and I feel words climbing my throat. Words I don't want to speak. But I'm helpless against them. They grind out of me with a growl. "I lied."

Bronwyn freezes, a hand on her mother's arm, eyes wide on me. *I didn't lie. I didn't! Please, so help me, someone has to know!*

Bronwyn's hand falls from her mother's arm and she rounds on the older lord with Dominic. "It's you."

"What is, dear?" Lord Greene asks calmly.

"Father resented you for what you did to us during our magic training," Bronwyn edges toward me like a shield. "Controlling us. Forcing us to..." She shudders.

Lord Greene's mouth twitches upward as he takes her in. Fury burns through me like red-hot fire. What did he force her to do?

"Mother, I wouldn't be here right now if it weren't for Vincent," Dominic says smoothly, inserting himself into the tense moment. "Come—"

"No." Bronwyn plants her hands on her hips. "If he is controlling you somehow..." She cocks her head as she studies her brother.

Bella leans close to Dominic and whispers something in his ear. Her fingers slide over his shoulder. He nods, and I recognize the look in his eyes as he meets Bella's gaze. The same adoration I've seen on Zephyr's face when he spoke of Paige. *He's in love with her.*

Bronwyn must have sensed my thought or deduced the same thing, because she steps back, pulling her mother with her. The queen looks torn between her children. She believes them both. Dominic has had years to perfect his word choice. He can speak the truth without telling the whole truth. Which means his mother will never know the difference, and her love for her son will blind her.

The princess places herself firmly at her mother's side, hugging her shoulders. Stroking her arm. Something passes between the queen and the princess. I don't know what's happened, but the queen's face contorts in conflict. Is the princess telling her something mentally?

Dominic watches all of it, and his mask cracks. He lost, and he knows it. "Mom?" His voice breaks.

Queen Elena stumbles back a step, clearly torn by everything that's happened. Bronwyn must have told her something, shown her something, and given her some evidence mentally that the Queen knew as the truth. "I don't know you," she says to her son. Then her voice hardens and cracks like a whip over one word. "Go."

Dominic looks like he wants to resist, to plead his case, but instead he dips his head and turns away, shoulders slumped. Bella gives his back a reassuring rub and murmurs in his ear. What is her Power? If she is an Influencer... No. The things he did to me were of his own volition. I won't believe the Greenes are manipulating him.

Dominic knows exactly what he's doing.

"I hope you will reconsider," Lord Greene says as the prince and Bella shuffle toward the carriage. "A son needs his mother." His gaze roves over the Queen and Princess.

Had I any control over my own limbs, I would rid us of his lecherous ambitions. Lord Greene is a snake coiled around a monster.

The envoy leaves, but I remain there at the gate as the others turn and sidle back inside the fort walls. This is far from over.

3

PAIGE

COOL SPRING AIR CARESSES my face as I stand on the balcony overlooking the palace entrance. A few hours ago, Dominic left with an envoy.

His royal carriage returns to the palace and Dominic steps out, fury trailing in his wake. Whatever he left to do, it didn't go the way he wanted. He storms up the palace steps, barking commands at his guards.

Bella murmurs something to him, which seems to placate Dominic, though only slightly.

"They will see reason. And they will come crawling back before this is over!" Dominic's anger brings a smile to my lips.

Bella reaches for him again, but he shakes her off, stomping up the steps and into the palace. She and her father trail in his wake.

It has only been two days since the insurrection, since Dominic's betrayal, but every hour has felt like a century. The days pass agonizingly slowly. My new room is both a punishment and a prison. One I can't escape from on my own. I have quite literally become one of those fairytale princesses locked in a tower. But I won't wait for a prince to come rescue me. I must do it myself. But how?

I cry a lot. Especially in this new suite... Zephyr's suite. Dominic must have assumed it would be amusing to put me in the room that belonged to Zephyr all his life.

I've lost my sense of self. It's hard to hold on to myself when someone else controls my moves, my Powers, and my direction. I'm floating in an abyss, and nothing will bring me back to who I used to be.

I can't leave the suite. Dominic's control over me has loosened, but the list of things I still have no control over unnerves me. I can walk around the suite at my leisure, but when I try opening the door into the hallway, an overwhelming headache blinds me. The same happens when I lean too far over the balcony rail. Somehow, Dominic doesn't just Control me. He has planted a web of directives in my mind that prevent me from acting out even when he isn't around. His skills are impressive...and disgusting.

Someone removed all the drinks from the wet bar in the suite. I know Zephyr would have kept it stocked. He has a weakness for alcohol, and I can't imagine him having a dry room. Which means Dominic doesn't want me to drink. I can't even use alcohol to drown my agony. Would the alcohol make it harder for him to Control me? I wish I could find out.

Zephyr's smell lingers on the pillow, though the sheets were changed. I am ashamed to admit that I spend a fair amount of time laying in his bed inhaling the scent of the lake—of him.

I only cry when alone. Showing weakness in front of Vincent, Bella, and Dominic is *not* an option. But when no one is around, all I can do is grieve over my situation. If I don't take Dominic to Elpis, he will torture and kill Zephyr—a fact that often gives me nightmares even while awake. If I *do* take him and save Zephyr, I am putting the lives of thousands of innocents in danger.

The truth is, I know there is no way I can ever allow Dominic to reach Elpis. Which means I've already chosen my duty to protect my people over my heart's desire. I've sentenced Zephyr to death. He knows. The look he sent my way revealed he understood the truth.

My fingers tighten on the arm of the chair I dragged onto the balcony. He will die, and it's my fault.

When I can collect myself long enough to think straight, I attempt plotting ways out of this situation, but all of them are fantasies. Nothing I've come up with so far would actually work. I can't get out of this room, no matter what I try. I can't get to Zephyr if I can't escape. And once Dominic takes me away from here, I won't be able to protect Zephyr or Easton from a distance. Even if I run away once we leave the island, they will still be trapped. Killed.

The suite door clicks and I jump to my feet, scrubbing away the tears before anyone sees them. My heart instantly hammers hard and fast against my ribs.

Worse than being locked in this suite with the lingering scent of Zephyr on my pillow is my roommate. Dominic told me Vincent would sleep in the adjoining room—a room that once belonged to Lady Emry, Zephyr's mother—to keep a closer eye on me. I try my best to lock myself in my private room whenever Vincent is around, but today I'm too distracted.

Vincent strolls out onto the balcony and leans against the doorway, cutting off my only means of escape. "I'm pleased to see you up."

My jaw twitches. I tried attacking him the first night. I snuck into his room with a butter knife I had pilfered off my dinner tray. But as I loomed over his slumbering body, knife in hand, my fingers numbed until the knife clattered to the bed. Vincent only smiled at me. It still turns my stomach.

"You leave soon," he says. "Dock inspections report the ice is weak enough for the ships to move."

I swallow and risk pressing past him to escape.

Vincent's arm shoots out, blocking me off. He straightens, and his fingers graze my bare arm, sending a shiver down my spine and revulsion through my body. His eyes slide over me like slime. "I hope you know how to behave yourself. I can be a patient man."

What is he talking about?

He reaches up and strokes my cheek. I jerk back. "My last wife died young. But I get the sense you are stronger."

Wife? Bile climbs up my throat. Does Dominic think he has *any* right to give me away?

Vincent edges closer. I shift away, but there's nowhere to go. I'm trapped against the doorframe. "My patience only stretches so far. After you return, I expect you will be obedient." The corner of his mouth twitches up in what would be a charming smile were he not so vile. "But I have ways to make you agreeable if you resist performing your duties. I need a son."

This settles matters. I can't drag this trip out until I find a way to help Zephyr and Easton—if there even is a way.

I can *never* come back here. Not with this man waiting in my bed—in *Zephyr's* bed. He's older than my dad!

Vincent allows me to slip past, and I hate how quickly I rush to my bedroom. I fumble over the lock, but can't make myself engage it. Is that Dominic's doing as well? If I can't lock the door, I'm vulnerable to Vincent creeping in whenever he desires. Tears roll down my cheeks as I press my back to the door. I don't know what awaits me on the road to Elpis, but it has to be better than this.

I lie on the bed, listening to Vincent's footsteps as he moves around our shared parlor. Eventually, he advances toward my door. I hold my breath, heart hammering against my ribs, willing him to go away.

And he does.

For now.

I don't want him in my bed, soiling the lingering scent of Zephyr or forcing me to do things I don't want to do. And he *can* force me. His Power is like Dominic's.

If he wants me to do something, I won't be able to stop myself.

4

EASTON

I LEAN AGAINST THE open window of the fort watchtower, eyes fixed on the activity along the roads around the distant palace. Dominic's troops have been active since the takeover. Goods and massive enclosed carriages continue moving in and out of the palace grounds with purpose. They are preparing for something.

The ships are definitely preparing to launch. What is Dominic up to? Reginald seems to think Dominic will send men to rally the troops on the mainland. The goods, he says, could bribe the communities into believing he is a benevolent king. Little do they realize these are the same goods Zephyr suspected someone was stealing—that Dominic was stealing. Hoard what belongs to them under a different king, then give it all back to show his mercy and win their affection. It will probably work, too.

I can't stop thinking about what happened to the missing Tributes either. The girls who were supposed to be in the Windsor are still missing. Dominic did something with them. I know it, but I can't figure out where they are. He wouldn't kill them. They are tools, somehow. Or fodder for his experiments. Not that I know where he experimented on me. My memory of leaving that place is just...gone. There are so many little mysteries surrounding his plans on this island that it drives me crazy that I can't see the full picture.

Everyone in the fort has had a turn examining the activity around the palace, but I find it hard to leave this perch. My worry for Paige, for what Dominic will do to her, has my imagination running in overdrive. It's driven me to nightmares that were once of Dominic's torture. Now it's Paige under his knife while I'm forced to watch. *Where is his lab? Is she there now?*

My nails bite into the wood and I clench my jaw, glaring at the palace as if I can see Dominic now. Vengeance will be mine. I *will* help Paige. I have no other purpose right now.

"This isn't healthy, Easton." Bronwyn's gentle voice tugs my gaze from the window.

The princess is unlike any girl I have ever met before. Kind, patient, compassionate, and whip smart, but with strength in her veins. Not to mention she's stunning. I can never look at her for long, afraid of where my thoughts will wander.

Today is no exception. Her world has crumbled, but she still has the bearing of a leader. Her pale blue gown hugs her curves and shimmers in the sunlight that streams through the canon window. But it's her face that always draws me. Perfectly angular, soft, and alive with color. My eye drifts to her lips, then I quickly turn back to the window.

"Your mother is taking too long planning the next stage," I say. "Bureaucrats drag their feet, bickering over the best course of action while their window of opportunity closes. We are running out of time."

"We don't know that." Bronwyn stops beside me, placing her hand on my arm.

I glance momentarily at her long, thin fingers. I thought having a crush on the Minister's daughter was bad enough, but falling for a princess is so much worse.

"You spend all of your time at this window."

"Not all of it."

"Enough." Though her voice is gentle, something about that one word draws me away from the window. I turn my back to it and lean against the frame instead, crossing my arms. "I know you are worried about her, Easton. I'm worried about Zephyr. Not knowing what is happening to them in there... I've had nightmares."

The confession cracks my heart. Bronwyn is so purely good that the idea of anything haunting her makes me want to destroy the source of her pain in the most agonizing way. Hopefully, her nightmares have nothing to do with what she's learned from me these past few days. I would hate to think I've made her pain worse.

"Zephyr has been through enough," Bronwyn says. Sadness laces her voice. "Our father was never good to him. I couldn't read Zeph's mind like I could everyone else, but I could read my father. He guarded a lot of secrets I couldn't quite decipher, but he couldn't hide his hate from me. That kind of thing is hard to hide." She edges closer. "Which is why I worry about you."

I swallow, looking down at my boots. "Why?"

"Because the only thing more powerful than your fear of Dominic is your hatred." Bronwyn pauses so close to me that I can feel her body heat. She reaches up and touches the side of my face, running her thumb along the edge of the eyepatch. "Vengeance is poison, Easton."

I tilt my head away. She shouldn't touch me like that. If she knew what it does to me... *She does know, doesn't she?*

Bronwyn is a Telepath. I learned to block my thoughts during training—though I was never as good at it as Paige no matter how hard I tried—yet even with my training my mind isn't bulletproof. My face heats and I look away.

"I don't fear Dominic," I say sharply, but my words don't even convince me. Because I do fear him. Terribly. And I've never been afraid of anyone in my life. I don't like the sensation. "But he's planning something, and Paige must be involved, otherwise she would have died with Cypress."

Bronwyn flinches, and I murmur an apology.

"Princess, soldiers have been moving goods in and out of the palace for a day now, loading things into carriages that disappear down the road." I wave toward the main strip of the city. "I lose track of them among all the trees and houses, but the docks are busy. And other carriages come to the palace from that direction." I point along the north road. "Massive carriages pulled by the biggest teams of horses I've ever seen. Each one of them is buttoned up tight to outside eyes and heavily guarded."

"My mother knows all of this," Bronwyn says. She's trying to reassure me, but it does little good.

"Then why are we just sitting here? Why aren't we attempting to intercept one of those carriages or take back the palace? If we knew what he was hiding, we might have a better idea of what he is planning." I glance out the window again.

Soldiers stream away from the palace in organized lines.

"Where are they all going now?" I ask in a huff.

"Easton…"

"No, Bronwyn! I won't be talked down. My field of study encompasses hostile takeovers and military strategy. I know he is preparing for something big. And now the troops are moving."

"What?" Bronwyn leans toward the window, peering out toward the palace. Her side brushes against me and I have to step back as my chest clenches.

I hand her my binoculars so she can get a clearer look. Bronwyn snatches them and peers at the palace. Her lips move, but I can't hear anything she mutters to herself. Then she gasps.

"He's leaving!"

"Where is he going?" I ask, motioning for the binoculars.

Bronwyn ignores me, turning them along the road. A minute later, she steps back, lowering them into my hand and shaking her head. Her stunning face has paled considerably. "The ships."

I scowl and press the binoculars to my eye, following the long train of soldiers and carriages as they snake their way toward town. Then I rush to another window facing south and adjust the focus on the docks.

Soldiers rush around several large ships, loading crates of goods and entire carriages. With a curse that makes the princess blush, I lower the binoculars. Anger laces my voice. "What did I say? The queen took too long planning her next action, and now it's too late."

It's no wonder this kingdom is falling apart with this kind of leadership to guide it along. I rush toward the stairs and out the door with the princess on my heels.

Queen Elena, Nat, and Commander Reginald are easy to find. They have taken up residence in the Officers' Hill Quarters. As with any other day, they occupy the dining room with a series of maps of the island spread out over the surface, along with a map of each level of the palace. An inventory book rests open on one side of the table near Nat. When I burst through the door, they don't even pause in their debate.

"Lady Nora's father promised to help distribute as much food as we can collect to the people, and I am meeting with Lady Maeve's father about the farmlands later today," Queen Elena says sharply as if this proves some point.

"Without mounts, we can't move those goods, and Lord Greene has control of all the horses," Commander Reginald says. With no senior commanders remaining at the fort, he became, by default, the highest-ranking member of their military. His Naturalist Creation ability is unlike anything I've seen. He can bind anyone in a cocoon of vines in a matter of seconds without batting an eye.

"It's too late for all of that," I announce.

They all blink at me, just now realizing Bronwyn and I have entered the building.

"Why is that?" Commander Reginald snaps.

"Because they're boarding ships."

"I saw it, Mother," Bronwyn says quickly. "Hundreds of guards and carriages boarding nearly a dozen of our ships."

"So many?" Queen Elena pales. "But why?"

A chill runs down my spine as the answer clicks into place. "Elpis."

They all stare at me like I've gone mad. Their dumbfounded expressions cement the fact that Paige never mentioned home by name. Nor have I. Until now, it was for the best. But the need to hide the truth about home is long gone. If we aren't all on the same page, Dominic has the advantage.

I move closer, sliding their maps aside, and flip one of them over to expose a clean side. "Elpis is where we are from. And it isn't small. I don't know what Dominic knows about the city, but he is sending an army, so his intention is clear enough. Paige is the only one who could have given him the information." As I explain this, I sketch out a quick map based on what I can recall of our journey here. From the island all the way to the borders of Elpis. I mark out the two cities I remember us passing through on the way.

"Old St. Louis," Nat says in alarm, pointing at the city where we met. "He can get that far without her guidance. Zephyr reported everything when he returned to the Capital. Dominic knows all about what happened there."

I nod, but don't stop drawing. "Paige wouldn't tell him anything more without...without force. If he knows anything, he had to have tortured it out of her."

"So far away..." Queen Elena mutters when she sees where I mark out Elpis.

I stab the dot where the city is, then drop the pen and meet each of their gazes. "We can cut him off. Paige wouldn't have given him straight directions. If I can get within five hundred miles of the city..." I slump and press my fists against the tabletop, hanging my head. A curse slips out.

"What is it?" Nat asks.

"I broke my radio in old St. Louis when you attacked."

"Why does it matter?" Commander Reginald asks. "If he is taking an army with him, your people don't stand a chance."

I snort. "You underestimate our size and strength. Your island is only a fraction of what our city is, and nearly everyone has Powers."

Bronwyn's eyes widen. "Everyone?"

"I thought..." Queen Elena stares at the Elpis mark on the map. "I thought that place was a myth. The city beyond the waste, full of magic. It vanished from the world." Her blue eyes rise to study me. I try not to squirm under that gaze, so much like Dominic's.

"We need Zephyr to stop him," Nat mumbles, rubbing at his temples. "And Paige."

At least someone here understands. Paige has knowledge Dominic will want if he hasn't gotten everything from her already. Zephyr's Negation Power will be critical to stopping Dominic and his troops.

I nod. "We need to break them out of the palace. Today."

"Hold on." Commander Reginald holds up his hand, then crosses his arms over his wide chest. "If your city is really that powerful, we should let them go. Elpis can deal with the military. We need to control the palace, and if Dominic is sending the bulk of his forces away, this is our chance to move in on the palace and retake control."

"You can't be serious." I glare at him. "Every one of those soldiers headed into the city will die."

"How do you figure that?" Nat asks, more curious than anything else.

"Because we have ways of tracking our perimeter. We didn't vanish. We put up a protective barrier. If there is a threat, the Minister and the Council will activate the barrier around the city, killing anything that touches it."

"Good." Commander Reginald nods as if that settles matters. "It means we won't have to worry about any of them coming back to attack us. Let them leave."

Bronwyn looks just as horrified as I feel. "All of them? We can't afford to lose so many. Besides, it would be as good as the Kingdom of Tides declaring war on Elpis. Even if they all died, Elpis would come for us... And let's all face the facts. Dominic wouldn't do this without a watertight plan."

I chew my lip as the horrible truth of Bronwyn's words settles over us. She's right. It's precisely my worry. None of us wants a war. But if it began, I know enough about both cities to know who would win. The Kingdom wouldn't stand a chance. Unless... Zephyr was worried about Paige being used as a weapon. Can Dominic use her Power against Elpis? The very idea gives me chills.

I glance at the princess from the corner of my eye. If war is coming, I can't let anything happen to her.

"We need Zephyr *and* Paige," Nat says once more, but softer as if his words could shatter the fragile mood in the room.

This time, no one argues as they study my hastily sketched map between here and Elpis.

---

*W*E SHOULD HAVE DONE *this days ago!* The Queen and commander's hesitation and plotting could have cost us the right opportunity. I grit my teeth and fight off a wave of frustration.

Our small group waits behind the cover of tall shrubs across from the palace, waiting for the officer Nat recruited for the mission. Thanks to his Power of Stealth, he can move quietly in places where others might be seen or heard. Before we attempt to break in, we need to know what security looks like at all the exits.

The princess sits on her heels to my left, focused on the palace. My gaze sweeps over her uniform. She looks even better in blues than in dresses. It gives her an air of command as if she is in charge here. Wearing a uniform instead of a dress had been my idea.

"Dresses are hard to maneuver in when we're in a bind," I told her. "And harder to run or sneak in."

She had grudgingly agreed. Not that I want her with us. But her arguments for joining the mission were so thoughtfully constructed that telling her no would have meant explaining why I didn't want her along. Because the idea of something happening to her fills me with dread. Because her presence would be a distraction I can't afford. But her knowledge of the nooks and crannies of the palace, coupled with her Telepathy, is critical to the stealth of our mission.

Our priority is retrieving Zephyr and Paige. After that, our group will split up to secure the palace, but only as long as it doesn't risk our capture. There's no guarantee that either of our targets are even in the palace. For all we know, they could have been shipped off with the troops. But the queen insists that taking back the palace is the first step. Once we have it secured, we can send ships after Dominic.

Please be in there!

Nat waits beside the princess, his eyes in constant motion as he studies our surroundings. Officer Cante volunteered to join us when he found out about our rescue attempt. Apparently, he owes some sort of debt to Zephyr and wants to balance the scales. The only thing that matters to me is his proficiency with Hematology in a fight. Blood control can change the tide for us in a pinch.

There are five of us in total. I stressed the importance of keeping our numbers down. The fewer, the better. It's easier to sneak around with five people than with fifty.

Jeff darts across the street and dodges behind the shrubs with us. "The back entrance leading right down to the cells below is heavily guarded. As are the two main entries in the front."

"What about the garden doors?" Bronwyn asks.

"If we can sneak into the garden undetected, we are all-clear at least through the doors," Jeff says.

"How far from the garden doors to the cells?" I ask.

Zephyr is our first target. While his Power Negation will make it harder for us to use our Powers to our advantage, it will do the same for anyone else we encounter. With any luck, Paige will be in the cells with him. If Paige isn't there, Zephyr likely knows where to find her.

"We will have to sneak down two levels from there," Jeff says.

"Right past the grand throne room," Bronwyn adds. "But with the guards depleted, I doubt anyone will be there. We can sneak down past the Council Chambers from there."

I've never stepped foot in the palace. Though Reginald went over maps of the layout with me several times in the past couple of hours, I still feel like I'm going in blind. Not that I haven't trained for this sort of mission. If anything, I'm more prepared than any of the islanders. But their knowledge of the palace is a boon to their chances of success.

I'm at a disadvantage no matter who I face off against.

Bronwyn motions for Jeff to use his Stealth on the group. A strange sensation settles over me, like a skin-tight blanket over my entire body. The princess takes the lead. I can't help but admire how quick she is to take charge—and so excellently, too.

Our team hustles across the street, slipping through the trees and around the back of the palace where maintenance access through the garden will grant us entry.

From here until we reach Zephyr, we are in stealth mode.

5

ZEPHYR

*F*ORTY-SIX.

I scrub my hands, unable to shake the feel of Baron's blood slick over my skin. Vincent forced me to shower like an animal while he watched to be sure the job was done. Then he threw clean clothes at me. Jeans and a thin, black T-shirt. But sometimes, I still find dried blood under the locking mechanism of my manacles.

Forty-seven.

I wonder what Paige is doing. The tremble in my hands opens an ache to touch her again, hold her in my arms, feel her lips against mine. Thinking of her in such a way when Cypress breathes in the cell beside me feels wrong, but I can't stop myself. I need her just as much as I once needed a drink. Perhaps more so.

Forty-eight.

Always forty-eight. The number of floor tiles never changes. I've counted them all at least ten times in the last three days just to keep my mind from wandering too far down the path of despair.

But when I finish counting, the horrible truth rears its head again. I'm a dead man. I brush my fingers along the cold gray tile, laying on my stomach on my cot.

"Cy?" My voice cracks. My throat is dry. The only food and water brought down to us has been limited. I will starve or die of dehydration long before anyone kills me.

Cypress grunts softly from his cot in the adjacent cell. He spends his time staring at the wall, curled up with his back to everything and everyone. Not a great conversationalist.

If I'm going to die, he deserves to have some truth from me. I need someone else to know the truth. Someone besides Dominic.

I swallow a few times to work up some saliva, then clear my throat. "Baron was my father."

Cloth stirs. I roll on my side, resting my head on my arm. Cypress half rolls over, staring at me over his shoulder. He says nothing.

Compelled to say something, driven to share this secret, I spill the entire story. How Baron fell for my mother. How Alric refused to let them be together. The mistreatment and punishments they both endured. The horrifying mission to destroy her old community. Alric even poisoned himself every time Baron tried to stop him from abusing me, just to make her heal him.

As I let it all out, Cypress rolls on his back and props his head on his arms, staring at the ceiling. When I finish the entire horrifying tale, how the King treated me, punished me for existing, hated me for representing something he could never have, neither of us speaks for a long time.

"How long have you known?" he mumbles.

"Mom told me the truth right before she died," I say, studying the smooth ceiling. "Baron filled in the rest the day you and Paige...announced your engagement."

Once more, Cypress falls utterly still. I don't pretend to know what he is thinking. It doesn't matter anymore.

"Guess I'm not so different from my father, after all," Cypress mutters.

I eye him, but he doesn't move, doesn't say more. The silence drives me upright until I'm perched on the edge of my cot. "That's not true."

Cypress scoffs. "Don't bother sparing my feelings, Zephyr. I think we're beyond that now."

"Cy..."

"You have never asked me for anything," he says sharply. "We fought over the years, sure. Because I was never enough for anyone and you were an easy target. I'm not proud of myself."

His confession hurts. He targeted me because he felt inferior. If he only knew I felt the same way about him. How different would our childhood have been?

"Then Dad picked you over me to become Captain of Tides," Cypress snorts. "By the tides, I hated you for it for so long. It feels even worse now. He knew you weren't his son, and he *still* picked you over me. Do you have any idea what that feels like?"

Cypress hated me? I sensed some displeasure and knew he resented me at least for a while after I was named Captain of Tides...but never hate.

He pinches the bridge of his nose and heaves a long sigh. "When they died and Mom put that crown on my head, I thought things might change. But everyone still tried to push me over. Mom still pressed her influence, dogged my steps, questioned everything."

Queen Elena is like that with everyone, but now doesn't seem like the time to point it out to Cypress.

"I suspected something about Dominic and Bella, you know," he admits. "They spent a lot of time together at that ball a couple of years ago. Then she was in and out of the palace regularly after that. Her appearance as a Tribute came as a surprise to me. At first, she was flirty and attentive, and I thought whatever infatuation she had with him was over with. But then she got...weird."

Cypress winces at some memory before continuing, "I'm pretty sure she spied on my dates with the other girls. And after the incident in the igloo, I thought she threatened Paige, but Paige never said a thing about it. Now I know that's just Paige being Paige." He snorts. "I was so busy thinking about what Bella's deal was that I utterly failed to notice the connection between you and Paige. Idiot." He mutters the last at himself, then heaves another dramatic sigh. "Then, when I learned the truth, I was so blinded by my jealousy that I refused to let go. I wouldn't lose Paige to you like I did the respect of everyone in this family. Like I did the captaincy."

Cypress meets my gaze. Tears shine in his eyes. I don't know if I've seen him cry in a long time. Years.

"Mom hated Paige from the start," he admits. "She wanted her gone. Something about that first meeting with Paige set her off and Mom couldn't let it go. Apparently, Mom couldn't use her magic on Paige, which, of course, meant she was hiding something."

He snorts and his face twists in disgust. "I should have known this was coming. I was warned that someone was working against me. For a bit, I thought it was you, then hated myself for suspecting you. After you kissed Paige—"

"I didn't—"

"Irrelevant. The point is, Bella was the one who told me it happened. She said she saw the two of you outside that night and thought I deserved the truth." He grimaces. "I wasn't just angry. I was betrayed, Zeph."

"Cy—"

"Doesn't matter." He waves my protests off and presses on. "It was Dominic who suggested maybe we should send you off instead of Paige. Mom wanted Paige gone, but Dominic was worried that was exactly what Paige sought. He also said we didn't know what kind of danger she would pose if we let her go. All the warning signs were there. I was just too blind to see them for what they were."

My heart twists. It shouldn't surprise me to find out Dominic wanted me gone. He admitted as much, but I still haven't come to terms with the fact that Dominic isn't the same person I grew up with. Aside from his hurtful comments at the ball, I can only recall a handful of times when Dominic might have revealed this darker side. And I easily excused even those moments. We all get angry sometimes.

"And all I could think was, yes, if I send Zephyr away, I can still have her. Maybe I can charm her. I can keep her away from you." He makes a sound of disgust. "So yeah, I'm like my father."

Once more, the two of us fall into silence. Minutes pass. Hours. I can't tell. I lie back on the bed again and catch myself examining the cracks in the ceiling. Thin, hairline fractures that would withstand even magical attacks. Not that either of us has the right magic to break through, even if we weren't in manacles, bound away from our magic. There is no escaping this cell.

The rustle of fabric draws my gaze toward Cypress' cell. He studies me through the bars. "I'm sorry, Zeph."

"For what?"

"For being so selfish when I should have been selfless." His voice drops as if he doesn't want to say what comes next. "You love her."

I wince. Those words twist the knife already driven through my heart. "Doesn't matter. I'm already dead. I have one use to Dominic now, and when that wears out, he will kill me. Paige and I were never meant to be together."

"You got that right." Vincent steps around the corner and leans against the outer bars of our cells.

Cypress surges to his feet and rushes to the bars like a raging bull, throwing his arms through at Vincent. Startled, Vincent stumbles back wide-eyed. Cypress bares his teeth in a vicious snarl. "If I had known *you* were her trainer, I never would have agreed."

Vincent smirks, smoothing out the sleeves of his coat. "Which is why you never knew. And why her memory of me from the ball differs from the man who helped train her? Those two sides of me could never coexist in her mind."

I'm not as quick to rush the bars as Cypress. It won't do any good. But I am on my feet, hands in fists at my sides.

"Dominic will take her home, conquer her people, expand his empire, and send her back..." His gaze darts to me. Vincent's smirk turns into a broad grin. "To me."

Our conversation at the ball surfaces. Vincent mentioned making a play for Paige, should she be dismissed. I assumed he meant he would ask Cypress, who would have laughed at him. But he must have struck a deal with Dominic instead.

I can't help but laugh at the audacity. The sound is almost manic from my lips.

Vincent scowls at me.

"You don't honestly think he will hand her over to you? Paige is his secret weapon." I shake my head. "You're insane."

"He will. I need a son, an heir. Especially with my daughter leaving my household to rule the empire at his side." Vincent slides his hands into his pockets, smirking at both of us like he's the most brilliant person in the world. *Arrogant prick.* "I gave Dominic two choices. If he wanted me to keep his secret, he could either give me Paige or the princess."

My stomach turns. As twisted as Dominic is, he wouldn't subject his sister to a marriage with Vincent, would he? No. Not while he has an alternative. Which means he *will* bring Paige back. Either that or the two of them will end up going head-to-head once Dominic has whatever he's after.

Anger supercharges my adrenaline. My breaths come in hard, and my blood pumps in my ears. For a moment, I fantasize about pinning Vincent to the ground and hammering my fists into his face until there's nothing left. Lost in my fantasy, I miss what he says next.

Then Vincent saunters toward the exit like a strutting cat.

The second he disappears, Cypress turns to me, gripping the bars between our cells so tight his fists go red and white. Anger turns his face red and renders him mute. I've never seen Cypress this furious before.

"Paige won't risk her people," I say, sagging against the bars. "Dominic asked her to choose, and I already know she won't give them up for me. She won't give anything up for me. And I don't want her to."

"She will." Cypress' words are more of a growl as he struggles to control his rage. "She's given up her freedom for you before. She will do it again."

I blink. "What?"

"She came to me the night before our engagement," Cypress confesses. "She told me everything Bella had done, showed me Easton's eye, and told me about the finger. The pieces fell into place that night and it terrified me that all the signs were pointing at Dominic. The next morning, I gave him a list of menial tasks to keep him busy so I could find proof. By dinner, I still had nothing concrete. Then Paige connected the dots firmly for me. She told me Vincent was the one training her. Dominic knew and hid it from me. Then Dom came to me at dinner with evidence against Baron. I played along, hoping to trap him, but he was already playing his hand. I fell right into his trap with my eyes wide open."

Cypress closes his eyes and takes a breath to steady his raging emotions. "Paige knew I needed help as much as I did when we talked that night. She begged for Easton's freedom to go home, and for you to come back here to help me. She was willing to give me anything. I'm not proud of how I used her to get what I wanted." He opens his eyes, watery blues peering at me with deep sorrow. "She agreed to marry me if I brought you back and gave you a rightful place in the family. That was the deal. Like I said, like father, like son."

I shake my head. His words register, but still shock me. And agreeing to marry him to bring me back into the palace differs from starting a war against her own people.

"She loves you, Zephyr."

My jaw twitches.

"And I know firsthand what she will give up for you." His fury slowly burns out. "We pulled her into this trap. We need to pull her out of it."

"How?"

E SCAPE.

     Cypress says it as if we haven't both thought about it a thousand times in the past few days. As if the idea were new. But the fact remains that neither of us knows *how*. The guards who bring our meals slide the food and water into the cells. Even if we tried to rush attack, the guard doesn't have the key. He won't be any more capable of opening the door than we are.

The manacles we wear lock away our magic. Apparently, I killed the only magic-dampening lights Dominic had created. At least we aren't sick. Just shackled and without magic.

There is no way to escape these cells. Not without help.

"It's past dinnertime," Cypress grumbles. He sits on the tile floor of his cell, back pressed to the bars facing the hallway.

"How can you tell?" I mutter.

Twenty-three.

If only I could lift a tile or two and use a sharp edge as a weapon. If I cut myself, would they heal me or let me die?

"Guard change in the hall outside," Cypress says, stabbing a thumb behind him. "Vincent probably wants to starve us to death." He rolls his head to the side, eyeing me. "I get why Dom wants you alive, but why me?"

Twenty-four.

"You're his brother."

Cypress snorts. He opens his mouth to retort but freezes. His brows draw together. I straighten from counting the tiles. At the same moment, Cypress shuffles back away from the bars and rises on shaking legs.

I follow his example when I hear a soft thump in the hall. The two of us take cautious steps back from the doors to our cells, uncertain of what is happening.

After the thump, all falls silent. The only sound is the hammer of my heartbeat as it bangs all the way up in my throat.

A familiar shock of blond hair emerges on silent feet from the stairwell to our right.

"Nat!" I rush toward the bars, wrapping my hands around them.

He shakes his head and presses his finger to his lips.

On his heels, four others enter the hall outside our cells, and each familiar face fills me with renewed hope. Easton emerges, his boots hitting the steps hard, but not making a sound. When I see my old fort buddy, Jeff, I understand why.

Bronwyn stands in the center of their quintet in military blues, gaping at Cypress. Tears well in her eyes.

"Wyn." Cypress edges toward the bars. "Get out of here. It isn't safe."

"They're here to rescue us, dummy," I grumble, feeling suddenly much lighter than I had a few minutes ago.

Easton glances at my wrists as he approaches the bars to my cell. "That explains a lot." His mutter isn't meant for anyone else. He grabs hold of the cell door beside the lock and yanks. It pops with a muted shriek, then swings open. As I step out into the hallway, he moves to Cypress' cell.

Bronwyn throws herself at her brother the moment his door opens, wrapping her arms around him in a hug so tight he winces. "We thought you were dead. They changed the palace spotlights, and..." Tears roll down her cheeks.

"No luck, then. I'm still here." Cypress pulls back.

Easton ignores their reunion, scanning the rest of the cells. "Where is Paige?"

Something about the fire in his eyes, the determination to rescue his friend, makes me sick to my stomach. I can't meet his gaze for long. Dominic took Paige with him, off the island, and back home. The last time I saw her, I had Baron's blood on my hands. What a horrible way to remember me.

"Steady, son." Baron's last words have echoed in my head for the past few days, haunting my dreams.

"Zephyr!" Easton snaps at me, but I can't snap out of it.

Not until Bronwyn appears in front of me. Her hand rests on my cheek, offering comfort and reassurance in that way only she can. "Oh, Zeph."

Those two words break me open. I pull Bronwyn into a tight hug, which she eagerly returns. I can't stop the tears as I fumble over the apology. She knows. Without my magic to block her, Bronwyn can read me as easily as an open book. She murmurs sympathy as she soothingly rubs at my back.

"We don't have time for this," Easton huffs.

"Calm down," Cypress snaps. "We have a minute to spare. Paige isn't here, anyway. Dominic took her home. They're probably setting sail right now."

"Home..." The terror in Easton's voice pulls me back from the edge. I retreat from Bronwyn's arms, eyes burning, and note how pale Easton is.

"Dominic plans on using her against your city, and she won't be able to stop him." My throat tightens and I swallow. "We have to go after her."

"We should move, Majesties," Jeff says from the stairwell.

Easton nods stiffly, reaching for the manacles around my wrists.

I jerk back and shake my head. "Not yet. We might need your magic to get out of here. Take these off, and my magic will negate yours."

Nat removes Cypress' manacles, then hands me the key he must have pilfered from the guard. Cypress flexes his wrists, then rubs at them with a wince.

"Let's get the King out of here where people can see him," Cante says, following Jeff up the stairs.

"I'm no king," Cypress mutters as he follows them up.

Jeff's Stealth falls over the seven of us as we climb, stepping over the body of an unconscious guard at the top of the steps.

The palace is quieter than it was when I was escorted to my cell. Jeff's magic masks our steps and breathing, enhancing the utter stillness. I trail along at the rear of the group, keeping a careful eye on Bronwyn. The others form a ring around her as if guarding her by some unspoken agreement.

Easton lingers far too close to her side. I want to shove my way between them, protect her from him. But the look she throws at him from the corner of her eye as he examines the adjacent hallway makes me hesitate. Easton isn't so bad of a man. Better than some of her other options. Like Vincent. Just thinking about that snake makes my jaw clench painfully tight.

My steps slow as we near the stairs leading up to the suites. A voice barks orders from the throne room to my left. The doors are only open a crack, but I don't need to see who is inside to recognize the voice. Anger and hate roll down my spine.

As the others slip past the stairwell, headed for the broadcast center inside the palace, rage seizes me. I pivot, guided by hate. Wrapped in Jeff's stealth, no one can hear me. No one can see me either unless they look directly at me. Once I'm spotted, his magic will fall away without him nearby to hold it in place. Jeff's magic let me approach the side entrance to the throne room. The same entrance where I waited for the Tributes to emerge from their meeting with Queen Elena months ago.

I test the handle and ease the door open, knowing exactly how much pressure to apply to keep the hinges from creaking.

The wall sconces glow with soft light, making the golden lions around the throne come alive. Lines of benches between the side door and the dais block me from sight, but just to be safe, I duck behind the back row.

"King Dominic left me in charge until he returns victorious," Vincent snaps at the officers standing at attention before him. "To question my orders is to question the King himself."

King. Dominic isn't a king. He's a tyrant.

"Now go, organize the remaining troops, and take back that fort." Vincent sinks into the throne, clenching his fist against an arm. The nerve to sit on someone else's throne! "Bring me the Queen and princess. The rest die. You were all promised certain spoils. If you refuse to listen to me in the King's absence, I assure you that you will receive nothing but your own head on a platter. Am I clear?"

The officers emphatically agree, then turn and march toward the main doors together. I duck lower to make sure they don't spot me sneaking around the edge of the room.

What did Dominic promise these men in exchange for treason? What could they possibly want?

Vincent sinks a little deeper on the throne. I keep low, slipping around the outer edge of the throne room. He mutters to himself, sipping his wine. I make a quick visual sweep of the room, but no one else is here. The corner of my mouth twitches as I grin.

Having my magic blocked by the manacles is both a blessing and a weakness. Vincent can't feel me in the room, blocking him off from his magic. But that also makes me vulnerable to his Operator skills. I've been at his command before, as a boy. It's painful and twisted. If I don't act quickly, he can use his magic against me.

That fantasy of punching his face into a pulp returns. How many teeth can I take with me?

I slip behind the salmon-colored curtains behind the dais and wait. Vincent gives no sign he's aware of my presence. I take half a step when he shifts. I freeze, holding my breath.

Then I see the knife on his belt glint in the sconce lights. The same knife he gave me to kill my father. In the same room. My gaze darts to the wooden floor, now scrubbed clean. But I see my sin all the same.

Determined to get my vengeance, I move as quickly as my feet can carry me, sneaking up behind Vincent. I snatch the knife from his belt before he realizes I'm in the room. I plunge the knife at his neck, but the movement caught his attention and Vincent jerks away. He tries blocking the blow, forcing my hand down instead of up. The knife plunges into his white dress shirt at his side. Vincent shouts. I have seconds before he forces his magic on me, so I twist the blade as I yank it out, opening a vicious, jagged wound that pours blood.

Then my feet are no longer my own. Intense pressure on my mind forces me in front of Vincent as he clutches at his side in agony.

"*You*," he snarls through his teeth.

I drop to my knees as if pressed down by physical force. The bloody knife gleams in my fist. Then it turns toward me. I fight against my own arm as the blade inches toward my throat. Gritting my teeth, I howl in a rage.

"Vile insect," Vincent hisses. He's losing blood. It spills far too quickly from the wound, despite the pressure he keeps on it.

"You can't kill me," I growl, forcing each word out with great strain. Hopefully, Dominic left orders only to torture and not kill.

"Accidents happen. You will die eventually anyway."

The blade presses against my throat. I crane my neck as if I can move away from the cutting edge. "At least I will take you with me. You won't touch Paige or Bronwyn."

Sweat beads on his forehead. He can't hold his control over me while he bleeds to death. "Do you know why King Alric hated me? Because he knew he couldn't kill me. I tried striking a bargain with him four years ago. I needed a new wife. He refused my proposed alliance between our houses. But dear, sweet Princess Bronwyn..." He clicks his tongue and shakes his head. The color drains further from his face.

My anger pushes back against his Operator control. Sweat trickles down my temples. *What did he make her do?* I snarl as his grip on me slips. He's trying so hard to make me kill myself, but his will isn't as strong as mine any longer.

"You're dying," I say flatly. "I will enjoy watching."

Someone calls my name from the hallway. I can't tell who it is over the thump of blood in my ears. But the distraction is momentary enough to break his concentration. I rush toward him, wrapping my hands around his throat and squeezing. His bloody hands react in a panic, clawing at my arms, slipping over my bare skin.

In a surge, Vincent hammers his magic back at me. The two of us tumble to the floor. I throw a punch into the bleeding wound. He howls, then grabs my head and slams it against the hardwood floor. As I dig my fingers into his side, pulling at the wound, Vincent pins me down and forces my other hand around my own throat. I pinch the tips of my fingers in so tight I can't swallow, can't breathe. His sweat drips on my face and I flinch, but can't move.

Suddenly, Vincent's body launches backward off me. My fingers hook into his wound, ripping it open further. Then his Operator magic winks out with a sickening snap. I grunt, cough, and drag in ragged breaths as my grip releases.

"Zephyr, are you alright?" Officer Cante runs into the room with the others on his heels.

I roll on my side, eyeing Vincent's vacant stare. His neck hit one of the lion statues and snapped on impact.

Cypress kneels beside me, checking for injuries, paying close attention to where Vincent's blood coats my arm. "Are you hurt?"

"Not really," I say, my voice raspy. My gaze falls on the empty throne. "Found your chair."

Cypress chokes on a laugh as relief washes over his face. "It's not mine anymore. I abdicated..."

"Under duress," Bronwyn adds as she joins us, working very hard to not look at Vincent's bleeding corpse. "And by force. It doesn't count, Cy."

He grimaces and shakes his head, attempting further refusal of his throne. He can say whatever he wants, but his actions prove differently. As half a dozen guards rush into the throne room, Cypress rises impressively. Our companions form a protective ring around him.

And his words are laced with a clear warning of death for any who dare oppose him. For the first time, he *looks* like a king.

"Stand down."

A hysterical laugh bubbles up my throat. Dominic has Paige, but we have his kingdom.

6

DRAKE

I'VE BEEN A SCAVENGER for the Haven since the age of fourteen. Until now, our missions have been either accessible by boat or no more than a hundred miles from the Haven. But after over two weeks of walking, I'm farther from the Haven than I've ever been before.

At the edge of the cracked, overgrown, and buckled highway, I breathe carefully. We are close to the Wasteland. I almost feel as if I could see it in the distance if I squinted hard enough. But the trees still bud here. Grass and weeds along the highway spring back from winter and begin thriving. A rusted, rotting sign beside the road only reads, "Sioux". Whatever else was there wore off over time.

Ahead, the crumbling and overgrown remains of a former city promise potential foraging. We need food, water, and shelter for the night. This is the first city we have seen in days. Not that anything edible remains in these ancient cities. Eating the food on the store shelves could end in sickness or death. But the odds of a wild garden or natural edible vegetation are better there than out in the great wide open.

A glance over my shoulder tells me everything I need to know about the state of the Havenites. Exhausted. Weak. Lost. Six hundred of them shuffle along in worn-out shoes, ambling like the dead walking. Gavin is supposed to be our hope. Our savior. I've heard the whispers, the doubt they try to hide from him out of fear. I spend almost as much time moving through the masses, lifting spirits, hope, and faith in him as I do at his side. Probably more, if I'm being honest.

Children cling to their parents, faces gaunt and pale. Tears streak a few faces. The youngest were carried in their parents' arms for the first few days. Now the parents are too tired to pick the children up. The older, weaker community members linger at the rear of our mass of refugees. Those with the strength help them along, gently encouraging them just one more step.

Gavin said Elpis is far southwest from the Haven. But how much farther is it? How much farther can these people continue?

I tuck my hands into my pockets and edge closer to him.

Gavin hasn't been himself, either. I'm worried about him. He's always been a talker, at least with me, eager to share everything he thinks about...well, everything. But ever since he destroyed the Haven, he has withdrawn further into himself. He hardly talks to me anymore. He spends more time fiddling with his radio and staring at the horizon than anything else.

I've heard the whispers from the people. *Does he even know where we are going? How certain is he that we are headed toward safety? How much farther?* Gavin has reassured me he knows where he is going, and I have no reason to doubt him. Not only can he remember everything—which sometimes frustrates me—but he has an innate sense of direction. One of his many Powers, he says. I trust he knows where we are and where we are headed, which means I have to reassure everyone else of the same.

"We need to stop here for the night," I say as I catch stride with him. "Everyone is exhausted, and our scavenging parties need to find supplies."

Gavin's stone eyes sweep the landscape beside the highway. He says nothing but picks his way toward an ancient, half-collapsed building with a few letters still proudly displayed on the outer wall. *"Can—ood Su—s".* The sign near the highway vanished behind a mass of creeping vines and weeds long ago.

As we approach, Gavin moves his hands toward the building. Broken remains rise and stitch back together again as we approach. Without a thought, and with remarkably little effort, he restores the building to something much safer and more stable for everyone. By the time we step into the dirty lobby, the old hotel is solid once more. Gavin climbs the stairs to the top floor without comment.

Every door clicks open in unison. He vanishes into one in the far corner.

Emil steps up beside me at the end of the hallway. "I'll get scavengers out to look for food, water, and other necessities. You need to talk to him. Find out how much farther it will be. These people can't go much longer like this."

What does he think I can do?

Before I can respond, he turns to Ally and Ajax and begins discussing the organization of the search parties. I heave out a sigh and shuffle toward Gavin's room.

The door opens at my touch, and I slip inside to find Gavin perched on the edge of the dusty bed facing the newly formed window. But his focus is on his lap. I know what he's doing before I see the radio in his hands.

As usual, Gavin mutters to himself as he fiddles with the knobs.

"Gavin?" I stop beside him.

He gazes out the window and squints into the distance. Instinctively, I follow his gaze, but whatever he thinks he sees, I don't.

"We must be getting close to range," he mutters to himself, returning attention to the radio.

I ease down on the bed beside him and reach over, gently taking his hand. I offer a reassuring squeeze. His gaze darts to mine, startled that I'm there.

"The people are tired, Gavin," I say as gently as possible.

"We stopped."

My heart breaks a little. He's so brilliant but often oblivious to anyone else around him. I don't have to ask to know he doesn't sense their worry. "That's not what I'm talking about. It helps, but it's temporary. We need resources you can't just magic out of the air. Food and water. Suitable clothing for this climate. It's hot, and we are dressed in pants with long sleeves. It's too much. Besides, we must have walked over five hundred miles already. The people are tired."

Gavin frowns, eyes darting back and forth as if calculating something. "We're close, Drake. If I could just get this radio in range, I can call my dad and the city and ask for help. We are so close."

"How close?"

Gavin licks his dry, cracked lips and peers out the window as the sun begins setting. Then he pulls a notebook out of his pocket and unfolds it. The page he opens to is filled with numbers. Calculations.

I don't understand any of it, but he clearly does. "Six hundred miles, give or take."

"Six *hundred*?" My jaw drops. I shake my head. "It's too far. We're only halfway."

"But the radio range is five hundred miles," he says quickly. "If we can find shelter in a hundred miles or so, I should be able to reach Elpis on the radio." He clutches it like a precious jewel.

A hundred miles doesn't sound so bad, but we don't know what's out there. What if we come into range but there is no shelter? We can't wait out in the open for the rescue to arrive. Gavin restored this hotel, but if there's nothing out there, can he create shelter out of nothing for so many?

Another hundred miles could put us in the dangerous part of the wasteland, too. The people could die before help arrives. With the current state of the refugees, a hundred miles could take us a week or more.

"What if…" I shift, hoping this idea isn't entirely foolish. "What if we send a group of our fastest or strongest runners into range while everyone else waits here? Then when the trucks arrive, they can direct help to the people who need it most?"

Gavin considers this for a long, quiet minute. "I would have to go with them. Elpis will want to hear from me personally. If we want help, they won't send it to just anyone."

"But it could work?" I don't like the idea of him leaving the people behind. Not with so much doubt lingering among them. And certainly not without me. But the truth weighs against my back. I must stay behind to keep morale up while we wait.

Gavin grudgingly nods. "It *could*. But the Council of Representatives was hesitant to allow us beyond the five-hundred-mile range when we left. I'm not sure how they will receive a request to send not just one truck, but an entire fleet of them."

"Especially after you all vanished months ago," I add, deflating.

There must be some other solution. Some way to keep the people safe.

"How long will it take them to reach the group at five hundred miles out?" I ask.

"A day."

So fast! "And how long do you think it will take you to make contact once you're within range?"

He doesn't answer for so long I'm not sure he heard my question. I'm about to poke him and ask again when he breaks his silence. "It's hard to say. It depends on how closely they are monitoring the radio waves. And how urgent they feel the situation is. It could be immediately, but it could be a day or two."

"So we are looking at anything from two to four days."

Gavin nods. "Longer, if the Council argues about..." He cuts off, glancing at me nervously.

That look in his eyes makes me uneasy. "About what, Gavin?"

His jaw twitches and he avoids meeting my gaze. "Whether bringing so many outsiders within our walls is worth the risk."

The admission startles me. I blink dumbly at him, utterly stunned. "But I thought... You said they wanted survivors."

"I said they wanted to *find* survivors. Build alliances. Restore this." He waves at the world beyond the window. "I don't know how they will feel about bringing those survivors inside our borders."

Disbelief, betrayal, and anger pulse through me. I surge to my feet. "Gavin, we followed you all this way, assuming you were leading us to a better life. Now you're telling me they might turn us away?"

His brows draw together in that way he does when he doesn't understand something. "Why are you angry with me? I didn't ask those people to follow me. All I wanted was to go home. *You're* the one who suggested it."

Rubbing my face with my hand, I try to shake off the frustration. It doesn't help at all. "By the Idols..." I groan. My stomach sinks as dread floods through me. Dread and terrible understanding. "And you didn't think to bring any of this up a few hundred *miles* ago? What did you think would happen, Gavin? You were ready to just abandon all those people, the same people who stood behind you in the face of the elders' persecution, *after* destroying the only home, the only shelter they had? Unbelievable!"

"That's not what I said," Gavin says lamely.

I can't look at him any longer. I can't stomach this conversation for another second. If I don't remove myself from the situation, I'm bound to lose my cool completely. I need a moment alone.

Fury follows in my wake as I storm toward the door.

"Where are you going?" Gavin asks. His voice trembles. "Drake, I can't do this without you!"

As I turn to face him, I pause at the door and clench my teeth. "I'm not going with you, Gavin. I won't abandon my people. If you want to go home, then go. If you care about these people, about *me*, at all, then I suggest you convince your council to retrieve us. Otherwise, you've doomed us all to a slow death."

"I will fix this." Gavin's desperation only makes me angrier.

"Good." I turn away. "Signal me if you do." I tap the button on my bracelet and hear his buzz in response. The door rattles against the frame when I slam it closed behind me.

My blood boils. My stomach writhes in agony. How can I face the rest of the Havenites after so staunchly endorsing him for weeks? I lied to them all, reassuring them he would save us, see us to safety.

Gavin's detachment since leaving the Haven makes so much more sense. He didn't expect everyone to follow him. He didn't *want* them to. And he knew, all along, that Elpis might reject us, leaving us abandoned in the wasteland. So he kept everyone at arm's length.

Tears slip down my cheeks.

Gavin has never made me feel betrayed before.

7

PAIGE

H OW MANY WOULD SURVIVE if I sank this ship? It's only one of a dozen, but Dominic and Bella are on board with me. Two hundred deaths. Only two who matter. If they died, would the rest turn around or would Vincent take charge? I suppress a shudder at the thought. Dominic might be a vile monster, but at least I know he won't force me into his bed. Without him in the picture, Vincent would likely take control of the Kingdom of Tides and insist on producing heirs immediately to secure his legacy.

No. Dominic is the better choice, as much as I hate to admit it. I just need to sort out how to stall and send a call home for help.

Celeste warned me against Dreaming. She cautioned that forcing people into my Dreams could catastrophically affect not only their lives but the world. Surely, it's worth a little risk, though. *Isn't it?* If I can just reach Mom or Dad, I could warn them. Maybe they could have the Department of Security in place to stop Dominic.

But they wouldn't be able to stop *me*. Not with Dominic Influencing my every move.

I sink back on the bench of the sun deck, gazing across the water where the island had disappeared a while ago. Hours, maybe. Despite the warm spring air, the breeze off the lake is bitterly cold. I close my eyes and imagine it freezing me into a solid block of ice, impenetrable even to Dominic's Power. It's a dumb fantasy, but I can't help myself.

When we left the island, Dominic kept me below deck where I couldn't see much. But as we came further out in the waters of the lake, I spotted a dozen ships. Nearly half that again joined us from somewhere in the south. Where did they come from?

The size of the fleet is impressive, but not enough. Not on its own, anyway. If each ship has two hundred soldiers, Dominic has assembled nearly four thousand in total. Not small, by any means, but Elpis could defend against four thousand. Especially with the barrier active.

It's my Powers that scare me. I've experienced enough to know that my strength could not only dismantle the barrier but also bring the Department of Security to its knees. Without the DS, Elpis will fall. I cannot, for anything, allow Dominic to reach the city.

Not for Zephyr.

Not for me.

The thought creates an agonizing throb in my heart. The pain calls out to my Powers, aching to break free and unleash my fury. But I can't use my Powers. I can't harm myself. I can't even jump off the ship—and I tried several times already.

A shadow passes over my face, blocking the sunlight. I open my eyes to find Bella standing over me. "Dom asked me to check on you."

Right. He probably knows my Powers are thrashing inside of me. I scowl at her. "What would you like me to say? That I'm fine? I think we both know that's bullshit."

Bella rolls her eyes and crosses her arms. The wind whips her chestnut hair over her shoulder. "We will expect you to talk. If not, my father is more than happy to use Zephyr to *make* you talk. We will arrive in old St. Louis soon. From there, you *will* guide us to your city."

The emphasis she places on that sentence makes my skin itch. Can Dominic force me to tell him the truth? I need to be prepared for that possibility. I can tell him the truth without leading him directly to Elpis.

"You are assuming I care more about Zephyr than I do all the people back home," I say with a coldness in equal measure of her own. "He already knows what I will choose. Besides, you will kill him anyway when you get what you want. I'm not a fool."

Bella smiles so sweetly at me that it makes my gut twist. "That's debatable. We have ways of making you talk, Paige. You will listen to him scream and beg for the pain to stop. And the only way it will stop is if you tell us what we want to know. Do as you are told, and we will see he is healed swiftly. Dig in your heels, and we will allow him to bleed to the brink of death before bringing him back to start all over again. I wonder how long you can listen to him scream before you break."

I want to tell her I won't break. Not ever. If they want to torture me, I've been trained to take it. But I'm not sure how long I will listen to Zephyr's screams before I can't take it any longer. Am I strong enough to put Elpis before him when they push him to the edge?

I have to find a way out of this.

There must be some way. Bella and Dominic cannot win.

———— ❧ ————

S HIPS CLUTTER THE SHORELINE, tied to anything heavy enough to hold them in place. The sight of the massive camp already occupying the green space around the broken arch of old St. Louis leaves me gaping in amazement.

I've returned to the place Zephyr captured me. I recall the way he laughed when I called myself Princess Powers. How he comforted me as we approached the island when I worried about what happened to the mutineers. Saving me from Tudor in one Dream. Kissing me in another. It breaks my heart open as I follow Dominic off the ship.

The camp is enormous. I trail in Dominic's shadow past thousands of tents. The force is much larger than I thought. My assumption was that the ships all could fit roughly two hundred men, giving him about four thousand. But there must be at least twice as many here. Panic grips me. My breaths become ragged. Where did all these men come from?

A guard holds open the flap on a large tent near the center of camp. Dominic ducks through, followed by Bella, then me. I want to run, hide, disappear. But his Control over me keeps me close.

Heat hits me the moment I step through the flap. Smoke pumps out through a side flap from the small fire inside. On one side of the tent, they stretched half a dozen sleeping mats out on the ground.

Shock hits me once more when I recognize the despondent faces occupying the mats.

The Tributes Cypress dismissed. January. Alice. Summer and River. Layla. Ivy—who was taken from the cottage and marked as too ill to mingle with the rest of us. Each girl has a collar around her neck that looks like the manacles Zephyr was bound in when he was dragged in front of Dominic. Zephyr asked what happened to the girls. Dominic never answered him, but clearly, he had been using the girls for something.

"Your Grace, we are ready," a soldier says from beside the table on the opposite side of the tent.

The girls flinch back, curling in on themselves when Dominic pivots and marches to the table. *What has he done to them? And how long has he been at it?* I assumed my imprisonment in Zephyr's suite had been bad, but seeing the state of these six girls makes me feel guilty for complaining. My heart goes out to them. I wonder if I will be allowed to talk to them.

Bella remains glued to Dominic's side, her manicured fingers curled around his arm possessively. She wants these girls to know who he belongs to. Does she think any of them are interested? Highly doubtful.

I hesitate just inside the door, uncertain if I'm supposed to follow Dominic or sit on one of the vacant mats like the other girls. My gaze meets Alice's and her already pale skin turns even whiter. Layla glares daggers at Bella's back. *I wonder what that's about.* I need information, and hopefully, these girls can fill a few gaps in my knowledge. I move toward the empty mat.

"Paige!" Dominic's bark freezes me quite literally in my tracks.

My heart hammers wildly. The heat of my Power thrashes against his hold. I tremble, fighting against him, but my feet turn and march toward the table. The other girls watch me with mixed reactions, from fear to sympathy to anger.

An old atlas is open on the table when I stop beside Dominic. The corners are frayed from age and use, and the cover is ripped and wrinkled, but the contents are otherwise in fairly good condition. He nods toward the map. "You are here for a reason. Where is your home?"

My gaze automatically falls on the location of Elpis. This is the moment I've feared since Dominic announced his intentions. My entire body trembles from both fear and unused Powers burning inside of me. Tears blur my vision, making the lines on the map indistinguishable.

Bella scoffs on the other side of Dominic.

He ignores her, turning his back to her and facing me. Dominic takes my face in his hands, wiping away the tears with a tenderness that makes my stomach churn with rage. I blink furiously. I said I wouldn't cry in front of them, but the pain of this contained Power is torture.

"It's okay," he says with what he must assume sounds like a soothing tone. To me, it sounds condescending. I want to jerk my head out of his hands, but I can't move a muscle. "Paige, take a breath. In. Out."

I do as he commands, hating how it helps.

"Now," Dominic says softly. He smiles so innocently as my vision clears that, were I unaware of what a monster he is, I would believe the act. "I know what you are feeling inside. That fire. I can help you with it. But first, you need to help me."

If you would let me control my own Powers, I wouldn't feel like I'm burning from the inside out. Dominic would burn instead. Not for the first time, I'm thankful he can't read my mind but only control it.

I turn my attention to the atlas. Some compulsion in me needs to tell him the truth, to point right at the city. But I can't. And I can't lie either. As the words form in my mind, I catch a loophole in the Control. I can skirt the truth as long as it isn't an outright lie. I lean closer to the map as Dominic and his commanders await my answer.

My voice shakes. "I'm... I'm struggling... I wasn't in charge of the navigation."

Pain hammers against my temples as a headache forms. I grit my teeth. "But it's almost completely due west."

"How far?" Dominic asks as if he isn't torturing me, as if he is the most patient man in the room. Maybe he is...

"I...don't know."

"She's useless if she can't show us the way," Bella grumbles. She pulls some device out of a pouch hanging at her hip. *Is that a phone? How does it work out here?* "I'm contacting my father. Maybe Zephyr's screams will motivate her."

My heart drops into my stomach. Will they make me listen to him? I don't know if I can handle it. I would rather let this fire inside of me consume me whole. A shaky breath escapes me. "Please... I don't know how far." Truth. I could hazard a guess, but I don't really *know*.

"Bella, calm down," Dominic says a touch sharper than I expected. "We aren't there yet, are we, Paige?" His sapphire eyes remain locked on me, sparkling with false compassion.

I shake my head, wincing as it makes the headache worse. I reach a trembling hand across the atlas and point at the city we passed before old St. Louis.

Kansas City.

"We tried passing through h-here," I say, glancing at Bella to play off my fear as concern for Zephyr. Not that it isn't. "But the city is...was dangerous." Not a lie. I twisted my ankle racing Easton in the stadium there. "We should take the long way around to be safe."

Dominic considers my advice, then glances at me from the corner of his eyes. "What kind of danger?"

I shrug. "Buildings ready to crumble any second." Not a lie either. "Sections of the ground collapsed." Also not a lie, though I say it as if it happened while we were there.

Dominic nods and pats my hand like I'm an obedient dog. "That will be enough for now. In the morning, we will break camp and march in that direction. Once we're around the city, we can try this again, Paige. Maybe something will jog your memory between now and then." Though his tone is compassionate, there's a clear warning there as well. He's giving me mercy here, but it won't happen again.

"Dominic..." Bella's voice hints she thinks they should force me, take more extreme measures.

Dominic slides a chilly hand into my sweating palm, encouraging me to follow him out of the tent. "See that the girls are comfortable, Bella. Paige and I will return shortly."

I want to yank my hand out of his, but cannot. Where are we heading?

We step out into the cool spring air. A litany of voices bark commands or share conversations. Dominic strolls past all of them without a second glance, though every man bows to him, acknowledging him as their king. I peer up at the golden crown perched on his dark, wavy hair. If I squint, I can imagine I'm walking with Cypress. The two brothers look so much alike, though Dominic is taller. I remember admiring once how strong Dominic is. Now I know why he kept himself strong. It was all part of his master plan. That crown belongs to Cypress. I want to rip it off Dominic's head.

The surrounding tents are small, only big enough for two men. My military training allows me to handle long missions. I know the men can only bring what they can handle carrying. I also know this is no small-scale request for alliances. Where did all the supplies come from? Dominic is marching an army right to Elpis. He's declaring war. I can't help wondering what he learned about Elpis from Easton's interrogation that would make him launch an invasion of this size. It can't just be about building an empire. Elpis is his first target for a reason.

Easton was the one who warned *me* not to say too much, to protect Elpis at all costs. Did he break under pressure? *Will I?*

I tug at the collar of my shirt—at least Dominic allowed me to don my old Specialist uniform. It's so much more comfortable. But the heat burning beneath my skin as my Powers fight to break free makes the uniform feel too tight. Did I gain weight over the winter?

Dominic continues escorting me, offering small reassurances as we go, as if that will contain my Powers or my anger. We don't stop until we reach the western edge of the camp.

Three men kneel in a line, guarded by half a dozen more. When they see Dominic approach, all three of them straighten their spines and glare at him before eyeing me. The way their faces fall and their eyes widen tells me they know what is about to happen. They fear me. Why? I've never seen these three before.

Dominic stops, still clinging to my hand. He's remarkably calm. "The crown is a heavy burden," he tells them. "It's more than a circle of gold and jewels. It's a symbol of protection, strength, and prosperity. To preserve this, the man wearing the crown must learn to stomach what others cannot to protect those he serves. I am working toward a better life, a stronger kingdom, for all."

His hand slips out of mine, and I nearly sag with relief. I wipe my palm against my pants as if I can scrub away his gentle touch.

Dominic is either oblivious to my relief, or he ignores it for the moment. I try taking a half step backward, hoping he won't notice me slipping away, but the familiar pressure on my head tells me he isn't worried because he knows I won't leave.

He crouches in front of the three men, eyeing each of them. "My officers tell me you attempted mutiny once the mainland force reached this camp. We lost a hundred good men because of your foolish charge."

One captive spits at Dominic, hitting him on the cheek.

Dominic sighs, casually pulling a handkerchief from his pocket to wipe his face. Once the deed is done, he backhands the offender so swiftly that no one sees it coming. The captive man falls backward but is caught and righted by a guard gripping his hair.

"We serve King Cypress," the man says through gritted teeth.

I straighten, wishing I could tell them I would help them if they could just help me break free from this Control. But my jaw is locked firmly shut.

"Cypress is too weak to wear this crown," Dominic hisses. "He knows it. That's why he abdicated the throne to me."

Abdicated... I close my eyes and take a careful breath. Dominic forced Cypress to give up the crown. That Dominic didn't kill his brother tells me there might still be hope.

Dominic rises without a care in the world as he delivers their judgment. It gives me chills. "Refusing to serve your rightful king, which I assure you I am, is treason. I see now there is no regret in your decision."

As Dominic turns to face me, the world drops out from beneath my feet. I shake my head.

"Paige..."

"No. Please." My vision flexes as panic sets in.

"I told you I would help you release some of that pent-up magic." Dominic stalks toward me.

I can't stop shaking my head, as if that movement alone will halt what I know comes next.

Dominic pauses in front of me. He takes my hand and kisses it tenderly, then gives me a small nod. "It's alright. Just a little. Focus, just like we practiced."

A sob climbs up my throat. I can't stop it. The moment Dominic gives permission, the Power surges to the surface. Red mist flows out of my fingertips. Tears blur my vision, but the Power has a mind of its own. It grows, spreads. The guards around the three men back away in terror. I whimper as sorrow and relief wash through me. The pain is gone.

But their screams hit me like a thousand needles in my heart. I squeeze my eyes closed.

Then silence. The fire inside vanishes. Dominic cups my face in his palm and kisses my forehead.

"You did beautifully, Paige."

My eyes blink open. A crowd has gathered around us.

And in the center, three piles of ashes mark the graves of Cypress' followers.

I double over, suddenly overwhelmed, and vomit until nothing remains in my stomach. Dominic barely steps out of the way in time.

My knees give out and I sink to the earth, shaking violently, cold to the bone.

That was barely a trickle of my Powers. I don't want to do that again. Ever. But I don't have control.

And if that was only a trickle, do I have the Power to level a city like Elpis?

8

EASTON

THE PALACE IS SECURE, and Cypress has given a broadcast to the islanders, informing them all of what Prince Dominic and Lord Greene have done. For someone who doesn't want to consider himself a rightful king anymore, Cypress has a lot of natural charisma. His speech even moves me, and what happens on this island from this point is beyond my care.

All my focus is on planning the return to Elpis before Dominic can get there. Paige is with him, which means we will meet up again before this is over.

I rub at my temple, resting an elbow on the desk as I study the prisoner lists and resource logs. Dominic must have left *something* behind to give me clues about his plans. Many people back home assumed that, because I'm a Strongarm I'm not as bright as, say, a Telepath. But I've spent my life studying everything I could get my hands on. If knowledge is power, I refuse to be powerless.

It means I also know that we can't go charging after Dominic directly.

Paige won't go straight to Elpis and will instead take a detour southwest to buy herself more time. That gives us a second advantage. There's a river flowing west and slightly north from old St. Louis. The ship will move faster than a small army on foot or horseback. We can use that river to cut up and reach Elpis in time to warn them of danger.

I groan and sink back into the seat as the door opens. Zephyr strolls in. He puts on a good front, acting tough and dedicated to this cause on the surface, but the strain of Paige's captivity reveals itself in his exhausted, shifty eyes, and the way he bites his lip. *At least he isn't drinking.*

I peek at the wet bar to my left. Zephyr breezes right past it without a glance. When we first met, he would have stopped at that wet bar before anything else.

"Any bright ideas?" Zephyr asks as he approaches.

"A few." I break down the idea of taking the boat along that northern river to get closer to Elpis faster. Zephyr nods in agreement.

"It's a good plan. It also means we need fewer resources. What can we expect from your people?" He sinks into the seat across from me.

"That all depends on who ends up in charge," I say. "You can be sure they will send out a force to stop you if we can't send them a warning that we're coming. And it may not be friendly fire."

Zephyr cocks his head. "How could we send them...?" His expression shifts, then he surges to his feet. "Hang on." He bolts for the door, leaving me to stare at the door dumbfounded.

What the hell just happened? As I wait for him to return, I peer at the closed bedroom door. There are two rooms in this suite. Last night, Bronwyn came to my door in distress over everything. We talked for a few hours—or she talked, and I just listened and did my best to behave myself—then she asked to crash in the spare room. How could I say no?

Zephyr darts back in and drops a backpack on the desk.

Paige's backpack.

My jaw slackens as our gazes meet. A second later, I pull the pack open and rifle through the contents. Her guns, which I am absolutely keeping. I slip them out and into my desk drawer. As I pull out her radio, my gaze once more darts to Zephyr, who is grinning for the first time maybe ever.

"You can contact them within five hundred miles, right? That's what she said." Zephyr nods at the radio. "We can send them a warning once we're close enough."

"Yes." I click the radio on. It makes a noise, just static. We won't get anyone from here. Boosting the signal off the Kingdom's tower could allow us to send a message from here, but it could be intercepted by Dominic. We can't let him know Vincent is dead.

"We can't just radio them with a warning," I tell him. "You have to send a mayday to Daliah and tell her to notify Doctor Brown."

Zephyr's brows crinkle. "Who are Daliah and Doctor Brown?"

I chuckle and click the radio off. "They aren't people. It's a code. That's how they will know who we are, and that trouble is coming."

Zephyr licks his lips and nods at the radio. "So, you can use that, right? To warn them and get help for Paige?"

"Yes, we can."

He nods. "Good. I want us ready to launch as soon as possible, Easton. We can't waste much more time, even if we will end up ahead of him."

"Agreed."

Zephyr's eyes glass over for a moment, and he rubs at his throat, then he pivots and marches toward the door. "I'll go talk to Cypress."

The second he's gone, the bedroom door clicks open and Bronwyn peers out.

"Coast is clear if that's what you're worried about," I say, clipping the radio to my belt. For the first time in months, I dare to feel hope. Real, deep hope that I will return home and all of this will end.

Bronwyn steps around the desk and leans against it, crossing her arms as she studies me. Being this close to her makes every part of me ache.

"Don't go." Her request is so quiet, so desperate.

I raise my gaze to meet hers. Those honey eyes pierce my soul. I swallow the thick lump that lodges in my throat. "I can't sit by while Dominic attacks my city. Paige needs my help. They all do."

"She has Cypress and Zephyr. And you said your city can protect itself. Don't pretend this is about either. This is about your need for vengeance again. It's about your hate."

"I need answers, Bronwyn."

"And I need you to be safe." Her fingers brush my forearm.

My heartbeat increases. My gaze drifts to her lips. Then everything inside of me shuts down as I slam a wall between us. I push back the chair and rise, needing more actual distance from her.

"Dominic picked me apart piece by piece and stitched me back together in all the wrong ways," I say, hardening my voice—anything to sway her away from me. I'm broken, and she's perfect. She deserves so much better than someone like me. I stop at the window, peering out over the water, and cross my arms over my chest.

"I like your broken pieces," she says. Her slippered feet hardly whisper over the rug.

I clench my jaw. This cannot happen. "Until Dominic is stopped, I can never move on."

Her slender hand slides across my back as she stops beside me. Her chin rests on my shoulder. I should pull away but can't make myself move. "But you don't have to be the one to stop him."

"Bronwyn, you don't know me."

She steps around me, placing her body between me and the window. The hand on my back shifts to my bicep as she moves. A charged heat rises instantly, but I can't break away. Her other hand reaches up and strokes my jaw. "I do. Easton, I know everything I need to know about you."

Our gazes tether to one another, like two polar magnets dancing around one another, waiting for the other to flip and create a collision course. Bronwyn *does* know a lot. I've shown pieces of my mind, my memories, to her. But there is still so much she doesn't know. There's been a darkness festering inside of me since my mother killed herself. A thing like that can take even the most beautiful, pure soul and tarnish it. That's not fair to her.

"Remember what I told you about vengeance and hate, Easton," she says softly. "Maybe it's time to put that darkness behind you."

I swallow. My gaze dips away. "I can't. Not yet. Not until this is over."

Bronwyn sighs. "Then I'm going, too."

I shake my head, taking her arms. "No. We aren't talking about a little skirmish, Bronwyn. Your brother has declared war. It will be big and brutal and ugly in every way. Battle has a way of closing in around you. Sealing you in a box you can only escape from by killing."

"I've been in battle," she says sharply. "Or have you forgotten what happened a few days ago?"

"It won't be like that. This will be worse. Much worse."

Bronwyn rests her hands against my chest, forcing me to meet her piercing, warm gaze. "I can handle myself. But I don't know how to make myself any clearer. If you go, then I go. Because you will need me to keep you from tumbling into that darkness. And if you do..." Tears shimmer in her eyes.

She's throwing herself into this because she's afraid I won't come back. Or that I won't come back the same, which is likely true. What will the others say if they find out she came because I refused to stay here?

"Please, Easton."

Without meaning to, I snake my arms around her. That push and pull of the magnetic field between us supercharges with frantic energy. If something happened to her out there, I would never forgive myself. It could be the very thing that finally pushes me over the edge.

And if I stay, I can search for Dominic's plans. Something *must* be on this island, in this palace, somewhere. Once I have answers, I can get them to Zephyr and Cypress.

Our eyes are locked. My walls tremble. Her lips draw me in. Then the magnetic end flips. Our lips crush together for one glorious, charged moment. When I try pulling back, worried I've overstepped, Bronwyn's grip on my face firms, pulling me insistently into the kiss. Her arms slide up around my neck, fingers tangling in my hair.

Our lips part for one agonizing instant as she breathes her desperate plea into me. "Don't go."

I press her back against the window. Her lips part, welcoming me, and a groan of delight climbs up my throat.

At this moment, I would give her anything she asks for, despite only knowing each other for a few days. Those days have felt like months. From that first moment we met, when I saved her from the Strongarm attempting to capture her, to this moment, it's like some invisible force has pulled us together. I've never been a romantic and often questioned the validity of love when I've seen it bend and break so many times in my life. And I don't know that this is love, but I know I could never do something while aware it would put Bronwyn in danger.

I will stay. But I will not do nothing. I will have my answers.

Then I will make Dominic pay.

9

GAVIN

I SQUINT INTO THE darkness beyond, trying not to tremble. But everything is so...unknown. If there's one thing I hate, it's not knowing something. An owl hoots in a distant tree, making my heart hammer even harder against my ribs. So hard I can feel it in my throat. The scent of damp earth reminds me of Drake's scent and my gut twists in agony.

He was so angry with me so quickly. How could I ever make him understand I didn't ask for this—*any* of this? Maybe I should have told the Havenites to stay, and helped them rebuild before going home, but all I could think about was getting back to Elpis. Back to my parents. Drake was the one who said we should go home. I'm not built for adventure or danger. Not like Paige.

A shadow moves through the trees to my left and I tense, holding my breath and watching for danger. Drake wanted me to make things right. But I can't help worrying that the Council will refuse so many strangers. A few of them, I could get them to accept without a second thought. But nearly six hundred? That's a lot of extra mouths and a lot of unknowns.

I wince. The unknowns are stacking up. It's almost as terrifying as wandering alone in the dark.

A deer sprints out of the trees. I yelp and stumble back, falling on my backside. But the emaciated deer doesn't give me a second glance as it darts off.

I remain on the ground, recovering my courage. Tears prick the corners of my eyes. I draw in a shuddering breath. There's no time to sit around and let my fear take control.

I waited until dark to leave the hotel, not wanting anyone to see me and follow. If Drake wants me to fix this, to convince the

Council, I would rather do this alone. Failure isn't an option. Not if it means losing him.

Before slipping out, I left a note for Drake on the bed. Hopefully, he doesn't try following me. I doubt he will. I've never seen him so angry with me. In fact, I don't recall him ever being angry with me at all. We've had debates before, but that was our first actual fight.

I don't like it. Not the way it makes me feel sick inside. Not the way he looked at me like some revolting excuse for a human being. And definitely not realizing I was the reason it happened. He's right though. Whether or not I like it, those people are following me, depending on me. I can't let them down.

Brushing dirt off my hands, I steady my nerves and continue southwest. Exhaustion creeps over me, threatening to swallow me whole. I haven't slept in days. It's been two days since I left the hotel. Two days of running, walking, and stumbling in turns. Sweat has created a horrible smell that permeates my clothes. Dirt kicked up from the ground has caked on my skin. My legs want to give out utterly, and I'm having a hard time keeping focused on anything for more than a minute. But I'm close. I have to be.

The moon casts bright light against the barren wasteland. Aside from the deer and some dead trees it must be using for food, or the owl that seems to follow everywhere I go, nothing else lives out here. No grass or shrubs. Not even weeds. I'm starving and thirsty.

Drake was right. Bringing those people this far would have sentenced them to death. At least at the hotel they can forage or hunt. The land there is dying, but it isn't completely dead. I hope they are doing better than I am.

I hope Drake isn't angrier with me.

Every hour—or what I assume is an hour—I pull out the radio again and send another call for help. My fingers fumble over the knob, shaking violently. I press the button and bring it to my lips.

"This is Gavin Powers, attempting contact with Elpis," I say. My voice cracks. "I am...about five hundred miles northeast." I rattle off my coordinates to the best of my knowledge. Typically, my Location Tracking would allow me to pinpoint where I am like an innate sense of direction, but the hunger and exhaustion are warping my sense of place. I clear my throat and continue. "I won't make it much farther without assistance. Please respond. Over."

I release the button and draw in ragged breaths as I trudge on-ward. Two days of endless walking and running should put me close to range.

The landscape is flat as far as I can see. Only squat, crumbling houses or abandoned and rusting vehicles break up the countryside. What was once a highway is little more than concrete baked by the sun and broken from a century of neglect and disuse. I blink as the sun rises to the east. Day three has begun. I haven't slept in so long.

"Gavin Powers here," I say, licking dry lips. "Elpis, please respond. Over."

The radio crackles. I'm about to switch it off to preserve the battery a little longer when a voice pops from the other end.

"...Powers... Respond... location?" The voice is so broken and foreign that I fear my mind is playing tricks on me.

I freeze, then my knees give out. I collapse to the ground and release a delirious cry of joy. My hands shake as I fumble with the button. "Elpis? Is this...home?"

"What is your location, Powers?" she asks.

I fumble for the notebook, noticing the dirt under my nails as I shuffle through the pages. "I...I'm not sure." My vision blurs and I can't read my writing, no matter how hard I blink.

An old road sign lies on the ground beside me. I brush it off, cutting my palm on a wayward stick. "The sign says 81, Norfolk 25."

The radio falls silent, and dread clenches me. Did that get through before the signal dropped? Do they even know what the sign means? I cradle the radio like a precious jewel, willing it to make noise again, to hear the girl talk.

But another voice responds instead. One I recognize despite months away. Aunt Bianca.

"Gavin, are you hurt?" she asks.

"No. But I'm...hungry. Thirsty." Tears blur my vision and roll down my cheeks. I've never been so happy to hear her voice before.

"Are you alone? Are Paige and Easton with you?" she asks.

All my relief washes away and I choke down a sob. "No. The Kingdom..."

"It's okay, Gavin. We know." Her voice soothes my frayed nerves, despite the rough edge in it. How do they know what happened to Paige and Easton? What happened to Olivia, Harper, and Doctor

Adams? Bianca isn't asking about them. Did they make it home? "I've notified your father that you've contacted us. How far can you make it to meet?"

Panic grips me. How far? They won't come get me. Not so far from the city. Which means they won't retrieve the Havenites either. Drake will die hating me. "No. I can't..."

"No problem, Gavin. Take a breath." Bianca sounds so calm. "Find a safe place to lie low. Leave a signal in the open for a drone. We will scout and send a truck."

"No, listen to me." Desperation tightens my throat. "I'm not alone."

"Are you in danger?"

"No. I brought...people. We are starving, thirsty. They need shelter."

"One step at a time, Gavin," she says gently, like reassuring a toddler. Her tone angers me.

My voice takes on a razor-sharp edge and the words pour out in a rush. It rises toward a fevered pitch by the end. "I won't return without them. They are out here suffering because of me. I won't leave them. If you don't send trucks for all of us, don't send trucks at all."

"Calm down. It's okay. We will see what we can do. How many did you bring?"

I swallow, blinking furiously to fight off tears. "Six hundred and eleven."

Silence greets me. My heart jumps into my throat. Moving so many with the vehicles Elpis has available will be a huge undertaking. And the longer this silence draws out, the more worried I am that they will refuse.

"Please." My voice cracks. I told Drake I would fix this. *I must.* "Help them. Most are Powerless. They won't survive out here. I..." The confession dies on my lips. I want to admit that I destroyed their home, their civilization, their way of life. I buried their crops and crushed their water treatment center. My grief caused me to lose control. My final plea is a whisper. "Please."

"We will see what we can do, Gavin," Bianca reassures me. "For now, we will send supplies. Then see where we can take it from there. One step at a time, Gavin."

I wish she would stop saying my name. It's like she thinks I'm volatile. The very notion makes me angry, but I'm too exhausted to do much more than sag.

"Sit tight," she says. "The drone is already on the way. We are getting trucks ready. Keep yourself safe."

I lay on the brittle, dry ground and close my eyes, clinging to the radio. I couldn't take another step if I wanted to. The exhaustion overwhelms me, and I drift to sleep there in the middle of the road. I don't even dream.

S OMETHING BUZZES ABOVE ME. I blink, shielding my eyes from the sun to assess the situation. A drone. It hums, circling over me, then darting around the area. I'm in range. That must be enough for now.

M OVEMENT JOSTLES ME AWAKE. As I shift, something tugs at my arm. In a panic, I reach down and rip it away. A needle and tube. An I.V. It's at this moment I realize I'm no longer on the road but on a gurney inside a truck.

No. No, I can't let them take me home. What will happen to the Havenites?

I thrash, bolting upright as hands attempt to hold me down. "Drake... I can't... I have to get Drake! I can't leave him. I can't..." My throat tightens and tears roll down my temples.

"Gavin, breathe." The voice stills me.

I blink furiously to try clearing my vision, not allowing myself to believe this is real.

Perched on the edge of a bench beside my gurney, Dad leans toward me, clinging to my wrist. His gaze is steady, but full of worry. His face is gaunter than I remember, and he has more gray hair along his temples. But it's Him. Dad is here unless hunger and dehydration have created this brief fantasy.

"It's okay," he reassures me. "Breathe."

I ease back down, sliding his hand into my own. "Is it really you?"

"It is, son. Everything will be fine." His grip on my hand tightens, but his gaze moves over me.

I follow it.

Doctor Adams and Dad's friend Rosie work together adjusting my meds, heads bent together. The truck moves so smoothly it takes a moment to realize we are moving at all. Dad never releases his hold on my hand. I should be relieved, overwhelmed, to see him, and I am. But I can't stop thinking about Drake.

"Where are we going?" I ask.

"You need proper rest and medical attention," Dad says.

"You're taking me back to Elpis?" I try pulling away, unsure how to stop them. Panic claws at my chest. *Drake...* I can't leave him. I said I would fix it. I must, otherwise I lose Drake and that's something I know I can't handle. If it came down to it, I would choose death in the wasteland over losing him.

"Gavin—"

"No!" I jerk my hand away. "We can't leave those people out there, Dad!"

"We need to proceed with caution," he says calmly.

This is it. *This* is what I feared. The Council will drag its feet while the Havenites starve. Tears once more well in my eyes. I will lose Drake. *No. Nonono....*

"Stop the truck." The words scratch out of my throat.

"Gavin..." Dad is trying to calm me like he's always done since I was little. But I'm not that boy any longer. I hate change, but I *have* changed.

A surge of Power surges through me.

"Stop the truck!" I thrust a palm against the wall of the truck. The Electromancy pulses outward on contact. The engine cuts out and the truck rolls to a stop.

Everyone raises their eyebrows as the drivers in the cab attempt to figure out what just happened. But I know what happened.

Dad does, too. He leans back, examining me curiously. I seize this moment to sway him before he can put too many arguments together.

"Dad, you wanted to know if there are other people out there. And there are. Far more than we thought. Some of those people need us. Need *me*. I told them we could help. They lost everything because of me and followed me hundreds of miles." I close my fist, feeling the hum of the engine in my grasp. It roars to life, then the truck turns northeast. In the cab, the drivers argue over what's happening, and how they can regain control of the truck. But they won't. "Bianca said she would send supplies."

"Gav—"

"Was that a lie?" My heart twists.

"No," Dad eyes the cab through a small window, watching as the drivers fight for control. A losing battle. Is that fascination in his dark eyes? "But we need to see that you're safe."

"I won't go without Drake. Dad, please..." I can't bring the words I want to say to my lips. That I love Drake. My Location Tracking guides the truck in a straight line toward the hotel where I left Drake. It's a long drive, but I won't be turned away.

"Your mother is waiting for you, Gavin," Dad says softly. "She...hasn't been the same since you disappeared. Nor has Gram or anyone else in the family. If you don't come home, I..." His voice cracks. He looks on the verge of tears. "We don't know what happened to your sister yet. Just that this Kingdom probably took her."

Paige. She's in danger, but I can't tell Dad that. Not yet. Last I knew, she was close to the king and that Bella girl was threatening her. "King Cypress won't let anything happen to her."

Dad frowns. "How do you know?"

I need his help, which means he needs to understand this situation. I tell him what I know about where Paige is, and how she has talked to me in dreams, though I leave out some of the more dangerous bits.

Dad's shoulders sag. "Then Paige is okay for now. And Easton is alive, at least." His eyes take on that look they always adopt when he is calculating something, putting puzzle pieces together to see how they all fit.

"Dad," I say, interrupting him before his mind can go too far from where I need him to be. "You want me home and safe. I want that, too. If we retrieve the Havenites and return to Elpis, I will come home. But I can't leave them. They..." How do I tell him what happened, and why these people are following me? I can't. Not yet. "It's a long story, Dad, but they are depending on me. We have a moral duty to help those in need."

I expect Dad to flinch as I throw his lessons back at him. All my life he taught me about moral duty, equality, and fairness. But what they are doing right now to the Havenites isn't fair. Instead of flinching, Dad smiles.

"Who are you and what did you do with my son?" he asks. Pride shines in his voice. "Is it safe between here and wherever they are?"

"Safe as anywhere could be without food."

He nods. "Okay then. Let the drivers take over so Doctor Adams and Rosie can treat you. Then you can explain it all to me."

"Fine."

10

DRAKE

I *WILL FIX THIS*. It's all Gavin left in his note, but it's enough for me to know where he's gone. Alone.

Days have passed since he vanished. His departure hurt worse than I care to admit to anyone. I'm not angry that he left to do what I insisted he do. I'm not even surprised he did it. But I am worried. Emil tried reassuring me that, if anyone can take care of themselves, it's Gavin. But Emil doesn't know Gavin like I do. His gifts won't save him from everything. There are dangers out there that could swallow him whole—and leaving with the memory of my anger in his heart could be the most dangerous of all.

I'm not exactly proud of how I reacted. A few hours later, after wallowing in my regret over my outburst, I returned to his room to apologize. But he was already gone.

When I brought the note to Emil, Ajax, and Ally, I wanted to go after him. The three of them wouldn't allow me to leave. It isn't safe out there and they insisted Gavin could handle himself. I'm not so sure.

Every day has been agony. What if I never see Gavin again? What if my last words to him were anger?

The hotel isn't big enough with so many people here. I've taken to my room, hiding from everyone while they send scavengers out for supplies and hunting parties to forage for edible foods. Ally was angry when I refused to help with the hunt. She thought the distraction would do me good, but I would be more of a danger to the hunting party than a help. Not when I can't stop worrying about Gavin.

Ajax has pleaded with me to reassure the people. Gavin's disappearance has caused a ripple of confusion, fear, and anger through the Havenites. Ajax worries they will turn down dark paths without assurances that Gavin is out getting help. But I can't face the people. Not knowing that Gavin had known all along that Elpis might not come to our aid, that they might abandon us to death. How can I possibly reassure them when I no longer feel certain of anything, either? A better leader would give hope even when they had none for themselves.

I never claimed to be a leader at all, let alone a good one.

As I sit in the musty armchair beside my bedroom window, I sniffle and wipe away tears. I was too hard on Gavin. We thrust so much onto his shoulders so quickly. I should have been more understanding. Being the Idol of Creation can't be an easy burden to bear.

A knock on the door makes me jump. "Drake, a scout caught sight of three vehicles approaching."

My heart stops. For a moment, I don't breathe. *Did Emil just say vehicles...approaching?* I surge to my feet and rush toward the door, yanking it open. "Vehicles?"

Emil smirks and nods. "His doing, I assume?"

"Let's hope." I brush past him and run down the stairs.

The lobby is humming with energy as the people gather and speculate. As I cross the floor, all eyes fall on me, but I ignore them, rushing toward the entry.

Guardians post themselves around the entryway. They're our only source of protection against attacks, and we have far too few of them. I stop under the awning and watch the large trucks drive closer. Only the dust cloud that the trucks kick up gives away their approach. The vehicles are larger than I expected, resembling large boxes on wheels. How many people could fit in just one of those? Twenty? Fifty?

The trucks stop twenty feet from the door. The air around us tenses in anticipation and fear. It could be Gavin. It could be enemies, and we are just standing here waiting for their attack.

Emil waits beside me, arms crossed, studying the vehicles with intense curiosity—and something guarded as well. I peer over at Ally on his other side. Her hands twitch at her sides, ready to grab her lightning and whip it at the newcomers.

A door opens in one cab. My heart jumps in my throat, praying for Gavin to appear. I have so much to apologize for.

The man who steps out isn't Gavin. The cut of his hooded green jacket fits his form in a trim, collected way. His pants have more pockets than I've ever seen before, and the boots gleam in the sunlight. While his clothing clearly marks him out as a leader, that isn't what strikes me about him.

It's his face, his eyes. While he is older—perhaps in his forties—the angles of his face are agonizingly familiar. The kindness in his eyes tells me who he is.

Gavin's father. The Minister of Elpis.

His gaze sweeps our collective group guarding the doors, but he doesn't seem concerned that we might start a fight. The air of calm around him is so at odds with the constant agitation of Gavin that, despite the obvious resemblance, he seems cut from an entirely different cloth. If anything, Paige's mannerisms mirror him more than Gavin's do.

Emil glances at me from the corner of his eyes, then steps forward. He must notice the resemblance, too. "Can we help you?"

"Maybe." The Minister's gaze settles on me, calculating something. The way he looks me over makes me uncomfortable, but again, he reminds me so much of Gavin. Before I squirm, he turns his attention to Emil. "We came to help you."

The crowd of Havenites pushes at our backs to hear everything. No one else has emerged from any of the vehicles.

I want to ask about Gavin, but if I'm wrong, it might give something away.

The Minister gives a subtle nod of his head. The doors to other vehicles open in unison and a few men and women step out. They move toward the back of the trucks. I chew the inside of my mouth anxiously and wait to see what will happen.

"How do you suppose to do that?" Emil asks.

"We have food and water, for starters." The Minister peers past us at the haggard people. "Is there somewhere we can speak in private?"

I can't contain myself any longer. Emboldened, I take a step forward, only stopping when Emil emits a low sound of warning.

"Where's Gavin?" I ask.

The Minister's gaze once more falls on me. A ghost of a smile plays over his lips. "In the truck." He motions over his shoulder at the truck he emerged from.

"You're his dad, then?" I ask.

He cocks his head and raises a brow. "I am."

Ajax relaxes at my side as if this revelation has removed all suspicion. "It would honor us to speak with you!"

"Ajax," Emil hisses in warning.

I'm already moving toward the truck. If Emil wants to stop me, I dare him to try.

"Do not insult the revered father of our Idol," Ajax replies.

I give wide berth to the Minister, afraid he will stop me if I get too close. His gaze tracks my movements. I stare at my shoes but dare a glance in his direction just in time to see him give me a nod of understanding. He knows. My heart lifts a fraction at his open acceptance.

By the time I reach the back of the truck, the door whips open and Gavin emerges, growling at the other two inside the truck about feeling fine. But he is so thin, and his lips are so dry. Did he look like that when he left? What happened to him?

The sight of him stops me dead in my tracks. Gavin doesn't see me at first as he eases out of the back of the truck. When he spots me, he pauses.

"I'm sorry," he says. His voice sounds regretful to me.

"It was wrong of me to get so angry." I want to run into his arms, but don't know if he wants me to. "I'm sorry, too."

For a tense moment, neither of us moves, even as everyone else does. Then our resolve shatters and both of us close the gap in a heartbeat. I pull him into a fierce hug, which he returns with just as much force.

"Don't *ever* leave me again," I murmur against his shoulder.

"Never." He pulls back, holding my face in his trembling hands. The intensity of his stone-gray eyes sends a thrill through me. "You're stuck with me from here out."

"A burden I'll have to learn to live with, I suppose," I smirk.

Forgetting the world around us, and his father ten feet away, I kiss Gavin slow, gentle, eager to prove just how deeply I love him. To my delight, he doesn't pull away.

11

PAIGE

STRONG ARMS HOLD ME close, protecting me while I sleep. I squeeze tighter against his body, taking comfort from the warm security of his embrace.

"Paige..." Zephyr's voice draws me from my slumber.

I nuzzle closer.

A hand on my arm shakes me awake.

"Paige, wake up." Dominic peers at me in the hazy light of dawn.

I shuffle back away from him, worried that it had been him I snuggled up with in my sleep. My heart races a mile a minute as my gaze sweeps the large tent. All the girls are waking up and packing up their sleeping mats. Noticing the pillow's position, everything suddenly becomes clear. I had been snuggled up to the pillow, dreaming of Zephyr. Was it a regular dream or an actual connection? Would I remember it if it was Dreaming?

Dominic raises a brow at me but says nothing about my reaction.

In no time, troops pack everything and the army marches southwest. After leaving a skeleton crew behind to protect the ships, we have been headed in this direction for two days. Most of the soldiers walk. A few of us are given horses. Not for the first time, I notice the lack of carriages and supplies. How long does Dominic think this will take? How much food did he pack and where is it? If I can draw him far enough out of the way, maybe we will run low on food and water, and it will weaken the army.

Then the only problem remaining is me.

I will have little choice but to use my Dreaming to try contacting someone back in Elpis. Mom or Dad. Bianca. Even Levi. I can only do so much, but maybe I can convince them to use a Power stone on me. It's better than the alternative.

The stone will kill me, which makes me delay contacting them. Bianca or Levi would probably be better than Dad or Mom. My parents would never agree to use the stone to weaken me. But if I can make Bianca and Levi understand, they will see there is no other choice. My life for hundreds of thousands. What choice do I have?

Every step I take brings me one step closer to my fate. I know it. I've Dreamed it before. Locked in a cage outside of Elpis, fighting for control of my strange Powers. Fleeing the city for fear I would destroy it. This was always inevitable.

In every one of those Dreams, Zephyr appeared to help me keep my Powers from spiraling catastrophically out of control. He won't be there when the time actually comes. I will be lucky if he survives once this is over. Or unlucky. Because even if he survives, I won't. Hopefully, someone can help him through losing me. I don't want him to turn to drinking to hide his pain as he has done before. *God help me, I love his stupid face*.

I won't reach out to Elpis in a Dream until we are closer. At the rate the army is moving, giving Elpis at least three days' notice should be more than enough time for them to prepare.

River edges her horse closer to me, shooting a glance at Summer. "Paige, are you... I mean... Of course, you aren't alright."

I wipe away tears, only just now realizing I'm crying...again. "Everything will be fine." My words are meant to reassure me as much as her. Because it will be fine. It must be.

I spot Dominic and Bella riding alongside one another up ahead. Layla easily follows them, confirming my suspicion from weeks ago when she had trouble riding with Cypress. She only wanted his attention. Now she appears more proficient than I am.

"Do you mind if I ask you a few questions?" I keep my voice low.

River picks up on the secrecy, giving Summer a subtle nod for her to get closer to us. The other girl joins.

"What happened to you when you were dismissed?" I ask.

Both girls flick terrified eyes toward Dominic.

River pales and licks her lips, whispering so softly I'm uncertain I would hear were we not riding so close together. "Cypress was so kind once he realized... Well, he knew..."

"I know." I reassure her with a pat on the arm. "My brother is gay. It's not a big deal where I come from."

Both girls widen their eyes, but I'm not sure which part shocked them.

"Cypress told me he would dismiss Summer in a few days and set us up in a place together," River continues. "But once I was alone in the carriage with Dominic..." Her voice trembles as she fights for control.

"Did he...force...?"

"No!" River's eyes widen, scandalized. The outburst catches the eye of a nearby guard.

I smile sweetly at the guard, and his dark skin turns green. He fears me.

"He asked me if I wanted to serve the Kingdom, and I didn't realize what he meant. Plus, I didn't want to insult the royal family. So I said yes." Her voice cuts out as tears carve down her rosy cheeks.

Summer eyes River with concern. "It was about the same for me. I agreed without realizing what I agreed to. Then his hand brushed the side of my face. I wanted to punch him, thinking he was gonna force himself on me. But he pulled back almost as quickly. Next thing I knew, I couldn't tell him no. And I couldn't warn anyone else. He put me on this... Well, I dunno what it was. But we rode it across the frozen lake."

He asked for their permission and cooperation first...just like he did with me. Does our agreement strengthen his grip on our minds or bind us to him somehow?

"You rode to the mainland?" I ask. Where did he send these girls when he was supposed to give them housing on the island?

River shakes her head. "Another island just south of the main one. He had an entire facility set up there in the middle of the island. It's surrounded by trees. No one would ever notice it unless they walked the island. Which apparently no one does."

"No one but his guards," Summer mutters bitterly. Did she attempt to escape and fail?

A facility. "You mean experiments?" My stomach lurches. How long did it take him to realize what I can do? Did he know about my Powers before I did? What did he do to *Easton*?

Both girls shrug. "I guess," Summer admits. "He had doctors there who took all kinda samples. And once a week he would come and inject us with something, then force us to use our magic, push us to our limits. He said he needed to know how dangerous we would be to the Crown."

River sneers at Dominic's back, practically growling, "Liar."

Summer nods in agreement. The two of them share a look that tells me they have discussed all of this at length with one another before.

I don't want to push for too much information too soon, but now I know Dominic took those dismissed girls off the island so he could prepare them to fight in his army, at his will. Who would come looking for a few mainland girls? Whatever he injected the girls with couldn't have been good. Maybe he was looking for a way to harness their Powers or use Control without using his own Influence. It must be exhausting Controlling all of us at the same time, which is probably why the other girls wear collars.

I peer up at Dominic, who rides tall and confidently. He shows no signs of exhaustion on the outside, but this must be taxing. How long can he keep it up?

Dominic has a research facility on a secret island, an army at his beck and call, and alliances with some of the powerful lords in the Kingdom. Just how long has he been planning to steal the throne? It can't possibly only go back a couple of years to when he fell for Bella, as he told Zephyr. This takes years of planning. It's not a stretch of logic to believe he is using Bella just like the rest of us. Maybe he singled her out, targeting her at that ball the night they allegedly fell in love. Whether or not that's true, I certainly could use it to plant seeds of doubt in Bella's mind. If I can fracture their relationship, it might give the girls and me a chance to escape all of this.

The level of conniving it takes to orchestrate all of this gives me a whole new respect and fear for our leader.

Elpis couldn't have been part of his original plan. If he tortured Easton for information or compelled it out of him, he could know anything about Elpis. Easton was good at resistance in training, but someone as powerful as Dominic might have been able to break him without him even knowing it.

What is it we have that he wants badly enough to declare war? Or is it simply that he sees us as the biggest threat to his ultimate goal? This must be about more than building an empire.

Elpis must possess something he needs.

12

ZEPHYR

I WAIT ON THE front palace steps beside Cypress for the rest of our group to join us. Once we disposed of Vincent and Cypress broadcast his passionate speech to the people, retaking control of the island had been easy. Too easy for my comfort. Easton agrees with me.

Commander Reginald gathered only the men he trusted most to apprehend those still loyal to Dominic. Discovering what he promised those men had been easy enough once we had a few in custody. Their loyalty only went so far and once they realized they were being tried for treason, it took little to get them to talk. Easton insists there's more those men didn't tell us, or that they can't tell us because of some compulsion to keep certain secrets. I don't disagree, but his fevered argument bordered on obsession.

"I have to find out what he's hiding," Easton had growled. When I had pressed, he dropped it utterly.

One promise we uncovered is that, in exchange for their service, Dominic vowed to remove some constraints on soldiers. Only ranked officers are allowed to marry. Consorting is against the rules. Easton had grumbled about the rule weeks ago, stating that some men were not happy with it. Once the men confessed this aloud to us, Easton grunted and called the rule archaic, reminding us all in his very Easton way that we created this mess ourselves. He isn't wrong. The rule had been intended to allow the royal family control over the lower class—men with magic who bred with women were more likely to have magical children. What would happen to the ruling class if everyone had magic?

The rule hadn't bothered me much before. Honestly, I never gave it any thought, having no actual interest in marriage. Now that I know what it means to need someone, I don't blame the men for wanting what should have been their free right.

And apparently, Dominic told the soldiers that Paige's home is full of women like her. I doubt that very much. *No one* is like her. But the promise of meeting magical women must have appealed to many of the soldiers.

Temperatures have increased enough for several days for the waters to thaw. Dominic took most of our ships, limiting our ability to give chase.

But I only need one ship to reach Paige. Once I can get close enough, Dominic's hold over her will vanish.

Unfortunately, our plan doesn't allow me to run straight to her. Easton came up with a brilliant plan that Cypress fully backed. I was helpless to refuse without overplaying my hand. I feel for Cypress' need to overpower Dominic—really, I do—and Easton's determination to organize the best plan to protect his people. But my priority is Paige, a fact they will learn eventually when I have no choice but to go after her and leave them behind.

Because I will leave them if they take too much of a detour. The moment I feel her magic push at my own, I'm following the trail straight to her.

Cypress adjusts the jacket of his uniform, glancing toward the doors. He shed his usual suits for military blues. It's strange seeing him in uniform.

"I wish you would stay behind," I say again.

He chortles and shakes his head. "I'm sure you would prefer that. Then you can run off and claim all the glory for yourself."

I glare at him, but his smirk tells me he's ribbing me. "Very funny." I've never cared for glory and he knows it.

Cypress slaps a hand on my shoulder. "I told you: my brother and I have a score to settle. I can't let someone else fight this battle for me. If I will ever get the respect to rule, I must do this. I need to defeat him. I need to pass his judgment."

"And what judgment will that be?" I raise a brow, genuinely curious. Cypress has given no clues about what he plans to do to Dominic once he catches him.

Cypress' expression sours and he turns ice-cold eyes to the road. "That all depends on him. He didn't kill me. That must mean something."

It means Dominic had a spare to torture Paige with, but I don't say that out loud. I study Cypress as he examines the soon-to-bloom garden across from us. He talks himself down a lot these days, but I think he will make a better king than he realizes. That speech he gave to the people was far more moving than anything his father ever gave.

"All set!" Easton strolls out the palace doors with Bronwyn and Queen Elena. He shoves his hands into his pockets, and I notice he isn't in his uniform.

"You aren't ready," I say, nodding at his clothes.

Easton nods, then his face contorts into conflicting emotions. He grimaces as he glances at Bronwyn. "I'm staying here."

"Why?" Cypress asks.

I observe Bronwyn's reaction. She knew this already. She doesn't display the slightest bit of surprise. On the contrary, she eyes Easton with a glimmer in her eyes. They discussed this. *What else did they do?*

He notices my stare and clears his throat, averting his gaze. "I told you, there is something here. My gut is telling me to keep searching. I will find the answers and bring them to you."

Bronwyn scowls at him. He ignores her as he continues, "Besides, your mother and sister need extra security from someone you trust. Reginald can only do so much. I've told you everything I can about Elpis. The rest is up to you."

Cypress' face screws up in confusion, but he shrugs it off. "I guess. We could use your knowledge once we get close, though."

Easton steps forward, pulling Paige's radio from his pocket. "Thanks for letting me examine it. I checked to make sure it still works, and I tuned the dial to the correct frequency." He looks at me, sliding it into my hand. "You remember what I told you?"

I nod, taking the precious device and pocketing it. His radio is more advanced than the old remnants we have here on the island. Just one of many clues about his city. "Give the code phrase," I say, "then once we're in contact, ask for the Minister."

Easton nods. "I promise he will understand. He's much more level-headed than his daughter." The corner of his mouth curls up in a smirk. "Make sure he knows I sent you and that I gave you the code phrases. And for the love of God, don't tell him about my interrogation or torture. That won't help your case." He reaches out a hand to shake. I take it. His grip is firm, confident. "I'm trusting you to get her to safety. If I have my way, you will hear from me soon, somehow."

I promise to protect Paige. I would rather die than allow her magic to be used for destruction.

"Too bad you don't have the Knockout needles anymore," Easton says as he shakes Cypress' hand. "She would be much more agreeable if she didn't talk."

Cypress laughs as he shakes with Easton.

When we first captured Easton, he had a pouch in his pocket containing two mysterious needles. Knockout needles. Touching them renders one instantly unconscious. The Minister had slipped it to him before leaving home, asking him to use them on his children if they refused to return home and were in danger. Unfortunately, both were used during the mutiny on the return trip to the island. One on me.

Bronwyn steps forward to give her brother a hug. "Please come home to us. We need you."

Cypress kisses the side of her head as he hugs her. "I will do my best to bring him home, too." He steps back and meets his mother's gaze. "I promise. Just hold it together for a few weeks. That's all I ask."

Queen Elena embraces Cypress like a mother who is about to lose her only child. I understand her fear. If Cypress dies and takes Dominic with him, that only leaves Bronwyn. Who will rule then? Bronwyn could if they allowed women to wear the crown. *Another archaic rule.*

Bronwyn hugs me next and whispers in my ear, "Don't forget to look out for yourself, too."

I hug her and nod.

The two of us load into the carriage and ride to the dock in silence. The carriage is guided right onto the ship. Cypress hesitates inside as I open the door. Worried, I glance back at him.

"It's not too late to stay," I say.

Cypress shakes his head. "I just need a few minutes alone."

"I'll see to departure."

Climbing the steps, I steal a glance back at the carriage. We crammed hundreds of soldiers on the ship. With only one vessel, we had to pack in as many as we dared. The ship will travel for two days around the lakes to the Great River. Then we head south on Dominic's heels.

Per Easton's strategy, another river travels west off the Great River. Navigating this beast of a ship through the shallow, narrow waters will be tricky, but it will get us closer to Elpis faster than Dominic. Then we can send the message to the Minister and plead our case.

Hopefully, it isn't too late for an alliance. Easton seemed convinced that kidnapping the Minister's daughter wouldn't win us any trust. Cypress and I will have to prove ourselves to him.

Once Minister Powers hears my vow to bring his daughter back safely, I'm convinced he will see reason. He must. Everything hinges on getting Elpis to help us against Dominic's four thousand soldiers.

Cool spring air smacks my face when I step out onto the deck. Nothing feels quite like being on a ship over the waters.

Nat jogs over. "Ready when you are, Captain."

"Pull the hawsers and hoist anchor," I command.

Nat grins. "Aye-aye, Captain."

13

PAIGE

I VY AND I HUDDLE close together with our rations, avoiding the watchful gazes of the soldiers all around us. Of all the girls, I like Ivy the most. Her spunky personality is only inhibited by our terrible situation, but she has a dark sense of humor that I appreciate.

The camp bustles with activity as thousands of soldiers set up their sleeping tents, patrol watch routes, or grab their meals. There are no campfires. Dominic is worried about smoke signals giving away our location, but he still has what they call Firestarters who can create a smokeless heating orb. I need to get a better handle on what his army is capable of. These men are all trained to use their Power in combat, but I don't understand the organization of the army yet.

The air around the camp is tense, as usual. Or I could just be projecting my fear. Dominic and Bella have vanished from our shared tent. I've noted how they make rounds throughout the camp each night before turning in. The two of them are probably making their evening rounds. It's one of the few moments of peace we girls get each day. Not that a dozen guards aren't lingering nearby to stop us from running.

The other girls have formed their own friendships in these close quarters. River and Summer cling to one another ten feet away, whispering to each other folded over their meager meals. Layla and Alice chatter amicably, but occasionally a flash of anger shines in Layla's eyes. January gravitates toward Layla and Alice most of the time, but tonight she seems uncertain before settling close to where Ivy and I sit together.

Ivy shares the story of what happened to her when the guards removed her from the cottage months ago. January less-than-covertly eavesdrops as she eats alone.

Ivy's story isn't much different from the other girls. She spent a couple of weeks in the hospital under tight quarantine as she recovered from an illness she called the flu. Based on her symptoms, I don't think it was simply the flu, but I don't know what it could have been either.

"The doctors stressed the importance of my isolation because, apparently, whatever flu it was, it wasn't something the islanders were accustomed to," she explains.

That makes sense to me. The islanders would not be protected by herd immunity if they were not introduced to the virus before. Do they have vaccines?

They kept Ivy isolated until she was no longer contagious. The girls trapped in the cabin with Ivy didn't catch the illness, probably because they were already naturally immune to whatever it was. Elpis has so many immunizations I've probably already been inoculated against it.

Once her quarantine lifted, men dressed as royal guards collected Ivy from the hospital under orders from the King.

"I thought they might be returning me to the palace as Tribute," Ivy says, lowering her voice. "But they took me to a different island."

She explains the passage of water between the Capital and the other island where Dominic held the girls captive. The water was shallow enough to freeze solid during the winter. None of the girls have been able to give me an appropriate description of the two-person vehicle used to transport them. Just that it has skis and only fits two. The closest I can imagine is a motorcycle.

Ivy spent weeks there alone, with only the guards and doctors who studied her. "I was so relieved when River showed up, then Summer not long after. I wasn't alone, even if we couldn't talk much."

"What did they do to you while you were there, Ivy?" I ask, lowering my voice as a guard marches past.

January shifts subtly closer. Ivy doesn't notice, but I do.

Ivy waits for the guard to move farther away before responding. "Blood samples, mostly. A few injections, but I don't know what it was. It made me groggy for a few minutes, but never knocked me out." She flexes her fingers, staring at the tips of them. "One injection made me sick for about two weeks."

If only Dad or Gavin were here. They would understand all this better than I do. I'm military trained and have never taken to medical knowledge. But some of what Ivy describes to me reminds me of the stories Dad told us about Paragon. Could Dominic have been attempting to increase the Powers of the girls? It seems to work with what River and Summer have already mentioned. Dominic was trying to turn them into weapons. *Just like me.*

"Summer and River mostly kept to themselves. We all did." Ivy rubs her hands together, then glances at me. "Every now and again, Dominic would show up and force one or more of us to push the limits of our magic. It was horrible." Tears well in her eyes.

"What can you do, Ivy? What is your skill?" How is this a thing none of us talked about before?

"Mimicry," she says. "I could never do it on a large scale before. Not until they started injecting me with something. Not until I got sick. Before, I could mimic little things, like making my hands into stone. Now... I can take the form of almost anyone close to my size. I can't make myself taller or shorter, and dark skin is hard to mimic." She turns her caramel-colored hands as if that explains it. "But I can turn to stone. I could even become you."

A shiver runs down my spine. "Promise me you won't do that unless I give you permission."

Ivy bites her lip. "I wish I could make that promise and keep it, Paige. But...some things..." She dips her gaze.

I nod. I understand what she means. Dominic Controls all of us. I suspect I'm the only one he Controls all the time. I had hoped that using his Power on all of us would weaken him over time, but after watching him, I've already accepted that assumption was wrong. The collars keep the girls from using their Powers, just like the bracelets did, only stronger. I'm the only one the collars can't contain. I'm the only one he must hold on to all the time.

The assumption I'm operating on is that Dominic's control over me is only possible because it's already established. But if he loses that grip, Gram's psychic wall should stop him from getting in again. That's my hope, at any rate. If I can slip his hold, maybe he can't Control me anymore. The moment I'm freed, I will destroy those collars the other girls wear. If we are all unleashed, all hell will break loose.

"They injected me, too," January whispers.

Both of us peer at her and her face heats.

"Did you get sick, too?" Ivy asks.

January nods. "Not until the fourth or fifth dose, though." She shifts even closer to us, adjusting the skirt of her riding dress. Her gaze follows three guards who march past, giving us all cocky smirks. One guard doesn't hide his leering at January's ample chest. Her cheeks heat even more.

For the first time, I see the vulnerable girl beneath the tough front. For months, January acted high-and-mighty like Layla, and often used sharp words and nasty comments to put others down. She walked around with her head held high and her chest puffed out like she wanted attention. But circumstances have changed for all of us. Wanting Cypress' attention isn't the same as these men.

"I overheard the doctor telling Dominic that Layla remained isolated, per his instructions, but we saw her sometimes, too." January glances over at Layla across the small clearing, deeply engaged in a conversation with Alice. "And every time she emerged, she acted like she was in charge of...everything. Like she thought she was there to watch over the rest of us for the King or something."

The confession draws a frown from my lips. Why would Layla think she was there serving the king? Her dismissal from the palace had not been easy for her or Cypress. I remember watching her cling to his arm, begging to stay. And that night, I overheard a conversation between Dominic and Cypress about Layla's dismissal.

Cypress had asked if Layla resisted the entire way to her new apartment. What had Dominic told him? I slowly chew my venison as I try to pull the memory back. He said something about giving in. Like the others. And keeping her distance. *You need not worry about her causing trouble.*

I study Layla and Alice. The air of comfort around the two of them. The certainty. Layla has been like that since she stepped off her boat in old St. Louis. The hate she throws at Bella is so visceral. I'm missing something. What did Dominic do to Layla? Or what did he promise her in exchange for compliance?

I can't trust her. None of us should. I turn my attention to January, who is studying the ground so hard it almost appears she's trying to disappear into it. "Don't trust Layla," I murmur to the other two girls. "Let River and Summer know if you have a chance."

"What about Alice?" January asks. "I like her."

What *about* Alice? Is it too late to help her, or is she in cahoots with Layla? "Not yet."

January frowns but doesn't argue. The topic changes to something more girly, friendlier. January opens up to us in a way she never has before. *She just wants friends in this horrible situation.* River and Summer are content to keep to themselves, mostly. Alice is glued to Layla, who January has never liked. For the first time since I met her months ago, my heart opens to January. She's just seeking a place to belong in this disaster.

The meal passes with friendly conversation. January tells us about her Power. She's Divinic with Cellular Activation, meaning she can use the cells inside someone else's body, manipulating them. It should make her a healer, but January insists her Power only hurts people.

As we finish, January asks a question that makes my heart stop. "Is it true you were engaged to the King?"

Ivy's eyes shoot up to me, wide and intensely curious. All the girls are listening now.

I clear my throat and lick suddenly dry lips. "Cypress and I had an agreement, yes." And he still lives. If this nightmare works out in our favor and we both survive, will he hold me to that promise?

"That sounds so clinical." Ivy giggles. "No swooning for this girl."

"Why would she?" January asks. "I heard a rumor she kissed his little brother."

My cheeks flush. Before I can defend myself, Summer curls her nose and says, "Dominic? Really?"

"No, dummy, the other one," January says, applying her trademark sharpness. "The handsome captain." January grins roguishly at me. "Did you really have both of them on the ropes?"

Zephyr. Thinking of him rotting away in a cell, suffering who knows what kind of treatment because of me, makes a pit of agony open in my gut. My eyes burn, then blur. I attempt to steel myself against the fear and sorrow enveloping my heart, but it pulls me under no matter how hard I try to stay afloat.

"Oh, no! Don't cry, Paige." January kneels in front of me, taking my hands, then she pulls me into a hug. "I'm sorry."

"Dominic's going to kill him." I can't stop the pitiful words from escaping. "No matter what I do, I can't help him."

"You poor thing," Ivy says, rubbing my back as January hugs me. "You love him."

Frustrated that I can't control my own emotions, or that I would let *any* guy create such helplessness in me overwhelm me. I pull back, roughly wiping away the tears. All the girls are staring at me now. As well as a few guards. I focus on the men, glaring at them through my tears as if each of them is Dominic. As if my gaze alone could burn them.

The fire of that anger spreads through my body swiftly. My Powers push painfully against the web of Dominic's Control. One guard winces and presses a hand to his temple. The other guard checks on him and then turns his attention to me.

"Paige," Ivy hisses, "calm down. You're getting their attention."

"Good."

January pulls back suddenly, glancing over her shoulder at the guards.

The concerned guard stomps toward us so quickly January can hardly shift out of his way in time. He draws his sword, extracting cries of alarm from all the girls. They scramble back.

But his gaze is locked on me. The Powers pushes through me, fiery and fierce. I grit my teeth against the intensity. His gaze flicks momentarily at my hands in terror. I barely register the red Power pulsing to life in my fingertips as Dominic charges into the tent. The guard hammers the hilt of his sword against my skull to knock me out cold.

14

GAVIN

AFTER A THOROUGH CHECKUP from Doctor Adams, I clean off days of sweat and dirt. Once that's done, I head to the conference room on the main floor of the hotel.

While I cleaned up, Dad worked alongside Emil and Ajax to distribute the food and water they brought along. It's little more than nutrition bars and water pouches, but far better than nothing at all. Especially the water.

When I enter the conference room, Dad is sitting close to Drake. Their heads are together in deep conversation. A solar lamp lights the conference room as the sunlight outside dims beyond the horizon. My stomach twists with worry. What did Dad say to him?

Then Drake grins in that way that makes my belly drop. "There you are. Looking much better, I gotta say."

Dad nods. "Agreed. Drake was just telling me all about your amazing *gifts*." Pride shines in his eyes. I'm not sure why he is proud of me. Drake must not have told him what I did to the Haven, to the people who tried to kill Drake—who *did* kill Drake. "Seems you might be more important than I am."

Did Drake tell him about the Idols and the prophecy?

I choke on a laugh, eyes widening. "You're messing with me, right?" I glance between the two of them.

Dad shakes his head and leans back, resting an arm on the conference table. "Not in the least." He studies me in a way that makes me uncomfortable. What does Dad think he sees? Finally, he approaches and pulls me into a hug. "I'm relieved to see you doing so well." He pats my back as I hug him, then whispers, "I like him."

I flush, withdrawing. Having Dad's approval means a lot—more than I can express—but it still feels strange.

Dad turns toward the newcomers, all business. The Major from my Department of Security briefing enters alongside Ally. It makes sense that the two women would take to one another amicably. Both hold similar positions in the military.

Drake rolls his chair on squeaky wheels toward me while the others file in. "I think he likes me," Drake whispers the moment Dad is too distracted to notice.

I only offer Drake a smile.

"The supplies are all rationed, but they won't last more than a day with so many people," the Major reports, taking a seat at the table. Ally settles across from her.

Emil grimaces as he leads Ajax in. As they take their seats at the far end of the table, Emil's eyes remain locked on Dad, skeptical to the core. As always.

Dad offers them an easy smile. "Drake has told me a little about what your minister did in the Haven, and I want to reassure you that my title differs from his. I'm elected by the people, not selected by a few."

Ally relaxes a little at this, as does Ajax, but Emil remains rigid.

"My son has likely already told you a bit about what I've done for my people," Dad continues.

I nod, but no one is watching me—except for Drake.

"If it makes you more comfortable, you can just call me Ugene. I've never been one to stand on formality."

"You said you're here to help us," Emil cuts in. "Like offering us shelter in your community instead of just bringing us food and water?"

The subtle press of Dad's fingertips against the tabletop is the only outward sign of irritation. Dad rarely loses his cool.

"I have to talk to the Council of Representatives to sort out those details."

Drake's head snaps up to my dad. Fear springs from him. He's thinking about our argument. About what I said about possibly rejecting their admission into the city. I told him I would fix it. I must. Their struggles now are my fault.

I clear my throat. "But we can start a slow integration, can't we? Even somewhere on the outskirts, like in the mountains near the Greenhouse. I can create housing for them there."

Dad glances at me, his face a mask of professional patience. "Gavin, I'm sure they understand why we might be worried. Especially after what their community leaders did."

"But they aren't here," I argue.

"I am." Ally sags in her seat.

She isn't to blame for what happened. Ally was horrified by what they were doing, and begging forgiveness for sins she didn't even commit. Emil never would trust her if there was any reason to doubt her.

I shake my head. "No, Ally—"

Emil crosses his arms and leans back in the chair. It creaks under the strain. His hard eyes are locked on Dad as he speaks to me. "It's alright, Gavin. If they will send us supplies, we can manage protection. For now."

"I can take your weakest and your injured back with us," Dad offers. "We have doctors like Adams who can help them."

"And their families," Emil adds. "You can't take a child from a parent."

"Of course not." Dad winces, glancing at me. "Which brings me to my next request." He weighs each of the Havenites around the table with me. "The Kingdom has my daughter and I want her back."

"Good luck," Emil mutters.

Dad's jaw twitches. It's odd. I've not seen him show anger often. Or maybe Drake has made me more aware of the emotional reactions in others. I slide my hand over his under the table and squeeze it. He clings to me.

"What can you tell me about the Kingdom?" Dad asks.

The Havenites all glance at Emil as if worried about how this subject will make him react. Admittedly, a vein in his neck pulses with wild life.

"They steal girls and little boys with gifts, and we never hear from any of them again," Emil snaps. "They keep to themselves on their little island unless they need more boys for their army. And it's an enormous army. From what I've gathered over the years, a large portion of their population is military-trained from childhood. They have forts on the mainland near the coast to monitor potential invasion, and dozens of ships to patrol the water. The island is impenetrable."

Dad takes everything in like pieces of a puzzle. "And what *is* their population?"

"We don't really know," Ally adds.

"Nearly a hundred thousand," I say.

Everyone freezes and stares at me. No doubt, they wonder how I even would know such a thing. I lick my lips, anxious, and consider how to explain.

"The dream?" Dad asks.

I nod.

Dad relaxes as I tell the others what Paige told me, excluding the more intimate details.

Dad reabsorbs everything in studious silence, reexamining each morsel. He clears his throat when I stop. "I'm relieved she's alright, and Easton as well, but we don't know how long that will last. I need to bring her home."

The Major takes notes on her tablet of everything. Is she recording the conversation? Probably. I'm happy I left out the personal details. My sister deserves some privacy.

The meeting continues. Emil and Ally have a few requests regarding integration into Elpis and how the city can help them. How big is the city? What will be required of them once they are integrated? Will they have voting rights? Dad hesitates with that one. Logically, giving newcomers voting rights immediately seems like a dangerous idea. But there are so few of them that the votes wouldn't really make *that* much of a difference.

Once they have exhausted questions and Dad has done his best to smooth out ruffled feathers in the way only he can, everyone agrees to get rest. In the morning, the weakest and the injured will go back to Elpis with the trucks. He will convene with the Council of Representatives, then return with more supplies and a response.

Dad waits outside the door for me to emerge, then falls in step beside me. Drake trails in our shadows.

"Your mom will be relieved to see you tomorrow, Gavin," he says. "She's been a mess ever since Adams and Harper returned."

A lump lodges in my throat. He already expressed Mom's distress, and I don't want to make it worse, but I made a promise to Drake.

She will understand and must at least be relieved to know I'm alive. I will get back to her eventually, but the trucks have limited space, and I want to be sure they can take as many of the Havenites as possible. Besides, I can't leave these people to go home. Not after what Drake said.

Drake shuffles a half step closer to listen.

"I'm not going, Dad."

Dad's brow wrinkles. He doesn't understand. He probably expected me to leap at the chance to go home. For just a second, his gaze flicks to Drake. "I can't leave you out here. Your mother—"

"I can't leave these people. I think both you and Mom understand that. They need protection. I can provide it. Until they are *all* integrated into Elpis, I stay with them." It also allows me some leverage to hurry the process along with the Council of Representatives.

Dad stops, taking my arm and forcing me to face him. Drake nearly walks into the two of us. He mutters an apology and shuffles a few steps back.

"Gavin, the Council might not agree. You know I can't force them."

I nod but square my shoulders. "I understand. Even so, I want to protect them. I need to. And once they're safe, I'm going after Paige."

"You can't stand against a force that size. It's impossible." The forcefulness in his tone shocks me. Dad spoke like that to Paige sometimes, but never to me. Does that mean I'm doing something right? Or very wrong...?

"Not for him." Drake's voice startles me. I was so buried in my thoughts I lost my sense of place. Drake edges closer to my side, and I admire the way he stands up to my father. Few people have the courage to do that. "Gavin can do far more than you could ever imagine. I've seen it. And I think he can do even more. I believe..." Drake trails off, swallowing what he intended to say. His gaze darts to me, then the floor.

Yes, I understand that look. Despite everything, he still thinks I have the power to remake the world. He still believes in me.

"I can get to the island *without* ships."

Dad takes a step back. "Not everything can be defeated with Powers, Gavin. And Powers don't make you invincible. If anything, they make you vulnerable."

"You haven't witnessed what your son is capable of." Drake slides his hand into mine. I swallow. Earlier, Dad gave Drake his stamp of approval. This could undo that.

But does it matter? I love Drake, and Dad can't change that.

"No, but I've seen what happens when a large army of Powered individuals work together in battle." Dad pales a little. "It's horrific."

"I know I'm not invincible." The memory of being weak as the Elders burned me rises to the surface. I swallow it down. "But I took on dozens of their soldiers already, and that was without understanding what I'm capable of. And I won't be alone. Easton is there, and Zephyr will help." Probably. "And who knows how many allies he has on the island? Until Paige is safe, I won't hide in my bedroom in Elpis. I will help these people, help my sister, then take my promotion and live in peace." I squeeze Drake's hand, hoping he supports me through all of it.

Dad turns and marches toward the steps. "Just sleep on it, Gavin." He hasn't accepted my answer. He just doesn't want to fight about it tonight.

I agree to sleep on it, but one night won't change anything.

15

PAIGE

KANSAS CITY IS BEHIND us now. Dominic called for a halt farther west, once we found an open field large enough for his army to make camp. While we gave the city a wide berth, Dominic kept his army as close as he could, not wanting to skirt too far off course, I assume.

The girls lay out their sleeping mats without comment. I stretch my back, watching as Bella and Dominic stand to the side of our shared tent, their arms around one another. If I could just get a few minutes alone with her, I could plant the seed of doubt in her mind. Tearing them apart will weaken both.

Bella's fingers slide the hair away from his face, tucking it behind his ear. He grins at her and murmurs something that makes her cheeks turn red. My stomach dips as they kiss. Envy surges through me, making my wild Powers kick at the reins holding them in check. Zephyr and I never had a chance to have that, to hold each other without judgment or danger breathing down our necks. I turn away as sorrow clenches my heart. We never had that and never will.

Only a day has passed since the guard knocked me out. January whispered that he was worried my Power would break free and kill them all—which she seemed to think is a ridiculous notion. But she doesn't know what I can do. She didn't see what I did to those three men. His worry was justified.

"Paige." Dominic's sudden appearance at my shoulder makes me jump. He slides his hand into mine. "Let's walk."

I glance at Bella as he escorts me from the tent. She doesn't seem the least bit bothered that I'm taking her place on patrol tonight.

I hate the feel of Dominic's hand in mine. It fills me with anger and disgust, but I can't pull away. Part of me wants to stubbornly reject walking with him. His Control will win, but I can dig in my heels and make it harder. The problem is, the results hurt me more than him, ending in a pounding headache the harder I resist him. So, I don't bother fighting him tonight. This is not the time to pick my battle. That day is coming, but we aren't there yet.

The two of us meander through the camp toward a tree-lined hill to the west as the sun sets. Neither of us speaks. The silence is a brewing storm between us. A pulse of something slides through me, subtle and nearly undetectable. I dare a glance at our hands as I feel it again. It's him. Dominic is reinforcing his Control through direct contact.

What would happen if I broke that contact when he tried strengthening the bond? Is this how he keeps his hold when he isn't touching me, by reinforcing it when he has a chance? What would happen if I didn't allow it anymore? Could I stop him?

Before I test my theory, Dominic releases my hand and dips below a low-hanging branch. I follow obediently on his heels as if I had any other choice. He ducks and weaves deftly around trees, forcing me to keep up.

I step into a clearing around a small body of water. Dominic already stands at the shore, hands in his pockets, staring westward across the water to the trees on the other side.

"It doesn't quite match the beauty of sunsets over the lake, but it's still a beautiful view," he says serenely.

I stop, not wanting to stand next to him like this is an ordinary day and we're friends. He doesn't force me to join him.

"You miss him a great deal," Dominic says, stating the obvious. I don't need to ask. We both know who he's talking about. "I'm sorry that my happiness causes you distress."

"No, you aren't."

His shoulders lift and he heaves out a sigh. "You must think me a monster, but everything I do has a purpose, Paige. Stop fighting against me and start fighting for me, and I will give you what you want when this is over."

My teeth grind and I ball my fists tightly at my sides. "I'm not a complete idiot. I know about the deal you made with Vincent."

Dominic peers over his shoulder at me and then holds out his hand. He doesn't force me to join him. This is a test. He wants me to obey on my own. If this small acquiescence helps save Zephyr, I can swallow my pride.

I edge closer, placing my hand in his. He smiles sweetly, that innocent smile I adored when I thought he was someone else.

"Vincent has always been a snake," Dominic admits. "I'm offering you a chance at happiness, Paige."

"You made me kill those men."

"It doesn't have to be this way." He kisses my hand, then releases it and edges closer to me. Wind whips between us, throwing my long hair in my face. Dominic pulls it back over my shoulder. "Despite what you might believe, I love Zephyr and Cypress. I want them to be happy, as long as it's not at my expense."

I snort and roll my eyes. "That's some declaration of love. How do you imagine I could ever be happy after what I've done?"

"We are far from finished, Paige. It will get worse before it gets better. For all of us. But if you work with me instead of against me, I can make sure you and Zephyr end up together."

"If you are so willing to go back on your word to Vincent, why should I trust that you wouldn't do the same to me? Dominic, I don't trust you anymore. Everything you say and do is coated in layers of deception."

Dominic places my fingers against his temples, sapphire eyes blazing in the setting sun as he peers into me. "See for yourself."

"What?" A trickle of my Powers rush through my veins.

"You can See for yourself. Trust in your abilities, Paige. Stop trying to fight them. You know how to Dream. I've caught you in the act when you eavesdropped on Cypress and me weeks ago. Now it's time for you to see my dreams."

He knew I overheard that conversation? I've never knowingly tried delving into anyone else's dreams before. Each time, it's been an accident. But as Dominic's gentle voice coaches me, I sense the link moving between my fingertips to his mind like a tingling connection.

A sea of memories flow past in swift succession, as if Dominic carries me on the current of his life, offering glimpses into his childhood. Playing with his brothers and sister. Fights and games and love and anger. His father worshipping a boy who could only be

Alric, followed by him shouting at the other three boys for breaking a priceless relic.

One memory morphs quickly into the next like wisps of smoke, giving me a clearer picture of the life that shaped Dominic. The way he adored his brothers. The moment he felt betrayed by them. His pain becomes my pain and I cry with him. The love for Bella is followed swiftly by his father terrorizing him, then his uncle—the one I never met—consoling him while simultaneously threatening to tell the King for his own good. Dominic's desperation, loneliness, anger, fear. Hate. His agony as he slipped into his uncle's room and smothered him with a pillow. The grief that followed.

All of it passes in a matter of seconds, but I feel what he felt. I understand his pain.

Then a vision of the future flashes past at a sickeningly fast pace. My stomach churns like I'm about to be ill. Flashes of armies, fire, destruction, creation, and communities falling before his forces. His flag rising above them all.

The images move faster and faster until they become a blur. Then everything grinds to a halt on one image.

Paradise. A restored earth. Peace.

Dominic, on a throne overlooking his empire.

"This future doesn't have to be only mine, Paige," he says inside my head, an echo that resonates everywhere.

I see Zephyr standing on a beach, feet in the warm water as waves lap the shore. My heart stops and I breathe his name. An ache opens in my heart to fold myself into his arms.

Zephyr turns, and a grin splits his face. He's dashing in his summer clothes. Cradled in his arms, a toddler with a shock of curly hair slumbers against his chest. I edge closer to him, reach for him, but the moment our fingers meet to lace together, the image disappears.

I'm standing on the shore of the pond with Dominic once more. All the warmth of the summer sun fades away as the real world washes over me again. Agony rips at my heart. Tears roll down my cheeks.

Dominic eases my fingers off his temples, hope in his eyes. He wipes away my tears. "Help me, Paige, and that can be your future, too."

I hadn't realized until that moment how much I want that future...just how much I want *Zephyr*.

But at what cost? The destruction passed swiftly, but there was no mistaking the pain and fire and fury that consumes the world before we reach that end. How long would it take? How many would die? I love Zephyr. If I doubted before, I know it absolutely now, down to the very matter that creates me. But I can never live that happily ever after with him on the heels of so much death. Especially not by my own hands.

Dominic cradles my head in his hands, studying me with that terrible hope in his eyes.

I can't give him that future on the heels of such mortality. But he doesn't need to know that. He can't read my mind. Nor can Bella. If I agree, will he loosen his hold on me?

"What do you say? Help me fix this broken world, and we can both have what we want."

Regret catches in my throat. I nod stiffly.

Dominic smiles as bright as the sun and kisses my forehead. "Thank goodness. You had me worried." He steps away, turning toward the water. His hand touches the small of my back, encouraging me to join him on the edge. "You're capable of more than you realize. Let's see if we can unlock one more skill set. For this to work, you need to learn to sink or swim, Paige."

"Sink or swim on your own." Tudor's angry voice surfaces, and I nearly choke on a hysterical laugh, but a pulse of terror surges through me.

"Ready?" Dominic asks.

"For what?"

Dominic doesn't answer. Instead, he shoves me into the water with all his might.

I scream as I flop into the icy cold water, plunging beneath the surface. My clothes are soaked before I break the surface, paddling my arms toward the shore.

Then my arms refuse to paddle. My legs stop kicking. I gulp down air seconds before I sink below the surface again. I struggle against the cold that penetrates my skin and break the surface. Dominic crouches on the shore, hands folded in front of himself, frowning at me.

"No, Paige." He lifts a hand, turning it slowly as if twisting an invisible knob. "Powers only."

My arms won't move. Nor will my legs. I fight for breath as I sink below the surface, catching a mouthful of water. Dominic won't *let* me swim. Panic grips me as the murky water grows darker and I sink toward the bottom like a stone.

Claustrophobia kicks in. My heart rate increases, and with it, panic surges through my body. Without thinking, I attempt to pull in a breath, only to have my lungs flood with water. I close my eyes, grasping at my Power as it slips through my fingers. Flashes of the collapse in the Greenhouse surge to the surface. Mom curled around me, stroking my hair and wiping away my tears as I cry. Panic clawing at my chest. Every second of that agony repeats inside of me.

"It's okay, Paige. We have air to breathe. You are not alone." Mom's voice echoes from the memory.

But I don't have air, Mom! I can't breathe. I'm alone. So utterly, impossibly alone.

I can't tell if everything darkens, or if that's just the surrounding water. Mom vanishes. Stars wink into existence. I reach out, fighting for breath, and grasp a star.

"Focus on me, Paige," Gavin says as we lean against each other for support. His strength ebbs through me as he takes my hand. *"Together."*

I close my eyes, allowing Gavin's strength to flow through me, and feed my own.

My Powers surge. Heat rushes through my veins, chasing away the chill. Once more, I'm surrounded by half a dozen pulsing stars. I touch another star.

Zephyr cuts through the water with powerful strokes of his arms. Some purpose drives him forward. Is he reaching out to me?

The image vanishes as the stars reappear. I'm drowning. Dying. Time slows. Stops. *Moves backward.*

I'm standing on the shore beside Dominic, his hand on the small of my back. My clothes are dry. Only air fills my lungs. I bask in the glory of life.

"Are you ready?" Dominic asks.

"No!"

Dominic shoves me under again.

Once more, I sink, unable to swim to shore. Then warmth wraps around me. The stars. *Dad, marching alongside Uncle Alex in the wasteland.*

Rewind.

I'm on the shore.

Dominic shoves me.

I sink. Am I controlling time? *Mom is curled in her recliner under a blanket, holding a picture of the family and crying.* "No. Mom, I'm alive!"

Rewind.

"Vincent has always been a snake," Dominic admits as he stands near the water. My lungs remain void of water, yet I continue to gulp down breaths. I can't get oriented quickly enough. "I'm offering you a chance at happiness, Paige."

I blink and speak without meaning to respond at all. "You made me kill those men."

"It doesn't have to be this way." He kisses my hand, then releases it and edges closer to me. Wind whips between us, throwing my long hair in my face. Dominic pulls it back over my shoulder.

I've done all this before. My gaze darts around, seeking some way to escape this loop.

"Despite what you might believe," Dominic says, oblivious to my distress—or not caring about it, "I love Zephyr and Cypress. I want them to be happy, as long as it's not at my expense."

Stumbling backward, I shake my head. "I already agreed. Stop this! *Please.*" Tears roll down my cheeks as I peer at the water in terror.

Dominic frowns, then eyes the water. It only takes a second for him to put the pieces together. His face lights up. His grip on my hand tightens, and he launches me in once more.

I sink. I'm definitely controlling time. Does he know? Did he always know?

Bianca and Levi argue in their living room, both looking furious. The swell of Aunt B's muscles makes him flinch. "They need our help, Levi, and I will not stand by and do nothing."

"We need to be cautious about this! Bianca, if—"

"I promised Ugene." Bianca's jaw clenches. Her hands tighten into fists.

"And what about me?" Levi sneers, shaking his head angrily. "That's it again, isn't it? You never let go."

Rewind.

I step into a clearing around a small body of water. Dominic already stands at the shore, hands in his pockets, staring westward across the water to the trees on the other side. I can avoid him throwing me in again if I don't let him take my hand. I step backward.

"It doesn't quite match the beauty of sunsets over the lake, but it's still a beautiful view," he says serenely.

Another step backward.

"You miss him a great deal," Dominic says. Zephyr. He's talking about Zephyr again... "I'm sorry that my happiness causes you distress."

"No, you aren't," I snap, filled with fury. "And if you throw me in one more time, I will take back what I said. I won't help you. I will break from this Control or die trying."

Dominic cocks his head curiously as he studies me. "It worked. I wasn't sure, but based on what we observed with your samples and magic..." He edges closer, hands up like he's trying to calm a startled animal. "Paige, you and I are going to change the world. Help me, and your people won't have to suffer."

My people. What is he planning to do to Elpis? I saw flashes of his grand plan, fire and death, but I couldn't get a clear beat on what he plans for Elpis. Though, I understand his endgame now.

Dominic wants to conquer the world and believes that, once he does, he can reforge it in his glorious image.

16

ZEPHYR

NORMALLY, I LOVE THE open water. The sense of peace it offers; the utter calm. But ever since we cast off from the Capital, I can't stop thinking about Paige, dreaming about her. Even standing at the rail of the ship gazing out at the moving water reminds me of her.

Months ago, Paige and I stood on the deck of *Wave Slicer* as the Capital approached. It was the first genuine conversation the two of us had without layers of sarcasm or anger. Months have passed since then. Everything has changed. Every*one* has changed, too. Myself included.

The closer we get to the fork in the Great River near old St. Louis, the tighter I grip the railing. I finally understand what my mother was trying to tell me the day before she passed away. Her words were understandable, but the emotion they carried was foreign to me. I assumed my feelings for Paige were simply primal. But I was wrong. The consuming need. The unyielding drive to risk everything to fight for Paige, to protect her and hold her...to have her. I've felt nothing that grips me so absolutely.

Without a doubt, I know now how I feel about her. I only hope I'm not too late. *I can't be. I* won't *be.*

Cypress marches over to join me, but he doesn't bother looking out at the water. His gaze is fixed on me, expression drawn tight. Something's wrong.

"What is it?" I ask, straightening from the rail.

He tucks his hands into his pockets and peers at his feet. "If we find Paige and stop Dom—"

"*When* we do," I correct through gritted teeth.

Cypress nods sagely. "When. I won't do what my father did. I won't hold her to her promise and subject all three of us to misery. She deserves the right to choose, free of any meddling."

My heart seizes. He's just letting her go? I've never known Cypress to do anything selfless. Not on this scale. Little things like sneaking me his muffins when Dad refused to feed me, sure. I don't know how deep his feelings for Paige go, but I know he has them.

"Cy..." But I don't know what to say to him. I certainly won't tell him not to do this. Paige would make her own choice no matter what we said or did, anyway.

"Fighting over a girl nearly destroyed the Kingdom. If I had just recognized and accepted your feelings for her way sooner, if we had both admitted the truth to each other, Dom wouldn't have been able to do as much as he's done. I can't let this distract me any longer." He swallows, lifting his gaze to the parting water. Then he chuckles and shakes his head. "You would probably make a better king than I would."

He can't really believe that. I would make a *terrible* king.

Before I can respond, Nat calls to the two of us from the bridge above. "Cap, we have ships!"

I pull the scope from my pocket, adjusting the focus until the ships come into clear view. Well over a dozen ships are tethered to the old St. Louis shoreline. Twenty of them. All the ships appear empty. Did Dominic just leave them there?

The scope slowly sweeps along the shoreline, working up toward the park where I first met Paige. Nothing. Not another soul in sight. Could Dominic have brought a Mirage with him—a soldier with the magic to make his army invisible? It would take an entire team of Mirages to mask such a large force. But that doesn't mean one isn't on the shore guarding the ships, even if the bulk of the army has moved on. I counted on a skeleton crew or darkness here, but we don't know what waits on shore, and it isn't dark out. The fork in the river is close to us, but we won't pass Dominic's ships without notice. We have to assume someone is guarding the vessels.

"How bad is it?" Cypress asks.

"Twenty ships," I report. "Not a soul in sight."

"There's no way those ships are unguarded."

"My thoughts, too." I turn, lowering the pocket scope. "Nat! Stop the ship. Find Jeff."

Nat responds, then disappears.

"What are you thinking, Zeph?" Cypress asks, holding out his hand.

I place the scope in it. "We might slip past, but there's a chance someone could spot us turning westward and give chase. We can't risk our only ship. It's important to uncover what's hiding over there. Jeff and I will swim to shore and get as close as we can. If there are Mirages there, hopefully, my negation magic will reveal the size of the force hiding on the ships. If we can take back those ships, Dominic will be trapped on the mainland with nowhere to run."

Cypress frowns as Nat and Jeff make their way through the crowded deck toward us. "So, what's Jeff for?"

"Stealth."

"But..." Cypress cuts off his protest as I pull a single manacle from my pocket and snap it on my wrists. "You want to go ashore with just Jeff and try taking back the ships without assistance? Zephyr, this is an epically terrible idea."

"No one will notice us until it's too late."

The ship groans as the engine cuts out and it drifts to a stop. Then the anchor drops into the water.

"Once the mirage is down and we've secured the officers in charge, you can come in with our men and finish the job," I say, motioning for Jeff to follow me below the deck where the wetsuits are stored.

"I don't like this," Cypress protests on my heels. "You'll freeze!"

"Have blankets and a healer ready, then." I slide out of my boots, then take off my coat.

This *is* a bad idea, but we can't just attack without knowing what's out there. Stealth is better.

———— ⬧ ————

T HE WATER IS FREEZING and the swim is far too long. Though Jeff and I donned thermal body suits reserved for cleaning hulls in the summer before diving in, the frigid temperatures still wreak havoc on our nervous systems.

Within twenty yards of shore, Jeff nearly drowns as his arms refuse to cooperate any longer. I do my best to drag him to shore with me. Thankfully, the sun is warm enough today that despite the cold water, our skin, at least, heats the moment we flop on the bank. His Stealth masked the sound of our arms slicing through the water, and now the drip of the river as it slides off our soaked bodies.

"I c-can't...move." Jeff's teeth chatter like drums.

I roll only my hands and knees, then force my aching body upright, tucking my hands into my armpits. "Rub your hands together, then tuck them in like this." I wave my elbows.

"The g-ground is i-ice."

"We have to move, Jeff." I reach over and help him upright. "Heat up our blood."

Jeff follows my instructions to warm his body. Not that it will stop hypothermia from setting in. We don't have long before the need for medical attention takes hold. Every second counts.

The two of us stumble, leaning against one another for heat as we make our way in a crouch along the shoreline to the nearest ship. Once we reach five yards from the ship, we pass through some invisible veil.

At least a hundred men mill about, scattered across the twenty ships. They shout back and forth to one another, clearly with little supervision.

"So m-many," Jeff mutters through his chattering teeth.

On the shore, four men enter a dock house. The door closes behind them, but not before I notice the insignia on their jackets. They are the officers of this skeleton crew. Our targets.

"How close can you get us to that dock house without notice?" I ask, nodding toward the building. "If we can get inside, the two of us can subdue the officers. From there, taking over should be easy."

Jeff half chatters, half laughs. "In our s-state?"

I grimace. He might not be useful in a fight, except as a distraction. The cold is impairing me as well, but not nearly as badly. I've done arctic plunges on a dare with Cypress before. I know how to handle the cold water and the aftereffects.

Maybe if Jeff and I get close enough with his Stealth, I can remove the manacles with the key tucked in my suit, then cut the officers off from their magic. That only leaves hand-to-hand combat. I can manage that with only four enemies. *I hope*.

"Let's go." I tug his arm, then slip close to the ships, keeping out of sight of the primary force still on the vessels.

Jeff follows, moving a little better now. If he can take care of just one of those officers, I can probably handle three of them. *Maybe*.

I can't help worrying these ships have some way to report to Dominic. With Telepathy, maybe? I don't know of anyone powerful enough to send telepathic messages very far, but I also don't know how far away Dominic is.

We reach the ship closest to the dock house, and I fumble in my pocket to retrieve the manacle key. It slips out and hits the ground, nearly falling into the water through my trembling fingers. With a curse, I retrieve the key more carefully. It takes several attempts to unlock the manacles, but when it pops open, my magic springs to life. Jeff gasps.

"Don't like this feeling, Captain," he mumbles.

No one does. Some get used to it as the price of being around me. But I've lost friends because they don't like the way my negation magic cuts them off.

We tip-toe close to the door and listen with an eye on the ships.

"...something," one officer finishes.

"Reminds me of the old captain," another grumbles.

Crap! We don't have time to dally. They'll figure it out quickly. I signal for Jeff to follow me in and head to the back of the dock house—or as near to it as the farthest officer is. I will take the nearest out as quickly as possible. Jeff nods, shifting his feet.

I count down with my fingers, hand on the doorknob. Then I thrust the door open and barrel into the closest officer. He stumbles backward, knocking another into the wall. Jeff rushes in and runs straight at the farthest officer in the back corner.

The last man surges forward with a string of curses, reaching for his discarded sword. I'm faster, moving on pure adrenaline. I seize the weapon first. As my fingers wrap around the hilt, one of them tries grasping my wetsuit, but their grip slips right off. I shuffle back, swinging the sword in an arc between myself and the three men.

Jeff has the fourth on his knees in the corner, pinned to the wall.

"I would rather this transition goes smoothly," I say. I shift into a defensive stance, ready to slice them down if they attack.

Two of them raise their hands in defeat, backing against a wall. The final officer studies me as if probing for weakness. Hopefully, he can't tell how weak my limbs really feel at this moment.

I drop my manacle at his feet. "Put that on."

His eyes bulge, but as I shuffle closer, he raises a hand and bends to retrieve it. He glares at me as he snaps it over his wrist.

"If you want it removed, you will do exactly as I say," I order, motioning for him to move toward the other two. "You alright there, Jeff?"

"High and tidy, Captain."

I glance over for just a moment. Jeff ties up the officer with a thick rope he must have found in the office.

"Order your men to stand down and submit to their king's inspection," I command.

"*Their* king?" the second officer hisses. "Or yours?"

"All of ours," I snap, inching closer like a hungry predator. Two of them press their backs firmly to the wall. I get in the face of the third. "Reject King Cypress. I dare you."

His mouth twitches. "Long live King Do—"

The declaration cuts off with a grunt as my blade pierces his gut. I jerk it out less than kindly and glare at the others.

"King Cypress has zero tolerance for *any* form of dissent," I declare.

The officers watch as their comrade grasps his gut and slumps to the floor, then pitches forward on his face. I step back out of range of the pool of blood spilling beneath him.

"You have your orders," I growl.

Our small party edges out the door toward the ramps.

———◈———

ALL TWO HUNDRED SOLDIERS are disarmed and rounded up on one ship by the time Cypress climbs the ramp. In his military blues, he cuts an imposing figure. I stand at attention, wrapped in a warm fleece blanket and eyeing the subdued crowd for signs of an attempted assassination. No one can use their magic right now, which means those of us with weapons have the upper hand. Any attempt on Cypress' life will be smothered immediately.

Cypress marches in front of the crowd, taking them all in with one calculating glare. "The Kingdom of Tides has stood for a *century*. My ancestors have expanded our territory beyond the safety of our island and given hope to those on the mainland who had no hope. In less than a day, you have destroyed our peace and strength with your greed and division. You should be ashamed."

His voice raises above the breeze that rips across the deck. I tighten my grip on the blanket.

"You have committed treason against the crown," Cypress announces clearly. All the captive soldiers react with apprehension or silent defiance. He presses on. "I will *not* have my reign stained with the blood of my own people! But I also cannot allow such insurrection to go unpunished." He raises his chin, glaring at the gathered soldiers. "Rejoin your fellow soldiers right now, and you will be regrouped and given a second chance under close surveillance. Rise and *beg* my mercy."

No one dares to move or breathe.

"Now," Cypress growls the word out.

A few men cautiously rise to their feet, offering terrified apologies to their king. Then a few more. And more. More than half of the soldiers beg his forgiveness. My heart lifts with each plea, but a knot of worry remains in my gut. How far can we trust these men? Will they turn against us again in favor of Dominic's promise of wives and a life of their choosing?

The repentant soldiers were forced away by Cypress' loyalists, and only a few dozen defiant stares remained.

Cypress gives them another moment before his gaze sweeps those who swore themselves to him. "I know what my brother has promised you. My first act as your king, once we defeat my brother and return to the Capital, is to abolish the marriage laws. Soldiers will, from that day forward, be allowed to court and marry whomever they wish, no matter social or magical standing."

A gasp of shock moves through not only Dominic's followers but also ours. *I hope Cypress knows what he's doing.* Some of our traditions could use a refresh, but to undercut a core practice of our kingdom could have adverse effects.

"It's just one of many laws I intend to amend once we deal with my brother," Cypress continues. "Remain loyal, and your lives *will* improve to your liking."

The defiant soldiers glance at one another as if weighing whether it's too late.

Cypress turns his cool eyes to his own soldiers. "Kill the rest."

Several of the defiant standouts rise, begging forgiveness, but it's too late. They had their chance and only turned against Dominic once they knew there was a reward for them. That isn't loyalty or trust. That's greed.

Cypress turns his back on them and marches over to me. His jaw clenches as the death cries of Dominic's men shatter the air behind him. His face pales. Cypress doesn't like what he had to do. That's good, I suppose. We don't need another heartless king. But what he did is necessary. We can't leave them at our back. We can't bring them along as prisoners to turn against us later. Death is our only option.

"Looks like you commandeered a fleet," Cypress says to me, drawing me to the rail with him. He glances at me and the corner of his mouth tips up in a forced smirk at odds with the pain in his eyes. "Organize your armada, *Admiral*."

17

Paige

Dominic rests casually against his command table on the other side of the tent with Bella standing between his legs. None of the girls have Enhanced Hearing to know what the two of them say to one another. Not that I'm sure we want to know some of what they share. The public displays of affection between Dominic and Bella rip open the ache in my heart further each time.

He pulls her closer to him, hands on her hips, until their chests are nearly flush. The charming smile he bestows on her would be enough to melt any girl's heart—were he not a hideous monster underneath. He nuzzles his face into her neck as she wraps her arms around his, sliding her fingers into his dark, wavy hair.

My heart aches. My stomach twists. *"If you work with me instead of against me, I can make sure you and Zephyr end up together."* Dominic's promise is worthless, but as I watch him with Bella, I want it to be true. I want to be with Zephyr. I want that future with him on a beach, without a care in the world to hold us back.

I rip my gaze away from the two of them and finish straightening my sleeping mat, using far too much force to flatten out any bumps beneath it. One patch of uneven ground pushes up against the mat and I punch it ruthlessly into submission.

"What's wrong?" Ivy asks softly so no one else hears.

I just shake my head. How can I tell her what Dominic has asked of me? How do I admit that he asked me to help him burn the world to rebuild it? Or that I might consider it if that means having Zephyr hold me like Dominic holds Bella? Not that I really would agree, but the fantasy eases some of the pain in my heart.

Ivy doesn't press the issue.

By the time I stretch out on my mat, all the girls are casting worried glances my way. All of them except Layla, who glares at Bella like she wants to burn her alive.

The tent is cramped, which does nothing to help my claustrophobia. Ivy is too close on one side; Alice is too close on the other. I flop on my back and stare at the ceiling, but it looks lower tonight than usual. It can't be. That's my imagination running wild. My lungs tighten. I focus on regulating my breathing, but the more I focus on it, the harder it becomes. Between the close quarters and the suffocating sensation of being harnessed, my claustrophobia kicks into high gear. Nothing I do seems to help. My vision swirls. I whimper as I gasp for breath.

Alice's face hovers over me, worry drawing her brows together. But she's close. Too close. I shove her away, and my hands tremble violently.

Raised voices call for help. I fight for air like a fish out of water. I close my eyes, but nothing works.

Dominic hovers over me, his hand on my forehead like he's checking my temperature. Glorious air fills my lungs.

"What happened, Paige?" he asks. "You lost consciousness. Were you trying to break free again?" His fingertips press painfully against my head now.

I shake my head a little. No part of me wants to admit weakness to him. He already knows enough, and the idea of baring any more of myself to him makes me nauseated. But I have no choice. If I don't tell him the truth, he's likely to tighten his hold. I don't know if I can handle that.

"I... I'm claustrophobic," I admit. "All of this, the tight quarters, being smothered and constantly surrounded, the way I can't..." The pressure returns, threatening to grip me again. "I can't control myself or these Powers..."

Dominic grimaces, trying to gauge the truth in my confession. The healer shifts back and shakes his head. I hadn't even noticed the healer with Dominic crowding my vision. His grimace tightens when he meets the healer's gaze, then he nods and waves the man off.

The girls linger nearby, watching me with a variety of concerned expressions on their faces.

The moment the healer is gone, Dominic's expression softens. Were it not for the captivity and emotional abuse he's subjected me to, I would buy this act of compassion. Instead, it makes me want to punch him in the face.

Dominic slides his fingers along my temples, then holds them in place for several agonizingly long minutes. But the longer he remains glued to my temples, the less my panic grips me. He remains in this position, melting away my fear. How is he doing that? Is he somehow Controlling my reactions? I don't like that at all.

At last, he lets go, stroking my hair back away from my face like Gavin would, full of brotherly compassion.

"Is that better?" he asks tenderly.

My gut churns. *No, jerk!* Any hold over me isn't better. It's just different. But I nod because I just want him to go away.

"Paige, if we are going to do this together, you need to be honest with me about things like this." He doesn't scold me. His voice is gentle like my mother's when she wants me to see reason. "Understood?"

I offer a weak nod.

"Good. Get rest." Dominic rises and marches to the other side of the tent where Bella waits.

I averted my eyes before he reaches her. Watching them so happy together is unbearable. I need to tear them apart.

"What are you doing with him?" Layla hisses from her mat.

"Nothing more than we all are," I say. Admitting the truth to her is not an option. I trust Layla less than any of the girls here—except for Bella.

Layla huffs like she doesn't buy what I'm selling, but she drops it.

It takes forever to fall asleep. I don't drift off until the others are already softly breathing in sleep themselves.

I can't Dream anymore. Not like I used to. I still have dreams, but they don't leave me with a sense that any of it was real when I wake. Often, I can't remember them. Sometimes hints of the dream remain. The lingering sensation of Zephyr's touch. The feeling that something great has been lost. Blood on my hands. A flaming heat burning beneath my skin. I wake up crying sometimes and don't even know why.

Ivy comforts me when I wake in tears. The next morning when we break camp, Ivy and January ride beside me as we traverse the wastelands. I don't say much. I don't have anything of value to say, and my worry for Zephyr consumes my thoughts.

Both girls are more than happy to fill the silence with stories of their childhood. It casts a light on life on the mainland that I hadn't been aware of before.

The royal family's assertion that they protect the mainlanders and that there are bandits seems accurate. Ivy lost an older sister to bandits who invaded her village, dragging her sister away. The elders found her body four days later, abused and abandoned. They struck after the Kingdom soldiers checked in, then left. When January was a little girl, the soldiers hunted down a small group of bandits north of her village and eliminated everyone they found.

I can't help wondering if that's true. If any of those men had Powers, would the Kingdom have forced them to join service or die? So much about their system is broken, but not beyond help. *Cypress could have helped fix things. His compassion and calm intelligence would have made him an excellent king. And a good ally to Elpis.*

18

GAVIN

FOUR ELPIS MILITARY SHUTTLES pull in front of the hotel where the Havenites and I have taken up residence. Dad has been gone for a couple of days to work his magic on the Council, though he did once more beg me to come home with him the morning he left. It was hard telling him no when his request was so heartfelt. But not that simple. He swore he would have more supplies sent.

We've heard nothing for two days. The resources that were sent earlier have been depleted.

"I was starting to think they abandoned us," Drake mutters as the shuttles roll to a stop.

"Dad wouldn't leave me here."

Drake stands beside me, glancing at me from the corner of his eyes.

Before one vehicle has come to a complete stop, the passenger door opens and Uncle Alex hops out, his shock of shaggy blond hair instantly recognizable to me. A grin splits my face, and we rush to greet each other with a firm hug.

"Thought I lost you, kid," Alex says when he steps back. "Glad to see you alive."

"Is Mom here?" I ask hopefully, watching as the other truck doors open.

"Not this time. Sorry, Gav." Alex places a reassuring hand on my shoulder. "Not for lack of trying, though. She tried to get on the shuttle, but Levi kicked her off. Apparently, she isn't deemed *essential* to this undertaking."

Men and women in uniforms march toward Emil, Ajax, and Ally. I track their movements just in case there's trouble.

"But Mom can create environments," I argue, not that I don't understand the logic behind the decision. Mom's Powers have always been weak. She would be of little use to us. "Never mind. I'll see her soon enough. Wait, how did you end up being essential?"

Alex smirks. "Levi wouldn't dare stop me, and Bianca wouldn't let him." Electricity hums between his fingers, making his meaning clear enough.

I laugh, my heart lifting as I can picture the scene playing out. No one stands in Uncle Alex's way once he makes up his mind.

Alex's gaze slips past me. "Who's this?"

I peer at Drake as he strolls over to join us. My cheeks heat. "Um, well, this is... I mean, he..." Why can't I just say it? Uncle Alex would understand. He's the one who helped me understand the challenges that being gay presented. He knew before anyone else.

Alex raises his brows pointedly.

"Drake." Drake stretches a hand to Alex. "And you are?"

"Alex Miller." He shakes Drake's hand, and his eyes rove over Drake like he's picking him apart one cell at a time.

I waste no more time. "You brought a lot of supplies this time?"

Alex shakes his head. "We brought a lot of shuttles, genius."

Drake's eyes widen. "Wait, does that mean...?" Hope sparks in his eyes. "Are we going to Elpis?"

Alex opens his mouth the respond, thinks for a moment, then his shoulders sag. "Not just yet. Your dad is working hard on getting everyone access at least to the outskirts, but you know how the Council can be. Bunch of stick-up-the-butt bureaucrats."

Drake chuckles. I don't. It's just Uncle Alex being Alex. He has a deeply rooted mistrust of any form of government. I can't really blame him after everything he went through, though I would have expected him to be at least a little more open to this new government with Dad playing such a critical role.

"So no supplies or entry to the city," I say flatly. "Why bring four shuttles?"

"Bianca has been scouting the land between Elpis and here as best she can ever since your radio signal reached us," Alex explains. "She found another location closer to Elpis with easier access for everyone. It's still pretty far out, but at least radio communications will be open. They restored an old hotel along a river, and there's a bridge nearby that's in good enough condition for the shuttles to cross. We came to move these people to the new location. All the supplies are already there waiting for your arrival."

Four shuttles. Each carries thirty people, maximum. We have six hundred.

"That's five trips," I exclaim. "How far is this new hotel?"

"A little over a hundred miles that way," Alex says, squinting as he points southwest. "At least five trips. The sooner we can start loading people up, the better. You should climb in a truck now so you can be there to organize everyone at the other end."

I shake my head. "Emil and Ally can handle that. I'm not leaving here until everyone is moved."

Alex nods. "I'm going wherever you are, kid. I'm not letting you out of my sight for a second."

Drake shuffles his feet and mutters, "Hopefully at least for a *few* seconds."

Alex smirks, then clears his throat. "Let's get people loaded up, Gavin."

Easier said than done. First, we have to gather everyone together and explain what is happening. Then we need to form groups so there are Guardians and acolytes evenly distributed to protect the Havenites who have no Powers to protect themselves.

Emil doesn't like being sent in the first wave, but his arguments die a slow, painful death when Alex puts his foot down. The glowering the two do at one another would amuse me if I wasn't worried they might actually try tearing each other apart. I always thought Emil was like Alex. Seeing them together now only solidifies that assessment.

By the time the shuttles leave with the first group of Havenites, we've already lost hours of daylight. The trucks can't travel at night, or they won't get a proper solar charge as they drive. When they leave, we all know we won't make a second trip today. The trucks will return here, then leave at first light tomorrow.

At this rate, with a round trip that should take just under four hours, depending on conditions and how long it takes to unload everyone, it will take us three days. One group today. Three tomorrow, and the final groups the day after.

———— ❀ ————

B Y THE THIRD NIGHT, Drake and I are settled into our
suite—one of only a few in the hotel. The location is secure
enough for our needs at the moment. It won't serve long-term.

I close the door on Uncle Alex after another *"Just checkin' in, kid,"*
and turn to Drake, releasing a puff of air. Getting Alex to take a room
across the hall had not been easy, and Drake had stepped in and
convinced him. I still don't understand how he did it. Few people
can talk Alex out of an idea.

Drake shrugs. "I mean, aside from not wanting to share a room,
because we *need* our privacy, I don't see the problem. I like Alex, and
I can see why you get along. He doesn't pull any punches, does he?"

I shake my head. "No, he doesn't."

"If he doesn't like me, this is over, right?"

The question startles me.

Drake chuckles. "I'm joking."

"I don't like the joke. And I don't get it."

"Because he... Never mind. Not important." He moves toward
the minibar Elpis has been kind enough to stock with non-perish-
able snacks. I smile as I watch him tear open a packet of jerky with
feverish hunger, then I step out onto the balcony overlooking the
river.

The air is cool, and I can't complain about the scenery, either. We
have a pleasant view of the river, though the barren landscape across
the water leaves something to be desired.

"This is a far cry from being cooped up in cramped apartments
underground," Drake says around a mouthful of jerky. He drops
into a patio chair that looks ready to snap at any moment. I wince,
but nothing happens. "So how long do you think your council will
take?"

I shrug, easing cautiously into the other chair. It holds. "Dad will
do everything he can to sway them as quickly as possible. Especially
knowing I won't come home until the Havenites are safe." I glance
at him. "This isn't a terrible place to be stuck with you."

He peers out across the river. "I guess. But what if they don't agree, Gavin?"

"They will."

"But what if they don't? And then, say, one day they stop sending rations. We can't farm that land. No one has seen any wildlife. The river has no edible fish. How do we survive then?"

I study the wasteland across the river. Drake isn't wrong. That land is dead. The few trees that remain alive barely cling to life. They're twisted, nearly barren versions of what they should be. If trees can't survive with roots deep in the soil, crops won't stand a chance. I'm not sure even I can fix that.

"Dad won't let it come to that. He will go against the Council before he lets these people starve."

Drake snorts, swiping his sleeve across his lips. "He didn't seem too eager so far."

"He's done so much already," I point out. "This hotel..."

"You set us up before he came along."

"The food and water rations."

"Which could stop at any time."

I fight off a retort. "The endless stream of Department of Security people to help protect us."

"*Their* military."

My fingers twitch on the rusty arm of the chair. "The regular updates from the city."

"Vague, at best."

I huff. Drake is right. The updates we received haven't given us a lot to go on. Reassurances that they are doing everything they can, that it shouldn't be long, that more supplies will arrive in a few days. The Council of Representatives has been locked in meetings with the major departments in Elpis for hours each day. None of the information sent to us gives us a lead.

"This level of negativity from you is something I'm not accustomed to," I admit. "I don't like it."

"It's important to me that you see this as some of us do. We are getting by on the whims of your council. If they change their minds, we'll have nothing."

I need Drake to believe me. Partly because I know I'm right—Dad won't leave me out here, and I won't leave without the Havenites.

Partly because it hurts me that Drake thinks so little of my people. Especially after what *his* people did to us. Another fight like our last one might destroy me for good. Terrified we are headed down that road, I shift out of my chair and kneel in front of him, taking his hands in mine.

"Everything will work out," I say urgently, desperately. "I need you to keep faith in me. I may not know the Council, but I know my people *and* my dad. Not only will he not want me to stay out here any longer than necessary, but he won't want these people to come to harm. Especially not when he could do something about it. No one will."

"But he can..."

"And he is. I promise you that." My thumb brushes the waves on his bracelet. I stare at the medallion as a small smile creeps across my face. "Dad will exhaust every viable argument the Council can raise. He will state our case better than anyone else. And if they still refuse, he won't leave us here."

Drake leans forward, sliding his hand along my neck. It sends a shiver of delight down my spine. "You better be right, Gavin."

"I'm betting my life on it."

"You're betting *all* of our lives on it." His lips brush mine, creating a ripple of heat across my face that spreads like fire throughout my body when he deepens the kiss.

At that moment, I accept the truth. I would rather die out here with him than go back to Elpis without him. His lips move away from mine and I groan in disappointment. But he blazes a trail along my jaw, then whispers in my ear. "We should go back inside."

I rise, clinging to his hand and pulling him with me through the suite to our bedroom. Heady excitement floods every molecule of my body as his hands tug at my shirt, then slip beneath the fabric. Weeks of unspent desire pour out with each kiss and touch until I can't take it any longer. My Powers buzz like electricity beneath my skin. Can he feel it, too?

The knock on the suite door hardly even registers over the hammering of my heart. I never knew that intimacy could feel like this.

"If that is Alex again, I swear..." Drake mumbles between kisses.

Another knock. I growl and tear my lips away. He's right. Uncle Alex needs some clear boundaries. Drake doesn't give me a second to breathe before turning my face back to his.

"Don't." Then he's kissing me again and I'm helpless to refuse.

Another knock, followed by a familiar voice.

"Gavin?" Dad calls through the door.

All the excitement building inside crashes down on me. I pull away from Drake.

"No. Gavin, it can wait." He grabs my waist and pulls me back.

I ease his grip off, holding his hands. "I wish I agreed. Believe me. But we were just talking about how important getting to Elpis is. He came out tonight instead of tomorrow for some reason. I can't ignore him."

Drake mutters something under his breath while I make my way toward the entrance. The door to our bedroom thumps closed. I wince. Hopefully, Drake won't be mad at me for too long.

I pull the suite door open, my face still heated. "You're back a day early."

Dad's gaze sweeps over me. He appears ready to say something, then thinks better of it and slides past me into the room. And he isn't alone. Uncle Alex is, of course, hot on his heels. Dad examines the room, then stares at the closed bedroom door. Embarrassment rushes through me. Does he know what nearly happened?

Alex does. The smirk he cannot hide says he knows exactly why it took me so long to answer the door.

Dad clears his throat. "The Council wants to hear from you in person."

Memories of that horrific meeting with the Elders bubble to the surface. I fumbled like a fool and didn't know what to say. The humiliation still haunts me. Not to mention how I lost my temper with them. What if I do that in front of the Council of Representatives? "I...can't."

"Sure you can, kid," Alex says gruffly. He eases down onto the sofa.

Dad eyes him but dismisses whatever thought has popped into his head. He turns his attention fully to me. "They just have a few questions about the Havenites and how they propose to become functioning members of Elpis." Dad slides his hands into his pockets. Even standing casually, he has an air of control that I've admired all my life.

"Oh, that's all?"

Alex raises his brows at my snide comment. "Sarcasm. That's new." Is that pride in his blue eyes?

Drake jerks open the bedroom door and rushes out onto the balcony. We watch him, distracted by the odd behavior.

"Gavin!" Drake's panic makes my gut twist.

As Dad, Alex, and I join him on the balcony, the warning booms all around the hotel.

The Havenites shout a warning, "The Kingdom approaches! Everyone hide!"

I peer down to see Havenites scrambling for shelter inside. Doors slam closed. Locks click in place.

Drake trembles, clinging to the balcony rail. "That's a lot of ships."

"That's a lot of *soldiers*," Alex corrects.

My stomach sinks as I watch a fleet of ships sail in a line upriver...straight toward our hotel.

The radio attached to Dad's belt crackles to life, making all four of us jump.

"Mayday Daliah. Notify Doctor Brown," the male voice calls from the radio.

19

ZEPHYR

I HOLD MY BREATH, waiting for a reply. Paige's brother is nearby. The intensity of his magic has been reaching out to me for miles, growing stronger as we creep closer through the water. The sensation of his magic reminds me of the magical power thrown at my men in old St. Louis. It *must* be him.

Only ten minutes ago, that magic surged and nearly knocked me out cold. Were it not for the time Paige spent training on the island, giving me a chance to acclimate myself to the vicious assault, Gavin's magic would have been like a hammer directly striking my skull. It feels different from her, but just as powerful.

"Are you sure we're close?" Nat asks.

"Look at that building," Cypress says, nodding at a sprawling three-story structure. "It's clearly been restored recently. Everything else is in ruins."

We can barely see the building from this distance without the pocket scope. But what we can see makes it clear Cypress is right.

I press the button again. "Mayday Daliah. Notify Doctor Brown." Easton assured me these words would get someone's attention once we are within range. Does Gavin have a radio, too? "Nat, have the helmsmen on each ship kill the engines. We can't appear aggressive."

Cypress raises the scope and gasps. "There are definitely people there. They're all scrambling inside. They've spotted us."

Come on. Someone answer!

Just as I'm about to press the button again, the radio crackles and a man responds. "Daliah responding. Doctor Brown is on alert."

My heart leaps. Is this Gavin? I press the button. "Requesting permission to dock."

"Easton?"

All three of us stiffen. Nat's eyes widen.

"Tell him who you are," Easton had advised.

"Negative. This is Admiral Zephyr Strong. Easton sent me to speak with the Minister of Elpis." I release the button and hold my breath.

The silence makes me uncomfortable. Cypress' lips compress. The longer the silence draws out, the more he eyes me like I screwed something up. I did what Easton told me to do.

Nat shifts his feet. My shoulders tighten so much I'm worried they will snap.

"You can only bring ten men ashore, yourself included," the man finally says. "Our guards will disarm you at the dock and escort you to the patio to meet."

Nat puffs out a breath and sags so close to the ground he nearly collapses. Cypress nods in agreement.

THE GUARD UNIFORMS REMIND me of the ones Paige and Easton wore when we captured them, except bulkier, with extra pockets and a thicker vest. The gear is more sophisticated than anything we can create in the Kingdom.

Each guard shifts uncomfortably before we even step off the ship. They can feel my block against their magic and they don't like it, but they don't seem to realize I'm the cause. I say a quiet prayer of thanks. Something tells me that if they knew it was me, I would be either in chains or dead.

Unlike our military—which consists solely of men—these guards are a mixture of men and women. While none of them are anywhere near as strong as Paige or Gavin, each is nearly as strong as Easton. The Elpis gene pool must be saturated with magic to have so many at such a high class.

I'm thankful Cypress is dressed like I am, though with a few more stripes on his jacket. We can't afford for this to go wrong. We need Elpis to help us fight Dominic. Everything we have planned banks on the Minister of Elpis wanting to join us to get his daughter back.

The guards escort our meager group of ten to the patio the man on the radio mentioned, their positions surrounding us on every side to trap us in. Not that we intend to start a fight.

The patio overlooking the river has flagstone flooring, rusting metal tables and chairs, and a firepit with no fire. The guards accompany us to a circle of chairs around the low firepit.

Dozens of faces peer through the tall windows lining the building walls. Women and children. Pale-faced men. Some are curious. Others are mistrusting. Who are these people? Are they from Elpis? Based on what Paige said, I expected her people to be heartier, like the guards. These people are all gaunt and pale.

A door opens, and a man in his forties, with dark skin and keen eyes, emerges ahead of a small group. Most of them have magic. Gavin's magic hits me before he steps out on the older man's heels. The resemblance between the two is immediately recognizable. I hadn't connected the older man as Paige's father because she looks almost nothing like him or her brother. Were it not for Gavin's magic, I might not believe it either. *She must look like her mother.*

As Gavin passes the firepit, he runs a hand through the air over it. A pulse of magic bucks against me, making me grit my teeth. A fire springs to life.

I gape. That shouldn't be possible with me so close.

Nat leans closer. "How did he do that?"

I can only respond with a subtle shrug. Gavin's magic didn't even fight to break free. It simply surged to light the fire. That doesn't bode well for my chances of helping Paige keep hers from roaring out of control.

Minister Powers approaches with a certainty that indicates he knows we won't attack. Something about the way he moves reminds me of Paige. Either he is confident in himself, or they have something up their sleeves. I certainly hope it's the former. He stops a few feet away, inside the circle, eyeing the ten of us as if picking the group apart. He stops on Cypress.

"Zephyr?" he asks Cypress.

My cousin shakes his head, amused by the mistake. We agreed he wouldn't announce himself as the king until we are certain we can trust these people.

"That's Zephyr," one of Minister Powers' men says, nodding toward me. He's older, with an angry face.

I frown. *How does he know me?*

A dark-haired young man edges closer to Gavin and whispers something. Gavin nods in response. The other guy examines me like he's judging a pound of flesh on the scales of justice. My guts twist in a knot. What are they saying about me?

I clear my throat. "I'm Zephyr."

"A bit young to be admiral, aren't you?" Minister Powers asks.

I can't answer. Baron's dying eyes pierce me. This title shouldn't be mine. Not yet. I wanted it, but not like this. Baron should be standing here, not me.

"He's up to the task," Cypress says, sensing my distress.

Minister Powers eases into a chair, his gaze fixed on me. My palms sweat under his scrutiny. As he sits, the rest of his group follows his lead. I make note of who sits at his side—Gavin and a blond-haired fellow about the Minister's age—and how the rest fan out. The dark-haired guy sticks close to Gavin's side, and his gaze keeps drifting to Cypress.

"Where are Easton and my daughter?" Minister Powers asks.

The blond-haired man glowers at our group with far more mistrust than anyone has ever looked at me before. His fingers twitch and his scowl deepens. Then his hand tightens in a fist. His magic is strong. He's the closest I've ever felt to a class ten mage. His magic pulses like electricity against mine but can't break free. In seconds, he deduced I'm the cause of his block, and the hate in his blue eyes reminds me all too much of Dominic.

I avert my gaze and jerk my head to our own small party. Everyone takes a seat across from the Elpis people.

Cypress leans forward, resting his elbows on his knees while meeting Minister Powers' stare without flinching. I admire that.

The Minister has no magic to speak of, but he commands the surrounding air like Vincent or Dominic. Obedience to him doesn't come from forced subjugation or fear. These people respect him that much. *No wonder Paige wanted to go home.*

"Easton is back at the palace," Cypress explains. "We asked him to come along to make this easier for all parties, but he insisted on staying in the Capital to tie off a few loose ends and protect our family while we are away." Cypress' face falls as he examines his hands, slowly rubbing his palms together. "We came hoping to forge an alliance."

The blond grunts as if the idea is ludicrous, folding his hands across his stomach as he lounges back without a care. But the guy is a wolf. We would be foolish to underestimate him.

"Let me stop you there, young man." Anger burns in the Minister's voice. "The *only* reason we're speaking right now is because my son insisted we give Zephyr a chance to explain." His dark eyes dart to me. "So explain. Where is my daughter?"

The anger in his eyes differs from anything I'm used to—far unlike the former king. Sweat beads beneath my collar and trickles down my back. This is a father ready to move heaven and earth to get his daughter back. And more than anything, I want him to approve of me. Because I know Paige well enough to know that if he doesn't, nothing I say or do will sway her to choose me.

"Paige is with our brother, Dominic," I say. The words ease the tension in Gavin, and he sinks back in his chair. I lick my lips. He knows something about us, but not enough to understand what that means. Last he heard from Paige—I assume in a Dream—Dominic must have been helping her. "He...is not who we thought he was."

"Not your brother?" Gavin asks. His brows tighten as he examines Cypress. He's putting it together.

I attempt to keep my body language open, but more than anything, I want to cross my arms and curl in on myself in front of this crew. Instead, I grip the arms of my rusty chair. "That's...complicated. But not the point, either. Dominic plotted insurrection against the crown and seized control of the island. By the time we retook control, he already left with a substantial army, and Paige."

Minister Powers rubs his fingers over his forehead, chin dipped to his chest. "Why her?" But the way he asks makes me think he already knows something.

Gavin's eyes widen. "Because she's like me, Dad."

The Minister opens his mouth, ready to say something to his son, but thinks better of it and clenches his jaw.

"We only recently discovered Dominic's magic is much stronger than we were led to believe," I continue. "He's controlling her and marching his army to your city."

The blond's already angry face turns red. The electric pulse of his magic thrashes against mine. Who is this guy? "Controlling her?" His words are little more than a growl.

"Isn't it your army?" Gavin directs his question at Cypress. "You are the King, aren't you?"

Cypress eyes the Minister warily as he answers. "Dominic has been planning this longer than I've had the crown. It goes back years. Paige served as a catalyst for his plans."

At first, the Minister's eyes shine with rage, but as he lifts his gaze, I notice they're tears. "Since he is marching on my city and my people, you think that gives you the right to request an alliance after you attacked both of my children and abducted one of them?"

Cypress gulps loudly. He sinks back in his chair.

I lean forward to draw some of the anger off him. "I admit, we have made some mistakes. Some big mistakes. But Paige and Easton have changed us. Easton has been level with us from the start. His objective view of our life has opened our eyes to truths we were blind to. And Paige has been quick to point out every way we are doing things wrong." I can't help a small smile from curling the corners of my mouth as I remember the shade she threw my way about the entire pageant. "Including the notion that any girl forced into her situation could ever accept life on the island or find happiness there."

Discomfort at the thought of what might be happening to her right this moment writhes in my stomach. Dominic won't hurt her, not physically. But emotionally, he will tear her to shreds. Could Paige have found happiness with me if the situation had been different, or would she have chosen Cypress?

"Happiness. You mean like your mother?" An older man with dark hair and darker eyes glares at me from his seat—the same guy who picked me out without hesitation.

My heart stops. His hard eyes pierce every fiber of my soul like a thousand needles. Then anger burns in my veins. What does he know of my mother? "My mother loved my father."

He recoils, then glances at Gavin and turns his head away.

"Look, we are aware there is a lot of bad blood between us," Cypress says diplomatically. "But we are here to take the first step toward building a bridge instead of burning it for good. Isn't that why you sent your children out of the city in the first place? I will deal with my brother and get Paige back to where she belongs."

Minister Powers opens his mouth, but before he can speak, Cypress presses on, "In Elpis, with her family. But we don't have the strength to do this alone. Paige and Easton insist your city has a lot of power. From what I've seen so far, I think they're right. We are hoping you can help us defend your city and end this quickly. None of us want war."

Silence falls over us, punctuated only by the dull roar of the firepit. It stretches into eternity before the Minister rises.

"Walk with me, King Cypress," he says.

But he doesn't wait for Cypress to agree before he moves toward the path along the waterfront.

Cypress rises to join him.

I surge to my feet. "Cy..."

He rests a hand on my shoulder and gives it a small squeeze. "I'll be fine. Talk to your uncle." He nods toward the dark-haired man.

My jaw slackens. *Uncle?*

Cypress chuckles. "It's so obvious. He made the comment about your mother. She talked about her brother. He looks just like her. I'm surprised you don't see it."

"Just...stay close."

Cypress knows what I mean. No farther than fifty yards. I can't protect him with my sword, but my magic can protect him. Without further comment, Cypress strolls away to join Minister Powers. The angry blond lumbers in behind the two of them at a suitable distance. He is ready to kill Cypress to protect Minister Powers. The way he carries himself, tensed and ready for a fight, hands at his sides, tells me as much. Not that Cypress will do anything dumb... I hope.

I blink dimly after him, then glance from the corner of my eyes at the dark-haired man. Cypress is right. Though he wears a perpetual scowl, the man has the same jawline, the same eyes, as Mom.

The group on the patio breaks up. What remains of our group of ten men shuffles away from the others under Nat's watchful eye.

Gavin strolls toward me, hands in his pockets. The young man follows closely at his side.

"Paige told me about you," Gavin says.

I tense. What did she tell him?

"He's worried now," the dark-haired guy says, amused by my nervousness.

Gavin cocks his head. "This is Drake. He's my, um…"

"Boyfriend, Gavin," Drake says with a chuckle. "The word you're looking for is boyfriend."

Boyfriend? I glance from one to the other. I've heard of same-sex couples before, but never on the island itself. Except, I suppose, for Summer and River. Cypress told me about the two of them on the way here when we had a little time to waste, along with the other girls he dismissed.

Gavin waves the correction off. Do I look uncomfortable? I'm not. It doesn't really matter. Did Paige tell me he's gay? Maybe. It's hard to recall among everything else that's happened.

"Not the point," Gavin says quickly. "I just… I'm glad to meet you. To put a face to the name. And to tell you I'll do whatever I can to help get my sister back. No matter what Dad says."

Paige talked about Gavin like he is the other half of her coin, like he depends on her. Their sibling bond differs from the one I had with my cousins. Maybe because they weren't my siblings, and I knew it deep down somewhere.

I draw in a breath, asking what's been bugging me for several minutes. "How did you use your magic to start that fire?"

Gavin frowns as if he doesn't understand the question.

I wave a hand at the firepit. "My magic negates others. Not even Paige can use it around me. But you didn't even break a sweat."

Drake beams at Gavin, dark eyes sparkling. The older man—my alleged uncle—groans as if I've struck a nerve.

Gavin simply shrugs. "I feel your Power, but I've dealt with worse than you."

Worse than negating his magic?

"Paige told me about your mom," Gavin says, motioning the older man forward. "I wish we could have helped her. The Kingdom took Emil's sister years ago. You aren't her, but you are her son. I hope that counts for something. There's nothing more important than family."

Family. I peer over my shoulder at Cypress as he strolls alongside the Minister. I've already accepted that Cypress is my brother, even if we don't share parents. But Dominic... "I wish I had the heart to believe that."

"Dad taught us that the true quality of a man is tested when he is at his weakest," Gavin says. "Some fold. Others fight. Don't blame yourself for what Dominic has done. You can only control how you respond."

I raise a brow at Gavin. Those are some wise words from a guy who must be close to my age, though I suppose if they come from his dad, that makes more sense.

The older man, Emil, remains off to the side, somewhat aloof in his stance. But every few seconds, he eyes me like he wants to say something but doesn't have the words.

Gavin and Drake hold hands as they walk away, leaving me alone with my uncle.

Emil stares at his boots now, hands buried so deep in his pockets he could reach his knees. Neither of us speaks. I don't know what to say to him. Mom talked about her brother, but never named him—a fact I hadn't thought odd until this moment. Was she trying to protect him?

He clears his throat. "I hated you for a while once I found out who you were."

I flinch. It shouldn't hurt. I don't even know the guy. But it does. "Why?"

He shrugs, nudging the flagstone with the toe of his boot. "All I've wanted for the last twenty-three years was my sister. You're, what, twenty?"

"Nineteen." *Barely.*

He nods, finally straightening to meet my gaze. "I resented you because those were supposed to be my years with her. But you got 'em instead."

How do I respond to that? It's not *my* fault they took her from him, even if I am part of the same system. "She never forgot about you. But she loved my father right up to the day she died." The pain of losing her claws at my heart. Of the anger she saw in me before she died.

Emil nods. "And your dad?"

My throat tightens. "Dead," I croak.

Silence. Emil's lips thin, looking at everything except me. Does it hurt to look at me? I've always been told I look like my father—which I had assumed meant Alric the Third—but I have my mother's eyes.

Emil sighs. "I've scrounged up some *really* old whiskey if you want to share stories in my room."

My mouth waters. I'm about to accept. "I don't drink." The words alarm me. I've not had a drop since Easton poured everything down the drain. Emil's offer is the first chance I've had at a drink since. I *should* want it. Some part of me does, but a larger part of me doesn't. Not if it inhibits my ability to help Paige. She needs me to break free from Dominic, and I can't risk that for anything. I can't let myself fall back down that hole.

"I have water rations, too," Emil offers with a reserved smirk.

I squint down the riverfront. Cypress and Minister Powers are engaged in deep conversation. The blond remains some distance away, watchful.

"He'll be fine as long as he doesn't try anything dumb," Emil reassures me. "Ugene's not rash. If anything, he's annoyingly patient and smart. He wouldn't attack first. Plus, no one here would dare bite the hand that feeds them." Emil pats my shoulder, then turns me away. "Come on. They're fine."

I trail along after my uncle, glancing at Cypress once more before slipping inside. He meets my gaze for a moment and gives me a subtle nod.

20

PAIGE

W E MAKE CAMP AGAIN for the night and I peer over at Dominic perched on the edge of his bed—he is the only person with an actual bed. Bella sits beside him, holding his hand. The two of them speak in hushed whispers. Then he shakes his head as he responds, then rises and stretches his limbs, and kisses her on the cheek before marching out of the tent.

Bella watches him go. Then her gaze darts to me, determination burning in her eyes. I don't dare look away first.

"Paige," Ivy hisses. "You'll get yourself into trouble. Stop glaring at her."

"Let her bring trouble my way," I grumble, sitting back on my mat. Dominic needs me. If Bella hurts me, it's as good as causing a fight between them.

We've traveled further southwest, but at some point they will demand more direct answers to my vague directions. "I want to take her eye out and give it to Dominic as a gift," I grumble.

Which one of them took Easton's eye? It must have been Dominic. He had access and the means while she was trapped in the palace.

Bella marches toward us. The other girls shy away—except for Layla and me. Layla glares at Bella, as she always does, as if she would love nothing more than to put a dagger in the girl's heart.

Bella nudges me with the toe of her boot, arrogantly peering down her nose at me. The walls around me close tighter.

"Get up, Paige." It isn't a request.

I grit my teeth and fight back against the compulsion to obey her. "Dominic seemed to disagree with whatever you said."

"Don't pretend to understand what we were talking about," Bella snaps. "*Get. Up.*" While her words don't force me to obey, I still do. What does she want with me?

Bella turns on her heel and marches toward the exit. I don't want to follow her, but I *do* want to get out of this tent and have a few minutes alone to inject doubt into the happy couple's relationship. Divide and conquer.

The night air is cooler than I expect and a chill crawls across my skin.

Bella walks me around the tent into a small clearing, then pulls a device from her pocket that looks a lot like an old cell phone. They don't have those, do they? I don't recall seeing anyone with a cell phone anywhere on the island during my stay. The ones in Elpis only work in or around the city. Anywhere we can set up a tower. How does Bella's phone work?

"We've been walking for days with no signs of your people anywhere," Bella says, casually flipping the device open and closed. "Dominic is certain you can't lie to us, that you will work with him so you can get what you want in the end, whatever that may be. None of that means you can't stall us for as long as you like. Which has me wondering what you think you have to gain by stalling."

I cock my head. This is my chance to plant seeds of doubt between her and Dominic. Fracturing them might help Zephyr—it might help all of us. "I find it interesting that he clearly instructed you not to do something, yet here we are. You don't trust his judgment."

Bella snaps the phone closed, glaring at me. "Dominic and I are of one mind."

I shake my head slowly, exuding a cocky arrogance to match her own. "No, he and I are. He showed me everything. His childhood. How his plans began forming. What he intends to do. I've seen it all."

Bella's lips thin, but I press on before she can speak, "You are just like me, Bella. A means to an end. His desires for control go farther back than you. He needed your father's help, and what better way to secure that help than by using you, Vincent's one and only weakness?"

She sneers. "Dominic loves me. He adores me."

"Oh, I'm sure he's more than happy with the company you provide him between the sheets, but his vision doesn't include an empress at his side. He will use you and toss you aside when your usefulness has worn out."

A slap stings my cheek before I've finished speaking, jerking my head to the side.

"How dare you accuse me of being loose," Bella growls, leaning close and baring her white teeth. "I'm not the one who jumped from one Strong brother to the other."

I flinch. "Didn't you? What about Cypress?"

"He was nothing to me, and we never so much as kissed. But you..." She shakes her head.

I hate the way her words make my insides twist; hate how right she is. I care deeply for both Cypress and Zephyr, though in very different ways. It makes my blood boil. "All I'm saying is that you should be wary of Dominic's affection. He's an excellent actor, and terribly patient when he wants something." I dare to take a step closer to her. "Do you know what he offered me to get my compliance? Zephyr."

"He's playing you," Bella snorts.

"Maybe. Or maybe not. He didn't seem bothered at all by the idea of removing your father from the equation the moment his usefulness has dried up. He called him...what was it?" I inch another step closer, hissing the insult in her face, "A *snake*. If he is willing to get rid of your father, no doubt he has considered how you will react and what he will need to do, then."

Bella slips her hand into her pocket, then pulls something out. "Enough of your poisonous words, slave."

Slave! But the word strikes true. I am a slave, harnessed and forced to perform for my master.

I glance at her hand. Vines shoot out from her palm as quickly as bolts of lightning, binding my limbs to my torso. Then they creep up around my neck and tighten. I can't even reach up to relieve the pressure as the vines slowly cut off my air. I've made a mistake forgetting her Power.

"You've been stalling us, and I want to know why," Bella hisses.

"I...can't...breathe!" Spots float in my vision.

"How far away are we?" Bella rams a fist into my gut, knocking what little air I have out of my lungs. The vines hold me up as she grabs a fistful of hair and yanks my head back. "I will get my answers, slave. Tell me how far we are and what waits for us, or I place a call to my father and you can listen to your lover scream."

My heart lurches. Anger flares in my chest, but my Powers remain just out of reach as they rage. My vision blurs. "I can't... I can't..." There's no breath to speak, even if I wanted to.

Bella sneers, flipping the phone open. For a moment, I can't see anything at all, but I can hear her voice as she holds the phone to her ear. "Answer, dammit!"

My fingers twitch. If I don't get out of this, I'll be unconscious in seconds, and who knows what will happen to Zephyr if I don't get that phone away from her.

"Answer," Bella grumbles as the other line continues ringing.

I don't need much of my Power. Just enough to breathe and get that phone. Or destroy it. Were I not suffocating, I might be able to focus enough to harness just enough to destroy the phone before Dominic's Control knocks me out.

The sound of booted feet approaches. I can't see clearly to distinguish who it is. I've never wished so hard for Dominic to appear.

The vines slacken at the same moment Bella snaps, "Watch it!"

The distraction, whoever created it and whatever it was, is just enough for me to regain the focus I needed to grasp a trickle of Power. With the vines loosened, I concentrate on the phone in Bella's hand. I can hear it ringing from here.

Bella yelps, then screams at me, but before she tightens her hold again, I destroy the vines and stagger to my feet. My vision slowly returns to normal and I prepare for a fight. A headache hammers at my skull, momentarily blinding me. I stagger.

But Bella is already on the ground being punched mercilessly by Layla.

A guard wraps his arm around Layla's waist as she kneels over Bella and hammers her fists into Bella's face.

Dominic rushes around the tent, taking in the fight with a sweep of his blue eyes. "What in the name of the tides happened?" Dominic snaps. He grabs my arm in an iron grip as he pulls me away. "Paige, we had a deal." His fingers dig into my arm.

"I didn't..."

Layla screams and kicks wildly, but the guard hoists her away firmly in his arm. He must be a Strongarm.

"I'm sorry, Your Grace," the guard says quickly. "She needed to use the restroom. I didn't expect her to attack Lady Bella."

Was Layla trying to help me? No. She's always been selfish, and ever since she first laid eyes on Bella out here, she has been glaring death at the other girl.

"He was supposed to be mine!" Layla growls at Bella.

Dominic releases my arm to attend to Bella. I want to run, hide, and escape further interrogation, but I can't move. His Control tightens, intensifying my already pounding headache. He kneels beside Bella, helping her sit up and pressing a handkerchief to her bloody lip. There's so much tenderness in his attention to her injuries that it makes me feel like I'm invading their privacy. It also threatens to undermine any doubt I might have planted in Bella's mind.

"I was right about her," Bella mumbles.

Is she talking about me or Layla?

"I told you to leave it be," he says.

Bella whispers something to Dominic and he stiffens, then shoots a curious glance at me over his shoulder. For a moment, he weighs me as if considering his options. I'm in big trouble if she told him what I said. If I'm right, I've exposed his plan. If I'm wrong, he will want retribution.

Dominic helps Bella to her feet, sliding his arm around her. Layla growls in a rage and starts kicking like a wild animal against the guard again.

"Bind her and put her to bed," Dominic tells the guard.

He grunts as Layla's foot connects with his shin, but he doesn't let go. "Gladly, Your Grace."

"Bring out January when you're done," Dominic commands.

As the guard struggles with a wild Layla, Dominic turns his full attention to me. "I thought we had an understanding, Paige."

Without the phone, they can't contact Vincent or hurt Zephyr. I straighten with a renewed sense of confidence. He might Control me, but my ability to grasp my Powers for even a second revealed the truth. He doesn't have absolute Control over me. Perhaps with enough time and finesse, I can break free.

"What understanding?" Bella asks, frowning at Dominic. Her lip is bleeding and swollen. I can't hide my smirk.

He ignores her, which only fans the flames of doubt. I watch as the realization strikes her. I may not be wholly right, but she knows I'm not entirely wrong, either.

"If you intend to undermine me and keep secrets, this will not work out the way you want," he tells me like a father lecturing a child. I want to strangle him.

I embrace the sensation of his Power over me, feeling along its corded tendrils for some point of weakness. He's wrapped it around my mind like a deep, invasive net. I can feel it, trace it, but I can't remove it. Not yet.

Dominic's oblivious to my gentle probing. "I think it's time for a little honesty, Paige." I hate the way he says my name, like we're friends. "Let's start with something simple, shall we? Tell me what we are up against when we reach Elpis. How many people live there?"

My jaw twitches as I fight against answering. The headache expands along my temple, spreading like a slow-burning fire. Then I sense it. The thread of Control is connected to this one command. I snap the thread, and a surge of agony shoots across my skull, forcing me to my knees. I grip my head and groan.

Dominic grunts. "It will only get worse the more you resist, Paige," Dominic says patiently. "How many people live in Elpis?"

All my fury burns in my gaze as I snap a fierce glare at him.

The guard rounds the tent with January following obediently. She stops beside me. I gulp for air, for cool relief, but it offers none.

"Right on time," Dominic says. He releases his supportive grip on Bella and glides toward January. "I need your help, January." His fingers slide along her collar until meeting the lock on the back. It pops open. "Paige believes she may resist commands, even when it causes her so much pain. She refuses to answer our questions and destroyed our connection to the island."

Zephyr is safe! For now, at least. As long as Dominic is here and Zephyr is there, he cannot hurt him. Which gives me more space to fight back.

"Get her to talk." Dominic sounds bored as he gives January the command.

January pales, shaking her head. Her lips tremble, but she reaches out for me against her own will, unable to disobey. The moment her fingers contact the skin on my collarbone, her Power pushes through me. Every fiber of my body feels like it's being slowly peeled apart. Sweat rolls down my temples. It collects on my upper lip. All I can do is scream.

January whimpers as tears roll down her cheeks.

Minutes pass—or maybe only seconds—before Dominic directs her to stop.

My body collapses beneath the weight of sudden relief. January murmurs an agonizing apology to me as she hugs her arms tight to her ample chest. I don't blame her.

Dominic crouches in front of me. "How many, Paige?"

I can't give him any information. This is one request I *can* refuse. I broke his tether forcing me to respond, so I clamp my jaw tight.

He sighs sadly, then waves to January. She whimpers, and her movements are unnatural as she reaches out this time, like she's trying to resist and fails.

I tense, readying for her Divinic Power to tear through me again. But nothing could prepare me for the intensity of torment. A scream rips from my throat for so long that my throat goes raw. January will kill me if this keeps up. I feel stretched out, as if she's healing me, but it isn't healing. Every cell in my body activates in a frenzy, trying to pull apart. I black out for a second from the pain.

Each breath is a gasp, small and desperate.

"Paige, answer the question," Dominic growls. "This will all end once you do."

My limbs twist as close to unnatural limits as possible. But I can't give in. I would rather die. I'm prepared to die to save my people.

Dominic's icy fingers pinch my chin, forcing me to look at him. Tears roll down my cheeks. "How far are we from your city, Paige?"

My lips part to answer. *No! I can't. I can't!*

Again, I feel that tendril of his Power linked to my compliance with this request. If I'm already in agony, a little more won't matter. I snap it like I did the last one. Dominic gasps in alarm.

If I thought I knew what was in store for me, I didn't know what genuine pain is. January cries at my side, begging me to answer him. Her Power pushes through me. I feel my joints pop as my limbs stretch out away from me. A muscle tears in one shoulder. Then another.

I scream like I've never screamed before, loud enough to wake the entire camp, the entire world. Sweat pours off my body. My teeth grind so hard against one another I fear they might break.

"How big is your military, Paige?" Dominic's voice is muffled by the blood rushing through my body.

Even if I wanted to, I wouldn't be able to answer him.

As I look at January, I hope she can sense that I don't hold her responsible for any of this. I pour as much apology into my gaze as I can under the circumstances.

Fighting to remain focused and conscious, I struggle to locate the thread leading to the question. When I do, I can't seem to break it like I did the other two. Blood drips from my nose. Prepared for death, for the worst, for this fire inside to consume me whole, I release a roar and tear at a chunk of the web he's placed over my mind.

The agony swallows me whole, and I welcome sleep as it engulfs me.

21

GAVIN

M Y HEAD HURTS. I would rather go back to bed than sit in this conference room any longer. Eleven of us are crowded into the room to plan the next steps; representatives from each of the three communities. The tension is so high even I can sense it.

Cypress, Zephyr, and Nat—Zephyr's second in command—sit at one end of the table. Though the three of them hold up well to the incessant grilling and backhanded comments thrown at them, it's obvious they are fighting the urge to lash out. Zephyr faces intense fire from the Elpis representatives who arrived this morning. He has pressed his back hard into his chair, fingers wrapped tightly around the arm of his seat.

Directly across from the three of them, Emil and Ally glare their way. I had hoped that, after catching up with his nephew, Emil would warm up to the Kingdom royals. I don't understand why he's still angry. Even Drake is standoffish toward them. I guess after a century of being hunted by the Kingdom, old animosity is hard to cast aside.

Dad sits at the head of the table, flanked on one side by Uncle Alex, who seems to hate Zephyr and Cypress for reasons I don't fully understand. On Dad's other side, Bianca—Paige's colonel and a family friend who's like an aunt to us—leans back in her chair with her arms crossed and thick lips tight. Levi, the Director of the Elpis Department of Security, sits beside her with his hands clasped on the tabletop.

The historical significance of this moment isn't lost on me. It's the first time these three communities have met, let alone attempted hashing out an alliance—even if it's short term. I just wish *they* understood the significance. No one seems able to make headway without kicking off another long-winded debate from a different community that takes forever.

Zephyr may be close to losing his cool, but his aptitude for military planning is apparent. Every time he proposes an idea that seems logical, either Ally or Alex shoots him down. Not that Alex is even part of the Elpis military. He just hates Zephyr.

Drake slides his hand over mine under the table, giving it a reassuring squeeze. He doesn't say a word, not wanting to interrupt the debate. I realize at that moment that I've been tapping my fingers against my leg impatiently.

"Your entire plan hinges on you getting close to Paige," Alex snaps sharply at Zephyr. "But if you think I'm letting you anywhere near her again—"

Dad heaves out a sigh. "Miller, remember what I told you."

Alex sneers at Zephyr like he wants to rip Zephyr's throat open with his teeth. "Oh, I remember." Does all of that hate stem from Zephyr kidnapping Paige and taking her to the island?

"Minister, you told us your mother put a protective barrier around Paige's mind," Zephyr says, ignoring Alex's hatred. Still, his jaw twitches ever so slightly. "The only way Dominic could use his magic on her is with the Control already in place. If I get close enough to her, my magic should negate his and free her."

"Should." Alex snorts.

Cypress shoots a glare at Alex. "Do you have a better idea, Mr. Miller? We're all ears. Because so far, you've only offered us snide comments and naysaying which hinder our progress more than help it."

Dad groans. Alex uncoils his crossed arms like a predator readying to strike at its prey. "Just point out this little bastard and I'll fry him before he knows what hit him. No leader, no invasion, no Control."

Zephyr grunts and shakes his head. He leans forward, not backing down from Alex. I don't think I've ever seen anyone challenge Alex like this before. Not since his partner, Jayme, left him. And Dad, but it's different with him. Dad's challenges are gentle and soothing. Zephyr is all hard edges. I'm seeing why Paige likes him.

"First, Dominic is too smart to make himself visible until he's breached the city to find whatever he's after," Zephyr says firmly. He stabs a finger at the table with each point. "Second, even *if* he shows his face, he will have protections around himself to prevent anyone from *frying* him." He air quotes Alex's words, which makes Alex's neck muscles tense. "Third, there's nothing preventing him from Controlling *your* mind. I can get close to him, walk right through his walls of magical protection, and he can't Control me. He's tried. It doesn't work."

"Magic..." Alex mutters. "Bunch of heathens."

Zephyr's jaw twitches. Cypress scowls at Alex. Neither of them rises to the bait.

Levi scrolls through something on his tablet as the two of them debate. As Zephyr winds down, Levi clears his throat. Bianca slides a holoprojector onto the table. With a few taps, he brings up the eastern 3D perimeter of Elpis. The hologram doesn't reveal much about the city, aside from a few buildings on the eastern edge. But the buildings are big, modern. What does the Kingdom's capital look like?

All non-Elpis members of the war council gape. Ally leans away from it. Drake's hand tightens on mine. Ajax murmurs a prayer to the Idols. All three of the Kingdom men lean closer, fascinated. Emil seems unphased.

"First, I think we need to discuss security," Levi says, cutting off anyone else from speaking first. "Keeping the people of Elpis safe is our top priority."

"What about the Havenites?" I ask. "They need to be moved safely inside the Elpis borders before this starts."

Cypress and Zephyr eye the Havenites curiously. I wonder why.

"That's a big ask, Gavin," Levi says. "Where will we put hundreds of refugees?"

I ease my hand out of Drake's and lean forward. "Bring them within our borders, and I'll take care of the rest."

"You can't—"

"I can and I will." I meet Dad's studious examination of me. "Just get them to safety. They can't fight in this battle. They don't have the Powers or battle skills. We only have a few fighters among us."

Dad's brows rise. "Us?"

Cypress reaches out to touch the hologram, and his fingers pass through it. Alex snorts and rolls his eyes.

Bianca nods at me. "We will do what we can. No one wants to see innocents harmed here, Gavin." She shoots some kind of look at Levi that I can't read. He grimaces.

I relax back into my chair a little. *That's something.*

A red ring appears along the eastern perimeter. Cypress snatches his hand back, drawing a look of amusement from Zephyr.

"Bianca and I will activate the DS and the Specialists to protect the border," Levi continues, ignoring the reactions around the table. "Once we have our troops along the border, we will activate the barrier."

Dad groans. "We don't have a lot left in it, Levi."

"We only need enough for the Kingdom to do their job," Levi says. "Our troops will guard the border. Theirs will distract Dominic's army and draw them away from the city. Zephyr will slip into the camp with a team of our best Specialists to find Paige and Dominic, free her, and capture him if we can, kill him if necessary."

Cypress stiffens. His gaze shoots at Dad. For a moment, Dad meets his gaze. Then once more Dad heaves out a sigh. "Capture only. Cypress and I have agreed that he has reserved the right to deal with his brother."

"Dominic will use Paige's magic against everyone," Zephyr adds. "I'm not even sure he would have launched this invasion if she hadn't...if I didn't..." His words trail off as his face contorts. Zephyr slumps back, pulling his hands into his lap as he studies them.

Cypress pats him on the shoulder.

"So you admit this entire mess is your fault," Alex says snidely.

Zephyr nods. "I do."

Cypress shakes his head. "Zeph, it's not—"

"It is." Zephyr's dark eyes lift, boring straight into Dad. "And I will do whatever I can to fix it. I'll stop him. I'll bring her back to her family. Until she's safe and Dominic is in custody, I won't stop."

The implication of his vow weighs heavily on my chest. Zephyr would rather die than fail her again. He's not seeking approval, but absolution.

No one speaks. No one even moves. The weight of Zephyr's words has smothered all protests.

Dad is the first to clear his throat and speak. "You keep speaking of her Powers. How strong do you think she is?"

Zephyr glances in my direction only for a second before answering. "At least as strong as Gavin. Maybe more. She's afraid of her magic, too."

Alex sighs in irritation. "Stop calling it magic like it's some sort of mystical thing. We aren't magical or chosen for special gifts." Drake flinches. "They're just Powers."

Zephyr raises his chin, avoiding Alex's gaze. "Her *Power* is dangerous and destructive." His sharp emphasis only increases the tension in the room.

"How destructive?" Bianca asks, her own voice strained with worry.

Zephyr doesn't answer at first, glancing at Cypress as if seeking approval, or maybe help. He fidgets with his own fingers. Does he not want to tell us?

When he breaks the silence, his voice is hushed, ominous. "World-ending."

My heart seizes. Time seems to freeze as everyone absorbs the implication. And I know what the first words out of Ally's mouth will be the moment her lips part.

"Desolation."

Drake's eyes widen and his entire body becomes rigid beside me.

"Trust in the vision of the Idols together," Ajax murmurs. "Break the back of Desolation alone. Do not face Desolation head-on, for only Creation can balance the destruction sure to come." His attention turns to me, then lifts his chin as if he just acknowledged some noble quest.

I swallow the lump lodged in my throat and steer the conversation away from this dangerous road before anyone can ask questions. "If she's that strong, the barrier won't stop her. Just like the Power stones didn't stop me. And she knows right where the source of the barrier is, so she can target it if he makes her."

For the first time since the meeting started, Dad deflates, pressed down by the burden of all of this.

"If that's true, we need a backup plan in case the barrier falls," Levi says.

Dad nods, but his heart isn't in the meeting any longer. He's put the pieces together already. Drake, Ajax, and Ally have told him enough about the Havenites' beliefs for him to understand what Ally means.

"Let's get the Havenites mobile," Dad says. He sounds so much older than he did a few minutes ago. "Enid is already working on something. The sooner we can get them settled within the border of the barrier, the better."

Mom is trying to help the Havenites? I smile to myself.

22

ZEPHYR

I EXPECTED THE HAVENITES and the Elpis people to hate us, but the level of unyielding animosity quickly wears on me as the meeting goes on. It seems like they have it out for me, personally. Cypress comes under fire, but not nearly as often as I do. What is it about me that makes me a target?

The technology these people have is far more advanced than anything we have in the Kingdom. It sends a pang of regret through me. Back at the ball, Paige told me her people could slow or stop the illness that killed my mother. I had not believed her completely and had not wanted to cling to hope. *Could* she have saved my mother? I can't afford to let that regret bury me with the rest. I have enough of them already.

The meeting finally ends, and I can't get away from Miller fast enough. The guy looks like he wants to chew me up and spit me back out. Unfortunately, the funnel of people leaving the conference room pushes me toward the back of the crowd—right beside Miller and the Minister.

Cypress escapes a moment after Nat. Miller cuts me off as I try to leave through the doorway, forcing me to step back. I halt, glaring at him while simultaneously worried he intends to inflict some horrible pain on me. I still don't understand who he is to Paige, or why that should make him hate me so much. Not that their hate isn't deserved.

"Zephyr, may we talk in private?" the Minister asks. "Miller, let him be." Is the Minister amused by Miller's antics? I'm not. Teaching this old man a lesson would be a pleasure for me.

"I've got my eye on you, kid," Miller hisses before turning and heading out the door.

I freeze, meeting Cypress' gaze on the other side of the doorway, willing him to help me.

Cypress simply nods his head back toward the Minister. He wants me to talk to Paige's dad. Alone. I gulp, then square my shoulders and turn, assuming an at-ease military stance.

"Sir?"

The corner of the Minister's mouth curls up in a way that reminds me of Paige. She doesn't look much like her dad on the surface, but she certainly has some of his mannerisms. What is he so amused by? Have I done something wrong?

He pulls two chairs over by the conference room window, motioning me toward one of them. "Have a seat, Zephyr," he says.

As I shuffle closer, he eases down into the other. I sink into the other, facing him.

"I would ask if I've done something wrong, but I think my list of offenses speaks for itself," I say, pulling an ankle up on my knee. "Once I've returned your daughter and dealt with Dominic, I'll submit myself to your council for punishment, sir."

His brows climb his forehead. "I'm not sure that will be necessary."

Shock rips through me. Considering the coals these people raked me over, I assumed it was what they wanted. A scapegoat to punish. I can't allow it to be Cypress. He must go back and assume the throne again.

"And please call me Ugene. I get enough of that *sir* crap at work." Ugene assumes a casual position in his chair, his dark eyes curious as he examines me. I've never felt so picked apart. "I would like to learn what you know about my daughter's Powers. Dreaming, I assume already. Influence of her own?"

I frown, trying to recall any hints of it. "No, I don't think so."

Ugene almost seems disappointed. "Hm." For a second, he draws into himself as he calculates something. This guy is intuitive. I can sense it. Not like I can sense magic in others, but by the way he considers everything. "World-ending Power is dramatic. Are you sure you aren't overstating her capabilities? We haven't had anyone that strong since before the Collapse."

I swallow, peering out the window at the river, wishing I could be on the ship instead of stuck in this room with Paige's dad. "I wish I were."

"Can you give me a few examples?" Ugene asks. He's not interrogating me. There's a soothing nature about this that makes me want to talk and relax. And again, it isn't magic. This guy is the definition of charisma and charm.

I lick my lips, wishing I had something to drink. "When I... When we...met." I swallow again. Sweat beads along my hairline. "She caused an earthquake. On accident. And she didn't even realize it was her. On the way to the Capital, some of the men..." What will he think of me after admitting this? "They mutinied against me. I now think that they were under orders from Dominic, but I didn't know it at the time. He wanted me out of the way because he can't manipulate me like he can others."

I'm rambling, but Ugene listens patiently. I carry on. "The men took the three girls with them when they fled, Paige included. Easton and I went after them, but what we found was... I've seen nothing like it." The memory firms in my mind as I describe the scene to him. The ash and smoke and fire and death. Only the three girls escaped the destruction. "And I felt it. The surge of magic was intense and quick."

Ugene's distress is clear in the wrinkles creasing the corners of his eyes. "How quick?"

I rub the back of my neck. "Thirty seconds, max."

"And you think it was Paige?" Ugene asks. He wants to doubt his daughter's capable of such destruction. I can see it in his dark eyes.

"The other two girls told us it was her," I admit, unable to meet his gaze for more than a second. "They were hysterical, but not delusional. I believe them."

"What else?"

I hesitate, glancing sideways at Ugene. This is her father. I should trust him. But I trusted Dominic and look how that turned out.

He intuitively senses my hesitation and shifts gears. "I've studied Powers extensively almost all my life. When I was a kid, everyone developed something. Everyone but me. I wanted to know why I was different, why I was a freak." He grimaces. "It's hard being the only Powerless person in such a big city. Especially when our entire social structure revolved around Powers. Being different terrified me. It hurt me."

Their *entire* population has magic? Why would they not want them all to fight, then? Just how big is their city?

"The point is, if my daughter is suffering because she is different, I want to help her. I can't allow her to face this alone."

"She won't."

He nods. "I admire your determination. Not many people can stand up to her uncle. And your willingness to accept responsibility for what's happening says a lot about your character. The greatest journey in life is not where you stand as much as in what direction you move, and it begins with a single step. You have taken steps in the right direction, Zephyr."

Something about his words tickles my memory, but I can't immediately recall why. *Easton!* He asked me to send a message to Paige when she was in the palace. *It begins with a single step.* I almost laugh out loud. Easton was quoting her father back at her, and she received his message loud and clear. Clever. Both of them.

Ugene gives me a strange look but doesn't question me as he continues, "I've studied everything we know about Powers. But I can't help my daughter if I don't understand the extent of what she can do. Can she control the Powers herself?"

I shake my head. "Not as far as I know. Which is why she's so scared of it."

He nods sagely. "Understandable. And knowing my daughter, she will worry herself into a hole of despair before she asks for help."

Yes, that sounds like Paige.

Ugene is right. If we are going to help her, we need to all be on the same page about what she can do. If I can't trust her father, we are all doomed anyway.

I break down and tell him everything I've noticed her capable of. When I tell him about her Dreaming, I leave out some of the more personal details: the intimacy, our kiss. Somehow, I doubt he would appreciate hearing about it. Nor do I want to tell him about the dream of the monster. But I do share details about her locked in a cage, shaking and scared. Her red magic taking control of her. Her terror at being unable to stop it. I also admit Dominic had her trained—though I don't tell him about my exile. I figure that won't go over well with her dad.

Ugene takes every detail in stride, making mental notes of each piece like he's putting some giant puzzle together. When I have nothing more to report, we fall into deep silence. He stares out the window, at the land across the river. It's a dead, barren landscape. A true wasteland not much unlike the place in Paige's dreams. How have his people survived in this place?

"The world may be ready for restoration at last," he says. I'm not sure if he's talking to me or himself. He finally pulls his gaze from the landscape to stare me down. "We need to be ready to help her, even if she doesn't ask."

We?

"I need your help with that, Zephyr," he admits. "I know you've learned by now just how stubborn she is. She gets that from her mother." He smiles at the mention of his wife, but something else haunts the smile. "Cypress told me how much he admires Paige, and how he feels about her."

I swallow, watching the boats anchored to the docks downriver. Pain burns behind my eyes; sorrow clings to my heart. Cypress said he would let her choose, but did he go back on that once he spoke one-on-one with her father?

"He also told me that nothing he said or did could charm her." Ugene chuckles. "It surprised me when he told me Paige gave up her freedom and her happiness to help you, which is a very Paige thing to do. But she wouldn't do it for just anyone."

My face heats. From anyone else, these comments wouldn't bother me. But this is her dad. Having him know the depth of our feelings, even just a fraction of them, fills me with dread. Does he already know about my exile? Will he like me or hate me?

"Cypress also told me what you risked for her," Ugene continues. "What you did for her."

What did I risk for her? Exile, sure. But that can't be what he's talking about.

Ugene leans forward, placing a comforting hand on my forearm. "Zephyr, no one should have to do what you did. I can't even imagine the strength it took or the way it haunts you. But you did it so she wouldn't have to. You spared her that pain. I don't have words to thank you for that."

Baron. When we were locked up, I told Cypress what Dominic nearly made her do. What I had to do to spare her. I killed my father to protect her. Tears burn in the back of my eyes, but I refuse to cry in front of her father. I clench my jaw so tight my teeth hurt.

Worse yet, I know I would do it again. And again. And again. As long as it protected her from this pain.

Ugene doesn't let go of my arm. His fingertips press into my shirtsleeve. The pressure is light, supportive. It creates a fissure in the wall I've built around that entire nightmare. He nods perceptively, knowing he struck the nail dead on the head.

"It was pointless," I say, surprised by the thickness in my voice. "Because she will suffer so much worse if I don't stop Dominic. It won't just be my...my father. It'll be your entire city. And once that's done, where does he stop? With her at his command, Dominic will crush the world under his heel. No one else seems to understand that. And Paige..." My voice cracks. I curse myself for being so weak in front of her dad.

Sadness pours off Ugene. He nods in understanding. "Which is why I can't trust anyone else with this task. And you can't tell anyone. Not Cypress. Not Miller. Not even Gavin."

My heart lurches. I want his approval, but I don't really know him. Cypress is a brother. That Ugene stresses three people most important to him, me, and Paige makes my head spin. What could he possibly want from me?

"I swore to my wife I would get our kids home," Ugene says, drawing back. Suddenly, the haunted look in his eyes makes sense. She blames him for all of this. "But I'm not as young as I used to be. Paige gets so stubborn with me, but she will let you close enough."

Ugene glances at the door before reaching into his pocket and sliding out a small black case. I gape at the familiar package. Knock-out needles. He presses it into my hand. I try to resist, pushing it back toward him.

"You obviously know what this is." Ugene closes my hand over the case. "Just as a last resort. Because if it comes down to it and she loses control like you seem to fear she will do, it might be the only way to save her from a bullet. I can't control the military. They won't risk everyone for her. Even if some of them want to." A tear rolls down his cheek. "Please. You are the only one I can trust with this."

I stare at the small black case in my palm. Will Paige resent me for using this on her, or will she thank me for saving everyone? I have to believe that she would understand.

"I know I'm asking a lot," he adds. "But you cared about her enough to help her before. I hope you care enough to do it again."

I don't see what choice I have. If Ugene is right—and he probably is—then I will gladly knock her out to save her life. I offer him a stiff nod and slip the pouch into my jacket pocket.

Pain hits my skull like a hammer. I groan, leaning forward and cradling my head instinctively.

"Zephyr, are you alright?" Ugene leans closer, tipping his head to peer at me.

Vomit climbs up my throat. I take a few breaths through the nose and swallow the sickness back down again. She must not be far from us. Otherwise, she is using far more magic than I've ever felt before.

I prop my arm on the arm of the chair and rub my temples. "It's her."

Ugene frowns. "You can sense her? How far away is she?"

I grit my teeth. The pain ebbs slowly away. "I don't know. But that can't bode well." I lift my gaze to meet his and immediately regret it.

Worry creases his forehead. Not for me. For his daughter.

"It's gone now. A small burst. But if she's far away, that burst was strong. Really strong."

A thousand questions shine in his eyes as he watches me, waiting for more. I don't have answers, though.

"How can you sense her like this?" he asks.

I shake my head stiffly and grimace as my head swims. "My magic. I can sense the strength of people, and sometimes what they can do. She's strong enough that proximity isn't a prerequisite."

"And you can negate it." Ugene eases back, appeased that my head won't explode. I'm not so certain, though. "New Divinic Powers. Fascinating!" He offers me a fatherly smile. "You're special, too, Zephyr. It's no wonder you're drawn to one another."

Special. That's not a word anyone has ever associated with me before. "What's Divinic?"

I regret ever asking as Ugene launches into an enthusiastic explanation of how magic works in Elpis—and what each of the Four Branches of Powers are...for an hour. *Is he always like this?*

By the time it's over, I have a clearer understanding of how magic divides itself. The alignment of what he tells me compared to what I know of our magic is crystal clear. We call it different things, but magic is all the same, and it all falls into the same four branches.

Except Paige and Gavin don't fall into any of these categories. It's more like they fall into all of them. Or none of them.

23

PAIGE

S OME INVISIBLE FORCE CLOSES on my head like a vice, slowly twisting tighter and tighter. I blink awake, gripping my blanket. My stomach twists in revolt at even the smallest movements. How did I end up in the tent? Did someone carry me back inside?

My nightmares resurface as I wake. Gavin at gunpoint as the shot is fired. Dad nearly crushed by a massive boulder until Uncle Alex shields him, shattering the projectile with lightning only to be killed by the debris. Aunt Bianca and Levi taking out a full battalion of soldiers, but unable to stop the ground from swallowing them whole. Zephyr's blood on my hands as he bleeds out from a wound in his chest. My Powers engulfing me, consuming me, annihilating everything as my grief overwhelms me. The burst of those Powers exploding outward, destroying the world.

Tears slip from my eyes as the remembered agony rips my heart apart. A sob climbs up my throat. The grief from the nightmare remains raw and devouring.

Someone sits beside me, pressing a cool, damp cloth to my forehead. I appreciate the gesture, but considering how hot I am, how overcome with sorrow and pain, the effort seems futile. I'm dying. I must be. I *want* to be.

"Don't move, Paige," Ivy whispers. "There's some swelling on your brain. The healer couldn't fix it properly unless Dominic removed his Control, which he refused to do. River, Summer, and I are taking turns caring for you."

Of course, he refused to remove his Power from me. Dominic knows I would never let him in again. He would rather risk my death than give up Control.

"How...long?" My throat is dry, making my voice raspy and weak. I crack my eyelids open.

"A day," she says. "Let me help you take a drink."

Ivy gently slides her hand behind my neck, supporting me as she tips a cup to my lips. Water dribbles from the corners of my mouth and down my cheeks and neck, but most of it hits the mark. It rushes through me, extinguishing the fire inside for just a moment. Once I've drunk the whole cup, she eases me back down again.

"January?" My gaze sweeps the tent, but I don't see the other girl with us. Alice is sleeping on her mat. River and Summer are nearby, watching Ivy and I with keen interest. "Layla?"

"No one has seen Layla for a day, and Alice has been a mess over it."

I try to remember what happened to Layla. She came out and attacked Bella. They dragged her into a tent and tied her up. *Did they kill her?* "And January?"

"Don't worry about that right now," Ivy says tenderly. "You need rest." As if to punctuate her point, she checks that I'm tucked into my blanket snugly, then adjusts my pillow under my head.

"Ivy," I snap at her. It makes my head hurt, but I need to know what happened to January. Last I remember, he forced her to torture me with her Power as she sobbed and begged Dominic to let her stop.

Ivy's caramel skin mottles, and she continues avoiding my gaze.

"She died," Summer says from where they are huddled together nearby.

Died?

"None of us blame you, Paige," River says as if the words will offer reassurance.

But they confirm what I already fear. I killed her.

A sob rips from my raw throat. The grief makes my already aching head hurt even more. I only just befriended her. Now she's dead, and I'm responsible. Something must have happened to her when my Power surged to burn some of Dominic's Control away. Maybe January was caught in the crossfire.

Ivy just curls up with me, holding me and murmuring reassurances as I cry. But nothing will mend my broken soul. Between my nightmares and this terrible reality, there is no escape but death.

I'm a killer. First, the three men loyal to Cypress. Now January. Four victims. I can't let Dominic use me like this again. Zephyr tried to spare me from this pain. He killed his father so I wouldn't have to kill against my will. But what good was it if I've killed four people since?

Zephyr.

I would give anything—everything—to have his arms wrapped around me instead of Ivy right now. As soothing as her presence is, I need him. And I can't stop picturing him dead by my own hand. Agony grips my mind, heart, and soul as I cry myself back to sleep.

A GALAXY OF STARS, but one pulses with light, calling out to me. I reach out and pluck it from the sky, holding it in my hand as warmth bursts outward from it. It agitates in my palm, buzzing around like a firefly in a repeating pattern. An infinity symbol.

Then I'm elsewhere.

Zephyr stands at the rail of a balcony, gazing out at the water beyond. His military dress blues stand out in the night sky, with the jacket loose and the top buttons of his shirt undone. His hair ruffles on the breeze. He's beautiful. My heart stops beating as I gaze at him. Where are we? This isn't the palace.

I glide toward him, and my Elpis uniform transforms into the dress I wore to the winter ball.

He spins around when he hears my shoes scuff the balcony decking. The bright light from the moon makes his dark eyes shine as they sweep me over from head to toe. "Paige? But I'm awake." His brows furrow.

For a moment, time stops. Even the breeze ceases to caress our skin as we stare at one another. Tears well in my eyes as I recall the feel of his blood on my hands in that nightmare, of his lifeless eyes staring at the burning sky. Now those eyes flame with life.

Zephyr closes the gap in a few long strides. His hand slides along my neck and his lips capture mine. It's glorious and everything I want and need. When he breaks the kiss, a surge of disappointment rolls through me.

"Are you okay?" he asks, both urgent and breathless. His fingers trail my jaw.

Tears burn in my eyes and I shake my head, unable to tell him what I've done.

"Where are you?" he asks.

"I don't know." I cling to him, feeling the very real flex of his muscles beneath my fingers. "Southwest of Kansas City. I could tell you on a map, but I don't know otherwise."

"A map..." Zephyr slides away, but he doesn't let go of my hand. Is he as scared as me that if we break contact this will end? "Gavin!"

The call to my brother startles me. My heart beats harder as Gavin steps out from a room nearby, rubbing sleep from his eyes. "What...?" Upon seeing me, he freezes.

Am I Dreamwalking in the walking world? I've only done that once before with Cypress and Dominic.

"We need a map," Zephyr snaps. "Now. She could be gone any second."

"How...?" I ask. "How?" *They're together?* No. That can't be right.

As Gavin scrambles for a map, Zephyr spins to face me, and his words come out in a rush. "We may not have much time, so please listen. Easton broke us out of our cells in the palace. Vincent is dead, but Dominic can't know that. Not yet."

Dead... That explains why he didn't answer Bella's call.

"We took back the island, then Cypress and I set sail with as many men as we could." He pulls me toward a counter inside the suite. "By the time we found the ships in old St. Louis, you were already gone, so we took them back. We sailed up the river as far as we could until we encountered this hotel. Your brother and dad are here with us."

"Dad?" I glance around as if he will step out from around a corner.

"Yeah, and some guy named Miller who I really don't like."

I can't help a small smirk despite the hope and terror in my pulse. Uncle Alex rubs most people the wrong way. But when he loves, he does so with the fierceness of a dragon.

"We're planning the defense of the city, but if you can help us pinpoint Dominic's path, that will go a long way." As Zephyr says this, Gavin rushes out of his room with a map.

Gavin spreads the map out on the countertop. Drake steps out of Gavin's room, his hair mussed and eyes blurry.

Zephyr slides his arm around my waist, holding me close to him as if afraid I'll vanish. And I might.

"How is she here?" Drake mumbles groggily.

"Later," Gavin says.

I peer at the map. It's different from the one Dominic is using, so I take a minute to locate Kansas City, then our trail from there. They already covered the map with markings in Gavin's handwriting. I don't understand most of them, but I can tell where they are located.

"Here." I stab a finger at the map. "Or close to it."

"That's only three hundred miles from Elpis," Gavin mutters, then his eyes widen. "He's in range. We can track him now!"

"I can't...I can't go there." My voice trembles and my body shakes. Zephyr's hold on me tightens, and he rubs at my arm. "I'll kill them all. I can't do this, Zephyr. I would rather die."

"No. You won't kill them, because I'll be there waiting for you. Gavin, how fast do you think we can get there?" Zephyr turns his dark eyes away from me, and I feel empty once more.

"Digging channels and creating a river the whole way?" Gavin scratches the back of his head, frowning at the map. "Four days."

"Paige, how long can you stall Dominic's arrival?" Zephyr asks, rapidly firing at each of us.

"I don't know. Gavin said we're three hundred miles..."

"Three hundred twenty-nine, to be exact," Gavin says. "If they are making a good clip of it, we are looking at about nine days. Twelve if they are moving a little slower. That gives us time to get there and set up defenses."

Zephyr nods, then turns toward me, still clinging to me. "Stall him, but bring him to the eastern border of the city. We will be there."

I grimace, not liking that part of the plan, but nod. "He has all the mainland Tributes," I say. "Dominic was experimenting on them on another island. He did something to them, Zephyr. I'm not entirely sure what, but it made all the girls horribly sick for a week or so."

Zephyr sighs. "Easton's smarter than he wants people to think. He told me something was wrong and suspected Dominic was involved."

"Is he safe? Is he with you?" I glance around them as if Easton will pop out of nowhere.

"He wanted to stay behind on the island to dig for clues, but I don't know what he's looking for," Zephyr smirks a little. "I suspect there's something going on between him and Bronwyn."

Easton and Bronwyn? He stayed with her instead of returning to Elpis and finishing his mission? That's very...unlike Easton. There must be some other reason he stayed. What clues would he want?

"And Cypress?" I ask, then bite my lip, remembering my kiss with Zephyr just minutes ago. I kissed him, then asked him about my fiancé.

Zephyr cups my face in a hand, stroking my cheek with a thumb. "He's with us." His glance slides past me toward a closed door. Is Cypress on the other side? What would happen if he opened the door and found the two of us like this? "Don't give up yet, Paige. We are coming to help you. Both of us. All of us. Stall Dominic but lead him right to the eastern edge of Elpis. We will meet you there to stop him." He presses his forehead to mine, lowering his voice as he gazes at me with hooded eyes. "I will find you there. I promise."

Celeste's warning suddenly hits me in the chest. It creates a ripple of fear in my heart. I've pulled Zephyr into this. I've changed his fate by dragging him into my Dreams. I should run, but as his lips brush mine, I can't pull away.

24

GAVIN

"YOU'RE SURE ABOUT THIS, son?" Dad asks as he settles back in his chair, arms crossed.

The alliance council crowded into the conference room early this morning, after Zephyr and I said we had updates. As Zephyr, Drake, and I explain what happened last night, the rest of the Council falls into deep silence. Of course, we left out some of the more personal details, like the excessive kissing between Zephyr and Paige, and the way he refused to take his hands off her. No one needs to hear that. I'm not even sure I needed to *see* that. But it at least served one purpose. I now know beyond a doubt how the two of them feel about one another. Which means I can trust Zephyr.

"The Kingdom's ships are the easiest way to move so many so quickly," I say.

"And the ships have cargo space that will fit the vehicles you have here," Zephyr adds.

I nod, shooting him a thankful smile. "Between my Powers and those that the Kingdom's Builders possess, we can tunnel a new channel straight to the Elpis border."

I'm not looking forward to the task.

They all appear dubious. All but Drake and the Havenites, who have seen what I can accomplish with my Powers.

"We can do this," I insist. "*I* can do this."

Drake shifts in his chair at my side. He agreed to the plan, but he doesn't like how it might drain me.

Uncle Alex eyes Dad from the corner of his eyes, lips drawn in a tight line. He wants to say something but doesn't. That's unlike him.

Dad's gaze slides to Levi and Bianca. "What do you think? I know Enid has been working on establishing the triage and organizing help. Do you think you could expand that area for command?"

Levi's eyes darken as he meets Dad's gaze, but he nods tightly. "It wouldn't take long. I can send word to Higbee and Pearlberg to focus the drones around the area Paige showed until we find this army. It might be the best way to gather intel before the invasion begins."

"And we can put out a call for Naturalists with construction experience to help expand the channel toward the ships as the Admiral's team and Gavin fill it to meet them," Bianca adds. "How long do you think it would take?" Her gaze turns to me.

I shift in my seat as all eyes turn in my direction. "Um, four days, with Cypress' Builders helping. But we need water, too. Which means we need to use anyone who can create environments or draw from the water table."

Dad rubs his jaw. "The Council won't like this. Bringing so many into our borders is risky."

Alex snorts. "Come on, Ugene. What's worse, bringing in these people who propose an alliance, or waiting for an army to swarm our streets? Because if what you've told me is true, even in the slightest, we can't stop them even with the barrier."

I glance across the table at Cypress and Zephyr as Cypress studies his cousin from the corner of his eyes. His lips thin slightly and he taps a finger on the arm of his chair. I'm not good at reading people, but the tension between the two seems more intense today than it has before. They have been joking with each other and working off one another in tandem since we met, but today is...different.

"Okay," Dad says at last. "Admiral, organize your ships and your men. Collect those we will need for the front ship." Zephyr nods. "Levi, contact Pearlberg about the drones. Bianca, organize the military triage. Emil and Ally organize the Havenites into groups to spread across the ships. Miller, gather the supplies and work with Cypress to get it all aboard the ships. I'll contact the Council with an update." He leans forward, preparing to stand. "We have only two days to get ourselves organized before we leave."

Everyone shifts to stand. I lean forward, placing a sweating palm against the tabletop. "What about me?"

"Rest," Dad says. "You'll need it for this to work."

As the others filter out of the room, I sink back into my chair. Rest. Like that's even possible. Zephyr pats my shoulder in sympathy as he passes.

Drake's eyes follow Cypress out, but he remains fixed in his seat beside me.

The plan sounds simple but requires far more working parts than anticipated.

Four days of travel. Another day to set up the Havenites safely away from danger. Another day to prepare for Dominic's arrival. We *should* have time.

Drake rolls his chair toward me, turning mine to face him once we are alone. "Gavin, promise me you won't burn yourself out."

"We've already been through this—"

"Promise me." His dark eyes penetrate me, unrelenting and worried. For someone who has faith that I can remake the world, he's awfully worried about me doing something as simple as creating a channel. Granted, it will be about five hundred miles long.

"I won't burn myself out," I say.

"That's not a promise." He leans closer, gripping the arms of my chair, sliding his knee between my legs so we can draw tighter. "Everyone else can worry about the army and what might come our way. My only concern is you, because if anything happens to you..." He bites his lower lips and shakes his head. "Please, Gavin. I'm begging you. Promise me."

I slide my hand along his jaw, stroking his cheek. "Don't lose faith in me now."

His eyes search mine, digging, but I don't know what he's looking for. "What did the *Book* say would happen to you once you fulfill your purpose?" he asks.

I flinch, understanding what Drake implies. To do what the *Book of the Prophet* promised, I could very well die. "Nothing."

Drake grimaces. His hand slides along my neck, drawing our foreheads together. "Promise me, Gavin. You are capable of the most amazing things I've ever witnessed, but I can't lose you."

The love and desperation in his voice tug at my heart. I'm helpless to do anything but obey if for no other reason than to ease some of his suffering. "I promise."

The kiss he plants on my lips is soft and sweet.

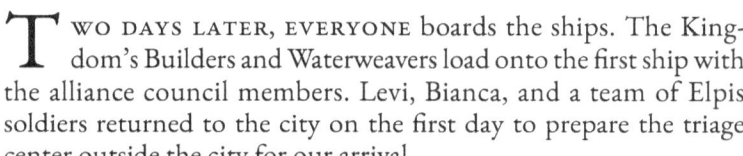

T WO DAYS LATER, EVERYONE boards the ships. The Kingdom's Builders and Waterweavers load onto the first ship with
the alliance council members. Levi, Bianca, and a team of Elpis
soldiers returned to the city on the first day to prepare the triage
center outside the city for our arrival.

As final checks on the ships are completed, Dad and Zephyr stand
near the helm together, conversing with one another. Does Dad have
any idea how Paige feels about Zephyr? It isn't my place to tell. Paige
has scolded me in the past for telling Mom and Dad things she didn't
think I had the right to tell. I learned my lesson.

Zephyr nods at whatever Dad says, holding up an arm. Dad pulls
something out of his pocket. I squint, edging a little closer for a
better look. As Dad closes it around Zephyr's wrist, a blue light activates. Power-dampening cuffs! It's logical. Zephyr's Power negates
the others, which would leave me to undertake this endeavor alone.
Zephyr winces, rubbing at his wrist along the edge of the cuff.

Dad holds something out, placing it in Zephyr's hand. The key?
He pats Zephyr on the shoulder and says one more thing, which
Zephyr nods to even as Dad strolls my way.

"What was that all about?" I ask.

"Just offering him my thanks for what he's doing," Dad says. But
something about his tone doesn't sound wholly right. I don't know
many people, but Dad is one of the few. Why is he hiding something
from me? What does he think he needs to hide from me that he can't
keep from Zephyr?

He offers me the same pat on the shoulder he gave Zephyr a
moment ago, then moves farther back on deck toward Cypress.

The Builders and Waterweavers join me on the upper deck as the
rest of the Havenites and Kingdom soldiers move out of the way.

I embrace my Powers and envision a straight line to Elpis, the task
ahead overwhelms me.

"You sure about this, kid?" Uncle Alex asks, watching Dad as he
speaks in low voices with Cypress.

I glance at him and notice the tension in his shoulder, the way his fingers twitch against his legs. He bites his lip and seems to fight off some uneasiness. It only takes me a moment to connect the dots. I've heard all the stories from his youth, as well as Dad's. Alex nearly lost his partner to burnout from using too much Power at once. But I'm much stronger than Jayme ever was.

"Just step back and give us space." I sense the tendrils of my Power in everything. The very atoms of the world respond to my touch. The sensation leaves my head spinning. Is this what it feels like to be drunk?

Blue light emits first from my fingertips. Alex watches with intense curiosity—and grave concern.

I don't dare move as I address the men assigned to help me. "I will carve the path. Your job is to secure the shores so the earth doesn't flood back into us. Waterweavers, draw the water from the air, and deep in the earth. Make sure it's deep enough for the ships to pass safely."

Though the orders sound simple enough, the reality of what we are about to do is much greater. I've done the calculations. How wide and deep the trenches need to be. How much water we need to summon from the earth and atmosphere. The water is down there. I can sense it, even if water manipulation isn't my specialty. I feel it flowing deep beneath the surface. It's a herculean task, even for a team of forty people using their Powers in cooperation with one another.

Silence falls over the ships. All men and women hush, watching dozens of us use our Powers to change the world.

The blue glow in my fingertips intensifies the harder I pull at the Powers. They flood through me, invigorating and beautiful. I can see *everything*. The atoms that make up our world lay bare before me. I wish I could share this with Dad. He would love to see this. But no one can see what I see.

The earth rumbles. A few cries of alarm arise from somewhere behind us. But I don't stop. I can't. I pull at those atoms, clustering some together while tearing others apart. The ground doesn't just open. It parts before us. The gap widens enough for the ships to pass safely. Unearthed dirt rolls up the banks like waves. Water from the river floods the opening chasm.

Then the air dries out. Rain falls from the sky. Water bubbles up from beneath the fresh soil. The first ship floats into the new channel.

Somewhere behind those of us creating the path, murmurs of amazement echo among the people. Among their voices, I hear Dad and Miller expressing their awe at my skills. It fills me with a sense of pride, and I want to pull harder, do more to impress them. But pacing myself is critical. We have to do this for four days. I can't overexert myself.

The passage of time becomes irrelevant. There is only me, the ship beneath my feet, and the fabric of the cosmos heeding my call. While others take breaks and set up shifts to avoid exhaustion or burnout, my Power continues without end like an infinite expanse of sky. I've never pulled so much before. Not when I opened the temple beneath the Haven. Not when I buried the Haven beneath tons of earth. My physical body weakens, but the Power holds me upright, filling me with energy. I no longer feel like flesh and bone. I feel like part of the fabric of the cosmos.

Time is irrelevant. The rise and fall of the sun mark its passage, but I lose track of the days. I'm one with the framework of the earth, bending it to my will like a master craftsman.

Yet still, I know I'm capable of more. So much more.

25

PAIGE

DOMINIC KNEELS IN FRONT of me, resting his arms on one knee while his icy blue eyes plead with me. The soft lines on his face are at odds with my situation. There is nothing gentle about this monster.

"I thought we had an understanding, Paige," he says. The sorrowful act of desperate hope might sway me, but it's hard to buy into his act when he has me tied to a chair, bleeding in the open arid field. His guards have tied my arms so securely to the back of the chair that my shoulders ache. My torture is out in the open on full display for any who cares to watch.

And they do. Some men, anyway. A few turned their backs and stomped away in disgust long ago, though I'm not sure if that's toward me or what they are doing to me.

Actual torture differs greatly from what the Department of Security imagined. Apparently, the creative minds at the DS couldn't imagine true evil. I can take a punch. I can handle a few cuts or swollen limbs. But the blood trickling from my nose, ears, eyes, and mouth wasn't brought on with fists or knives.

One of Dominic's officers looms behind Dominic, arms crossed over his lean frame. The guy doesn't look like much, but his Power has slowly pulled me apart from the inside. The pressure from his Power builds inside of me each time he attacks. It isn't Hematology because he isn't manipulating my blood. There is something else inside of me he reigns over. The agony is worse than anything I've ever felt before.

Sweat rolls down my temples. Dominic hooks his finger under my chin, forcing me to meet his gaze. "Every time you resist, it will get worse," he says, as if trying to reassure a child. "I can make it stop. I made the mistake of not making you speak the words before, Paige. I won't make the same mistake again. Give me your binding vow that you will work with me and obey me. I tried reason. I even offered you exactly what I thought you wanted, but it seems the only thing you truly understand is pain." He tips his head, making the crown shift but not fall. "I don't want to hurt you."

I grit my teeth, glaring over his shoulder at his officer.

"Look at me, not him." Dominic shifts to block my view of his officer.

He doesn't force me to obey, but I meet his sympathetic gaze with a hate-filled one of my own. I know why Dominic wants me to speak the words that will bind me to him. Because he can then reinforce it with his Control so that I can never break my promise. I won't do it.

"Wanna know what I think?" I ask, fighting to control my breathing. "The thought of losing Control is terrifying you. I've severed part of your Control, proving that you can't hold me forever. I think you know you can't fulfill your vision without me, and you're worried I will break free before you are finished. Instead, you will brute force me to swear an unbreakable vow of obedience." I lean closer, enjoying the way his sapphire eyes cloud over and become stormy. "Make me do it."

Dominic heaves out a sigh and stands, turning his back on me.

Agony instantly rushes through my veins. I scream, unable to control my response. The pain is like a thousand microscopic needles rushing through my blood, trying to break the surface. I reach out with my Powers by instinct for something, anything to help me, but the attempt does nothing more than create a headache so brutal and swift it's like a sledgehammer to my skull. I can't breathe, can't see, can't think. Still, I reach out, praying for anything to relieve the misery. I black out.

A slap jerks me alert, and I groan as my entire body aches. My muscles spasm for a moment before calming down.

Once more, Dominic is crouched in front of me. He wipes my face with a cool, damp cloth. "It's okay. We can circle back to this in a minute." His touch is so tender it makes my skin crawl. "Let's try something else for now, okay?"

Like this is really a request.

Dominic drops his arms to his knees. "Let's talk about Elpis."

I scoff, but he ignores me.

"How many soldiers do your people have?"

I clench my jaw as the urge to answer him rises. I won't tell him anything even if it kills me. And I can't give away the truth that Zephyr and Cypress have joined forces somehow with Elpis against Dominic.

The Dream with Zephyr and Gavin rushes to the surface, a soothing balm on my anguish. They're safe, and I would love to throw that fact in Dominic's face. I want to see the look in his eyes when he discovers his brilliant plan to use Zephyr against me didn't work. That his brothers are coming for him. But I can't tell him. Surprise might be their only chance to enact whatever they're planning. I wish I had learned more from them. *Maybe it's best I don't know more*. Dominic can't force me to tell him what I don't know.

"How much farther, Paige? And what will be waiting for us?"

I jerk my chin out of his grasp, then spit blood in his face. But the compulsion to tell him the truth pulls at me. I seek the thread and pluck at the connection between the two of us until it snaps. My vision darkens once more as an anvil of pain hits my skull.

All the tenderness vanishes from him in a flash of fury. Dominic pinches my face in his hands, baring white teeth in rage. "Stop doing that," he growls.

Panic seizes my chest as his command wraps around my mind like a horrifying blanket meant to smother me. Claustrophobia kicks in as I realize what he's done. Dominic has tightened his Control over me, removing my ability to seek those threads and snap them. A tear rolls down my cheek, mingling with dirt and blood.

In my panic, as I gasp for breath, for control, for anything to help me, part of my Power breaks free. I close my eyes as dizziness overpowers me and makes the world tilt. A cacophony of noise overpowers me, like thousands of voices all screaming for help. I follow the voices in my mind. They branch out in all directions, interconnected over and over again, much like the web of Control Dominic has over my mind. Farther and farther, I reach. The screams get louder, a mass of white noise buzzing louder with each passing second.

"Paige," Dominic's voice is breathless. "St..."

But he doesn't finish his command, and I can't stop it. I squeeze my eyes closed, trying to shut them all out. "Stop…" I groan. "*Stop!*"

Silence. Utter stillness.

I blink slowly to focus my darkened vision. Dominic's half bent over me, clutching his head as blood trickles from his nose.

And all around us, bodies litter the ground. Some groan in agony. Others shift as if regaining consciousness. A few don't move at all.

"What happened?" Dominic asks, breathless as he rubs his temples. Realizing he's bleeding, Dominic pulls a cloth from his pocket and wipes the blood away.

"Your Grace," an officer staggers over, unsteady on his own two feet. "It was a psychic attack."

Dominic mouths the words like he's trying to put the pieces together for himself. Then he eyes me. "Oh, Paige. You are far more useful than I ever dreamed."

Laughter bubbles up from somewhere deep within as the brutal truth hits me. It's a mad laugh, even to my ears. Tears of glee and dread roll down my cheeks. Dominic can't kill me, even if he wanted to. I already knew that much. He needs my Powers. And no matter how well he has woven a web of Control over my mind, I will always find little holes to poke at, little ways to break free. Knowing that Cypress, Gavin, and Zephyr are coming for him only confirms the truth Dominic doesn't yet see.

He's losing.

Everyone freezes and stares at me like I've gone mad. Maybe I have.

"What is so funny, Paige?" Dominic hisses.

"You can lock me in a cage, but I've seen the future," I say madly. "And I always break free."

His jaw clenches, and those blue eyes harden. Before he can react, one of his men rushes over.

"Your Grace!" Two others follow the soldier carrying something in their hands.

Drones…

"We used Electric magic to shoot them down," one soldier says as he tosses the broken drone on the ground. "They were hovering around our camp."

I bare my bloody teeth as I grin at Dominic.

His expression hardens. He stands, smoothing out his coat as he peers at the broken drone. "They know we're coming. We must be close." He glances at me, flinching at the manic grin I throw his way. "Find someone to heal her. We need her at full strength for the fight."

"You have no idea what you're up against," I call after him.

26

ZEPHYR

E VEN WITH THE POWER-DAMPENING cuff Ugene gave me secured around my wrist, Gavin's magic makes my gut churn
with nausea. I can't sense anyone else around me, but Gavin stands
out like a beacon. The fact that he's enveloped in a blue haze only
adds to the effect. Those blue tendrils flow out of him toward the
ground in front of the ship and dig into the dirt. It doesn't simply
move the dirt. It recreates it in waves that crash along the shore of
the newly formed channel. From there, our own Builders take that
earth and secure it in place.

Watching them work for days with only a few rests has been one
of the most amazing things I've ever witnessed.

Not everyone is as pleased with how hard Gavin is working his
magic. His dad watches him like a hawk, constantly perched on
a nearby bench. The pride and fear in Ugene's eyes fills me with
envy that I know Cypress feels as well. His father never looked at
us like that. The King demanded perfection, and anything less was
a failure. How different would our lives have been if the King had
been anything like Ugene?

Ugene's sidekick, Miller, paces the deck like a caged animal. His
worry for Gavin is more apparent than Ugene's. I heard him mum-
ble something to Ugene about burning out. Miller tried to stop
Gavin for food and rest, but Gavin didn't even flinch. It was like
Gavin existed on a whole other plane than our own. Drake has
managed to get food and water into him, at least.

Cypress returns from his trip to the restroom and settles back on
the bench beside me, watching Gavin work. "I've been meaning to
talk to you about something that's bothered me for a while now."

I glance at him from the corner of my eye, trying to keep my focus on controlling the swirling nausea in my gut. "What's that?"

"The night of the insurrection," Cypress' voice catches for a moment. That was a terrible day for all of us. He still hasn't told me all of what happened between him and Dominic before they threw him in that cell. I doubt he ever will. "You came down to the cells and fought off those guards. And you did something. You used their magic."

I recall that moment with striking clarity. The misery and fear. The overwhelming sickness caused by those lights and my desperation to get rid of them. Normally my magic is a push against others, but in a panicked moment outnumbered by swords and weakened by those sickening lights, I pulled instead of pushed. Somehow, I pulled the guard's magic into me, harnessed it, and used it against him and the lights. It's something I never knew I was capable of, and I haven't done it since.

"How did you do it?" Cypress asks.

As if the magic is present, I flex my uncuffed hand, ready to unleash it. "I'm not entirely sure. I was desperate and scared and I pulled instead of pushed."

"Is it something you can do again?" His gaze drifts to Gavin.

My shoulders tense. I don't like the way he's looking at Gavin. "Cy, be careful. The Kingdom is holding onto this alliance by a thread. Breathe on it the wrong way and it could snap."

"I'm not thinking about him completely." He shifts on the bench to lean closer and lowers his voice. "He's just as strong as Paige, isn't he?"

I rub at my temples to dull the ache forming there. "I don't know. He might be stronger. I can feel his magic even with this cuff on."

Cypress eyes Gavin again. "Imagine what he could do for the Kingdom."

"Forget the Kingdom," I snort. "Imagine what he could do for this *world*. You realize he isn't just moving the earth. He's reforging it."

Cypress leans back, crossing his arms. "Maybe those Haven zealots weren't so crazy after all. Dad must be rolling over in his grave. He spent his life searching for them, and we stumbled across them by accident. Talk about a knife in the old man's rotting corpse."

I chuckle, enjoying the idea that we accomplished by accident what he couldn't accomplish in a lifetime. I hope he *is* rolling in his grave, wallowing in the knowledge that we have done what he never could. *Eat that, jerk.*

The clouds shift, allowing the sun to peek through. A long shadow falls over the two of us from behind. I turn on the bench to find Drake looming behind us with his hands clenched into fists at his side. Anger and hate burn in his dark eyes. How did he sneak up on us like that? I usually hear... *He's a Stealth mage.*

I offer him a stiff nod. "Drake."

Cypress stiffens as he glances back at our eavesdropper. He drapes an arm over the back of the bench casually.

Drake's feelings for Gavin are clear, and if he thinks we are a threat to Gavin in any way, he won't hesitate to pick a fight. I can't blame him. I would do the same for Paige. But if he tells Ugene—or worse, Miller—what he overheard, this tenuous alliance could shatter before we meet Dominic on the battlefield.

Drake's jaw twitches. "Say what you want about us *zealots*, but we were right." His gaze drifts past us to Gavin, and a soft smile of affection curls his lips. "And thanks to us, he's starting to understand what he is capable of, too. So you can take your opinions about our religion and stick them—"

"Everything okay over here?" Ugene strolls over, hands tucked casually in his pockets. His dark eyes sweep over the three of us. This guy doesn't miss anything.

If Drake opens his mouth and tells Ugene what he overheard, Cypress and I are in trouble. Ugene's trust in me only goes so far. Especially with Miller always looming nearby with his sharp tongue.

"We're good," I say, staring at Drake, begging him not to say anything.

Before Drake can say anything, an intensely blinding headache slams into me. I buckle over, squeezing my head in my hands.

Paige...

The pressure is intense, familiar, yet also different. She isn't just using her magic. She's reaching into my mind and squeezing. I can't breathe. Sweat beads on my forehead, dried by the breeze that blows past.

My ears ring. When I've adjusted enough to raise my gaze, gritting my teeth, I gape at the sight before me.

Everyone feels it this time. Soldiers and refugees all clutch their heads, wincing or crying in pain.

Then it ends, and only one person is unaffected by the psychic attack.

Gavin.

He has stopped working but otherwise stands tall, and his gaze focuses sharply southeast of our location. I rise and rush to the rails, whipping the pocket scope out to peer in that direction. Is she that close? Dare I hope to see her there?

I sweep the scope across the horizon, seeing nothing but the same barren wasteland. When I lower it, Ugene, Miller, and Cypress are all at my side.

"It was her, wasn't it?" Ugene asks.

I nod.

"How does he know?" Miller asks, glaring at me.

"Because they're linked somehow," Ugene replies.

I glance at Cypress, worried about how this news will affect him. He was upset to find out Paige had visited us in a dream and I didn't wake him. He frowns and stares straight southeast, as if breaking focus will shatter him into pieces. His voice sounds too hard when he breaks his silence. "Zeph, if that's true, and you can do what you did in the palace cells, we all need you to get to her. If Dominic can Control that magic, he can selectively kill us all."

Miller grunts, eyeing Cypress with grudging respect. "I wonder how far she managed that attack. Ugene, do you think...?"

Ugene grimaces and marches away from us, pulling his radio from his pocket, and calling to someone in Elpis.

This attack only makes more urgent that which we already know. We need to free Paige as soon as possible. Every day we waste, Dominic could grow stronger through her.

27

GAVIN

I HAVE NEVER FELT so alive. The Power that moved through me for the past four days fueled my body just as surely as the food and water Drake insisted I consume. I wonder, though, if that atomic fuel in the very air around me would have been sufficient. I'm not sure what else to call it other than atomic fuel. The atoms, the very fabric of reality, are everywhere. While the logical part of my brain already knew as much, to see it and *feel* it brings my understanding of our world to a whole new level.

And it's far more broken than we thought, but after what I just did for days on end, I'm starting to believe I might be capable of fixing it. I bite my cheek as I reluctantly let go of the Power. Drake will never let me hear the end of this. If I tell him what I think I can do, he will surely give me that crooked smirk that tells me he was right all along. Maybe he is. The Prophet had visions of the future, after all. Maybe he saw me doing this.

By the time I release my Powers—regretting the loss of its embrace—the ships have already docked and people are flooding the ramps to disembark.

Dad and Uncle Alex move toward me as Drake reaches for my hand.

"How are you feeling, Gavin?" Dad asks.

I grin. "Amazing."

Drake gives my hand a subtle squeeze.

Dad's gaze sweeps over me, prodding for signs of exhaustion or danger. Satisfied that he sees nothing, he nods. "I have a few things to check on. Your mother will be in the camp waiting for you. We will catch up soon."

"Dad, wait!" I lunge for his arm.

He pauses and turns back to me.

"We need to help Paige."

"We all felt it, kid," Alex says with a grimace.

Dad nods sadly. "We will help her as soon as we can. Meanwhile, I have a few matters that require immediate attention, and there's a tent awaiting the arrival of their new senior analyst."

He and Alex hustle away, heads bent together conspiratorially.

The promotion I was promised if I went on this mission months ago is mine. I should be thrilled, and I am pleased, but it's still hard to recognize being back in the safety of Elpis borders.

From the deck, I watch Drake as he peers at the distant skyline. The skyscrapers of Elpis are just visible, dwarfed by distance but still impressive. We are perhaps ten miles out from the city itself.

Beside the ships, a sea of camouflage tents dots the landscape as a thousand men and women from all three communities disembark and mingle, following directions from the Elpis guards.

"Is that...Elpis?" Drake breathes.

I squeeze his hand. "Let's go. Mom is waiting."

Even from this distance, I can feel the buzz of the city like a living, breathing thing. Before I left, I could always sense certain things when I wanted to: how much concrete was used to pour a sidewalk; the wires inside a room and where they connected to a main power breaker; the buzz of the stoplights and electric vehicles around me. All that pales compared to what I feel now. It isn't just the little pieces that make the whole. It *is* the whole. Despite the horrors I suffered in the Haven, I cannot deny that it has strengthened me.

We join the growing crowd eager to disembark. Nearly everyone steps aside to make a path for us. Even the men from the Kingdom. They nod to me respectfully and my grip on Drake's hand tightens as I pull strength from him. The Havenites gawk at me in awe, which only fuels my discomfort. Partly because I can already feel that I will fulfill their prophecies. I'm becoming what I refused to be. Their savior, and the man who will fix this broken world.

The moment our feet hit the dirt, Mom's voice calls to me. I perk up, peering over heads to find her among the milling masses. A wave of bodies shifts as someone pushes against the flow.

"Mom!" I jerk Drake along with me as I rush toward Mom's familiar face, only releasing him when she is a few steps away.

Mom barrels into me, pulling me into the fiercest hug she's ever given me. Her body is much thinner than before. Her complexion is pale and her black hair has more gray now. Tears roll down her cheeks as she refuses to let go.

She tenderly strokes my cheek, beaming with so much relief and affection, it makes me uncomfortable with Drake lingering just behind me.

"My sweet boy," she gushes. "I was so worried. I thought... I mean, when you didn't come back..." Her voice catches.

"Mom," I groan, jerking my head away from her as heat rushes to my face. "You've lost weight. Are you feeling okay?"

"So much better now that you're back," she replies.

I edge another step back and lace my fingers through Drake's, pulling him closer. "This is my mom, Enid. Mom, this is—"

"Drake," she says. Her gray eyes sweep over Drake, picking him apart. "I heard all about him from your father."

Drake shifts uncomfortably. Is he nervous? His Adam's apple bobs as he glances sidelong at me for...what? Guidance?

Mom rubs Drake's arm warmly, then pivots and calls over her shoulder as she marches away. We follow without instruction.

"Your dad said you refused to come home until the refugees are taken care of, so I organized a task force of volunteers to help. They're in good hands." She leads us through the bustling camp with apparent purpose. I admire her confident strides. Mom has always been a force to be reckoned with. Shy and introverted, but able to dig in her heels and get things done when the chips are down.

"Tonight, they will rest in some tents here and get full bellies," she says. "Tomorrow, we will shuttle them all to the Greenhouse. They should be safe there until the worst passes. Then we can talk about what to do next."

"Mom, I'm not so sure they will want to be in the Greenhouse," I say, tightening my grip ever so slightly on Drake's hand.

Drake frowns. "A greenhouse sounds delightful."

I glance back at him, lips set in a grim line. He wouldn't know. I didn't give away many details about Elpis during my stay in the Haven. "It isn't what you think, Drake. The Greenhouse is an old, pre-collapse missile silo that was converted into living quarters. It's underground in the mountains." I point west to the mountain range looming in the distance.

Drake eyes the mountains uncertainly, suddenly tense. I understand why, for once. The Havenites just escaped one underground community. They may not look too fondly at the idea of being herded into another when a massive city clearly appears on the horizon to the south.

"It's only until the invasion is over," Mom reassures us. She peers over her shoulder, noticing Drake's anxiety. "I promise, it's only temporary. The Greenhouse is the safest place in Elpis. Far to the west away from what will probably be a nasty battlefront, in the ground protected from Powered attacks."

"Not from Paige," I mutter. I felt her Power, her cry for help on board that ship. If Zephyr is to be believed, and if I trust my instincts on this—which I do—she can bring the mountain to the ground.

Mom stops outside a tent, and her brows draw into a tight line. Crow's feet crease the corners of her eyes. "Do you know what's happened to her? Your dad wouldn't say much. Only that he has a plan to get her back."

I glance at Drake. What should I say? There's desperation in her gray eyes, a fragile balance between confidence and collapse.

"She's strong, Mom." Words fail me utterly. I can't be the one to crush her soul.

Drake clears his throat. "Her gifts are as impressive as Gavin's. If anyone can help her, it's Gavin and Zephyr."

"Zephyr?" Mom frowns.

Zephyr and Cypress stand outside a nearby tent, speaking to Aunt Bianca. Mom follows my gaze, scowling at the two men.

"I don't trust them, Gavin," Mom whispers.

"Me, either," Drake mutters.

I jolt, turning to him with wide eyes. "Believe me, if there are two men who want to protect her more than we do, it's them."

Mom bites her lip as she watches the two men. Zephyr must sense her watching because his dark eyes scan the crowd, then fall on her. A flicker of recognition crosses his face, and he gives her a respectful nod.

"He will walk to his death for her," Drake says. "Maybe not for the rest of us. But her, for sure."

"How do you know?" Mom asks.

"I heard him say it to his cousin." He nods at Cypress. "Among other things."

Mom sighs heavily. "Well, we will see, I suppose. Meanwhile, I need to make sure your refugees are taken care of properly. And you have an analyst team waiting for their boss to direct them."

Boss. I glance at the tent she indicates as she marches away. Time to face my promotion head-on.

Drake ducks inside after me and freezes in place as his gaze sweeps the analyst command center. Screens scroll data and video feeds from patrol drones. One feed shows as static. Another hovers high in the sky, recording the movements in a massive camp below. It isn't our camp, though. There are no ships. That must be Dominic. My gaze darts to the corner of the screen where the coordinates display. He isn't far.

Analysts occupy each station, making notes and collecting data on their own tablets. My fingers twitch to touch the technology. It's been so long, and I hadn't realized how much I missed the work until this moment.

I don't even realize I'm moving until I'm standing in front of a holodisplay projecting the known map around Elpis. My fingers dart over the display, entering calculation points to determine exactly how far Dominic is from us. In seconds, I've fallen back into the old rhythm, collecting, examining, deducing.

"Gavin!" Aron rises out of a chair across the tent and rushes over to me. Before I can properly react, Aron pulls me into a tight hug. It lasts a little longer than I expect.

Feeling awkward, I hug him back, then extricate myself from his arms.

"I was worried I wouldn't see you again," Aron says. He lowers his voice and leans closer. "I'm so relieved you made it back." He doesn't let go of me completely when I pull away. His hand slides down to take my hand. "I've been watching the data and listening every day since your teammates returned without you."

That devilishly charming smile graces his face. It used to make my insides melt, but not any longer. Interesting.

"There was so much I wanted to say before you left, but I couldn't summon the courage," Aron says. He bites his lower lip. "Then you were gone, and I was terrified I'd made a horrible mistake."

Mistake? My gaze darts to the data screens and he chuckles. The sound is low and heated. I've missed something here, and it makes me uncomfortable. "What mistake, Aron?"

Drake appears at my side, glaring at Aron. "He has a crush on you," Drake says sharply.

Crush? On me? I can't help a small laugh. That I pined over Aron for months when he had a crush on me is ridiculous. Aron is confident. If he had any interest, he would have been clear about it. "I don't think so."

"Yes, I do," Aron says plainly. "I couldn't just ask you out. You're so skittish about everything that I knew I had to lay a trail for you to pick up on yourself. I thought it was obvious. I thought for sure you knew, but you never said a thing." Aron steps closer and his green eyes dart to my lips.

My stomach twists in knots. I take half a step back.

"Gavin, is there any chance we can talk over drinks tonight?" Aron asks. And I hear it. The hope and heat in his voice.

My heart is racing like mad. I wanted Aron so badly it hurt, but so much has changed since I left Elpis. I've changed. Anxiety twists my insides into knots as I ease my hands out of Aron's, then nervously wipe the sweat on my pants. Drake is standing right beside us, which only makes me more uncomfortable with all of this. "Aron, I...don't think that's a good idea."

"Why not?" Aron's face contorts in confusion. "I thought we—"

"Because he already has a boyfriend," Drake interrupts. He steps closer and slides his hand into my own. "And just so we're clear, it's me."

My face heats. I don't want to hurt Aron. He doesn't deserve it. This is all a misunderstanding.

Aron stares at our hands and his shoulders slowly slope downward. My heart aches for him. This isn't what I wanted. He takes a step backward. A forced smile stretches the corners of his mouth as he meets my gaze. "I'm happy for you."

As he turns, Aron's green eyes sweep analytically over Drake, as if collecting data points and coming to his own conclusion.

28

PAIGE

RIVER CURLS UP AGAINST Summer's side while Summer holds her close on their mats. Both women watch Ivy clean me up, worry in their eyes. And pity. I don't want their pity. At least they have food and water to offer when I need it.

Ivy's touch is tender as she wipes away the blood with a cool, damp cloth. Her dark eyes sparkle in the dim lamplight. The sable skin of her face is flawless, framed by a few long stray wavy locks of her hair. She's a beauty. Too bad she never had a chance with Cypress. He would have liked her intelligence, gentle temperament, and simple beauty. Maybe, when this is all over and if we survive, I can help them connect.

The swelling in my head has gone down. The healer did all she could for me, but my remaining wounds are more emotional than physical. No one can fix those.

Alice munches on a fresh loaf of bread, peeling off chunks before popping them into her mouth one bite-sized piece at a time. How did Dominic acquire fresh bread out here in the middle of nowhere? Come to think of it, a lot of our food supply has been fresh. Does he have someone with food preservation abilities who might keep the food from rotting as we cross the broken landscape? Feeding this many people requires a lot of food, and we certainly won't find it in the wasteland.

Even the water has been fresh, passed around in cups from large jugs. Where *are* these supplies? Even the wagons carrying the tents disappear once we break camp, only to reappear when it's time to set up. I'm missing some critical piece of information.

"Why do you insist on antagonizing him?" Ivy murmurs as she focuses on cleaning one of my eyes.

I close my lids to make her job easier. "Dominic thinks he's smarter than we are, that he can control us."

"He can," Alice mutters from her nearby mat. We still haven't seen Layla since the incident with Bella.

"Everyone has limits." I open one eye and peek toward Alice. "When the fighting starts, he will try using all of us. Whatever he did to you made you all stronger."

Each gives a grudging nod.

"The stronger we are, the harder it will be for him to Control us all at once," I say. "Those collars will come off once he thinks he has that Control. You need to let him think he does."

"Because he will," Alice snaps. "It won't be an act." She drops her bread in her lap, glaring at me.

I ease Ivy's hand away from my face, glancing at the closed tent flap before turning to face the other girls. "Listen to me, please. I know we have our differences. I know what I did to...to January. And I don't expect you to forgive me."

"We don't blame you," Ivy says firmly, like she needs to be the peacemaker in the group. But Alice doesn't seem as forgiving. Even Summer and River act tenser around me than they used to.

"I do." I meet Ivy's gaze without flinching. My heart aches. Nothing they say will ease the agony of knowing I killed January, a friend. Not to mention the pain I caused each of them with my accidental psychic attack.

The appearance of the destroyed drone tells me Elpis knows where we are and that we're coming, just as Zephyr and Gavin promised. I'm no longer sure how far we are, but I know that Dominic no longer needs me to lead the army to Elpis. He immediately sent the drone to one of his trackers to find the point of origin, a clever move.

Nothing I do will stop our march to the city now. Nothing short of destroying this entire army. My consolation is knowing that Zephyr and the others have a plan. Zephyr's promise from my Dream echoes in my head. *"Don't give up yet, Paige. We are coming to help you. We will meet you outside Elpis to stop him."*

My heart aches just thinking about it. When we reach Elpis, Zephyr will be right there waiting for me. But we need a plan of our own. We need to help bring Dominic down. Which puts me in charge of this part of the mission.

You've trained for this, Paige.

I take stock of the girls around me. How can we use our Powers against Dominic? Our attack will need to be swift, beginning the moment he removes those collars. The girls may only have a split second of control to take him by surprise before he issues his commands. The collar clearly doesn't stop whatever he has laced on their minds any more than distance does for me. He doesn't need to hold on to constant Control until he needs us to act. That's when we need to strike. In the second before that happens. It leaves no margin for error.

Only a few of these girls will risk their lives without knowing there's a safety net nearby. If I want them to trust my plans, they need to know more about me.

"Before I left home, our military trained me for special missions," I tell them.

Ivy sinks back, cocking her head curiously at me. All of them are listening now.

"My city is massive, even compared to the Capital," I continue. "Hundreds of thousands of people, all with Powers like each of you and then some. Technology the likes of which the Kingdom has never seen. Dominic does not know what he is marching his army into, and I've done everything I can to keep it that way. But he got his hands on one of our drones, which means some of our advancements will no longer be a surprise."

River's jaw slackens. "Did you say hundreds of thousands?"

I nod.

"What's a drone?" Ivy asks.

I watch the door to be sure no one will enter. The guards outside will say something to give away Dominic's arrival, but not Bella's. We have little time before they finish their evening rounds.

"We are short on time," I say urgently, lowering my voice in case anyone with Enhanced Hearing is nearby. "I wish I could answer all of your questions, but if we want to form a plan, we need to do so before he returns for the night, because it won't be long now." That silences their questions. I press on. "Elpis will have an army waiting to stop him. They already know he's coming. If we can cause a distraction or interrupt his plans for the attack, it will give my people the time they need to close in and strike. We need to act *before* Dominic."

"How do we distract him?" Summer asks.

We spend the next few minutes discussing each of the other girl's Powers. They share what his particular interest in them seemed to be, the strengths and weaknesses of each. Once they have finished, I have a clearer idea of how I could use their Powers to our advantage.

I wave Alice closer to the rest of us. "There's no way to know who he will release first, so we need to prepare for every combination of Powers," I whisper. "If he orders his command, there's a loophole in his Power. He can tell you what to do, but if you think fast enough, you can do as he asks without doing as he asks."

Alice shakes her head. "I don't understand."

I chew my lip. "When he questions me, I'm compelled to answer. But if he asks me how many people there are, I don't have to give him the right number, as long as I don't give him something false. For instance, telling him five thousand isn't a lie. There are at least five thousand. But definitely more. However, I can't tell him there are a million because there aren't. It isn't easy and usually comes with a killer headache, but it works. If he commands you to open a hole in the earth to swallow enemy lines, your perception of the enemy may not be the same as his."

Alice's lips part as it dawns on her. "So I could open a hole under his men because, to me, they are the enemy."

"Exactly." I grin. "Twist his words in your own mind."

The other girls catch on now, nodding or murmuring in understanding. "To force us to do exactly as he wants, he has to take full Control." I shudder, remembering how he forced me to kill those men, to nearly kill Baron. "But he can't take full Control of us all at the same time. One really good distraction is all we need."

We continue plotting in haste, and each girl grows a little more confident in their role.

I'm feeling much better once we've completed our plans. "If we all want to make it out of this, follow my instructions. Enact your part of the plan, then the second the Control has slackened or released, run."

"He won't release us," Alice mutters.

"He will, because if we do this right, he can't hold all of us at once," I say. "Dominic can only do so much. I will try to keep him distracted so you all can escape straight east."

River scoffs, shaking her head. Her red ringlets wave limply around her pale face. "To *your* army? They don't know who we are. Why would they help us and not attack?"

I chew my lip once again. Zephyr insisted I not tell Dominic anything, but he didn't mention the girls. I could tell them the truth, but one of them might tell Dominic. Or more likely, he might force it out of them. Not that he has tortured any of *them*, to my knowledge.

"Please trust me," I try pressing urgency into my words. "They will know who you are. Once he's distracted, he won't stand a chance. Elpis will crush him."

Silence settles between us. Alice glances at the space where Layla's mat used to be. No one knows what happened to her after she attacked Bella. Dominic wouldn't kill one of his assets, which means Layla is still a wildcard at play. One we can't be certain will help or hurt us. Worse, none of us know what her Power is. In the palace, she was simply a Navigator, able to locate people or objects and create a mental map of the area. Who knows what Dominic did to her?

"What about you?" Ivy whispers. She sounds so small, scared. We all should be.

I throw her my most confident smile, even if I don't feel it. "Dominic doesn't scare me. Let me handle him. The moment those collars are off and you are free of his Control, promise me you will run."

Each girl meets my gaze. Ivy is the first to voice her promise. River and Summer follow shortly after, holding hands with resolute determination. I peer at Alice.

Her lips thin. It takes far too long for her to begrudgingly agree.

29

EASTON

*S*OMETHING IS MISSING FROM this puzzle. I've felt it ever since the prince seized control of the palace. We've all missed some critical piece that brings everything together. That piece will be the key to stopping him. I let Bronwyn believe I stayed on the island for her, but it wasn't really her. This puzzle has been itching at my brain obsessively.

We have all grossly overlooked something important, and I need to find it.

Dominic's suite is a disaster. I spent all day tearing this place apart without knowing what I'm even looking for. But a clue has to be around somewhere.

At first, when the others sailed away, I followed the paper trail. As Keeper of Tides, Dominic had access to all the information the Kingdom offers. Histories, supply runs, farming reports, grain depot reports, military reports...*everything*. The list of information at his fingertips is endless. Everything is funneled to the king through his hands, which makes it easy to fudge the documents. A little clerical error here or there can easily be overlooked—especially if he doesn't report the errors.

I noticed the discrepancies in those reports. He had been stealing from goods storages and military personnel for a long time. But none of the answers I'm looking for are in the records.

Dominic had something else up his sleeve. Something he didn't leave behind a trace of in the palace. One of my burning questions is, where did he conduct his experiments on me? I know now that he could slip me into the fort seamlessly because of his inside connections. But from *where*? It isn't the hospital. I've inspected that building thoroughly. And it definitely wasn't the fort or palace. He wouldn't put that much power in Vincent's hands by conducting anything at the Greene Manor, nor would he leave any evidence there for Vincent to use against him. He's too smart for that.

I've searched the King's council chamber, the throne room, various suites, the library, and his own room. I even checked the officer's quarters and medical building in the fort. Whatever he was hiding, he hid it well.

I flip through pages in one of his notebooks. I've read it a hundred times now and nothing new strikes me. Frustrated, I toss the notebook into a wall. It leaves a dent in the purple wallpaper.

I lean forward at the desk, gripping my hair in a tight fist. This jerk will *not* outsmart me again. I need to find answers before it's too late. That psychic attack a few days ago left all of us dazed. Is it already too late? Would we know if it was?

Irritated and in need of release, I step into his bedroom attached to the suite, then yank out the drawers in the bedside table, flipping each upside down, dumping the contents, and checking the drawers for hidden compartments. Nothing. I heft the mattress off the bed and lean it against the wall, then shove the frame away and check the floorboards. The information must be here somewhere.

My rampage continues for another hour, tearing everything apart, searching under rugs and in the floor, seeking trap doors in the closet, the pockets of his suits. Everywhere.

Exhausted, I sink down on the sofa in the bedroom and glare at the ugly wallpaper. Frustration wells powerfully inside me, making my Strongarm muscles twitch.

"Easton?" Bronwyn freezes in the bedroom doorway, her honey-colored eyes sweeping the ransacked space. Her shoulders sagged. "We talked about this."

"It's here, Bronwyn. I feel it. I *know* it. Dominic couldn't possibly have taken every scrap of evidence with him. Why would he? We are missing something and it's right under our noses!"

She picks her way through the room, kneeling in front of me. "I don't like what this is doing to you. I know he did terrible things to you, and I wish I could fix that, but this..." She glances at the surrounding disaster. "It isn't healthy."

"I can't just sit here while the others fight," I say, and my voice cracks over the words as the weight of my failure presses down on me. "We don't know what's going on out there. What if they lose? What if he comes back, and I still can't—" I bite off the words the moment I realize I'm only proving Bronwyn's point.

Bronwyn takes my face in her warm hands. "You are not alone anymore, Easton."

I hold her delicate wrists in my hands, keeping her touch on my face, then lean my forehead against hers. "I know."

She strokes my jaw with her thumbs and I close my eyes, breathing in the lilac scent of her. We fall into silence, taking comfort in one another. When we break apart, I stare up at the wall, at the painting of the islands that's been here so long the wallpaper has discolored around the now crooked frame. The answer is staring right at me. It must be.

I pull away from Bronwyn and rise from the sofa to cross the room, eyes locked on the painting.

"What's wrong?" she asks, stopping at my shoulder.

"How old is this painting?"

"I don't know. Most of what's in the palace was original to the old hotel that stood before the Collapse." She takes my hand, resting a cheek against my shoulder. "Why?"

We haven't been able to find anything on this island. Not in the palace. Not in the fort. Not with any of Dominic's known accomplices. An instinct kicks my gut.

"It's not on this island." I groan, remembering one of Baron's old reports I read over a week ago. "I'm such an idiot."

"No, you aren't."

"I am." I tilt my head to stare at her stunning, smooth face. "We can't find anything because it isn't on this island. Which one is Round Island?"

Bronwyn points at the closest island, covered in a dense canopy of trees. "There's nothing there."

"According to whom?"

She pulls back, peering at me like she wants to answer, but her face pales.

"I need a small team and boats." I stare at the island in the painting. Nothing was there long ago. But Dominic has been planning all of this for so long, it's possible he had a team of men build him a hideout on that island. *What were you up to here, Dominic?*

30

ZEPHYR

TALL SPIRES GLEAM IN the distance. We are still miles out, but the tall buildings put our palace to shame. We have nothing even remotely close to that height. Even from here, their enormity strikes me with awe. Cypress stands beside me, just as slack-jawed.

"They're so tall," I mutter under my breath. I've seen buildings like those before, but they're broken, half-collapsed, abandoned in cities neglected for over a century. They don't shimmer with light from the dying sun, majestic and strong. New.

"Is that Elpis?" Cypress whispers.

I can only nod my head in awe.

"No wonder Paige wanted to go home." He shifts, subconsciously straightening his jacket. Does it make him feel as insignificant and small as it does me? Cypress sighs and pats me on the shoulder. "Let's get rest, Zeph. We have a long few days ahead of us."

I nod dumbly and follow him into a tent assigned to us. Nat is already inside, settling in for the night.

A good night of sleep would do me some good. Unfortunately, I haven't been able to sleep properly since Paige appeared on that balcony. She isn't far off. I can feel her magic sometimes. It squirms like a shark caught in a net, attempting to chew its way free.

The next morning, a woman retrieves us and escorts us to a command tent. When we duck inside, I struggle to keep my expression neutral. The technology these people have is leaps and bounds beyond what we can do! Computer screens occupy a full wall, feeding images from the area surrounding Elpis. Workers talk softly and it takes me a moment to realize they aren't talking to themselves. They have communication devices in their ears to relay information. Their military is impressive. While we have a sizable force, the organization and training of the Elpis military are very different and much more advanced. Hopefully, that will play to our advantage against Dominic. Easton was right. We need these people to help us stop him.

The three of us are the last to arrive. A team of leaders from each of the other communities has already gathered in a massive command tent. Cypress stands at my side, Nat on the other, as we crowd around the large table. Nearly a dozen men and women from Elpis have joined the strategy session, along with Gavin, Drake, Emil, and a few others from the Haven.

A man I haven't seen before, who I can only assume is a technician, swipes his hand over the tabletop and the image changes instantly to a video feed. Cypress gapes. I do my best not to look like a fool as much as he does.

The video shows an overhead view of a massive camp filled with soldiers, tents, and horses. I don't need anyone to tell me it's Dominic's army. *How did they get this footage?*

"The drones picked this up two nights ago," the technician tells everyone. "His men spotted some drones and shot them down with lightning, but not before we got the video relayed to us. The camp is twenty-three miles from the barrier. If we plan on stopping him before he gets to the barrier, we have to act right now."

Gavin nods. "I've tracked his progress and projected his arrival tomorrow by eleven-thirty-eight."

How does he know that so precisely?

Ugene studies the feed, his arms crossed over his chest and a hand pressed to his chin. His expression hardens as he watches the feed. Gavin eyes him and I wonder what is going through their heads.

"There's something else," Gavin says, eyeing his dad. "You see it, Dad?"

"I do," Ugene says.

"See what?" Cypress asks, leaning closer.

The moment he asks, I spot what caught their eyes and anger burns in my chest. I clench my hands into fists against the tabletop, pressing my knuckles against it. Dominic crouches in front of Paige, who is tied to a chair and looking worse for wear. Blood spots the ground surrounding her. My teeth grind as I suppress a fit of rage. I will rip him apart limb from limb.

"She's been trained for this sort of thing," Bianca says to Ugene as if trying to placate him. They trained her for torture? What else don't I know about her?

Paige raises her chin and spits in Dominic's face. I fight off a smug smirk.

Feeling as if someone is staring at me, I lift my gaze to find Ugene's calculating stare assessing *me*. I hope he can tell how much I care about her.

"That's when they caught the drone," the man explains.

"Two days ago," Cypress mutters. "That's the night of her psychic attack."

I nod. She was trying to fight back against Dominic. *Good girl. Keep fighting, Paige.*

"Wait!" Cypress squints at the feed, watching the playback again. He stabs a finger at the video. "River."

I peer at the feed. "She was right..."

"What is it?" Ugene asks.

Even Cypress eyes me with confusion. I rub at my temples, putting the pieces together. "The missing girls. The Tributes you dismissed went missing on the island. Easton and I went to check on them and they weren't at the Windsor. Easton suspected Dominic was up to something with the girls even then. Him or Vincent."

"You think he was hiding the girls somewhere for this purpose?" Cypress asks.

"I'm certain he did." All eyes are on me, wondering what I will say next. I wish they weren't looking at me like that. I glance at Ugene momentarily. "Paige told me he had the other mainland Tributes with him. That he experimented on them like he did to Easton."

Cypress' face turns red with anger. "All of them?"

I rub the back of my neck as I straighten. "Paige said he did something to them that made all of them sick."

Ugene mutters something, glancing at Bianca. They exchange grim looks I don't understand.

Levi grimaces as if he understands as well. "What can these girls do?"

Cypress huffs out a breath. "I can give you a full breakdown for each girl as we set up our lines for defense."

Levi nods in thanks.

The feed cuts out.

"Another drone picked up something else interesting," the technician says as he swipes the tabletop again and a 3D version of a report pops off the surface. Nat startles back.

"Is that a radiation report?" Ugene asks.

Gavin's eyes dart across the report. I'm getting a sense he's much smarter than anyone else here—his dad included. "That doesn't make any sense," he mutters to himself.

"What doesn't?" Cypress asks. I feel just as out of the loop here.

"There's a massive spike right where their camp is located," Gavin says, stabbing a finger at the report. "Right around Paige. But no one seems affected by it." Some data enlarges and becomes more detailed while other parts vanish. *How are they doing this?*

The technician giving the report eyes Gavin, nodding. The way he looks at Gavin is...strange. "Then it vanishes."

"No, it doesn't." Gavin scrolls through information faster than I can even see it. Not that I understand the significance of it. "I need more time with this."

"We don't have time for that right now," Bianca says. "We have less than a day to prepare for the invasion and get the troops in position."

"Unless you think Dominic can create a radiation device?" Levi asks.

Cypress and I study one another for a moment. We can't really rule out anything anymore, but it's highly doubtful.

"I don't think so," Cypress says at last.

They all accept it at face value and move on. The report vanishes, and both the technician who brought it up and Gavin groan in disappointment. The technician grins at Gavin, who averts his gaze and shifts closer to Drake. *Strange.*

A map appears in its place. But not just any map. It's a massive 3D map of the terrain. As Bianca talks, her finger presses parts of the map that light up, creating a clear image of our defenses. A red ring blinks into existence around everything as she explains what the barrier is and how it can keep the army out. No one even comments on the massive city nestled in the heart of it all.

"Based on his current trajectory, we expect his army to arrive here," Bianca says, marking out a location on the map to the southeast. Gavin nods in agreement. "We will have men and women in these critical positions to defend the city in case anyone breaks through." She touches two more points on the map that light up. "The barrier will be in place to hold him back. It's forty miles from the barrier to the city, so odds are he won't make it that far. The bulk of our forces will be out there to greet him."

"Cypress." Ugene's voice draws both of our gazes away from the massive city. "You will work in collaboration with Bianca and Levi to organize your men for defense on our side of the barrier. They shouldn't be able to get through, so with any luck, we won't even have to lift a finger."

Cypress shakes his head. "Nothing is ever that simple. Zephyr is our strategist. You need him there."

"He has another mission," Bianca says.

I nod. Getting to Paige is my priority.

"You're right, though. He won't be so easily defeated." Ugene nods grimly. "But Paige and those other girls are still out there. I won't leave my daughter to his whims. He will torture her to break down our barrier."

"He won't have to," Gavin says.

All eyes dart to him. He shifts anxiously.

"It's just a theory, but...Zephyr said she's like me."

I nod. "She is. I'm not sure if a barrier can stop her. Which is why I'm going to get her before he can use her against anyone." And I'm not asking permission.

"I'm going with you," Gavin says, but his voice trembles.

"No," Ugene says quickly. "You aren't, Gavin. You can do more to protect our forces from attack than anyone else can. We need you with the army."

Gavin grimaces but nods. I can't argue with the logic. Besides, I don't want to be responsible for both of the Minister's kids. Especially not if I have to choose between them. I know what my choice would be. It's better not to have Gavin with me.

Director Levi clears his throat, sliding his finger along the map. A path through the city and around to the south of Dominic's army appears. "Zephyr, you will join a hand-selected team of our top Specialists to slip around the side of Dominic's army to find Paige and get her safely away."

"I have a Stealth man to bring along," I say, thinking of Jeff.

Levi shakes his head. "We have our own, and they are highly trained for these kinds of missions. The only reason you are part of the team is because..." He glances sideways at Ugene, seeming unhappy with what he's about to say. "Because some people here think you are the only one who can break her from Dominic's Control. When we adjourn, you'll be escorted to another tent to change and prepare. You will have twenty minutes until the rubber hits the road. They *will* leave you behind if you don't make it. The timing here is critical."

They would just leave me? How do they think they can stop her without me? My gaze darts to Ugene, and I see the worry in his eyes. Terror grips my chest as I recall our private conversation back at the hotel. Without me, they might kill her to stop her. I can't miss that ride.

Bianca doesn't look pleased either. Her copper eyes glint with anger, but she stuffs it down to continue the strategy session. "We will send out a second team to act as a distraction and engage his forces, giving you a chance to slip in and find the girls. Our aim is to ensure all of Dominic's focus is on us."

They continue breaking down how they will go about distracting him. What magic to use, where, and when. How to draw his troops into the barrier. How to group magic groups together.

When they call the session to a close, I hustle toward the exit to find out where I can get ready. I won't miss that ride.

Cypress swiftly catches stride with me. "Do you think Dominic has any idea how big or advanced their city is?"

"If he does, we know why he's invading," I say. The words slip out before I even realize it occurred to me.

Cypress curses under his breath, rubbing a hand through his wavy dark hair. "If he gets hold of their technology, if he takes control of their city somehow..."

"He won't." I sound confident, but I no longer know what Dominic is capable of.

We reach the prep tent, and Cypress grabs my arm, pulling me to a stop. "Zeph, be careful. They aren't telling us something. Don't you find it strange that no one mentioned how they plan on *stopping*

Dominic? I'm worried about what they will do once you give the all-clear that you have Paige secured."

"You're worried about *his* men?" I ask. Why would Cypress care? "They overthrew you, Cypress."

"They're my people. They deserve the chance we gave the men on the boats back in old St. Louis. And Ugene promised I could deal with Dominic." He sighs as he lets go and pulls me into a hug. "Just...be careful, brother. Get Paige and get out."

Brother. That word warms my heart. Despite everything, Cypress still accepts me as his brother. Maybe because I'm the only one he has left.

"You too," I say, patting his back. Then I step into the tent.

31

GAVIN

THE ANALYST TENT HASN'T stopped collecting data and tracking Dominic's movements. The data collection kept me up all night, searching for answers. Dominic will be near Elpis today before noon and his army is much larger than Cypress and Zephyr first indicated. More than double the size. Match that with Paige's Powers, and Dominic actually stands a chance of winning.

Everything hinges on Zephyr getting to her in time. I didn't see him leave camp yesterday, but the haste with which he left the command tent leaves me with no doubt he made it to the vehicle on time. I can use my Powers to hold Dominic off, but without knowing how he will use Paige against me, I don't know how long I can hold him. After the fights I had with the Elders in the Haven, I don't know how well I will hold up under pressure on such a large scale, either. I'm not built for this sort of thing.

Another worry haunts me. If I can destroy Power stones, Paige probably can, as well, which means the stone that powers the barrier around Elpis is vulnerable. Can she target the stone without touching it? I must assume she can. Not that she will unless Dominic forces her hand.

Worse than the dread of throwing myself into a battle—something I very much would rather avoid—is the knowledge that I might have to face off against Paige. It's kept me from sleeping and made me sick to my stomach. I can't hurt her. Somehow, I need to hold her off without harming her. I have a few ideas, but I don't know how well any of them will hold up if she's forced to target me.

I bite my thumbnail as I once more go over the data the team has collected. The radiation spike concerns me. How did it happen, and why? If our teams are caught out there unaware when another spike strikes, it could kill them. The others dismissed it the moment the royals said there would be little chance of a radioactive bomb. There is a reason for it. There must be.

Strong hands massage my shoulders from behind my chair. I glance back, expecting Drake to be standing there as he often did in the Haven. Instead, Aron flashes a small smile my way. For an instant, I remember the way his smile used to make me melt. It's still charming, without a doubt. But my mind drifts to Drake. Panic surges through me. This is wrong, right? He shouldn't be doing this. Not after what he confessed. And I shouldn't allow it.

Before I can pull away, the tent flap opens and Emil ducks in, followed immediately by Drake.

My stomach drops, and I jerk away from Aron.

But not before Drake's gaze takes in the scene. I groan inwardly. That can't possibly look good, even if it only lasted a few seconds and I was ready to pull away. The set of Drake's jaw tells me all I need to know. I've been around him long enough to recognize certain expressions. Drake's angry.

Aron doesn't seem the least bit bothered, moving to stand beside me as I surge to my feet. Why is he sticking to my side like this? He knows I'm with Drake. I love Drake. Nothing Aron says or does will change that.

"The Havenites are all secure in the Greenhouse," Emil reports, shooting a dirty look at Aron. "Ajax is working with a security team there to make sure the people are looked after and protected. He didn't enjoy being positioned away from his precious Idol."

"And Ally?" I ask, clicking off the tablet in my hands. A glance at Drake cracks my heart. He won't even look at me, but his glare at Aron is clearly filled with hate.

Emil smiles ruefully. "She won't leave her Guardians to fight while she remains in the Greenhouse."

I shouldn't have expected anything else from her. Ally oversaw the Guardians in the Haven. She wouldn't leave them to charge into battle without standing at their sides. "What about you, Emil? Are you going back to the Greenhouse?"

He shakes his head. "Ally will be here." The implication that he wants to remain close to her isn't lost on me. "And I feel..." He rubs his neck and grimaces. "It's just, if others, if my sister's son..."

Drake pats Emil on the shoulder. "You're worried about your nephew. We get it."

Emil straightens. "I should go check in with Ally at the command tent."

"I'll come along," Drake says, glaring at Aron. He ducks out before Emil even turns around.

"Drake, wai—" I freeze a few steps away from Emil, watching the tent flap slap closed behind Drake. I edge closer to Emil, letting him read me with his Lie Detection. "Nothing happened. I wouldn't..."

Emil nods, but his eyes are on Aron. "I believe *you*, Gavin." He leans closer, resting a hand on my shoulder. He lowers his voice for only me. "But if you care about Drake, you need to distance yourself from Aron. And for the love of Creation, go after him *now*."

Now. Yes, I need to fix this before it gets out of hand. I sprint out into the sunlight and squint as my eyes adjust. Drake is only a few feet ahead, stomping straight toward the command tent. I jog after him, dodging an Elpis soldier carrying a menacing-looking crate.

"Drake, stop." I dart around him to cut off his path, holding up my hands.

He huffs and crosses his arms, but says nothing.

"I know how that looked, but it isn't what you think."

"No? Because it looked like he had his hands all over you."

"It was only a few seconds. I thought it was you at first, and when I looked back and saw him, it shocked me. Before I could pull away, you walked in."

Drake narrows his eyes, studying me in a silence that makes my stomach twist painfully. "That guy is trouble, Gavin. I saw the way he looked at me when I told him I was your boyfriend. He assessed me like your precious data points in seconds and decided I'm not good enough for you."

That makes little sense. How would Aron know that? He doesn't know Drake at all. Besides, it isn't Aron's choice. It's mine.

Drake snorts and rolls his eyes. "I know that look. You don't understand. Let me make this perfectly clear, Gavin. Just because you're with me doesn't mean he has given up. If anything, he will try to drive us apart so he can get what he wants."

I shake my head. "But that's ridiculous. My decisions have nothing to do with him. Whatever I felt for him is in the past. It's nothing like the way I feel about you."

Anger flashes in Drake's eyes. Is he mad at me? I didn't do anything, nor would I. Ever.

"Would anything have happened between us if Aron made his intentions clear before you left? If you two started dating?" Drake's question slams into my chest.

I flinch. "No, probably not."

Drake's lips thin, and he shakes his head, then steps around me. "We have work to do."

"Hang on, I think you misunderstood." I match his stride as he moves toward the command tent with purpose. "Nothing would have happened because when I'm in a relationship there aren't other options. There is no one else. I think that speaks more about my loyalty than anything else."

Drake snorts again but doesn't cease his relentless pace.

I grab his arm and pull him to a stop. "Drake, there is *no one* else. My love is and will always be yours." My fingers brush his rope bracelet and touch the wave medallion.

Drake's gaze drops to our wrists, to the bracelets. Some of his anger dissolves. His fingers lace with mine. For a moment, neither of us moves. Then he edges closer. My heart skips. This will not happen again. I won't allow it to happen again.

He brushes his lips against mine, then presses his forehead to mine. "I don't want to be the jealous type. I never thought I would be. But he's...assertive. Way more than I am. And Idols help me, he's way better looking. I couldn't help but think...maybe he's right and I'm not good enough for you."

"Don't be ridiculous," I breathe. "You bring out the best in me, Drake, and you understand me like no one else can. As far as looks go, don't sell yourself short. You are, without a doubt, one of the most staggering guys I've ever laid eyes on."

Drake chuckles, cheeks flushing. "Okay, okay. You win. As usual. But I think Cypress gets to hold that staggering award." This time when he kisses me, I slide my arms around him, ignoring the flow of the world around us.

Today could be the beginning of the end. I want to enjoy this moment of peace and fulfillment before everything comes crashing down.

32

ZEPHYR

I HAVE NO CLUE where we are going. The team leader, Camden, tracks our progress on some device while one of the other Specialists drives. Ten of us are packed into the vehicle. Everyone studies me when they think I'm not looking, picking me apart one flaw at a time, seeking points of weakness.

My only weakness is Paige.

There's only one girl in the vehicle. She introduced herself as Elly and asked how I know Paige, but I declined to answer. They know how Paige and I met, and her question feels loaded. I don't know any of these people and only trust them as far as this mission.

With one exception. Tudor makes a sport out of studying me from the corner of his eyes every time I look away. Like I don't notice his grim expression and calculating gaze. He hasn't said more than two words to me, but the moment we met, it became clear he recognized me from Paige's Dream in that locker room when he threatened her and I attacked him. I knew he was real and had an unpleasant history with Paige. But he likely didn't realize I was real until that moment. I wonder if he realizes I know him.

The gun holstered on his vest makes me uncomfortable. Would he use it against me? Ugene's warning rings in my mind. How long would Tudor hesitate before putting a bullet in Paige? How long would it take me to disarm him? Not that I know how to fire a gun, and they didn't give me one.

I shift in my seat, brushing my fingertips over the pouch of Knockout needles Ugene gave me, nestled safely in my pocket. My only weapons are my sword and magic. The Specialists eye the sword curiously, as if wondering how skilled I am with a blade. Hopefully, none of them have to find out. I will kill every one of them if they threaten Paige.

"Two clicks from the drop point," Camden announces from the front seat.

Like it triggered some unspoken signal, each of the Specialists checks weapons and secures their protective vest. I check my vest as well, but the garment makes me uncomfortable. If I have to use my sword, the vest might restrict my movements.

The truck rolls to a stop a short distance later, and a Specialist opens the back door. Everyone shifts toward the doors to exit.

Tudor brushes past me, bumping me out of the way. "Don't slow us down, *Admiral*." His sarcasm is so crystal clear that Elly clears her throat awkwardly behind me.

I hop out after Tudor and follow Mat, another Specialist, toward a nearby rock face. The team takes a knee to wait.

In this position, a series of rock faces guard us from the open, barren landscape, out of sight of the massive military camp. Our position is farther southeast than the bulk of our forces. The goal is to sneak around the back and take Dominic's men by surprise as we slip in and the rest of our army distracts them. The landscape is flat in every direction, with only a few dead trees and rock faces, like the one we huddle behind, to break up the expanse. It's the perfect place for a large-scale fight.

I glance cautiously around the rock face. We need to find Paige. I can sense her, but if I could lay eyes on her, that would be even better.

I pull my pocket scope out to get a better look at his camp. The tool draws a scoff from Tudor. *What did Paige ever see in this guy?*

I sweep the scope along the camp.

Dominic has grouped the soldiers together by magical abilities. At the front lines, men with the psychic patch on their uniforms check their weapons and organize into ranks. They will be his first wave, using mental attacks to weaken the front lines. I can predict what comes next. The Builders' deadliest weapon will be beneath our feet. At least one grouping of men is trained to turn the earth into deadly spikes. I saw them in action during the attack on the palace. Other Builders will work together, creating projectile weapons from the earth that the Telekinetics can use to attack. More than likely, this will be his first phase of the attack.

Once the Psychics and Builders have done their work, the muscle will move in to clean up the weakened lines. It's exactly how I predicted Dominic would fight. His training in military strategy isn't as extensive as my own, but I can't afford to underestimate him. Dominic had time to study independently. No doubt, he did.

I sweep the camp once more, searching for signs of Paige or the other Tributes. Nothing stands out.

"What do you see, Admiral?" Elly asks.

I hold the scope to her so she can look for herself. She puts it to her eye.

"Dominic is doing exactly what I expected of him," I inform the others.

"That's good news, right?" Mat asks. "It means our plan will work."

I grimace and shake my head. "Or we will play right into his plans. Dominic isn't stupid. The one advantage we have right now is that he doesn't know what's happening back home. He doesn't know an army of his own people is cooperating here."

"Any sign of Paige?" Tudor interrupts sharply, his focus on Elly.

She shakes her head, then lowers the scope and passes it down the line. Tudor snatches it from her, and I want to take it from him and stuff my fist down his throat. This guy's attitude gets on my last nerve.

"According to the video feeds, the girls will be in a central tent in the middle of the camp," I tell them. My gaze falls on a man named Carlos, a Specialist on the team. "Carlos can use his Stealth to get us into camp. Tudor's Hearing can listen for signs of trouble to help us find the best path. Once I'm within fifty yards of Paige, I'll drop the cuff and she should be free from Dominic's grasp."

Tudor lowers the scope and glares at me. "Just because your people call you an admiral doesn't put you in charge here."

"No, I think your *Minister* put me in charge," I reply, glaring at him.

"I answer to the Director," Tudor replies, using the scope once more, dismissing me.

Mat heaves a dramatic sigh. "This is why Specialists aren't supposed to date."

I pluck my scope from Tudor and pocket it before he can stop me, directing my gaze to Mat. "I wouldn't worry too much about that. Paige told me exactly what she thought of her ex."

Tudor straightens his spine and glares at me. "I'm sure you were more than happy to dive into my sloppy seconds."

The rage bubbles over. In a heartbeat, I pin Tudor to the rock face just like I did in that Dream, pressing my arm to his throat.

"Too bad she isn't here to save you again," I growl.

His eyes widen. *He didn't realize I knew about that Dream! Well, now he knows.*

Tudor's fist hammers into the side of my skull. He's stronger than I expected. I stumble back, but recover just in time to block a follow-up swing. My boots kick up dirt as I shuffle my feet and throw a fist into his exposed ribs.

"Stop!" someone shouts. Several of the Specialists grab each of us and pull us back.

My lip is bleeding. The coppery tang of blood touches the tip of my tongue. I spit blood on the ground and shrug off the men pulling my arms back.

"If you aren't ready for a fight, keep your opinions to yourself," I hiss. "And if you make comments like that about the king's fiancé again, it will be my sword in your gut. Do I make myself clear?"

Tudor clutches at his side, wincing in pain but still glaring at me. "Willing to kill for her, huh?"

"And for my King," I say, straightening my jacket and vest. "And you would do well to remember that."

For a moment, neither of us moves. Neither of us even flinches as we stare one another down. I would love to have him jump at me again, and I will shed this cuff and rip his magic right out of him.

"Guys?" Elly calls, her voice steady and full of warning.

Tudor's eyes glaze over. "I hear it." He adjusts his gun, then glances at me one more time before moving toward the gap that separates us from Dominic's army. "They're moving."

"Now or never," I say.

Carlos glances at me, then Tudor as he says, "Remember our orders. Get the Admiral as close to Paige as we can, then create a path for escape."

Goosebumps spread across my arms. *I'm coming, Paige.*

33

PAIGE

THE GIRLS AND I line up behind Dominic as he steps onto a makeshift stage and addresses the lines of his men. Once the tracker took over with information gleaned from the drone, I've been helpless to stall or direct Dominic into position like Zephyr asked me to do. Hopefully, Dad and the others have enough information now to know where we are and prepare accordingly. It's the best I can hope for now.

For the past few nights, Ivy lies beside me to monitor my health as I attempt to pluck away another thread of Dominic's Control. It's exhausting work that often leaves me in pain, but if I don't handle each thread delicately, he will know what I'm up to. It's all part of the plan. A plan that would be so much more effective if I knew what Zephyr and the others had in store. I've tried reaching out to him in a dream again, but the sensation that someone was watching me chased me away from contact with anyone I know. Did Dominic have another Dreamer who can monitor me? I can't take the chance.

We aren't far from the barrier. Elpis is only forty-some miles away, so close I swear I can feel the thrum of life ebbing and flowing along the streets. I wished to return home for so long, but not like this.

Dominic suspects something is amiss, but I don't know what he knows. A handful of his men have been reporting something to him discreetly for days. Whatever it is, Dominic isn't happy about the news. Hopefully, no one knows what's happened in the Kingdom.

Today is the day.

This morning, Dominic pulled the other girls aside one at a time to discuss his plans for them, but none of them could say a word to the rest of us about what he said. No doubt, he doesn't want us talking and conspiring against him. Dominic is smart enough to block us from sharing information. The frustration burns in my veins as I watch him put his head together with his officers atop the platform before turning to face the crowd of soldiers.

Ivy holds her head high at my side, but her gaze is shifty. Who would he have her Mimic? She doesn't really know anyone...except me. I peer at her from the corner of my eye. Would he use her as a decoy to draw out the Elpis forces? *Yes. That's exactly the sort of thing he would do.*

Alice hugs her arms over her chest beside Ivy, visibly trembling. The poor thing is terrified of whatever Dominic has in store for her, which probably puts her directly in the line of fire once the battle begins. Her Elemental Powers will be useful in a fight.

River and Summer stand at my other side, holding hands like nothing could ever tear them apart. My heart goes out to the two women. I hope this ends happily for them, but I know better than to offer such disillusionment. Until we are free from Dominic and his deadly quest, none of us will ever know happiness—assuming we survive what comes next.

Dominic steps forward, raising his arms above his head. A sense of calm pulses out of him like a great wave. I glance down the line again to see Summer sweating. She's a natural amplifier. Did he command her to increase his own Powers?

The soldiers all relax, watching their tyrant king as the sun glints off his crown. *No, not his crown. Cypress' crown.* I want to tear it from his head and bludgeon his face with it until he's no longer recognizable.

"The days are finally upon us!" Dominic says. His voice carries easily. Summer is definitely amplifying him. "We all have been oppressed by a system designed to keep us in line, and I'm proud to be your chosen leader who will break the system and reforge it in our image."

His words charm the crowd, but I'm not fooled like everyone else. This is his Power at work; his amplified Influence swaying them with false charm and charisma.

"Some of you have served me faithfully for years, waiting for this moment to come. Others have only recently seen the light. It matters not how you came to be here. What matters is that you are here, beside your fellows, ready to make a change, to seize opportunity, to control your own destiny!"

I scoff at that last statement. None of these men control anything. Dominic pulls all their strings like a master puppeteer. Once more, I glance at Summer. Her dark complexion has become ashen as she uses her Power to help his speech. I hope she has enough control over herself to carry out her part of the plan. I hope he doesn't exhaust her so that she cannot help us at all.

Dominic holds a hand out at his side, palm up. "No one and nothing will stop us from achieving our goals," he says.

My feet move toward him of their own accord. I cannot stop him from drawing me to his side. I slide my hand into his.

"And this," he continues, raising my arm into the air with his, "is our secret weapon! With the power to destroy any who resist, to control time itself, no one can stand in our way!"

I won't tremble. Not for him. Instead, I raise my chin and smile at the mass of soldiers. Let them think I'm on their side. The only thing I intend to destroy is Dominic's power.

Dominic distrusts me. The way he glances at me from the corner of his eye is suspicious. Though he pulled all the other girls aside to give them instructions, he said nothing of his plans to me, which tells me two things.

First, he doesn't trust me with his plans.

Second, he fears I might refuse.

Both broaden my smile as the soldiers cheer.

Dominic releases my hand and I fold them together behind my back, fighting off the urge to wipe his touch from my palm.

"Soldiers of the Kingdom of Tides, it's time! Officers form up ranks. It's time to move out."

The crowd gives another ground-shaking cheer of, "Ah-oo!" before breaking apart.

As they disperse, Dominic turns to face me, eyeing me like a curious bird. "Whatever you have plotted, Paige, I would abandon the plans now."

"I don't know what you're talking about," I say nonchalantly.

For just a moment, his lips curl in a rage, but it passes swiftly and is replaced by the calm composure of the innocent prince I once knew.

"Bella, dear," Dominic calls over my shoulder.

She appears at my side, hands folded demurely in front of her. "My love?"

"It's time."

She nods and marches toward Ivy. My eyes lock with my friend and the terror in her eyes makes my bones ache. What are they doing to her? Whatever it is, Ivy already knows. Bella unlocks the collar containing Ivy's Power.

The second Ivy is freed from her collar, her body transforms. It's the most incredible thing I've ever witnessed to watch the way her skin tone shifts to a slightly lighter hue. Then her eyes darken and her face morphs. The beautiful ethnic features of her face become much plainer.

"Ivy," Dominic growls in warning.

I throw my body against him as Ivy finished her transformation. An exact replica of Bella right down to the dress and haughty air, fights with the real Bella. Dominic and I slam into the stage and his stormy blue eyes bore into me. I throw a punch into his face that makes my own head hurt. My muscles resist every blow. But I don't need to do actual damage. My job is to distract him.

Bella screams, though I don't know which one.

"Stop!" Dominic mouths, but Summer's amplification suppresses his voice. I wasn't sure if it would work to keep his commands from forced compliance. For the moment, it does the trick.

I pluck at several threads of his Control all at once as we wrestle one another on the ground. My Muscle Memory surges to the surface and combat training tricks rush through my muscles, giving me an advantage in the wrestling match. My head hammers. Dizziness overwhelms me, but I can't stop. Every thread I snap makes Dominic flinch. He's sweating, struggling to keep his hold on me.

My back is pinned to the stage and Dominic looms over me, snarling as his hands reach for my temples to force his way into my head. I howl and bat his arms to the side, but the loss of his arms collapses his body against my own with a muffled grunt. His hot breath rolls across my neck and I hear his voice with crystal clarity in my ear.

"You will submit to me, Paige." The crooning of his voice makes me whimper as my body fights to obey. Every ounce of my energy is absorbed in this fight for control of myself.

A fight I lose before I can pull at the right thread.

Dominic jumps to his feet, dragging me with him as his arm wraps around my neck.

Summer is a lump on the ground with River draped over her, crying, begging the royal guard to leave Summer alone. I don't know what happened to her. Alice's hands tremble as she struggles to hold a frail wall around the stage to keep out more guards. When did her collar come off?

Two Bellas fight one another, pulling hair and scratching wherever their hands can reach. Dominic's breathing in my ear increases with his frustration. I smirk.

"Bellas!" His voice rolls out with that familiar caress of Influence. "Kneel."

"Dominic," Bella One whimpers as she struggles against the command forcing her to her knees.

Bella Two drops to her knees, eyes shining with tears. "Please, my love, it's me. It's me..." Something about her tone implies a familiarity between the twisted couple.

Dominic's grip on my throat tightens. His breathing increases. "Rev—"

I ram my head back into his face, cutting off the command before he can force Ivy to reveal herself to him. Dominic's grip loosens as he stumbles back with a yelp of alarm. The hold is loose enough for me to twist around and dip out of his grasp.

Dominic tips his head back to stem the flow of blood from his nose as both Bellas cry out to him in alarm.

I ball my hand into a fist, ready to strike, but Dominic's hand twitches at his side. My limbs slow. As he closes his hand in a fist, an unseen force thrusts me to my knees and knocks the air from my lungs. He's compressing me in a Controlling vice. It requires all his focus to stop me. *Good*.

"Dominic!" Bella Two rushes toward him, all concern and tears, her gaze sweeping over him critically for signs of injury.

My heart sinks. That's the real Bella.

"No!" Bella One shrieks, reaching for Bella Two's skirt.

Bella Two collides with Dominic, throwing her arms around him, hands roving over him as she asks about wounds. Dominic mutters that he's fine, aside from the bloody nose. Bella kisses his cheek, her hand on his neck tenderly.

Our plan failed.

"Please, Dom, that's not me," Bella One rises on shaking legs.

Something materializes in Bella Two's hand at Dominic's waist. Bella One shrieks. Dominic grunts and staggers back. Vines snap to life around Bella Two's body, tightening with sickening crunches.

Then the Mimic fades away. Ivy is bound in vines, mouth open in a silent scream as Bella's vines crush her like an ant. Dominic lowers a shaking hand to his side. I track his movements, noticing the blood seeping from a wound created by a jagged rock.

Alice appears nearby, her hand shaking in Dominic's direction. It was her. Yesterday, Ivy pocketed a small rock. Alice just transformed it into a jagged knife for Ivy to use against Dominic. It worked.

Bella cries, screams for a healer as Alice falls to her knees. Her protective walls crumble.

"Ivy!" I crawl toward my friend, fighting against Dominic's lingering command.

Ivy blinks slowly, her face ashen and contorted in agony. A surge of fury rushes through me and I burn the vines away in a flash, turning them to ash. But it's too late. Ivy's body is mangled, bones broken by the vines, thorns piercing the skin. Blood seeps from her wounds. But worse is the way she struggles for breath. Something punctured her lungs. Tears blur my eyes.

"Ivy," I want to take her hand, but the pain in her eyes is too much.

"Finish... it..." She whispers through each agonizing gasp for breath. Blood trickles from her lips.

"No. Don't die on me. Please..."

Dominic casts a long shadow over us as Bella supports his weight. "Let this be a lesson," he growls, clutching his seeping wound. "I will not tolerate disobedience." He lifts his boot and presses it down against Ivy's chest.

"Stop, you'll kill her!" I shout, reaching a trembling hand for his leg.

"She's dead already." He leans his weight down on Ivy.

I cry as Ivy takes her last breath, and a wave of anger I've never felt before turns my Powers into a wild hurricane.

"Hold on to that power, Paige," Dominic commands. "We aren't done."

I choke on his command as the fire in my veins threatens to consume me.

Dominic staggers toward a healer, leaning against Bella for support. "Collar all of them," he orders one soldier. "I will show them what true suffering is."

34

EASTON

TEN KAYAKS REST ON the shallows of the lake on the southeast corner of the island. Commander Reginald did not like my plan, but I stuck to my guns. Dominic is hiding something, and Baron had a report about that island to the south. Now, standing on the shore, I peer south and can just make out the tree-covered island in the distance. It will be a long row to reach the other shore, but my muscles can handle the task.

The men selected to join me are all trained in combat as well, and their strength is enough to ensure they reach the other side. I observe each of them as they wade into the shallow water and prepare to drag their kayak far enough from shore that it won't bottom out on the rocks.

Bronwyn hugs her shawl around her body as she stands beside me. "I expect to hear from you soon." Her tone makes it clear she won't tolerate a moment of delay.

"Yes, Your Highness," I reply as I turn to face her. "We'll be fine. If we encounter anything, we have the radio to contact Reginald. He's ready."

Bronwyn frowns, dipping her chin to her chest. She's worried about me. While I admit I have great affection for her, and our stolen kisses have grown a bit more insistent of late, this blooming—whatever it is—between us makes me want to be more cautious than I would have been in the past. If for no other reason than to see her face again.

I slide my hand along her jaw, marveling at the smooth skin, and tip her chin up to meet her delicious honey-colored eyes. "Not a moment longer than necessary. I promise."

Our bodies inch closer to one another, then our lips meet in a kiss so delicate it feels too fragile for my lips.

I reluctantly pull away and wade into the water. I don't look back until I steer my kayak parallel to the shore.

Bronwyn watches us as the wind catches her skirt and dances through the fabric around her legs. But I can't stare at her for long. My focus needs to remain firmly on the task ahead. The mission comes first.

The rhythm of rowing the kayaks across the lake instantly invigorates me. I pick up on it quickly, watching how the others row and steer. Cool spring air pushes past us. Drops of cold water splash every now and again against the inside of the kayak or roll lazily along my arms. But my shoulders take to the work like a machine.

The team swings wide to approach Round Island from the east. I hope anyone watching the shores is more concerned about the north—which faces the Capital—or the west, which faces the mainland. A team of ten men in kayaks should be able to slip past any guards.

By the time we reach the eastern coast and find a place to pull our kayaks ashore and hide them, the sun is high in the sky. I wanted to come at night when we would be harder to spot, but Queen Elena cautioned that the water would be too dangerous in the dark.

One man on the team has Enhanced Hearing that he has learned to use to track locations. I insisted he come along on this mission the moment I found out. His skills will be invaluable as we search this island.

Trees cover the island. We use them for concealment to sneak along. Another member of the team can muffle the sound of our feet, making it easier to use stealth. No one speaks. We agreed on hand signals only, in case one of Dominic's guards has Enhanced Hearing as well.

The tracker leads the group around the northern forest. I don't know why he chooses this path but trust his Powers to guide us.

Then I see the dirt-packed road leading deeper into the island. All ten of us crouch to watch the road. Patrols are light, and we make our way along the eastern side of the road, using the trees for cover. The road goes on for about half a mile before I spot the squat, domed building nestled beneath the tree canopy.

The guards are hidden among the trees. We're lucky we didn't accidentally stumble across one on the way. Either that or our tracker knew where to go.

I motion to myself and our stealth companion, signaling that he and I will sneak up to take out the guards around the doors while the rest of them wait. Once we secure the door, we will send the rest of the team the all-clear to follow. I tap my companion on the arm and nod away from the group.

We creep along the trees, making simple work of the guards. My companion smothers my steps. I sneak up behind a guard and slip him in a sleeper hold until his body goes limp, then we drag him into hiding and remove his weapons and radio, clicking it off. On to the next. Then the next.

It shouldn't be this easy to slip into the facility. By the time we've secured the doors, my brain has convinced me that something is waiting in the shadows, a trap ready to spring closed.

I signal the rest of the team, and they rush toward the doors, keeping low for cover. The tracker smacks my arm and points up. I follow his direction and spot the camera pointed right at the doors. *Crap.* I knew this was too easy. None of us can disable the camera with our Powers. We have two choices: find another entrance or storm the door and hope for the best. If we move fast enough, the element of surprise might benefit us.

I track the angle of the camera, hoping to find a blind spot. If there's a camera here, there must be a bunch inside as well. Even if we slip past this one, another one will catch us in the act.

Something else occurs to me. I make quick signals to the other nine. They scowl at me and two of them shake their heads. I hold up my hand to show a countdown from five. None of them say a word, but the protest is clear in each of their expressions.

I don't wait for them to stop me, slipping away through the trees, and darting across the dirt road, until I reach the other side of the door in the camera's blind spot. My insides are a mess. If this goes wrong, Bronwyn will never forgive me. I peer at the nine men hidden among the trees watching me. I give a tight nod and count down from five with my fingers.

When the countdown hits zero, I slip through the camera's blind spot and open the facility door. It gives without protest, but I was prepared to break the lock if necessary. Before stepping through, my gaze sweeps the inner corridor for cameras. One is nestled at the far end of the hallway. No doubt it can see this entire entryway.

I slide my big shoulders through the door and decide to go with cocky arrogance and confidence. I slip my hands into my pockets and finger the smoke bombs retrieved from our Elpis packs, then stroll along the hallways as if it belongs to me.

By the time I'm halfway up the hall, the door at the far end opens. I don't hesitate, swiping one of the smoke bombs from my pocket as I pull the pin. It soars through the open door and detonates. The shock makes the walls vibrate and smoke instantly fills the space.

I dart to the side of the hallway, rushing toward the open door as a guard staggers out, coughing. I hold my breath like I was trained to do—I can hold it for nearly a minute—and reach for the sword on the guard's hip before he even notices me at his side. He dives for his weapon like an idiot, impaling himself. I kick his body off and push forward through the open door as the room roils with smoke.

A hand clamps on my arm. I swing around as Zephyr taught me, swinging the sword in an arc across the body to avoid sticking the blade in flesh. The hand falls away. Shouts arise from deeper in the facility and booted feet pound tiles in my direction. I shift my grip on the hilt and move with brutal efficiency through the blinded, oncoming throng of guards.

By the time the smoke clears, I'm standing in a bloody hallway, dripping sword in my hand, with a dozen bodies around me. I breathe in a lungful of air, eyeing the two guards standing between me and the next door.

"By order of Queen Elena, stand down," I say. "I have been authorized to use any force necessary."

The two guards eye the dead men around me. I don't look at them. Witnessing the carnage I created is not something I want to do. I have enough nightmares as it is.

The men lower their weapons to the floor, holding their hands up in surrender. The rest of my team slips in. One of them emits a low whistle and murmurs something to another. I ignore their praise. Death is death.

"How many more are in here?" I ask.

"A dozen, but mostly scientists," one captive says.

"Most of the men are around the perimeter," the other adds.

"Well, we know they won't be a problem," the tracker mutters. "Not with Superman here."

I ignore them. I've heard of Superman and hardly compare. "Radio the commander and let him know we've secured the facility," I order. I turn to the captives. "Take me to the scientists."

They eagerly nod and rise, guiding me deeper into the stark facility. My insides are twisted in sickening knots as something familiar strikes me about this place. I've been here. Before I started training at the fort, I was here suffering at Dominic's command. I close my eyes as a flashback strikes me. Men in white coats slice off sections of skin, pierce my spine with massive needles, and take my blood. Everything hammers against me and I stumble into a wall, disoriented.

"Sir?" The tracker is at my side, supporting me as best he can.

I wipe the sweat from my brow and nod. "I'm fine."

"Are you injured?" he asks.

"I don't think so." Not physically. But the emotional scars of Dominic's experiments will linger with me for some time. Perhaps forever.

We pass labs and patient rooms, then my steps freeze as I peer through the window in one doorway. The room is massive, like a Department of Security hangar for supplies and transport. Inside, someone has stacked crates upon crates in organized lines. I push through the door and examine the nearest crates labeled "Medical".

Dominic has been stockpiling pilfered supplies for *years* to collect all of this. But how is he using it? He's over a thousand miles from here by now!

I edge deeper into the room and gape at what I see on the far side of the storeroom. A doorway. But not just any doorway.

It's a gateway to another location, operated by a young woman far too thin for her own good. A guard stands over her, hand on his weapon. Her hands tremble as she weaves the gateway.

"Hey!" I run at that guard as I call out.

He turns his head just in time for my fist to connect with his jaw. It cracks, sending him spinning to the floor. The girl yelps and the gateway snaps shut, severing another guard in half as it closes on his body.

"Lady Layla!" the tracker exclaims. "She's one of the dismissed Tributes."

My lips part as it hits me.

Dominic didn't just experiment on me. He did something to those girls. That's why Zephyr and I never found them. They were here all along.

I set the sword on the ground and raise my hands to show her I mean no harm. "Where does that gateway go, Layla?"

Her gaze locks on the eyepatch over my missing eye. "You're Paige's friend."

"I am." I edge closer with caution, afraid of startling the girl into running. "What can you tell me about that gateway, Layla?"

She bites her lip, fighting for words that won't surface. "I...I was with him, you know. He told me...he promised..." Tears roll down her cheeks. "He lied to me."

"He lied to everyone, Layla," I say gently. "Don't blame yourself. But if you want to get back at him, help us. Tell us what you know."

Layla hugs herself, her eyes darting around the room. Then she nods and starts from the beginning. And it makes my stomach curdle with hate.

35

GAVIN

E LPIS WAS BUILT A few miles from a massive mountain range, along a barren stretch of wasteland that could sustain nothing. Not until Powers were used to bring a small section of it back to life. Then the water was cleansed. Buildings were constructed from pre-Collapse remnants. A hundred years later, the sanctuary has transformed into a thriving city full of people with incredible Powers. I've always loved Elpis. The beauty of the green buildings. The life that flows through the streets.

I never imagined it would become my duty to protect her from destruction. I mean, I supposed on some level I knew I would have to do something someday to help the city continue to thrive and expand. But this, what I'm about to do today, is a very different Power use.

The faces hemmed in around me aren't all that familiar, except for a handful who refused to be far from my side. Drake among them. Without his constant faith and strength, I wouldn't have been able to do this. I wasn't meant for battle. I was meant for a desk.

But this isn't just about Elpis. It's also about my family. My sister. If I don't do my part, I don't dare consider what could become of her. Paige is my entire purpose right now. She is the center of my cosmic universe at this moment.

Our chosen battlefield is littered with organized chaos. Strategic lines of men and women ready to use their Powers to defend the city and hold the line. Ready to lay their lives at the foot of Elpis to protect her from desolation.

I shudder just thinking of the word related to my sister. If the Havenites believe I'm the Idol of Creation, then to them Paige would be the Idol of Desolation. They would kill her to save the world. I cannot allow that to happen. Somehow, I have to save her from them...from herself.

There aren't enough fighters. Not against Dominic's thousands of trained men. Not against Paige.

A flash of red light emits like lightning in the distance but makes no sound. I flinch, worried about what that could mean for us. If waiting is the hardest part, I look forward to getting this over with, because waiting is agony.

Soldiers murmur to the man or woman beside them about the display.

"They're approaching," Aron's voice says through the ear comm.

I wince, glancing at Drake. He simply reaches for my hand and squeezes it.

The play is simple enough. The front lines will draw Dominic's men towards the barrier, and I will use my Powers alongside other Naturalists to cause disruption in his ranks. Our attack will serve as a distraction for Zephyr to save Paige from Dominic's Control. Once that's done, he will have nothing left to bargain with. The battle will be done.

If all goes to plan.

Clouds gather in the sky to the east, moving in our direction like an ominous storm threatening to break. The color shifts from white to light gray to dark thunderclouds. I watch as the storm approaches.

"Windweavers!" Cypress' call booms from somewhere down the line.

A cluster of troops move their hands in unison, a sharp flow aimed toward the oncoming storm. The clouds break but don't scatter. Then the storm looms over our lines. The Windweavers continue their work with the help of some of the Elpis Naturalists, but it still isn't enough to break the storm, only scatter the clouds.

Thunder cracks across the sky, followed by lightning that zips straight at our lines. Clever. But not clever enough. Uncle Alex works with hundreds of Electromancers, redirecting the lightning into a protective wall of energy in front of our lines. It crackles against the barrier, and ripples of translucent rainbows streak outward upon contact.

Zephyr warned us this would happen. Dominic will test our lines, feel out the skills we have at our disposal, then use his own to gain an advantage. If I were Dominic, I would do the same. Then I would do exactly what we have planned. Move the earth to break the lines and create chaos.

I swallow, grasping Drake's hand in a death grip.

With the storm comes the mist. Dominic has shrouded his lines in mist to keep us from assessing his numbers. He must know by now that we already have his numbers and his structure. He captured some of our drones, after all.

"He's obstructing our ability to attack his lines," Dad says over the comms in our ears. He and Aron stayed in the command tent with the analysts, who used drones to monitor the battlefield and give commands. I know he hated being left behind, but I'm grateful I don't have to worry about him. "Hold steady and prepare for the attack. The barrier is in place."

The wind kicks up and suddenly the Windweavers who were fighting off the storm struggle to break apart tornadoes as they form and twist and spin toward us. Dominic's men outnumber ours, and someone trained them to coordinate their skills together.

"Hold the lines!" The shout that rings out belongs to Aunt Bianca. I can't see her in the chaos, but she's here just as surely as the rest of my family.

The tornadoes spin off into nothing as our Windweavers take control.

Something soars high in the air and hits the barrier, disintegrating upon contact. Still, I flinch, ducking as if it would protect me when I know better.

Utter silence falls over the battlefield. No one seems to breathe as we wait for the storm to break. Men and women holding the lines shift on anxious feet, worried about what might come next. The Elpis people aren't trained for this sort of thing, even if we have great Powers at our disposal. They're used for everyday purposes, not battle. We have more Elpis volunteers along the lines than we have actual trained soldiers. That alone unnerves me.

I hold my breath, watching the rolling mist.

The silence shatters. Thunder crashes overhead as lightning begins a fresh assault, but much more aggressive this time. It cracks endlessly overhead, creating a brilliant, deadly light show. Pellets to hail fire at us from the clouds instead of rain, and each strikes like a bullet. Men and women scream. Some fall dead as the hail hits just right.

At the same time, hundreds of boulders the size of DS trucks launch like cannonballs at the lines. Most hit the barrier and disintegrate. A few soar over the top of the barrier and tumble into the rear lines, crushing people.

Drake drapes his body over mine to protect me from the hail, but I can't help the terror that he will drop dead from one striking his skull.

In seconds, our lines have broken apart. Dominic's forces have the upper hand without even revealing themselves. The assault is relentless, endless. People die before they even have a chance to fight for their homeland or king.

Terror pulses through me and my Powers spark to life in my fingertips as a boulder soars over the barrier toward our location. Instinctively, I push my Powers out at the boulder. It dissolves into dirt and falls like rain over our heads.

I can't stand back here any longer. Someone needs to get into those lines.

"Dad," I call through the comm. "Shut down the barrier."

His voice hisses back at me. "Gavin, we can't allow—"

"Trust me. The barrier isn't helping anything. We need to advance. Now. Otherwise, we've already lost."

"He's right," Cypress says into the comm. "We're sitting ducks out here."

Silence.

"Dad!" I call.

"Barrier is down," Dad announces across the comms. "I hope you know what you're doing, boys."

That's my hope as well. I slide my hand out of Drake's and soak in the world's energy around me. It buzzes and pulses with life as my Powers grow until the blue glow has spread from my fingers to wrap around my body like a protective vest.

What am I doing? This is so stupid. But as I crush more boulders, I know I have no choice. Dominic's men have all the earth they need behind their lines. We don't stand a chance if we don't attack.

I use the surrounding energy to create a shield above the lines, protecting the troops from overhead assaults. The hail hammers against the shield but doesn't reach the troops. I rise, levitating above all their heads to get a clearer view of what lies beyond.

Boulders rip from the earth behind Dominic's lines and soar toward me. As they shoot in my direction, I reach out to their very core, their essence, and shatter the boulders apart, forming hundreds of rocky spikes. With a flick of my wrist, the spikes shift direction and fly at Dominic's troops. Troops I can see beyond the mist of cover he has created.

Men scream as the projectiles strike flesh. Others divert, dodge, or destroy the shards. The mist evaporates, revealing his army. In an instant, the earth beneath both lines shifts underfoot, and the lines break. Everything descends into organized chaos.

A distant call for a charge draws my gaze down. Cypress has his sword raised toward the sky like a lightning rod, shouting something to his men. I glide forward with his men, all my attention on shifting the ground out from beneath Dominic's lines. They scatter like ants from an anthill, but not everyone makes it before the hole in the earth opens.

I won't swallow them in a mass grave. I can't bear the idea of killing so many without mercy. They will have to climb themselves out, but it will at least slow them down. Flashes of the Haven collapsing hammer against my mind. Panic grips my chest. Screams. The thunder of the earth swallowing them.

Some force grabs hold of me. Then I'm being thrown toward the earth.

36

PAIGE

T EARS ROLL DOWN MY cheeks as Dominic forces me to abandon Ivy and follow him. The other girls beg for mercy as soldiers snap the collars back on their necks and drag them in the opposite direction. River struggles against the soldier hauling her away as she reaches for Summer, who is scooped up by another soldier and thrown over his shoulder.

Alice screams and kicks wildly, just as she did when those men mutinied against Zephyr months ago. Worse is the way she calls my name like I can help her, save her. My heart breaks for the other girls. For my helplessness. I try fighting Dominic, but his focus is completely on Controlling me now. I'm just as helpless as the other girls, forced against my will to trail Dominic like a shadow as he makes his way to a healer.

Dominic pauses, lifting his shirt to expose the wound to the healer. The toned muscles along his ribs twitch as the healer lays his hands on the wound. Dominic hisses in pain, his face paler than usual, but the wound stitches shut. Ivy died for nothing.

That realization makes my grief over her death amplify. The Powers raging inside of me buck and fight to release. Red energy emits from my fingers and I whimper, unable to stop it.

"Not yet, Paige," Dominic hisses through his pain.

The Powers don't stop raging, but those three words are like a master choking on the collar of a slave. I yelp as the Powers jerk back, waiting impatiently for release.

"Not until we reach our enemy lines," he adds.

Enemy lines... He intends to have me use this deadly Power on everyone who opposes us. Can I destroy so many so quickly? Maybe.

This fire burning inside of me is overwhelming, and it grows with each passing moment. I have to get out of his grasp. Soon.

In the distance, the rumble of thunder and lightning cracks across the sky. Dominic and Bella march toward the battlefront with me on their heels. The earth shakes as Naturalists rip boulders from the ground for Telekinetics to hurl relentlessly to the west. The barrier around Elpis ripples as lightning strikes it, creating a rainbow of colors. Some boulders hit the barrier and disintegrate while others soar over the top.

Nothing touches Dominic's lines. A wall of fog protects them from sight. But I can see them. If only I could grab control of this Power for a second. Would that be long enough to stop them?

Something overs over the battlefield. Is that Levi, hoping for an eagle eye on the situation? It can't be. His skin is too dark against the sky. The levitator raises his arms like he can block the boulders, then they shatter into hundreds of shards that rain death down on Dominic's lines. The screams of death and thunder mute the shouts of men charging into battle. It's horrific.

"What is that?" Dominic snaps, stabbing a finger at the lone figure in the sky. I'm not sure who he is asking. "Paige, take him down!"

The command sends a pulse of force through me. I clench my teeth so tight they grind together. Sweat rolls down my temples. I clench my fists and try refusing his command, but his hold over me is stronger than ever. Dominic grabs my wrist and thrusts me forward.

Whoever it is in the sky, he is more brutally efficient than a hundred of his men. He creates shields, breaks rocks, and launches attacks in quick succession and with brutal efficiency. He could be their strongest weapon. I don't want to take him down. I want to help him. But my hands shake as I fight off the Powers leaping into action from my hands. Without realizing what I'm doing, or how, I fire a Telekinetic blast in his direction.

Then the body tumbles haphazardly to the ground.

37

EASTON

I PACE THE STORAGE room as reinforcements arrive in the facility and join us. The rest of my team secured the building, as I wait for reinforcements. Reginald sent every man and woman willing to fight that the Capital could spare the moment I sent word about what we learned.

Now, a sizable army is gathering.

Layla sits on the floor, hugging her knees to her chest, rocking as if the motion soothes her. Dominic completely brainwashed the poor girl. He made her believe that, when all of this was over, they could be together. He twisted the poor girl's mind to *want* to be with him just so he could manipulate her and her Power. Then he convinced her he had to use Bella to get her help and to do that, he would have to play a happy couple. Layla bought the lie, though I suspect Dominic's Control has something to do with it.

The injections he gave Layla altered her Divinic Power. Before, she could read patterns using the stars to perceive potential changes, like a type of Psychic Navigation. He used her Power to plot his best course forward, then injected her with a serum that allowed her to create gateways. It reminds me of a study we were forced to complete during the early days of Specialist training. Something like this was done years ago in Elpis to a girl only known now as Vortex.

According to Layla, she can only create a gateway to a place where she has been. Naturally, Dominic needed to bring Layla along to Elpis so she could be the bridge between the battle lines and his resources here in the facility. It allowed him to travel light, moving in necessary supplies each day instead of dragging them along for more than a thousand miles. Another clever tactic on his part. I'm hating the way he remains smartly a step ahead like this.

When Layla couldn't take watching Dominic and Bella play the happy couple any longer, she lashed out and attacked Bella. Dominic didn't just make her cool off. I shudder as I recall what Layla told me next. The way he touched her face with affection while pressing his Influence on her weak mind, then told her she meant nothing to him.

He *gave* Layla to one of his top officers and somehow transferred specific control and obedience to that officer. After that, she remained separate from the other girls in a different tent, only emerging when it was time to transport goods at the officer's command.

Once more, Dominic proves his villainous cleverness. He left a Control on Layla's mind that prevents her from opening unauthorized gateways. Only one man has the authority here to command her to open it. The officer kneels nearby, hands tied behind his back, face a bloody mess. I couldn't help a few punches after I heard her story.

Layla is a broken, abused girl. I hate to use her more, but there's no choice. The battle has begun. I glimpsed it before the gateway snapped shut. If we can pinch Dominic off from his resources and launch a surprise attack from behind, his forces will divide and weaken.

Elpis *cannot* fall to that monster.

Officer Ody marches over to me and I cease pacing a few feet from where Layla rocks on the facility floor. "Everything is in order."

I nod, then turn to address my soldiers packed into the storage room. "Line up! Be ready. Move swiftly. Surprise is our best weapon, so the second your units make it through the gateway, strike hard and fast. No mercy."

The soldiers call out a booming, "Yes, sir," that makes Layla flinch.

I stroll over and crouch in front of her, careful not to touch the girl. "Layla, it's time. You don't have to follow us through. Wait for the last soldiers to pass through before you close it. Wait two days, then check-in. If I'm not waiting, close the gateway immediately. We can't let Dominic retreat here."

Layla nods, tears streaking through the dirt on her face. I hold out a hand to help her up. She hesitantly slides her trembling palm over mine. Her hand is like ice. I rise and pull her up, then give her hand a reassuring squeeze before letting go.

"Remember, the queen and the princess are prepared to offer you sanctuary and protection," I say soothingly. "Once you close that gateway, Miss Ingrid will escort you to the safety of the palace. Okay?"

Layla nods and sniffles. She's shaking like a leaf. No doubt she fears Dominic will come through and kill her.

I nod to our Influencer looming over Dominic's officer. The man would never open the gateway without being forced to do so. But after a whispered command from our Influencer, he raises his furious gaze to Layla.

The words grind out of him painfully. "Layla, open the door."

Her shoulders sag in relief and I realize she was worried that he would refuse, and she would have to fight through Dominic's firewall. Layla's eyes glass over as her hands begin the movements. I watch in fascination as the gateway sparks, then opens wider and wider until the entire storehouse wall is covered. It's a wide enough gateway for dozens of men to pass through in a long line.

"I don't know how long I can hold a gateway this big," she whimpers.

"Go!" I command the men.

The lines surge forward, eager to join the fight not only for my homeland but also for their king and kingdom.

38

GAVIN

Nausea claws at my throat. I push myself off the ground, rolling on my back as I fight off the sickness threatening to spill over. A shadow falls over me, blocking out the sun. My rope bracelet vibrates over and over. I press the face to contact Drake's bracelet. The vibrating ceases.

"Your work is far from done." Gramps reaches toward my chest. I don't understand. Where am I? It's the battlefield, but no one is here. No one but me and Gramps. Then why does my bracelet work?

His image flickers from the massive Somatic Strongarm with dark skin and darker eyes to a woman as pale as the moon with emerald eyes that shine like stars. It happens so fast as he presses his palm to my chest.

A shock rips through me.

I bolt upright as a cacophony of noises hammer against my eardrums. Thunder and rumbles and screams and shouts. A hand falls on my shoulder and I jerk away, scrambling to my feet.

Drake raises his hands. "Creation help me, Gavin, don't do that to me again!"

"Do..." I turn in slow circles as the noise assaults my senses. It's difficult for me to get a handle on my surroundings. I can't think. I can't breathe. I slam my hands over my ears and dip my head, squeezing my eyes closed. It's too much noise.

Drake's hands slide tenderly over mine. The noise dims. The sounds of the battle are still there but muffled like sound waves through water.

"Better?" he asks.

I can hear him perfectly. I nod, trembling from head to toe.

"Good, because if we don't get out of here, we're screwed." Drake takes my hand, and the two of us rush away from the roiling mass of bodies. Men and women fall dead all around us as others fight for the upper hand.

Rocks and lightning dominate the sky. Rain falls in heavy sheets here and there, only to rise as a wave on the ground to knock soldiers off their feet. Everything is chaos and I can't tell who is who anymore. I'm not built for this.

If I survive and get my sister back, I will happily spend my days living a completely ordinary life once more. Drake pulls me along as we huddle close to one another.

Cypress breaks through the mass of chaos twenty yards away. His men surround him as they fight their way forward. He shouts commands, but his words are swallowed by Drake's Power. Cypress' men have moments to react before an attack lands. Somehow, he is predicting what's about to happen and warning his men.

The sensory overload is too much. From above, I could handle it because I was separated from the fight, distant from everything. But down here on the ground, it floods me with terror and keeps my logical mind from functioning. How does Paige do this for a *job*?

Deadly spikes shoot up from the ground, driving Drake and me apart. I hear the muffled screams of agony and death all around me. "Drake? Drake!" Panic surges to the surface. I punch the face of my bracelet and follow the sound of Drake's vibrating in response.

The spikes vanish, followed by a wave that knocks me off my feet as I reach for Drake's hand. The water carries me away before I can react. It crashes over my head and I'm drowning on land, gulping down lungfuls of water instead of air. The water dissipates, leaving me soaked and puking up fluid from my lungs on my hands and knees. I turn slowly once my lungs are full of air again, but Drake is gone, washed away by the tide. Again, I hit the bracelet. But I don't hear his response.

Then the noise of the battle breaks over me once more. Why did Drake's Power cut out? Is he...dead? *No. No, I can't be alone. I can't handle any of this without him*. Agony and terror grip my heart, my lungs, my muscles. I can't move, can't think. Instead, I continue punching the face of my bracelet, praying desperately for a response until I can't take it any longer. I collapse beneath the weight of fear and sensory overload.

This is worse than anything that happened in the Haven, and a thousand times more intense. I cover my ears and curl up, unable to logic through a course of action. All I want is for the fight to be over, for our enemies to go away, for life to settle down for just a *minute* so I can think.

Energy surrounds me everywhere and I grasp it, harness it. Lightning meant for attacks streaks toward me, gathering in a brilliant orb of light like a protective shield around me. The blinding light forces me to squeeze my eyes closed. I'm not meant for battle. It's wrong for me to be here. I don't know what I was thinking.

Energy burst from me, radiating up and out in a sphere-like torus. Everything shakes.

39

Zephyr

T HE CAMP ISN'T COMPLETELY deserted, but most of the soldiers are on the front lines. Only the healers and runners remain behind. The team with me is terribly efficient at slipping through the camp without notice. They've clearly had a lot of practice doing something similar. I noticed right away that their uniforms resembled the ones Paige and Easton wore when we first met. And Easton's training was thorough and noticeable the second he came out of the carriage during the mutiny. A grudging respect grows in me toward these nine companions.

Well, eight. I won't give Tudor any credit. He works seamlessly with his team but ignores or undermines me every chance he has.

Paige's magic thrashes madly, creating an invisible tether between the two of us. I can turn directly toward her, even if she isn't visible yet. I motion for the others to follow me as we slip through the camp. But it seems like we can never seem to close the gap between us. She's moving away from me.

I freeze when we reach a hastily constructed platform. The twisted and broken body of Ivy, one of the Tributes, has been left in a pool of blood. Her body is so crushed and broken it makes my stomach churn.

Elly murmurs a curse, staring at Ivy. "Poor girl."

Tudor's feet are on the move westward, ignoring the dead girl as if she doesn't matter. "Blood trail goes this way," he says.

"Who are you?" A soldier rushes toward us, hands raised and primed to use his magic. When he sees me, his hands shake and he pales. "You... How...?" His gaze flicks at his hands as if expecting his magic to vanish or fail.

In seconds, we are surrounded by at least fifty of Dominic's men. Possibly more. This pit stop cost us the element of surprise.

The team backs into a practiced cluster, magic flexing to prepare for a fight as they face out in all directions. The cuff dampening my magic itches against my skin. I feel as if I've walked into battle with my eyes closed and hands tied behind my back.

The soldiers edge into a tighter ring around us.

"Zephyr, you will submit to the King for judgment," a soldier says, but the tremble in his voice gives away his fear.

I grit my teeth as magic from both Paige and Gavin hammer against me. Even from so far away, Gavin's magic is like a thousand needles under my skin.

An idea strikes me at that moment. I raise my hands in submission. "If I do, will you take me straight to him?" Paige must be with Dominic.

The soldiers exchange uncertain glances. No one knows what they should do.

"Enough of this," Tudor mutters. He reaches for the gun at his side.

"No, Tudor!" But my call is too late.

In seconds, everything erupts into chaos. Soldiers thrust rocks and wind our way as the team works with expert efficiency, mixing guns and magic in tandem. A thrust of psychic magic followed by gunshots. Bullets curve to strike targets attempting to dodge. A tempest of wind kicks up to knock away projectiles the soldiers toss our way.

I want to rip off the cuff and join the fight, try stealing magic like I did in the cells. The only other weapon I have is my sword and knife, but I can't fight in hand-to-hand combat when the team throws so much magic around.

Soldiers fall, but new ones take their place. They severely outnumber us. I must do something.

One soldier on my side of the ring breaks the line and rushes at me with his sword raised. Two more follow him. This I can handle. I edge out slowly, drawing my sword as they close the gap. The rest of my team is occupied fighting off the onslaught of Dominic's soldiers.

As soon as the first soldier is close enough, I arc the blade upward. His own clashes with a shriek of metal against metal. I kick at his knee, bringing him down, then ram my heel into the joint so he can't get back up.

But the second he falls, the other two are on me. One wraps up my arms, and the sudden jerk nearly makes me lose my grip on my sword. The other lifts his weapon, ready to spear me, when a bullet drives through his skull. As he falls to the ground in instant death, I ram my head back into the face of the man behind me, then kick out to throw him off balance. His grip breaks and he tumbles backward.

I spin toward the man who held me, nodding toward Elly in appreciation as she turns her gun on my final attacker and pulls the trigger.

Paige's magic hits me like a hammer and I stagger, then fall to my knees. I have to get to her and stop this. But I don't know how we will break through these overwhelming lines pinning the team in.

After a few measured breaths to regain control of myself, I stagger back to my feet and the fight surges once more in a flurry of bullets, magic, and swords.

The fabric of the Elpis uniform holds remarkably well against the soldier's blades. Not perfectly. I still have a few cuts, but it's like a thin layer of armor. How do they make such marvels? Though the material and the vest hinder some of my mobility, the armored layer certainly makes a difference in this fight.

Not that I have time to contemplate all of this for long. I'm just happy to have it as the press closes tighter around us. Paige is farther away now. Her magic still reaches for me, but with every second we are locked in this fight against Dominic's rear guard, she draws farther away.

The team is nearly out of ammunition. Guns will fail us soon, and something tells me that when the time comes, none of their magic will save us.

But mine will. I will unlock the cuff Ugene put on me and prevent everyone nearby from using magic. Then I will find out if I can steal magic from others again. We are losing. To Dominic. I can't allow it. The thought makes my stomach curdle as I slice down another soldier and stumble backward into Mat.

"I have to get out of here and get to Paige," I say over my shoulder to the rest of the team.

"Like we don't know that!" Tudor snaps. "Quit repeating yourself and do something productive."

A nasty, petty part of me hopes he doesn't survive. The guy is an ass. He's the kind of recruit I would have ground into submission.

"What is that?" Elly asks as an orb of lightning dances across the battlefield like a hungry monster.

"This is insane," Sam mutters. "I'm out of ammo."

Mat curses. "Me too."

I slip my hand into my pocket to pull out the key. "It's Gavin." His Power doesn't hit me like a hammer the way Paige's does. Instead, it creates a sensation under my skin like a thousand needles.

"Something is coming from the rear!" Tudor calls. "It's...another army."

"What?!" Elly's eyes widen as she throws her twisting wind along the line like a whip.

Soldiers shriek as the earth spikes up beneath them, impaling a few. Then the spikes wave outward, creating a gap to the west. It drives most of Dominic's men away from us.

"Daliah, you seem to be caught in a soup sandwich," a familiar male voice booms over the heads of retreating. "Doctor Brown is in the house."

I release a half-hysterical laugh as a few foolish enemy soldiers to our east pivot their attacks. But the lines quickly fall without mercy or hesitation. Most of them die. A few retreat, seeking safety somewhere. But there will be no safe place for them.

Easton steps through the shattered lines with hundreds of troops spreading outward to trap Dominic's forces as they retreat. Officer Ody is hot on Easton's heels, grinning at me.

"Easton!" Elly exclaims. Her gaze sweeps over him. "What are you wearing?"

"Never mind that. What the hell happened to your eye?" Mat asks.

"Dominic happened." Easton glances down at the Kingdom's military blues he's wearing, then eyes my Elpis uniform and snorts. "Well, that's an interesting turn."

"How did you get here?" I ask, striding toward him as his soldiers take out Dominic's stragglers. All he has left are his advance forces, thanks to Easton.

"Turns out the princeling was up to some pretty nasty stuff on Round Island," Easton says as we clasp hands and shake. I should have known Easton wouldn't leave things alone, even if he stayed behind. Once more, his Elpis training impresses me. His gaze tugs past us toward the real battlefront in the distance.

I notice three of the Tributes move up behind Easton and his officers. "Where did you find these girls?"

Easton glances over his shoulder at Alice, Summer, and River. "In a tent back that way, being treated less than kindly. The second we took off their collars, the men holding them were done for. These cats have some claws."

Summer raises her chin as if proud of this. Her gaze falls on Ivy's body near where we stand. Alice whimpers when she sees their fallen Tribute.

"Things are about to get real," Easton says. "Where's Paige?"

I turn in her direction. I can't see her, but I can feel her with striking certainty. She and Gavin. Her to the southwest, him to the northwest.

Easton snorts again. "I've seen snails that move faster than you. We will back you up."

My cheeks heat as I pull out the key. "Ready yourselves."

Everyone steps back like I'm about to throw a bomb. I unlock the cuff and tuck it in my pocket, then toss the key. A couple of members of the team mutter their confusion as my Negation winks out their magic.

Easton pats my shoulder. "Go get her, tiger."

I nod stiffly, ignoring the glare Tudor shoots in my direction.

Alice nods at me and raises her hands. Once I'm far enough away, she will help clear a path part of the way. The rest is up to me.

I take off at a sprint, sword in hand in case of attacks. *I'm coming, Paige, and nothing will stop me this time.*

40

PAIGE

LIGHTING AND ROCKS BOUNCE off my shield. Sweat trickles down my temples as I shuffle stiffly alongside Dominic. I still don't know exactly what Dominic has planned for me, but with each step, we draw close to Elpis. Will he make me use this burning Power to destroy the other army? How long before we're within range?

I focus on the thread of command that forces me to maintain this bubble of protection around the three of us. As long as I continue using this skill, Dominic is untouchable. I loathe the arrogance on his face as he strolls without a single attack coming close to landing on him.

I'm like the barrier around Elpis. The barrier they have, for some reason, dropped to attack.

There it is! I locate the thread woven over my mind that controls this command. Glancing sideways at Dominic, I slide my resistance along it until my grasp is firm.

Dominic is sweating, too. His face is drawn and pale despite his cocky strutting. Holding me is taxing him. How much blood did he lose when Ivy attacked? Maybe it weakened him enough to give me a chance to break free.

A tidal wave rises over us and crashes against my barrier, rolling off like water shedding off a smooth stone. I tighten my hold on the thread.

"Don't do it, Paige," he warns. "Break this one and it will cripple you."

I hesitate, recalling how I blacked out when I broke too much, too fast.

Bodies are everywhere. I can't tell friends from foes. The Kingdom uniforms are all the same. How do they even know who they are fighting against?

Dominic pauses, frowning at two of the soldiers. My heart seizes. *He knows those aren't his men!* He crouches beside them, inspecting the bodies, and curses.

Rocks disintegrate against my barrier. Bullets, too. Nothing can reach us here.

While Dominic is distracted, I snap the thread forcing me to hold up the barrier. A scream rips from my throat as the barrier collapses, and I collapse with it. Bella shrieks as I kneel behind Dominic. A net of vines cocoons the two of them in seconds, leaving me outside her protective bubble.

He can't see me!

Agony rips at my skull as I jump to my feet. My knees shake as my legs threaten to give out. But this is it. Pain or no pain, I need to run. It won't break his Influence, but if I can just get ahead of him, maybe I can find Zephyr. *Where* is *he?*

I stumble more than run. Sweat and tears of pain blur my vision. For all I know, I could stumble right into my death, but I can't stop.

"Paige!" Dominic's voice rings out in the air.

I whimper and pick up my pace. I bounce off bodies. Panicked, afraid they will bind me and haul me back to Dominic, I lash out with my wild, roaring Power, then tumble through soldiers as they vanish.

Toughen up, Paige. Sink or swim on your own. I grit my teeth and brush the tears from my eyes, then plant my feet and turn to face off against Dominic with my Powers wrapping like a red mist serpent around my limbs.

Dominic lumbers toward me, fury burning in his wake. His Control presses against me, but I feel something else. A familiar push against my Powers. My gaze darts around the battlefield. *Zephyr!* He's close. Where is he? *Just a little closer, please!*

My head is hammering louder than the noise on the battlefield. I blink more sweat from my eyes, watching as the tide of battle shifts all around us. Dominic's soldiers are pulling back for the retreat while others from the back are pressing forward.

A crowd of soldiers parts and Cypress steps out, closing the distance between him and his brother quickly. My heart leaps at the sight of him, but terror grips my veins. Cypress raises his sword, aiming the tip at Dominic's throat.

"It's over, brother," Cypress announces.

"You don't really believe it will be that simple, do you, Cy?" Dominic asks.

I tighten my hands into fists as I edge toward them, holding my Powers like whips wrapped around my arms.

"On your knees," Cypress commands.

Dominic raises his hands in surrender. "As you wish, brother." He eases down slowly, lacing his fingers behind the crown perched on his head.

Cypress reaches down and plucks the crown off Dominic's head, gripping it in one fist.

No. Something is wrong. Where is Bella?

ZEPHYR

THE FAMILIAR PRESSURE OF Paige's magic hits me in the chest, fueling my adrenaline. It shines like a beacon directing me straight to her. Relief washes through me when I spot her wrapped in her red magic.

Then my gaze slides past her to Cypress and Dominic. Behind Cypress, something flashes between the bodies of his guards.

Bella flexes her hand behind Cypress' men. My stomach drops. She's far enough away to be out of my range. I scream for Cypress, but it's too late. Bella's vines snatch Cypress from the ground like he's nothing, squeezing him tightly as she yanks him back to her. I spot the flash of the knife an instant before she strikes.

"Bella, no!" Dominic howls, stretching a hand out to her as if he can stop her.

Paige screams and her magic lashes out despite my proximity, killing Bella where she stands in a flash of heat and red light. Only a pile of ash remains.

I zip past Paige and skid to my knees beside Cypress as he struggles for breath. The knife missed his heart but must have punctured a lung. Tears blur my vision. "We need a healer!" I call, my voice cracking.

Cypress takes my hand. "It...was..."

"No. Don't." My eyes sweep the men, Cypress' guards. "Go! Get a healer, now! The King is dying!"

Several scramble into action. Behind us, Dominic stands in numb silence. What did he think would happen?

"Zeph..." Cypress slides a bloody hand along my jaw, forcing me to look at him. I can't. I can't watch him die like this. He drops his arm against his chest where the crown now rests. "It...was always...you."

I shake my head. What does that even mean? "Hold on, brother. We'll get a healer and you'll be good enough to tease me another time."

"Listen!" Cypress' voice hardens, then he coughs up blood. He pats the crown. "This..."

"No." I shake my head as tears stream down my cheeks, refusing to accept the crown, refusing to accept that he will die. This can't happen. It *can't*!

"...is yours." Cypress closes my hand around the crown as Paige kneels on his other side. Her trembling hand sweeps his hair from his face. Then she kisses his forehead. A weak smile traces his lips. Each word is a struggle for breath. "This is...as it was meant...to be. King...Zephyr."

A sob climbs my throat and agony like I haven't felt since Mom died overwhelms me. I can't think, can't breathe, can't see clearly. I'm only dimly aware of Paige shaking her head and crying silently beside him. Regardless of which of us she would have chosen, there's no denying her affection for Cypress. It makes me love her even more.

Cypress' body rattles with the last breath, sightless eyes locked on Paige's face.

I lean over Cypress, knowing full well anyone could come up behind me and kill me where I mourn over my brother. But I don't care. I can't leave him. Not yet. I need this moment to let all the sorrow and hate and rage spill out. Cypress' death is still too fresh, too much of a shock.

In my grief, I'm only distantly aware of Paige growling something. Then her red Power sparks to life, and she's gone.

The earth trembles.

41

EASTON

As ZEPHYR RUNS OFF to find Paige—and I'm certain he will—my old Specialist team turns to me with raised brows. They have questions and probably expect me to run back to Elpis to debrief and settle back into our routine once this is over. I can't tell them that won't happen. Not yet. Once the city is secure, I will return to the Kingdom with Zephyr and the troops.

"I don't like that guy," Tudor mutters.

I turn to find him glaring after Zephyr as he disappears into the mass of soldiers, cutting down any who impede his route.

"We've put our lives in his hands more than once already," I say. "I trust him. And he's charged into the fire and certain death for her before."

Elly smiles softly, her gaze fixed in the distance where Zephyr ran off, which is as close to a girly sigh as she ever gets. Tudor's brows knit together as he checks his weapon. His jaw twitches. I almost laugh. He's jealous of Paige's relationship with Zephyr. *How does it feel, ladykiller?* Not so long ago, I felt the say way toward Tudor's relationship with Paige. Except he had a chance and blew it. I never did.

"Let's finish this," I announce. "Guns?"

"We're out of ammo," Mat informs me.

I nod. "Powers it is, then."

"Any chance I can get one of those swords?" Carlos asks, signaling the weapon on my hip.

I grin at him. "I trained hard to earn this. Wouldn't want you accidentally cutting up any friendlies."

He scowls at Mat's chuckle.

In moments, the three Tributes, the Elpis Specialists, and the Kingdom soldiers resume our flanking assault on Dominic's lines. Elpis and Kingdom forces collapse on Dominic's army from all sides. It won't be much longer before this is over, assuming we can get our hands on Dominic. The Specialists join ranks with the Kingdom soldiers at my command, and everyone falls into rhythm seamlessly.

Just as we seem to gain the advantage, the lines shift and Dominic's soldiers turn toward us, away from the Elpis forces. *They're trying to retreat to a gateway!* I grin, sweat beading on my brow. They won't get far.

As I break through a line of enemy troops, I spot a flash of someone familiar angling away from the battle, and away from our lines. Shouts arise, and the lines part like the red sea for the figure darting away. Anger bubbles to the surface. Anger and hate.

My feet carry me toward Dominic before I'm aware I've decided to cut him off. He's headed toward Layla's gateway. A wicked grin curls my lips. He won't get away.

Fueled by a desire to make him suffer, I pick up my pace, ignoring the calls from my team and the Tributes. Dominic will beg for mercy. And I won't grant it.

Cutting him off is harder than I had hoped as his men attempt to block my path to protect their tyrant king. A gust of wind kicks up and thrusts me back. My boots slide backward over the dirt, kicking up dust. I have no way to get to him. A growl of frustration and rage explodes out of me.

Then waves of earth rise from the ground, throwing back the soldiers in my path. The wind stops pushing against me. A renewed sense of determination rushes through me and I charge forward, drawing my sword to cut down any who try to stop me. One soldier grabs my arm to wrench me back. I jerk the arm toward me, yanking him off his feet, and toss him into the men on the other side of me.

Alice is hot on my heels, throwing her Naturalist Power at the men baring our passage. But there are always more. So many. Dominic is going to get away. Not that he has anywhere to run.

A sonic shriek rips through the air, making my eardrums bleed. I duck instinctively, pressing my palms to my ears to block out as much of the sound as I can. When I dare to look up, the soldiers have been knocked down, dazed, or stunned. I glance back over my shoulder to see Summer and River rushing forward with the rest of the Specialists.

Those girls are wicked dangerous. Why did Dominic keep them back from the fight?

I rise, trembling from River's assault, and move through the crowd.

Dominic lies on the ground, spitting blood as he pushes himself to his feet.

I put the sword away, lower my shoulder, and ram into him with all my strength. He howls when we collide and one of his bones breaks. I don't know which, nor do I care. We tumble across the ground. As we roll to a stop, I yank a knife from my boot, pinning him to the ground with my knees. My lips curl in a feral snarl.

"Let's see how you like it," I growl, pointing the tip of the knife at his eye.

Dominic chokes on a laugh, baring bloody teeth at me. "Do it."

Instead of starting with the eye, I thrust the knife under his sleeve and slice it open, exposing soft flesh.

"One piece at a time," I hiss, digging the knife into his arm. With no care at all, I carve out a chunk of his flesh. He screams. It doesn't give me the satisfaction I need, which only fuels the frustration roiling inside.

I grit my teeth to carve another chunk when Bronwyn's voice whispers in my ear. Her warning. *"Vengeance is poison, Easton."* My grip on the knife tightens, but I can't make myself dig it into his flesh. *"You don't have to be the one to stop him."*

But I do, Bronwyn. I need this.

My hand trembles with the knife as I move it toward his eye. He deserves this. He deserves so much worse than this. I will take his cold, blue eye and shove it down his throat.

Dominic half grimaces, half grins at me as if he can't decide which is greater—his pain or the joy of watching me break down. His stormy blue eyes dare me to carry through with it, to carve out his eye like he did to me. I want to, so badly it makes my body tremor.

"It's time to put that darkness behind you."

I blink sweat from my eyes. Or are they tears of frustration?

"Easton?" The female voice is familiar, but I can't place it in my current state of anguish. Elly places a hand on my shoulder. "What are you doing?"

"He deserves this," I say, hating the agony in my voice, the way it cracks over those three words. "He tortured me, Elly." *And he's smiling at me!*

"Vengeance isn't the answer," she says.

Again, Bronwyn's gentle voice croons in my ears, *"Vengeance is poison, Easton."*

The storm of rage and hate and frustration inside of me breaks, and I emit a scream until there's nothing left. Dominic winces, closing his eyes and turning his face away from me.

I can't do it. I can't become like him. Damn you, Bronwyn!

I thrust the knife aggressively back into my boot, seizing Dominic's collar in the other hand. Then I yank him to his feet with me. He wraps his hands instinctively around my wrist but doesn't try pulling away as I jerk his face closer.

"You can thank your sister for this mercy," I hiss.

A ring of my own soldiers closes in behind me, shoring up our lines. Dominic opens his mouth.

"No," Summer growls, throwing a hand out toward him.

His lips move, but whatever he says cannot be heard.

I shove him a few steps away. He isn't going anywhere.

Dominic has lost.

42

PAIGE

CYPRESS IS DEAD. HE's dead. Bella killed him. Dominic did this. All of this is his fault. Calling these emotions raging through me hate or fury are tame words for what's truly pulsing through my veins.

I don't even have to track him. Somehow, I know exactly where he has gone, like he left a pungent scent of betrayal and death in his wake and I'm following it like a bloodhound.

His Control is gone. Surely, that's why he fled while we were distracted by Cypress' death. Zephyr's Power negated Dominic's hold on me, just as I suspected it would. Now, I will show Dominic what pain feels like.

I march across the battlefield after him. Untouchable, I move through powers and swords, leaving nothing but ash and death behind. I pull the rot from within the earth and cast it out at any who would dare try stopping me.

When I catch up to Dominic, a handful of his soldiers line up around him. Dominic faces Easton and hundreds of others—including the other three Tributes. I thrust a hand at Dominic's rear line. They vanish in a puff of faded screams and ash. The next line of soldiers turns toward me. I flex my muscles and leap into the air, hoisted in the air and held aloft by wings of fire. I assess the situation.

Easton's eyes widen as he gazes up at me. The rest of my former Elpis team is with him as well. All eyes are on me.

I reach a hand out and close my fist as if taking a fistful of Dominic's shirt, yanking him into the air with me until we are face to face. Dominic laughs manically, arms stretched out at his sides. He doesn't fight back. He just laughs like he's lost his mind.

"What will you do, Paige?" Dominic asks. His sapphire eyes glow with insanity. "Torture me? Punish me?" He smirks, baring bloodied teeth. "Kill me?"

"This isn't just about the woman you love," I say. "If it were, you would have been satisfied back in the Capital once you claimed the throne. This is about greed and power."

"You're right," Dominic admits. "It began as a quest for love, but once Layla showed me the future and I saw how it would end..." Dominic closes his eyes and breathes in.

Layla showed him? I never stopped to ask what her Power was. Why did I never ask?

A barrage of wind and earth Powers fly at me, attempting to break my hold over Dominic. I thrust out my free hand. A sphere of red light pulses to life around us, blocking everything else out.

Dominic eyes the sphere, then glances down at the mass of armed soldiers below. "When I showed you my mind, what did you see, Paige?"

I grit my teeth, Power pulsing like hungry wolves. "A monster set on burning the world."

Dominic shakes his head. "I am not the monster. I saw your chaos magic spreading, destroying, creating a world so broken no one would recover. And since I am the only one who can see exactly how broken the world is, how much worse it will become, I had to act. I am not a monster, Paige. I am a conqueror. A man of vision. A man prepared to do anything to fix what was broken and prevent our annihilation."

I shake my head. "I saw your path of conquest. You want to destroy everything."

"This is what conquerors do, Paige!" Dominic snaps. "Sometimes, before we can fix something, we have to tear it apart so we can build something better from the ashes."

I flinch. Doctor Adams said the same thing about Liberation Day months ago, as we left Elpis. "Elpis has already done that. Our city thrives."

"I'm not talking about a city. I'm talking about the world." Dominic motions everywhere, as if he can encompass everything in one motion. Then he sneers. "You are a bomb waiting to go off, Paige. We will *all* die when you do. You are an abomination on the face of this earth. I will use you to fix this broken world, Paige, but you have no future beyond that. You cannot."

I don't want to listen to him, yet his words strike my deepest fear that my Powers are only capable of destroying. The fear amplifies, pulling more Power into me. The red sphere around us buzzes with life.

"I wasn't only Controlling you," Dominic says. "I was keeping your magic in check." The smile on his lips is not the charming, confident smile I'm used to. There's insanity in it. Hysteria.

I lash out with my Powers, yanking that rot from the earth to send a spike of radiation through him. Dominic hisses in pain, then grins at me. "Yes, there it is. That destructive force is fighting to break free."

Below, voices call to me, begging me to release Dominic. I'm tempted to release him, to let him fall to his death.

Dominic's voice slides across my skin like slime. "It's in *your* best interest to spare me. Without me, there's no stopping you."

Liar! I bare my teeth at Dominic, then hammer another tendril of radiation through him. Dominic's scream is more of a howl that transforms into cackling laughter.

He grins. "Again, Paige."

My jaw twitches, and I oblige.

"Paige!" Zephyr's voice booms through the ring of onlookers below, amplified by Summer's Power. Most of the onlookers have fled to escape my wild, burning sphere. Only a handful of soldiers remain below, along with Zephyr. He pushes his way through the crowd. He clutches Cypress' blood-stained crown tightly in his fist.

For months, I've wanted to be near him, not just in dreams, but in reality. Now that he's here, I want him to leave so he can't see the darkness rising in my soul.

"He will die," Dominic says, far too calm for a man in his situation.

Terror pulses through me. I've seen Zephyr's death in dreams. I thrust Dominic away from me, but the two of us remain hovering a few feet above the heads of those who remain below. Easton and his troops are gone, running toward Elpis.

"Paige, let him down," Zephyr calls. "Please!"

My rage still burns, but I slam Dominic's body down into the dirt just hard enough to make his ears ring and his body ache. He winces and scrambles away, but there's nowhere to flee. Not any longer.

I touch down on the ground with ease, just a few steps from Dominic. My fiery wings fold and vanish. Zephyr rushes toward me, pulling me into his arms. I hug him back, grateful for the embrace—a real embrace—but wishing he would leave and not witness this hate in me.

When he pulls back, Zephyr cradles my face in his hand. "It's okay. It's over. You're safe."

I shake my head and step back. "No, Zephyr. None of us are safe as long as he breathes."

"None of you are safe if I don't," Dominic adds.

Zephyr pulls me against him again, leaning his forehead against mine. "Let me deal with my cousin." His dark eyes pull me in.

"I don't need you to be my knight in shining armor," I say.

He nods. "I know. But I still will. I always will."

Tears well in my eyes.

Dominic snorts in disgust. "How touching. But it's too late to be her knight, Zeph."

Zephyr kisses my forehead, then pulls away and turns to Dominic, his hand stretched out. His boots crunch over the earth as he edges closer to his cousin, then takes Dominic's wrist. *What is he doing?*

Dominic's face pales. "What...? How?"

"I learned a few new tricks, thanks to you," Zephyr says. His free fingers slide across Dominic's temples. Something about the slope of Zephyr's shoulders shifts. He straightens his spine and glares down at his cousin. "Dominic, you will surrender and submit yourself for judgment. You are forbidden, from this day until your last, from using your magic for any reason."

Dominic whimpers, yanking his hand back, but he can't break free of Zephyr's grip. I edge closer to Zephyr, wanting to touch him but worried that it might interrupt whatever he's doing.

"If you don't agree to these terms, there is always death," Zephyr finishes.

Zephyr releases his hold on Dominic's wrist and Dominic scrambles backward, rubbing at his hand like he can wipe away whatever

Zephyr did to him. He rises to his feet, and his entire body trembles, then his gaze falls on me and he goes still.

I don't like that look in his sapphire eyes. *Victory.* My breath catches.

"Death it is," Dominic says with an eerie sense of calm.

Zephyr's face falls. "What?"

Dominic's eyes remain locked on me as he pulls his knife from his belt, stabbing it into his own throat. His eyes flicker with satisfaction as he smirks at me.

Zephyr lunges forward to grab hold of the knife hand too late. The deed is done. Dominic yanks it out of his neck and drops it to the ground. He doesn't stem the gush of blood as he stares at me, grinning all the way to his knees.

"Dominic!" Zephyr catches his cousin as Dominic tips face-first toward the ground.

But there's no saving him. Dominic is dead before Zephyr lays him on the ground and tries covering the wound.

"No, come on," Zephyr whimpers, agony in his voice. Both cousins he grew up with as brothers are gone.

The crown rolls on the blood-soaked ground and comes to rest by Dominic's head.

I tread backward, hands over my mouth as the truth sinks in. He killed himself because he thought it would have some effect on me. What did Dominic think would happen?

All is silent as Zephyr mourns once more. My heart aches for Zephyr, but I feel distant from everything, trying to figure out what Dominic's ultimate act was meant to accomplish. Terror grips me, running hot and wild through my veins.

"I saw your chaos magic spreading, destroying, creating a world so broken no one would recover." I stumble another step backward.

The heat in my veins becomes the wild rage of my Powers burning their way through me, growing, consuming. I feel everything and everyone. Pain and love and agony and hate and death and fear and sympathy. A hurricane of emotions hammer against me. Emotions that fuel my already growing Powers.

I lower my hands from my face and stare at them in horror as the red tendrils pulse and glow, growing more intense with each passing moment. I whimper and try funneling the Power into the earth, but it only turns the ground beneath my feet brittle and dry.

"You are a bomb waiting to go off, Paige." What did Dominic do to me?

"Zephyr..." I whimper. Every part of me burns and trembles violently.

He lifts his gaze to me and fear flashes in his eyes.

"Without me, there's no stopping you." I shake my head as Dominic's taunt haunts me.

I run, and no one tries to stop me.

43

GAVIN

A FAMILIAR HAND STROKES my forehead. When I open my eyes, the ceiling of a tent looms several feet above me. I shift on the stiff cot to find Drake seated in a chair at my bedside. Relief shines in his dark eyes as he smiles warmly at me.

I shift to try sitting upright, but Drake places a hand on my chest and shakes his head.

"Give yourself a minute, Gavin," Drake says. "That was a lot of power you put on display."

I stretch a trembling hand to his face, cupping his cheek in my palm. Tears well in my eyes. "I thought... I..."

"Me, too." Drake grins sheepishly. "I do *not* like battle."

"Me either." I wince, recalling how easily the chaos overwhelmed me. "I don't know how anyone knows what they're doing."

He nods, and his grin slips, revealing the trauma he experienced out there.

"How did I get here?" I ask. "Last I knew, I was stuck on the battlefield."

Drake grabs a water pouch and offers it to me. I gulp it greedily, washing out the dust from the battle and allowing the cool fluid to coat my insides. There's something comforting about the water.

"Once that wave tore us apart, I thought I lost you," Drake admits. "The Silence I wrapped around you snapped back at me. My bracelet kept buzzing, so I knew you must be alive. When it suddenly stopped, I had a moment of pure fear until that orb of energy grew on the battlefield. I knew it was you, but I couldn't get to you. I couldn't even see you in the center. After your energy pushed the enemies back and our soldiers could finish what resistance remained, the orb vanished. You were cocooned in the earth. I had to use my bracelet to find you, then use a Builder to open the earth, and a team brought you back here. After your family and a healer named Rosie checked you out, they left the tent to finish whatever they're working on. I promised to monitor you."

I take his hand, squeezing it in my own. "I'm glad you stayed."

"It overwhelmed you, didn't it?" Drake asks. His thumb gently caresses my hand. "That's why you created that cocoon."

I nod, swallowing a lump in my throat. "I'm not as much like Dad as I thought."

Drake lifts my hand to his lips. "Not everyone has to be a fighter, Gavin. Some of us have to be lovers instead."

I grin.

The battle is over, and from the sound of things, we defeated Dominic. "I missed Paige, then?"

Drake's smile flickers. He chews his bottom lip. My stomach drops. He only does that when he's feeling anxious.

My body tenses. My Powers ease through my body like they can create a shield against the oncoming storm.

"Drake... Did she... Is she...?"

"We don't know." His voice is so small. "Last we saw, she was a glowing red ball of death to the east. Apparently, after Cypress died, she took off after Dominic."

My stomach releases the clenched knot until everything he said sinks in. "Cypress... the King?" Poor Zephyr.

Drake nods. "His people brought his body back to camp. Zephyr is missing, too. I'm choosing to believe the two of them are together wherever they ran off to."

I sit up so quickly my head spins. "Let's go after her then! Dominic is still out there. What if—?" I can't even ask the question. It's too horrible to imagine Dominic killing her and vanishing before we can catch him.

"We already sent teams out to find her," Drake says in that soothing voice he uses when he thinks I'm too agitated for my own good.

I don't want to listen. I want to push him aside and go after my sister, but flashes of that horrible battlefield flood through my mind, immobilizing me. Drake slides onto the bed beside me, hugging me close. I wrap my arms around him, thankful for his presence. Were it not for him, I would crumble apart right now. He's all that holds me together.

As he pulls back, Drake brushes a hand along my neck. "I'm so relieved you're okay." I nod, unsure how else to respond, then he kisses me. It feels like the wrong time for kissing, but the way it centers me, warms me, and completes me makes it impossible to pull away.

Someone clears their throat. My face heats as we break apart.

Emil and Ally are in the tent doorway bloodied and bruised, but alive.

"Glad to see you awake, Gavin," Emil says.

My eyes shift to the ground. "I hid like a coward, Emil. I'm not much of a soldier."

Emil shrugs. "Eh. Who wants to live the soldier's life?"

"We just wanted to check on you," Ally says, laying a hand on Emil's arm and encouraging him back toward the door. "We will give you some privacy."

Drake clears his throat as they slip back out the way they came. Then he laughs. "That was awkward."

Was it?

I frantically rub my hands on my pants, trying to push away the horrific recalls of the battlefield. Before I know it, I'm scrubbing my palms over my pants as if I can scrub away the memories.

Drake takes my hands. "It's over, Gavin. We're alive."

"But Paige..."

"They'll find her. Or she will find us."

I nod, fighting off the tears as another visitor enters.

"Gavin, I'm glad to see you alert."

I frown at the unfamiliar voice. The moment I see Councilwoman Howser I connect the face with the name. Though she's a pudgy little woman with bleached-blond hair and too-big eyes, Howser still has an air of compassion and confidence that many people find endearing. It's how she won her election to become a councilwoman.

"Councilwoman Howser," I say, sitting up straighter on the edge of the bed. "I'm...surprised to see you here."

"I wanted to speak with you if you don't mind," she says, pulling a chair over to face me and sinking in as if my acceptance is assumed.

It isn't.

"I want to help find my sister," I say. "I'm not sure if now is a good time."

"We have teams out there searching for her," she reassures me. "We will find her." She relaxes in the chair, dismissing Drake completely as if he weren't sitting right beside me. "I've spoken with a few of your refugees from the Haven. They told me some very interesting stories about your time there."

I flush and am glad she can't tell. Can she tell? "Over-exaggerated, I'm sure."

"So you didn't animate giant stone statues to open the ceiling and bring in the light?" she asks calmly.

I chew the inside of my cheek. "I guess I did."

"Did you also fix their entire water treatment center, expand some of the housing, and..." She pauses, pulling her phone out to review what I can only assume are her notes. "...bring back the dead?"

My hands shake. I fold them tightly into my lap. Drake must sense the uneasiness gripping my stomach because he places a gentle hand over mine. I can't answer her. Mostly because I don't want to confirm any of this.

Her lips thin, and she glances at her phone again. "According to them, you also levitate, create stone, fix electronics, which when listed after resurrection sound ordinary." She purses her lips, no longer talking to me. I don't understand where this is going. "You created a six-hundred-mile-long river."

"Not alone," I say, though the argument seems lame when stated aloud.

Her green eyes lift from the device, then she straightens again and tucks it into her pocket.

"What are you getting at?" Drake asks.

She eyes him up and down as if just realizing he's beside me. The cool way she dismisses him again makes me clench my jaw. Dad didn't trust her. He seemed to think she was after his job. Is she fishing for something to help her reach that goal?

"When I checked your medical records, I discovered something interesting," Howser continues. Her green eyes are no longer gentle as she turns that sharp glare on me. "A lot of your records are missing or redacted. You *and* your sister. It took a lot of work these past few months to uncover why your parents would go to all that trouble."

My gut twists. She knows the secret Mom and Dad worked so hard to protect. Paige and I aren't like everyone else. Our DNA is different, which is why we have these unique Powers.

"I fail to see why my medical records are the Council's business," I say. My voice trembles and I curse myself.

She leans forward in her chair, folding her hands together over her knees. "I had to dig *very* deep to find answers. What I found leaves me quite uneasy, Gavin. You shouldn't exist."

Drake shifts forward, attempting to draw heat off me. I appreciate it, but I don't think it will do any good against her. "'Those who lack faith will scoff at any truth that challenges their own desires'."

I wince as Drake quotes the *Book of the Prophet*. Even after all he's learned, all he's suffered, all he's seen, he still believes I'm his Idol of Creation.

The councilwoman rises from her chair, looking down her nose at me and ignoring Drake. "You are a danger to all of us, Gavin. Your display today combined with what I've learned is proof enough of that. And if this is in your DNA, then your children could be just as dangerous, if not more so."

As if I plan on having children of my own. "Danger?" I rise, swaying slightly on my feet.

"I'm left with no choice. I'm sorry, but this is for the best for everyone, for our future, our safety, and our security." Howser doesn't look sorry. Did I misread something again?

Before I even notice her movement, Drake pushes me out of the way. The gunshot hammers against the tent walls. I gape at Drake as he stumbles into me, clutching at my arms. Blood seeps slowly into his shirt.

"Drake...?" I ease him down on the bed. I will fix this. I have to.

Howser curses. As I wrap myself in my Power to remove the bullet and save his life, she fires another shot. Heat spreads through my body. My Power winks out. My fingers go numb.

I'm dying. I lay on the bed beside Drake, desperate to help him before I die. But my Powers refuse to answer my call.

Then everything around us vanishes in a cloud of fire and ash. I huddle close to Drake as the wave hits us.

44

PAIGE

IN THE DISTANCE, CLOUDS of smoke rise into the night sky. The last remnants of the battle are squashed as mountains rise from the ground and make boulders tumble across the earth. Waves of water rise and fall, cleansing away the last of the fight. The world isn't being remade like in that dream I had months ago. It's being cleansed of the filth of this horrible invasion.

The sound of boots running after me hastens my steps. I run far and fast, but the terror and grief overwhelm me. I hunch over with my hands on my knees and cry. This Power is fighting to get out, and it has only one path. Destruction. I don't know how to stop it. Dominic was right. I'm a bomb waiting to explode.

"Paige, it's okay," Zephyr pants as he comes up behind me. His hand slides over my shoulder, then down my arm to my hand as he steps in front of me.

Red energy pulses in my palms, growing so powerful it takes my breath away. My heartbeat increases. Panic clenches me as tears roll down my cheeks.

"I can't stop it!" I cry.

"I'm here," he says calmly. Affection and compassion pour from his hooded gaze as he inches closer. "I'm here."

The red light expands outward from my body. I dreamed this. More than once. Yet I never saw the conclusion of those dreams.

"It's okay," he murmurs in reassurance.

"I can't stop it," I moan pitifully.

"I can help," he says, holding out his other hand. "Just take my hands."

I peer up at him through my tears, marveling at his rugged beauty. Despite everything he has suffered, he's here before me, a crown perched on his head. King Zephyr. The last Strong in line to take the throne. What happens if he dies because of me?

I don't want to take his hand. I want him to run as far from me as he can get. This is it. This is that nightmare I had before I even met him. Zephyr is and always was the man who was supposed to be here to help me. But all I want is to save him.

Despite my desperation to get him away from me, I need him. I slide my hand into his. Something shifts. Power pulses like erratic red energy between the two of us, a tug of war just waiting to explode. Zephyr's face pales, but he holds me tight in his grasp. The red light shifts, swirling around our joined hands, up his arm. Is he...pulling in my Power? Is that what he did to Dominic? Terror grips my heart.

"Zephyr, no!" I jerk my hands out of his, wiping my palms on my pants. I can't let him take on my Powers. The red mist around his arms slowly dissipates. He can't hold it for long. It's a sure way to kill him.

"Paige, please," he says, stepping closer. "I can do this. I might be the *only* one who can do this. Let me help."

He slides his arm around me, pulling me tight against his hard body. His lips brush against mine and I'm helpless as the Power surges with wild life. He slides a hand up to cup my face and I wrap my arms around him. Once more, the red mist wraps slowly up and around his body as well. The two of us are caught in the eye of the red storm as it buzzes and zips and burns around us.

"I love you," he whispers. His breath rolls across my already heated cheeks.

Outside the storm, I'm psychically aware of soldiers forming a circle around us, guns ready. Terror pulses through me. If this fails, they will kill me. Maybe both of us. Then Zephyr brushes his lips against mine again and deepens the kiss, and my fear slowly dissolves as I lean against him. Our first confession of love, sealed with a kiss, is here at the end of the world. It's bittersweet.

Zephyr's Power works. Mine fades as a new sensation overtakes my senses. The red storm intensifies around us, cutting us off from the rest of the world. I cling to him, parting my lips. The kiss is glorious and warm and passionate. His tongue brushes past my lips. I breathe in the scent of him—lake water tinged with blood from the battle. It's gloriously Zephyr.

When we come up for air, I feel like I'm floating. Heat colors my face, and it has nothing to do with my Powers.

"I love you, too, your lordliness."

Zephyr chuckles and the sound lights up my nerves.

But as we pull apart, my Power surges back to life, blazing hot and ready to explode. The red mist becomes an instant inferno around me. I cry out, stumbling backward.

"Paige!" Zephyr reaches for me.

All the elation from our kiss crashes down as red tendrils of my Power flick outward from the orb of light that protected us from the outside. The soldiers find a way through the cracks, closing in around us, guns aimed and ready to fire. If I don't stop this Power, they will kill us both. I shudder, unable to control the hurricane as it lashes out in all directions like a live wire. Random soldiers around the ring vanish in a puff of ashes. Tears roll down my cheeks.

Zephyr rips his hand from his pocket as I ease another step backward, knowing I'm about to explode, about to kill him and everything I love. A scream rips from my throat.

A gun fires.

Zephyr shouts and jumps in front of me, then falls to the ground.

"No..." I cry and sink down beside him, pressing against the wound in his chest, just like in my nightmare a few days ago. His lifeblood pumps out as his heart slows, then stops.

"Paige," Tudor stands over me, gun pointed at my head. The ring of soldiers with him closes tighter around me. Members of my old unit, and others for the Department of Security. "Stop, or I will have to shoot."

A telepathic shield presses down on me as a team of Psionics work together to harness my raging Power. I whimper, but the agony of watching Zephyr die overwhelms all other emotions. I buckle over his body and release a shriek.

My Powers race out of me in all directions, exploding outward in a destructive wave, taking out Tudor and his gun first, then the approaching soldiers, onward and outward without end. Tears blur my vision as I pull Zephyr's limp body into my arms and cry until my throat is raw. Somehow, amidst my grief, I preserved him and him alone. But he's still dead.

The world falls utterly still. Not a sound. Not even a breeze. I kiss Zephyr's forehead, lifting my gaze to the red sky. The earth trembles violently, then the ground beneath me cracks outward in all directions.

A knockout needle lies on the earth inches from his limp fingers. As I reach for it, the needle falls in a crack of my own making.

I stagger to my feet, shuddering from head to toe, and spin in a slow circle.

The world didn't just fall silent. There's nothing out here. Nothing at all. All signs of the battle, the camp, it's all gone. In the distance, Elpis burns. Buildings collapse. Puffs of fire and stone rise high in the sky from downtown.

Everything is gone. Everything but Zephyr.

I drop once more and stroke his cold face, sliding his dead eyes shut. If only I could go back. I need to go back.

I curl up beside Zephyr's body, clinging to his Elpis-issued uniform, and close my eyes as tight as I can, picturing his smile, hearing his laugh, imagining the kiss we finally shared here at the end of the world. Then my mind drifts to my family. My brother and parents. Alex, who Zephyr said he didn't like, even though they are a lot alike. Easton and his stubbornness. Gram... Agony rips at my heart. They're all gone now.

I focus, will myself, all of us, everything, back in time. I've done it before. I have to do it again. It takes every ounce of my focus as the ability resists. After several attempts, I choke on a sob. Just *rewind*.

"Paige."

I jump at the sound of Zephyr's voice. We stand face to face as we did just after our kiss. I glance past his shoulder and see Tudor approaching, feeling the Power building within me once more, just like it did before. Tudor's gun is aimed at me.

"No. Not far enough." I picture Cypress being crushed and stabbed by Bella. I close my eyes.

"Paige?" Zephyr's confusion fades.

Rewind. I open my eyes as the wind whips in my hair. I'm running. *Farther, Paige. Go back farther!*

Rewind.

"No, come on," Zephyr whimpers, agony in his voice. I watch as he mourns the monster that was Dominic. But I haven't gone far enough. Tears spill down my cheeks. Cypress. I need to go farther. I need to save Cypress.

Rewind.

"Death it is." Dominic stabs his throat.

No! Come on Paige!

Rewind.

Over and over, the same horrific moment of Dominic's death plays back on a loop. I relive it a hundred times but can't seem to move any farther back. Agony shreds my heart to ribbons more with each repeat of Dominic killing himself, each realization that I cannot go back far enough to stop Bella. My body trembles so violently I'm certain I'll shatter into a million pieces and rain down against the earth like tempered glass. My breaths come in shallow gasps. Sobs rip out of me, but I can't seem to rewind past this point. I can't save Cypress.

Zephyr pulls me into his arms in front of everyone. I don't resist. I crumble into a million pieces against him. He holds me as I cry, but the Power continues to grow and this time I can't run away.

"Just do it," I moan pitifully. "I can't...I can't save him." I hyperventilate.

I slide my hand along his pocket and his body tenses. Zephyr snatches my hand away, but the moment he pulls back and our eyes meet, I see it. He knows I know about the knockout needle.

"We can't stop it," I whimper and my voice catches on the words as I fight to get them out. "We tried and failed. Please. Before someone else does something." My gaze flicks at Tudor, whose face has set in a storm of anger and confusion.

Zephyr pulls out the needle. "I love you, Paige."

Another sob climbs up my throat and this time all I can do is nod in response. He doesn't question how I know about the needle. His lips brush my temple as he presses the needle to my neck.

Then, blissful nothing.

45

GAVIN

I'M ON MY FEET, facing Councilwoman Howser. This is familiar. It only takes me a second to remember what happened before. Drake calls out to me, but I push him aside instead.

The scene changes again, going backward in time.

Drake shifts forward in front of the Councilwoman. I've been in this moment before. "'Those who lack faith will scoff at any truth that challenges their own desires'."

"Again?" I mutter, scanning the tent for some device or logical explanation for what's happening.

The scene changes again, this time a little further back.

"Give yourself a minute, Gavin," Drake says, sitting at my bedside. "That was a lot of power you put on display."

I rub my head. "What is going on?"

He frowns.

The scene changes, repeating the same moment in an endless loop. Am I dead? Is this some sort of punishment? I claw for control of the situation, but I can't do anything to change or stop it. The same moment of waking with Drake at my bedside repeats a dozen times. A hundred times. More. I scream for it to stop.

Then it does. At long last, when I can't handle it any longer, the loop closes.

I'm breathing heavily as I sit up on the edge of the bed. My head hammers. Drake shows only concern over me and no signs that it affected him at all. *Why not?*

"Give yourself a minute, Gavin," Drake says. "That was a lot of power you put on display."

I shake my head. "No. This is all wrong. Don't you think it's all wrong?"

Drake frowns, cocking his head to the side. "I don't know what you're talking about. Gavin, I think the trauma of the battlefield is messing with your head. But it's over."

"And Cypress is dead and Paige is missing, and in a few minutes, Councilwoman Howser will walk through that door to kill me." The words spill out in a rush.

Drake's jaw slackens and he just blinks dumbly at me. "Okay..." he says slowly, dragging the word out. He huffs a few times, rubs at his brow, then shifts onto the bed with me. "Maybe you're in worse shape than we thought."

I shake my head and pull away as he slides his arm around me. "No. Drake, I'm not crazy. Emil and Ally will walk in here in less than a minute to check on me."

He looks like he wants to say something, but the words are lost on him.

"Look, something happened. I don't know how or why. It wasn't me." I eye my fingertips just in case I'm wrong, as if they will show me the truth. But it wasn't me. I know that much for certain. "Someone is messing with time."

Before Drake formulates a response, Emil and Ally enter. The exchange goes exactly as it did the first time through, minus the embarrassment of being caught making out.

They leave, and I take Drake's hand. "We need to leave this tent right now."

"I don't understand what's going on," Drake says as he stumbles after me, clutching my sweating palm. "But you seem really confident, so I'm just going with it."

"Where is my dad?" I ask Drake as we step outside.

He shrugs. "Who knows? The command tent, probably."

I hustle through the crowds of injured soldiers and healers, bumping people out of my way until we reach the command tent.

"Dad!" I exclaim as I burst inside.

I nearly collide with Councilwoman Howser as she makes her way out the door. We step around one another, and I don't take my eyes off her for a second. Tension swells in my shoulders so tight it makes my neck hurt. I edge away from her, pulling Drake along with me until I reach my dad on the other side of the tent.

He smiles when he sees me, but the second Dad notices my anxiousness, his smile slips into concern.

I lean close to him and whisper, keeping a careful eye on Howser. "Dad, someone is messing with time."

"What?" His brows tighten and he shakes his head. "That's impos—"

"Please, just trust me," I insist. "I relived the same moment a hundred times and no one else seems to remember it but me. There must be a reason."

The Councilwoman lingers by the door, arms crossed as she watches the two of us with narrowed eyes.

"Explain," Dad says.

"I can't. But I can tell you this much for certain. The Councilwoman means to kill me. Possibly Paige, too, if we find her."

Dad stiffens, pulling away from me and lowering his voice so only I can hear. Everyone in the tent is watching us. "That's a heavy accusation, Gavin."

"She has a gun under her jacket that's not standard issue," I explain. "Just…have someone check her now before she can leave the tent. And take her phone. She has some information on that as well."

Dad grimaces, but he knows she's been up to something for a while now. While killing his kids probably wasn't her first instinct, no doubt she intended to use us against him somehow.

He pats my shoulder and draws away, turning his gaze to the soldier closest to the Councilwoman. "Remove the weapon from under her jacket."

Howser's eyes widen and she shoots a look at me with utter disbelief. That's one I'm very familiar with by now. Her feet shuffle back toward the door like she's readying to flee.

I snatch her with my Powers, holding her in place as the soldier checks for the weapon. When he reveals it, Dad's stunned.

"Confiscate her phone as well," Dad commands.

The soldier checks her pockets as she protests, then turns the items over. Dad immediately uses a device to activate her phone and unlock it, then digs into the files until he finds what he's looking for.

"Why are you investigating my children?" he asks, anger burning in his voice.

She glances at me, clearly wondering how I knew all of this, then raises her chin as she stares him down. "You have been tampering with medical records and keeping secrets from the Council and the city."

A fit of anger I've never seen before tenses every muscle in his body. Dad's voice is so angry and cold it terrifies me. "I have every right to protect my children's privacy, Councilwoman. But you do not have the right to dig into their medical records without authorization. Nor do you have clearance to speak with Prisoner Cass."

"I am protecting us all!" Howser snaps.

Dad sets the phone calmly on the table and edges around it toward her. "We do not have the right to invade the privacy of any citizen of Elpis without an official written warrant for information. I assume you don't have one of those, do you?"

She opens her mouth to respond, but he doesn't give her a chance. "Councilwoman Howser, you are to be placed in holding under suspicion of conspiracy, invasion of privacy, and collusion. The Justice Department can perform the investigation. Rest assured, I will have no part aside from being a character witness as is required by law. Your fate is in their hands."

"Minister Powers!" A soldier in a Specialist uniform bursts into the tent, winded. "She's here!"

"Paige?" Dad and I both ask at the same time.

The Specialist nods.

Dad and I exchange a glance, then both of us take off out of the tent. Drake follows close on our heels.

46

ZEPHYR

PAIGE IS HEAVIER THAN she looks, especially when her body is dead weight in my arms, and the walk back to camp is far. Thankfully, halfway there, a truck arrives to help. I climb in back with her. Easton climbs into the front cab of the truck, watching Paige with worry creasing his brows. I don't fully understand their relationship. But he cares about her, and for now, that's all that matters.

The truck moves smoothly despite the terrain destroyed by battle. The second the back doors of the truck open, a host of healers surge around Paige, pushing me into the background. I jump out of the truck and follow quickly on the healers' heels. I won't be separated from her again. Not unless she tells me that's what she wants.

"She doesn't need healing," I bark as I follow them toward the area where injured soldiers are being tended. "Don't wake her up!" Not that their healing magic works around me.

I peer over the shoulder of one healer as she hooks some kind of injection into Paige's arm. "What are you doing to her?"

"Sir, we need you to step back and give us space," she says, gently pushing me back.

I resist. "Don't wake her up!" I repeat the words, wondering if anyone hears me.

A forty-something woman with cropped dark hair hovers her hands over Paige's body, sliding them along her like some kind of medical scanner. She frowns, and I feel her magic push against me.

"She needs me close to her," I say. I'm not sure if it's true, but I need to be close to her, holding her hand, and making contact to be sure she isn't ripped away again.

The healer says nothing to me as she struggles to harness her magic, then checks the fluids they are injecting into Paige's bloodstream. Once more, she peers at her hands. I shift my feet, gritting my teeth, but my patience expires quickly.

"It's me. Just... Let me do it!" I snap, pushing forward. I place a hand on the healer's arm, then another over Paige.

The sensation of Paige's entire nervous system comes alive as if I can touch it. Her lungs, heart, mind, everything. I sense it all, and the overwhelming strain on her nerves makes me snap my hand back.

The healer glowers at me, her lips in a thin line. "Satisfied? Healing isn't something you can do with brute force. It takes time. Paige is in expert hands. She's like family to me. I won't let anything happen to her."

I gasp breathlessly as the healing Power dissipates. It was overwhelming. No wonder healers take the longest to train.

I shift the crown now clipped to my belt and kneel beside the bed they've stretched Paige out on, holding her hand between both of mine. Easton appears at my side, snapping one of those cuffs on to cut off my magic. I'm about to snap at him when the healer instantly works again. She pauses here and there to fix a wound, then continues her work. I observe the entire process with eagle eyes.

"Paige?" Ugene rushes forward, nudging his way through the crowd. Gavin is on his heels. "How is she?"

My throat clenches. "I had to use the needle. She knew about it. She told me there was no other way. I'm sorry. I..." The words choke off.

"You did great, Zephyr," Ugene pats my arm in reassurance. "But you need to let Rosie do her job without interfering if we are going to help Paige. There's no one I would trust with her health more than Rosie."

I nod stiffly, reassured by his confidence in this healer. But I can't let go of her hand. I don't want to. Yet I have no choice as Ugene edges me out of the way to kiss his daughter's forehead. Enid kneels at Paige's side as well. In moments, her family crowds her and I've been forced into the background.

My heart aches as I recall the terror in Paige's eyes. I blink back tears.

"Ugene, my exam revealed some kind of tampering on her mind," Rose says softly. "It reminds me of what we found on Bianca years ago. Only this is different. We can't get rid of it the same way."

I tense. I don't know what they're referring to, but I get the idea well enough. Dominic tampered with Paige's mind. He did something horrible to her. My breathing becomes labored as my anger toward my cousin rises in my chest.

Drake edges toward me and pats me on the shoulder. "They will help her, Zephyr."

I can't agree. He doesn't know that for sure. And judging by the look on Ugene's and Enid's faces, they aren't sure either.

"She needs to be moved to the hospital," Rosie tells Ugene. "There's only so much we can do for her out here, but if we get her back into Elpis, we can learn more and find some way to help her."

Paige once told me her people knew how to cure magical illnesses. I should have more faith in their capabilities. But this is Paige's life. If they screw up, could she die? The thought sends a bolt of terror through my core.

I shake as Ugene agrees and they move Paige to load into another truck headed for the city. I dart forward and grab Ugene's arm. "The city is the last place she will want to be. Let me take her away from here and we can sort this out." My voice catches as my despair closes its fist around my insides.

Ugene eases my hand off, sympathy in his dark eyes. His wife crowds close at his shoulder. My insides curl in a mess of nerves and fear. Tears slip out and I quickly brush them away. *Don't cry, Zephyr!* But I've lost so much today. I can't lose her, too. I'm barely holding it together as it is.

Ugene speaks softly, "I understand you can help her. And I admire how much you want to, but I need you to trust that we know what's best for our daughter."

Though I disagree, I swallow and nod rigidly. He's her father, and he's nothing like the king was to me. He loves her. I have to trust him, but I can't let go of my suspicions.

"The doctors will take her to the hospital and stabilize her condition while they examine whatever he did to her," Ugene adds. "Trust me, I do not take this lightly."

"Some of our doctors have experience with this sort of thing," Enid adds.

Again I nod, though I have no idea what that means. "Let me go with her. Please."

"Let him go, Dad," Gavin adds. "It can't hurt anything to have him close, and I'm certain Paige will want to see him when she wakes up. And he has the cuff on, so he won't stop them from helping her."

Enid rests a hand on her husband's arm, and they have an entire conversation with a single look. I admire their affection. Maybe not all love fades.

"Okay." Ugene nods. "But you will be needed here as well, Zephyr. We will need to debrief with someone in charge." His gaze flicks at the crown fastened to my belt.

My jaw twitches. *Cypress is dead.* I blink back more tears and fight off the grief. I can't go home and face that yet. "Okay. Cypress... He needs to be..."

"We already have him in camp and are preparing him for the return home," Ugene reassures me. "A trip you will need to take with him or we risk more trouble in retribution. We will talk more later."

I nod and step around them to follow Paige.

Tudor steps forward, cutting me off. "Sir, the rules of engagement here were made explicitly clear. None of the outsiders are allowed into the city."

Snarling and looming over Tudor, I bare my teeth. I would love any excuse to rip this guy's head off. I glare at him with my jaw clenched tight. "Try to keep me away from her. I dare you."

Ugene steps forward. "It's fine. He can go with her. Until she is stabilized at the hospital, it's probably best that he stays close to her, anyway."

I brush past Tudor, feeling his hateful glare on my back as I climb into the truck. Easton rushes over. "Found this. You might need it." He hands me the key to the cuff. I murmur in thanks and pocket it.

Enid joins me, as do Gavin and Drake—funny, Tudor didn't try stopping *him*. I expect Ugene will remain behind to clean up the mess my cousin has made.

The truck's ride is smooth, as if the ground were not destroyed by the battle. I sit on a bench near Paige on the stretcher, taking her hand in my own. With no one healing her at the moment, I unlock the cuff until we reach the hospital. Her magic remains there, pulsing like a weak bulb. I allow a trickle to flow into me. It burns through my veins like a trail of fire. Is this what it feels like to her all the time? How does she not burn up?

I want to lean close and whisper in her ear, but Enid watches me curiously across the back of the truck, holding her daughter's other hand. Paige resembles her mother so much. Though Paige's skin is tawnier than her mother's pale white glow, they share the same keen eyes and heart-shaped face.

I don't dare meet Enid's gaze for long. The woman doesn't scare me, but just as I wanted Ugene to like me, I want Enid to like me as well. If she decides she doesn't, what will that mean for my chances with Paige?

Gavin sits beside his mother, biting his lip like a dog with a chew toy as he stares at his sister. What does he see when he looks at her? I still don't understand his magic either. Can he use healing magic? I have a thousand questions for him, but the intense concentration on his face keeps me quiet.

Drake sits beside me since there wasn't space on the bench beside Gavin. He nudges me with his shoulder and nods at the window across from us. The glass is tinted to keep others from seeing in, but it doesn't obstruct our view out.

I gape.

I knew the buildings were large. But they're much larger than I expected. Elpis is nothing like the Capital. It's a bona fide city like I've seen in pre-Collapse movies. Pristine homes, organized streets, and people. *So many people!* Electricity lights up homes, streets, and buildings as the sun sets.

And magic is *everywhere*. I feel it like a constant press against my senses.

Drake presses his hands between his knees and bounces his legs. His expression is one of wonder and fear. His movement is subtle, but clearly this city—because it is definitely a city—is overwhelming to him.

No wonder Paige wanted to come home. The Capital never would have offered her this kind of life.

47

PAIGE

ONCE MORE, I STAND among the stars. The expanse calls to me, and I now recognize the stars for what they are. Each represents an individual, though not necessarily where they exist in relation to one another in reality. I slide my finger along one and glimpse Easton speaking with Nat about Cypress, Bronwyn, and the new King Zephyr. I quickly pull back from that one and run my hand along another. Mom is asleep at a lab desk beside Dad. Another shows Gavin curled up against Drake, wide awake and clearly troubled by something.

The last one I touch belongs to Zephyr. He sits in a hospital chair at my bedside, his head resting against the edge of the mattress as he sleeps. His hands wrap around mine, even in slumber. I won't disturb his rest. He's been through a lot.

I hesitate as I examine myself. I've never seen myself like this before. Monitors connect to my chest and my head, recording information. The knockout needle shouldn't have created such a powerful reaction. Are they keeping me in a coma?

"This isn't over for you, Paige." Celeste's now familiar voice draws my gaze toward the window. She stands beside it, her eyes glowing with green life. "Nor is it over for him. You have pulled him deep into your orbit. There's no escaping it now."

I reach toward his back, wanting to touch him, but I stop an inch from the back of his shirt. Touching him could disrupt him. "I didn't want any of this."

"While you had choices to make that determined the path you took, the ending would always be the same," Celeste says. "It was just a matter of who came along with you." She stares at Zephyr. "He will be there no matter what you do now."

I step away from him and we are out of his world and standing among the stars once more. "You mentioned another last time we spoke. Was it Gavin?"

Celeste nods as she raises her palms, and our three life loops appear between her palms. I easily identify my loop. The broken pieces are even more fractured than last time. The star moves along the loop just as agitated as before, catching in one place and sliding back. It repeats the motion on a loop. My time manipulation.

"You continue to play with forces you don't understand," Celeste says. "Time travel can be tricky when you change the course of lives. There's a reason you were locked in one place when you tried to save Cypress. You cannot undo some things or it breaks time."

Tears burn my eyes. "He deserved better."

"He played his part, as we all do."

I grit my teeth. How can she be so callous about his life? Cypress was a good man, and he had the makings of a great, strong king.

Celeste continues as if oblivious to my anger, which only angers me more. "You fear your Powers, but you need to learn to embrace them. They are not only those of desolation. Your Powers can cleanse the world. Red and blue in tandem, just as I told your father. Together," she arches her fingers, and the three loops merge, "they create balance." The moment my loop merges with Gavin's, the thick loop thins out as it feeds strength into my own. Zephyr's star and mine continue shifting madly toward and away from one another like agitated atoms. Then Zephyr's star and mine suddenly slow, moving toward one another until they follow the same path.

Hope lifts my heart. It's possible. We can still fix this. We can still be together. It isn't too late.

"What happens if I fail?" I ask.

She pulls her hands farther apart. Our loops separate and return to their original state. Gavin's loop thins and his star loses most of its shine. I don't understand what that means, but it can't be good, can it? Mine and Zephyr move toward one another. The stars collide, and slide along the loops together at a frenzied speed. Then they flash out.

My breath catches.

Balance is possible. Happiness is possible.

But only if I learn to harness and control this Power.

No pressure, Paige.

48

ZEPHYR

THE REMNANTS OF THE battle are a disaster. Most of the dead are from the Kingdom of Tides, as expected when Dominic brought so many men along. Apparently, Easton and Nat are not suitable substitutes for my presence. I spent as much time as I could beside Paige's hospital bed until the Elpis officials insisted I attend to the camp and my men.

My men. They don't feel like mine. Nor does the crown. However, for the time being, I'm in charge. Nat and Easton work with me to organize the ranks and prepare for the journey home.

I'm not returning with them. Paige's journey isn't over yet, and I will stay at her side every step of the way. We are fated to walk this path together. Or connection through her Dreams can't be a coincidence. It has a purpose.

Ugene doesn't like my decision to stay with her. He wanted me to return home and smooth things over, but Easton and Nat can handle that well enough, and I wrote a letter for Bronwyn explaining as much as I could.

The doctors in Elpis ran a myriad of tests on Paige, and all came to the same conclusion. Dominic left a kill switch on Paige's mind. Upon his death, she will, as Dominic warned us, become a bomb waiting to go off. No one knows how he did it. Some special skill he must have had that's unique to him. They can inhibit his kill switch for a time, but the inhibitor will wear off in a few days and the effectiveness of their solutions have all been short-lived. Without drastic action, Paige eventually will die and take us all with her.

It only took a day for everyone to figure out we had a serious problem. Gavin knew already. I suspect he knew the moment he saw her in the hospital, long before the rest of us figured it out. After only a few minutes at her bedside, he vanished, resurfacing a few hours later to ask me for biological samples. He had a working theory that linked her to me. The idea made my stomach twist anxiously. Gavin might be her brother, but I learn my lessons the hard way. That doesn't make him trustworthy. Except Paige trusts him. So, I gave in and gave up the samples he wanted.

Gavin vanished again for the rest of the day. He returned the next morning clutching a tablet and reporting what he learned. I don't know that I fully understand everything he said, but I got enough to know it's her only chance. And for her to have that chance, she needs me. We woke her and shared the information, giving her the choice, which wasn't really a choice at all. After hours of debate, we came up with a plan. It might work. It might fail miserably.

But it's our only hope.

The plan requires the Kingdom's troops to return home as quickly as possible. Bronwyn needs to know what happened so she can be ready for the next steps. Easton came up with a way to get everyone home quickly. In minutes, he says.

Layla. According to his post-battle report, Layla can open portals anywhere she has been. That will help the Kingdom get Cypress home. It won't help us get Paige where she needs to be.

The Kingdom's ships wait in the harbor. In a matter of minutes, Gavin created a loop that will enable the ships to turn around safely. It was like he snapped his fingers and it was done. He's getting stronger.

Now, all the Kingdom's soldiers have loaded onto the ships to prepare for the return journey. It should only take them minutes to reach the Capital's harbor. Summer believes she can amplify Layla's magic to make the return smoother, which also means River is returning with them. Alice moved on to help the Havenites, hoping to reconnect with long-lost family. Easton retrieved Layla from where he had told her to open a gateway two days after he stepped through before. She stands aboard a ship now, waiting.

I remain at the bottom of a loading ramp as the last of the soldiers board and I peel away the bandage from where Gavin extracted his samples.

"You sure this is what you want?" Nat asks. He's grown a thick beard since we left the island. It suits him.

"Yeah, Nat." I peer over my shoulder at the solar truck Ugene gave us for our own mission. Paige waits in the driver's seat, watching me. The inhibitor will only last three days, then we had better be ready. "I'll be back when I can. As Acting Captain, I expect you to keep this motley crew in check. Queen Elena and Bronwyn can decide what to do with the men we arrested."

Nat nods. "I hope this works out."

A grimace sets on my face. "Me, too."

Cypress' coffin stops beside me. Easton gives me a small nod of respect. I step toward the coffin and place a hand over it. I wish some profound words would rise to the surface, some last goodbye, but I come up empty. No words could ever express how deeply I love Cypress, or how—no matter our blood—he was and will always be my brother.

"Funny that the brother I liked least growing up turns out to be my best friend," I mutter. Grief clenches my stomach, but I can't cry anymore. I have been crying for days over all that I have lost.

I step back and motion for the guards to carry the casket on board. A hand slips into mine as Paige steps up beside me.

A second coffin follows Cypress. I don't give it a second glance. I can't. Forgiving Dominic may never happen, and if it does, it will take a while. The boy I grew up with never existed, and it still hurts all the way to my core.

Easton steps toward Paige and pulls her into a hug, though she never lets go of my hand. "Take care of this idiot," he tells her, nodding toward me, then he toes the ground reservedly. "Take care of yourself, too. I hope to see you *both* soon."

The meaning isn't lost on either of us. Paige now knows what's at stake. We made it clear, and she seemed to have an idea already of what was coming when we woke her from her induced coma. There's a good chance she could still die even if she succeeds. I will be there holding her hand either way.

I unfasten the crown from my belt where it has lived for the last two days. When I hold it out to Easton, he accepts it, attaching it to his belt under his jacket.

"You sure about this, Zephyr?" he asks. "Cypress gave it to you."

"If anything happens to me, that crown needs to make it home. Wyn will know what to do with it." I pull out an envelope and stare at the pure white paper wrinkled from being in my pocket for a day. Paige rests her head against my shoulder, offering me silent support. A lump lodges in my throat. I swallow it down and thrust the envelope at Easton. "Give this to Wyn, will you? Hopefully, she will understand."

Easton tucks the letter in his coat pocket and nods. "She will. But if you don't come back..."

I smirk. "I know. But I trust she's in good hands."

Easton averts his gaze as heat colors his cheeks.

"Commander!" Nat calls from aboard *Wave Slicer*. "Ready to hoist anchor!"

Easton pats my shoulder, then turns away and jogs up the ramp onto the ship.

I draw in a breath and release it slowly.

"Ready?" Paige asks.

I meet her gaze and some of my pain fades. "Yeah. Let's go."

We walk hand-in-hand to the solar truck, where her parents are saying goodbye to Gavin and Drake. Since this mission is extremely dangerous, we limited the team to just the four of us. It had been three until Drake dug in his heels and insisted he would never in a million years not be right there with Gavin, and Paige and I need Gavin to make this work. It will require all three of us to work together.

Drake slinks away to the solar truck, sliding into the backseat as Gavin finishes his farewells. Paige slips her hand out of mine and hugs her mom tight. Enid doesn't like me.

"Come back this time," Enid murmurs against Paige's hair. "Please."

"Mom..." Paige groans and pulls back, attempting to make light of the request. The truth is we don't know if any of us will survive.

Paige kisses Enid's cheek. "I love you. And I will always fight to get back to you."

Enid sniffles and wipes tears from her eyes. She doesn't give me even a cursory glance. We've hardly spoken to one another, and the few words she has thrown my way make it clear enough that she blames me for what happened to her daughter. Maybe she's right.

As the girls continue their goodbyes, Ugene stretches his hand out to me. I take it and we shake.

"I never thanked you, Zephyr," he says. "Despite everything, you saved her again. Asking you to do it a third time feels greedy."

"I would do it a million times," I admit. Saying as much out loud to her dad makes my nerves sing with nervous energy.

He just nods. "I know."

In a surprise move, Ugene jerks me against him into a hug. I don't know how to react, so I end up patting him awkwardly on the back. As good as it feels to be accepted by him, I know I have a long road ahead with Enid. Hopefully, I have a chance to walk that road.

When I pull away, Paige and Gavin are both grinning crookedly at me. As I flush, I step back towards the truck to allow them a moment with their dad. I've only managed a few steps before Enid calls after me, "Your Highness," which makes me wince. I almost don't hear her. Preparing for verbal combat, I turn towards her slowly and freeze.

Enid shuffles toward me, arms crossed. She looks...uncomfortable. "Bring them both back."

It isn't a request from her. It's a warning. If both of her children aren't returned to her alive, she will blame me. But if I can bring them both back, maybe she will forgive me for all that's happened to her daughter. It's the best I can hope for, so I nod.

As Enid pivots away from me, I slide into the passenger seat and close the truck door with a heavy puff of breath.

"That was intense," Drake says.

I eye him in the mirror. He's watching Enid walk away. His finger absently brushes over his rope bracelet.

"I wish there was some way to make her see how much her daughter means to me," I mutter.

"She will," Drake says nonchalantly. "Assuming we survive. At least you have a part to play in this plan. I'm just the arm candy."

I chuckle, enjoying this moment of reprieve. "Something tells me Gavin will need you, even if he doesn't know how yet."

"Oh, he always needs me," Drake says, and despite his jovial tone, there's a seriousness in his expression. "He's brilliant, but not without fault." His jaw twitches and he peers out the window at the Powers family. When he speaks, it's a mutter clearly not meant for me. "I won't fail him again."

We fall into amicable silence.

I watch the ships turn in the harbor. Something sparks in the sky like fireworks, then a massive gateway opens its mouth over the water. Water gushes through for a moment from the lake as the level balances out. On the other side, the harbor and buildings along the waterfront of the Capital shimmer in the sunlight. And in the distance, the pristine white pillars and walls of the palace stand proudly on the hill, overlooking it all.

49

PAIGE

F UNNY, I THOUGHT I outgrew hugs from my parents. Yet, as we say goodbye again, I've never been so happy to receive their hugs in my life. Mom offers the same brief but warm hug she always does, and I don't want to pull away as quickly as she does. I suspect that hugging for too long might make it harder for her to let me go. The moment ends far too quickly. It's a defense mechanism. I'm sure of it. She's afraid she won't see me again, so she's distancing herself. It hurts, but I understand. I don't know if I will come back either.

When I turn toward Dad, he's hugging Zephyr, who clearly doesn't know how to handle such affection. The awkwardness of the moment is endearing. Dad hasn't said he approves of Zephyr, but it's becoming swiftly clear that the two understand one another. Mom is a different story.

I practically jump into Dad's arms the second he opens them to me. For months, I thought I would never see him again. Now, I'm worried about how he will handle it if I don't make it back. There's every chance my Powers will kill me, but if this is what it takes to save the world, what's my life against a million or more?

Dad practically spins me in the fiercest hug he has given me since I was a little girl. When my feet touch down, he doesn't let go as quickly as Mom did. "No matter what happens, I'm proud of you for having the courage to do this, Paige."

I jerk out of his arms as tears flood my eyes. "I get it from my parents."

Both of us laugh through our tears.

"Your time is limited. You should make it in time to get yourselves situated, assuming the truck doesn't have any issues and the sun shines for you all the way there," Dad says. He's deflecting his fear and sorrow behind a mask of obligation and instructions. "You should arrive at the hotel tonight. Tomorrow night, sun willing, you should arrive at the site he marked out. Don't dally. Get it done and get home."

I roll my eyes and smirk at him. "I know, Dad."

"You are the strongest person I've ever met, Paige," he says, blinking to fight off his tears. It fails. "And that has nothing to do with your Powers."

"You're gonna make me cry," I moan, wiping tears from my eyes. I sniffle and take a breath to collect myself, but it's hard when I know this could be the last time I ever see him. "You and Mom are the most amazing parents I ever could have asked for. I'm sorry for being a pain in the ass kid."

Dad smirks, wiping away his own tears. "Don't be. That independence made you who you are today." He strokes my head and pulls me into another fierce hug.

I cling to him like the world will fall away the moment I let go. "Celeste said there's still a chance," I whisper.

"You saw her?" he says, croaking the words out as he holds tight to me.

"In the stars, just like you did," I whisper. "She misses you."

His hold tightens around me. The hug lasts far longer than any of the others before he clears his throat and withdraws. His gaze slides past me to Zephyr, who watches the Kingdom ships returning home through a gateway.

"He's a good man," Dad says softly. "You did well."

I snort, feeling awkward having Dad give Zephyr such acceptance and praise. We don't even know what we are, at this point, but I know how we feel about one another. "Not everyone agrees."

"She will come around." Dad waves my comment off. "As long as you come home." He pulls Gavin into another hug but lets go quickly this time. "Now go. You're wasting daylight."

I duck away around the truck and slide into the driver's seat. Zephyr tears his gaze from the ships as I start up the truck and follow the predetermined route. The truck will do most of the work. I just have to keep it on track.

"You alright?" Zephyr asks.

"Yup." I sigh and glance at him from the corner of my eyes. "So, Easton and Bronwyn?"

He chuckles. "Maybe. I don't really know if they even know. But there was something, which I suspect is why he wanted to go back with the ships."

"I think you three have a lot of explaining to do," I say casually, trying to shrug off the worry racing through me. "And we have a long drive ahead."

We could still die. There's a good chance I will, but I can't let that consume me now. I need this moment of happiness before I destroy the world.

50

EASTON

THE ISLAND LOOKS LIKE a whole other world in the spring. During winter, everything was covered in a white blanket or brown and dead, giving the Capital an ominous feel. Now, the trees are once again turning green as leaves burst from their buds. The grass is vibrant. Homes and businesses have potted plants blooming to life. In a matter of weeks, everything has transformed into a rainbow of colors.

Yet those colors assault my senses as the carriage stops at the bottom of the red-carpeted steps leading into the palace. There is no joy on this day.

Bronwyn stands at the top of the steps beside her mother, Queen Elena, and Commander Reginald. Excitement and hope light up Bronwyn's face as she watches the carriages. I hesitate to open the carriage door, absorbing that pure hope and delight on her face before I crush it.

"Ready?" Nat asks.

I draw in a breath, steel my nerves, and nod. Better to get this over with as quickly as I can.

By the time we open the carriage door, Queen Elena has already noticed the second carriage behind ours. The one that's covered and carrying two coffins inside. My gut twists with fear.

Bronwyn rushes down the steps toward me before my feet finish hitting the ground. She thrusts her arms around my neck and hugs me close. I wrap my arms around her, breathing in that lilac scent.

"I haven't slept for days," she murmurs against my neck.

After rubbing her back, I carefully edge away. We saw one another through that first portal Layla opened this morning, but Reginald had barred her from crossing over. That was for the best. The battlefield was a disaster, and I wouldn't want her to see that.

I take her hand and guide her up the steps.

"Where's Zephyr?" she asks as she trails alongside me. Her gaze is cast over her shoulder at the carriage as if she thinks he will emerge.

"He's not ready to come back yet," I say. "He had one more mission to complete."

She smirks. "Paige?"

I nod.

"Good."

Would Bronwyn still think it's good that they are together if she knew what he was about to do?

"And Cypress?" she asks. We reach the top of the steps and Bronwyn is bouncing on her toes, trying to spot her brothers. "Dom?"

Despite all Dominic has done, Bronwyn loves him. I suppose everyone deserves love, even if it isn't enough to save them. What will she think of me when she discovers what I did to Dominic, carving into his flesh? Shame washes through me.

Queen Elena's eyes shimmer with unshed tears, but her expression remains neutral. She eyes Nat for a moment before fixing her gaze on the second carriage.

"Easton?" Bronwyn's hopeful face flickers with fear. I can't meet her gaze for more than a second, looking away the moment the horrible truth hits her. Tears flood down her cheeks and my heart breaks. She covers her mouth to smother a sob.

Reginald places a hand on the Queen's shoulder. "I will see that they are brought around back until you are ready."

Elena nods but says nothing as he marches away down the steps. Nat accompanies the commander.

"I wish I had gotten there sooner," I say. My voice tightens around the confession. "By the time I arrived, Cypress had already fallen."

Elena's knees shake, and she sinks down into a deck chair. Bronwyn leans against me and I pull her into my arms. She curls against my chest, trembling like a scared animal. I clench my jaw as her sorrow bleeds into me and my own eyes water.

"Zephyr tried taking Dominic alive," I tell them. "But Dominic..." I swallow and shake off the rest of what I was about to say. "I can tell you the rest when you're ready. But Zephyr told me Cypress gave him the crown."

The news sends a shock through the Queen. She gasps and her eyes widen as her hands grasp the arms of the chair.

I pull back from Bronwyn and unfasten the crown from where it hides beneath my jacket. "Bronwyn, Zephyr wanted me to give this to you. He said you would know what to do with it."

Her trembling hands slide over the crown reverently.

"And this is for you." I hand her his letter.

Bronwyn snatches the letter from my hand, holding the crown out to her mother. I give Bronwyn the space she needs as she glides down the promenade deck that stretches the length of the front of the palace. For a minute, I just watch as she reads Zephyr's note, silent tears rolling down her pale cheeks. I have no clue what he wrote to her and admit that I'm curious. But more than that, I'm worried about her emotional health right now. If Zephyr told her what he was planning to do, it might be the last straw for Bronwyn right now.

"Thank you for bringing my sons back, Easton," Queen Elena says, her voice barely a whisper.

I stuff my hands into my pockets and nod grimly. "I wish I could have done more."

Elena says nothing else. She rises like a wraith and glides through the open palace doors, caressing the crown as if it were her son.

Fifteen yards down the promenade deck, Bronwyn leans against the white railing, clutching Zephyr's letter, letting her tears fall uninhibited. A gentle breeze stirs the skirt of her dress around her ankles and pulls her hair away from her face. I admire her for a minute before strolling over to join her. I stop a few feet away, gazing across the lawn and gardens across from the palace.

"Are you okay?" I ask when I see the stricken look on her face.

"Yes. And no." Her voice shakes. Bronwyn folds the letter and tucks it back in the envelope. "After Alric died, Zephyr stumbled in drunk one night and I tucked him into bed. He told me I would have made a good queen. I told him he would have made a good king, and Zephyr said the day he was king of this rock was the day the world ends again." Bronwyn smiles at the memory. I admit it's amusing. If she only knew. Maybe she does. I don't know what he wrote in that letter.

She draws in a breath, sweeping stray hair away from her face, then she waves the envelope. "He says the crown is mine now, old rules be damned, and the men of this family have screwed things up enough. It's time for a change."

I edge closer and lean against the rail beside her so we can stare out at the gardens and lake beyond. "He's right."

"I don't know if I'm cut out for ruling," Bronwyn admits. "I know what we need to do next, and which traditions should probably be shed to strength the Kingdom of Tides, but the list of tasks is daunting and I'm not sure who I can trust anymore."

I want to reach for her hand, but she needs space right now to process everything that's happened. "You have your mother. I'm certain you can trust her."

Bronwyn's honey-colored eyes pierce through me. "And what about you?"

"What about me?"

Bronwyn places her hand over mine atop the railing. My heart skips and my skin heats. "You know what I mean."

I turn my head to find her much closer than I expected. My breath hitches.

"I know how you feel about a ruling class," Bronwyn says softly. "That it's a breeding ground for greed and corruption, and we haven't exactly made a case against that fact. If I was queen, would you...leave?"

I don't know if I have it in me to leave her, but I also don't want her choice to be determined by her feelings for me. She needs to make this choice for herself. I lick my lips and turn, resting a hip against the rail. "Please tell me your acceptance of that crown doesn't depend on my answer."

Her face falls. "It doesn't. What remains of my family and my people need me. There's a lot of work to be done. A lot of wounds I need to heal, and a few bridges that need mending. It won't be easy work."

"I agree." If Bronwyn knew what I held close to my chest, the love and fear of losing that love, the shame for what I did to her brother, what would she say?

"But I *need* you." Her hand is so warm in mine. She is life and beauty and perfection in ways I don't deserve.

I can't meet her gaze. "That's not true. I've seen you in action. You can hold your own well enough."

"That's not what I mean and you know it, Easton," she says. "You're deflecting again." She pulls my hand closer and places it over her heart. My pulse runs wild. "Could you be happy as a Queen's Consort?"

Everything inside of me twists in anxious knots. Acid burns in my stomach while my heart races a mile a minute. The air thins, yet I feel light. *Did she just propose to me?*

I adore Bronwyn. Not her body—though that is a delightful bonus—but her soul. She's far more than I ever could have hoped or dreamed of. Certainly more than I deserve. But marriage...? We've only known one another for a few weeks. And, as she said, she needs to focus her attention on healing the wounds her brother created both on the island and in Elpis. Bronwyn has a lot of hard work ahead of her. I'm happy to be there, helping, but she doesn't need me distracting her, either.

I brush my thumb along her jaw. "Bronwyn, I value you more than you can understand. But I feel like it's a little soon to talk about marriage. I will stay with you, help you. And I'm happy to see where this leads. But we owe it to ourselves to take our time and make sure this is best for both of us."

Bronwyn dips her chin and nods. "But *could* you?"

Wrapping my arms around her, I gently stroke her cheek and hold her face. "I think so. I just need time. Can you give me that?"

For a moment, we just stare at one another as she weighs my question. The longer she takes to answer, the more anxious I become until her face tips up and our lips meet. And for now, that's all the answer I need.

51

GAVIN

THE DRIVE TO THE hotel passes smoother than expected. Zephyr sits up front with Paige, regaling his story from the prison break to how and when he found us at the hotel, and how that led him to Elpis. I allow him and Drake to tell the stories as I watch the data on my tablet, keeping a close eye on the inhibitors injected into Paige's bloodstream.

The inhibitor was designed to act as a beta-blocker that prevents her Powers from activating, originally created to slow or stop Power-related illnesses. The batch injected into Paige has been altered to increase efficiency and longevity. In a normal person, the inhibitor would last at least a month before they would need to follow up.

But Paige isn't like a normal person. Her body works faster in response. She's rejecting the inhibitor quicker than we expected, but we should still make it to the Haven before it stops working. The Power stone mine there will be critical to saving her life.

I know I shouldn't blame myself for her condition. But all that time I spent in the Haven attempting to carry out the mission instead of just leaving to help her left her alone at Dominic's mercy. The logical side of my mind knows it wasn't my fault, but that doesn't stop me from creating a hundred different scenarios where I could have done more.

Dominic put a kill switch on Paige's Powers. None of the Psionics in Elpis knew how he did it or how to remove it. His skill with his Powers is impressive. Upon his death, Paige is set to go nuclear—literally. If he can't win, everyone dies. Zephyr is certain that's why Dominic killed himself.

Seeing her in that hospital bed, unconscious as the doctors struggled to help her, pushed me into action. I had to do something.

So, I left the hospital to review the records of the mission and the statements from everyone from the moment we left until the battle started. Combined with what I read in Airen Mosheyev's journal and Zephyr's statement about how he absorbed a guard's Power and used it against him in the palace, I came up with a theory.

Zephyr wasn't keen on the idea of giving me any of his DNA, but I knew his love for Paige would convince him to donate what I needed.

I broke the samples down, along with samples from Paige and myself. I used DNA coding software to experiment with reactions and combinations, and everything led me to the same conclusion. A conclusion I absolutely didn't want to share with Drake but knew I couldn't keep from him.

The *Book of the Prophet* wasn't wrong. When all is broken down and examined scientifically and logically, Paige and I are capable of exactly what Mosheyev predicted. Calling us Idols who will destroy and create a new world is dramatic, but the basic idea is not. Mosheyev's work with the Power stones plays a significant role in our ability to not only fulfill his prophecies but also fix Paige. Unfortunately, that means returning to the Haven. It's the only place I know of where we can find the Power stones required for this task. Airen Mosheyev wrote about this in the *Book of the Prophet*.

> *"This is where the end will happen.*
> *This is where the future begins.*
> *This is where the new world is born."*

Paige laughs at something Zephyr says from the front seat of the truck.

He grimaces. "I don't find it that funny. Wyn is like a sister to me."

"Oh, he's not *that* bad."

I missed something as I worked on the Power stone calculations on my tablet. If I don't get these exactly right, I could kill Paige, Zephyr, and Drake...and possibly the world.

Drake nudges me with an elbow. "Hey, you alright?"

I nod. "Just thinking."

"When aren't you?"

Drake has been my rock through all of this. His endless optimism and ability to help me see what I miss in others have been valuable. He took over with the Havenites after the battle and gave me the space I needed to work on this solution. If it works, I will owe him for the rest of my life.

Last night, at Drake's insistence, I went to the Greenhouse to visit the Havenites. Most of them were scared, but hopeful. A few quoted the *Book of the Prophet*, "Take shelter in the mountains for only Creation can balance Desolation." "Trust in the visions of the Idols." Knowing I'm doing exactly what Mosheyev told them I would makes their words strike harder in my chest.

Drake had raised his hands and reassured all of them that the Days of Glory were coming, which made my skin crawl. He had promised them all a new Eden. I wish he hadn't done that. If I fail, we could all still die.

Mom promised to take care of the Havenites in our absence and to work closely with Emil, Ally, and Ajax. If the four of us save the world but still die, the Havenites are in her hands. I reassured them she would take care of them, just as she always did for me. If I succeed, they will have a new place to call home. Some will probably choose to integrate into Elpis once the Council of Representatives approves the motion—one Mom promised to work on with Dad to advocate for the Havenites. The others will be free to leave, expand, and explore. The choice is theirs. But unless I complete this mission, none of that matters.

After closer examination, I noticed that Paige's Power isn't destruction or desolation. It's restorative, like a hard factory reset on an electronic device. Paige can remove the radioactive rot and break everything down to its original matter. With Zephyr's help, she should be able to focus her energy and redirect it safely.

Unfortunately, the way it works brings fire, ash, and earthquakes, which means we need to have a way to protect the people while she lets her Power loose. I'm hoping to focus her Psychic attack and transform it into a sort of Psychic Net of protection over all living creatures. But to do that, she will require my help.

Theoretically, Paige will cleanse the world still infected by the Collapse. Dominic's kill switch won't go away once she finishes her task, which means Zephyr and I must remove her Power and funnel it into a less destructive source.

The Haven's Power stone mine. Sadly, that means we could all die unless I get the calculations right. Zephyr has already tried his best to use his Negation to contain her Power several times, but she's too strong for him. We both are. Removing her Powers is the only way to save her life. Those stones are our only chance when her body rejects all other forms of resistance to Dominic's meddling. The only other alternative is killing her, and none of us will let that happen.

The truck rolls to a stop and Paige cuts the electric engine. It can only charge when the sun is up, so we can't travel at night. We will finish the trek tomorrow. The morning after we reach the Haven, we will begin the task, which means I have one day to get everything figured out.

I slide out of the backseat and enter the hotel on autopilot, watching as a fresh batch of calculations scrolls across the screen.

"Gavin!" Paige calls after me. "Get your own stuff out of the back!"

"I got it," Drake says. A moment later, he's jogging to catch up with both of our backpacks slung over his shoulders.

I march up the steps to the room Drake and I shared before. Paige and Zephyr trail along some distance behind us.

Drake closes the door to our room, then marches over and pries the tablet from my hands. "You've been staring at that thing since we left." He clicks it off. "Take a break."

"I don't have time." I reach for the tablet, but he holds it away from my reach. "Drake, if I screw this up, we all die."

"It won't come to that." His confidence rubs on my nerves. "But even the brilliant mind of Gavin Powers needs rest sometimes."

I hesitate. Mom said that to Dad once, nearly six years ago now, when he was stressing about the barrier and couldn't sleep.

Drake places the tablet in the drawer of the bedside table, then pulls me down beside him on the mattress.

I curl up next to him and rest my head on his chest, listening to the rhythmic thump of his heartbeat. Of all the ambitious projects I've undertaken in my life, this is by far the most terrifying. Failure isn't an option. The pressure is overwhelming.

Drake wraps his arm around me and slides his hand up and down my arm. "This will all work out as you planned, Gavin. Don't let worries get in your way. I understand what's at stake. We all do. But I know it will work out."

I tip my head and peer up at his angular face. "How are you so sure of everything all the time?"

Drake smiles ruefully. "Do you really need me to answer that?"

No, I don't. Drake's hope and optimism are a part of him, but with me, they're boundless.

"It begins with hope and powers." I almost groan aloud as the passage from the *Book of the Prophet* surfaces. If I'm Powers, Drake must be hope, because after everything he's seen and all we've been through, he still believes in me and clings to hope. To him, I'm his partner, but I'm also so much more.

Drake pulls back and rolls on his side, leaning over me. "Anyway, if these *are* our last days, I can think of better ways to spend it than staring at that device."

The words make the butterflies in my stomach writhe. His gaze lowers to my lips, and heat burns in his eyes. I slide my hand up his chest, along his collarbone, then slide my fingers through the dark hair curling at the nape of his neck. Our lips edge closer and I breathe in the familiar scent of earth and charcoal that is Drake. My heart hammers against my ribs and I ache for the kiss I know is coming.

"Should the worst happen," he murmurs, and the deeper register of his voice makes my head spin, "I would rather die at your side today than live a single breath without you."

I chuckle softly, remembering how he used those exact words in the Haven. I respond exactly as I did then, grinning at him. "A bit dramatic."

Drake's hooded gaze pierces me, punching the air from my lungs. His lips angle over mine, sliding into place slowly. The kiss is soft, teasing me with repeated attacks that increase in urgency. My hold on the back of his head tightens, pulling him in place against me, holding him there. His hand slides along my throat, the touch delicate, then along my chest. The tips of his fingers electrify something deep in my core; an overpowering longing that wraps around us; a deeply rooted love that plants itself in my heart and bursts with life.

Our lips and hands move like explorers in a whole new world, seeking paradise. Together, we climb to the highest peaks of this brave new world until there is nothing left to explore.

52

PAIGE

Z EPHYR OPENS THE DOOR to a suite with two bedrooms next to Gavin and Drake. Zephyr leaves me standing in the doorway as he heads to one room and closes his door. My heart sinks. I don't know what I want, or what I expected would happen, but disappointment and rejection curl in my stomach uncomfortably.

Though there are two bedrooms, there is only one bathroom. I watch his door, wondering if I should knock, before deciding against it. I close myself in the bathroom to shower. Someone restored the plumbing in this hotel somehow...and the water heater. The hot water feels like bliss over my aching muscles.

Flashes of the battle, of Zephyr's death, crowd my vision as the water runs down my back. I gasp and fight off the anxiety that swells inside of me, pressing a hand to the shower wall. No one else remembers it. No one but me. He died saving me. In two days, he will probably do it again. I curl my fingernails against the tile wall and focus on my breathing.

A knock on the door is followed by Zephyr's voice. "Paige? Are you alright? Your magic is trying to surge."

I swallow hard and clear my throat, then turn the water off. "Fine. I'll be out in a minute."

Silence greets me.

Once I'm dry and dressed, I open the door and peer out into the suite. The balcony door remains open, allowing a warm breeze to blow through.

Zephyr stands on the balcony, arms over his chest as he stares out at the river. I pad out barefoot to join him in a fresh tank top and leggings. His brooding gaze sweeps over me as if seeking signs of weakness. What does it feel like to sense someone else's Power? I know what it feels like to have his press against mine, but it can't possibly be the same.

"I know you aren't alright," he says. "You don't have to hide from me. There's no way you can be alright considering what you've agreed to do."

I watch the way the warm breeze makes the tips of his hair shift. The white t-shirt clings to his muscles and forms tight around his chest. This is the first time we have been alone for real, with no danger looming around the corner waiting to catch us and no forced distance to keep us apart. This draws me closer to him. I slide my hand down his arm. When my fingers brush his, they automatically weave together.

"Zephyr, you don't have to do this," I say softly, staring at our hands, reveling in the warmth of his skin against mine. "In fact, I would prefer it if you didn't. Chances are I won't survive, and I think that's the way this is supposed to be."

He turns toward me, hurt shining in his eyes. "Don't do that. Don't push me away now. We both know this is exactly where I'm supposed to be."

I want to argue with him, but he's right. The Dreams we shared before we even met led us to this. Celeste told me he would be there, no matter what. A sad smile perches on my lips.

"I don't want anyone else to die because of me," I say. January's tear-streaked face as she apologizes flashes through my mind. Ivy telling me to finish this. Hundreds of faceless soldiers I vaporized with radiation I pulled from the earth during battle. Tears prick the corners of my eyes. "If I could just..."

Zephyr places a finger against my lips, shaking his head. "Don't even say it. I won't let you fall on your sword when we can still save you." His other arm slides around my waist, pulling me closer. My pulse quickens and heat rushes through me.

I take his finger from my lips and kiss his hand, then place it against my cheek. For so long, I have suppressed these feelings, this longing for more, for him. Now, all I can think about is how I can save his life. That he wants to save me so desperately only makes my heart swell with love.

Celeste gave me hope, but she didn't promise we would succeed. There's a chance we could die. I can't allow it. "I need you to promise me—"

"Paige…"

"—promise that if this isn't going to work, if it comes down to me or everyone we know and love—"

"You can't ask me to do this."

"—that you will kill me quickly."

Zephyr tries pulling away, but I cling to him, gripping his wrist as my other arm holds him close. He shakes his head. "I can't."

"You can. I think you are the only person who can." I press my cheek into his palm, holding his gaze firmly with my own. "Promise me."

His Adam's apple bobs as he swallows hard. Fear and love and anguish make the lines on his face harder than normal. He nods. "I promise. But I decide when you've reached the point of no return. Not you."

Agreeing to his terms means he might wait until it's too late to stop my Powers from exploding out of me, but how can I argue and still get any kind of agreement from him? I nod. I trust Zephyr. Not only with my life but the weight of this horrible duty. He is the only one among us who *will* have the strength to do what needs to be done when the time comes.

Zephyr dips his head closer to mine. His penetrating gaze drills into my soul. It makes me ache. Of all the boys I've taken an interest in over the past couple of years, none of them are anything like Zephyr. There's something steadfast and immovable about him, like a mountain where I can find shelter. I love him more than I ever imagined I could love someone. And I've already watched him die once. I don't know if I can handle it again.

Zephyr's knuckles graze under my chin, tilting my face up toward his. "What's wrong?"

"What?"

"You looked like you were a million miles away." The intensity of his stare supercharges my adrenaline. "You can tell me."

How do I explain? "I…saw your death on the battlefield."

"I'm here." His thumb strokes my jaw.

"Now you are." I bite my lip. Zephyr will understand if anyone would. He won't try to judge me or placate me. "I can manipulate time. When you died, I lost control. I know what this world looks like when my Powers explode because I did it once already." My words catch in my throat.

"That's why you said you tried to save him," Zephyr breathes. His voice is deeper, and his gaze keeps shifting to my lips. "You tried to go back and save Cypress."

I nod and the tears expose my shame and failure to him. But Zephyr doesn't condemn me with a look, doesn't fault me for a moment. His rugged features soften. His gaze caresses me as gently as his fingertips.

Zephyr is rugged beauty. A lakeside breeze on a hot day. An ancient demigod sculpted of the mountains. It terrifies me how much I want him, need him...love him.

"No one blames you," he says, but the heat in his voice doesn't match his words. He is thinking about the same thing as me. I can see it clearly over every inch of his tense body.

My pulse quickens. We stand a heartbeat apart. I can't breathe with him so close, can't think, can't blink. His hot breath rolls along my neck, intensifying the pulse of need racing through me.

Zephyr presses against me, slowly squeezing out any space between us. His bristled jaw brushes my cheek. The surrounding air supercharges with a fiery energy that tingles every part of me. The fingers on my jaw slide along my neck and I shudder in delight. Then his lips brush my jaw and create a trail down to the tender skin of my neck. Every nerve in my body is on fire, but this time it has nothing to do with my Power and everything to do with his power over me. I cling to him, breathe him in.

His fingers press into my lower back, hugging me close. I half expect that any second I will be ripped out of this glorious dream and thrust back into reality. But this moment is real. It's ours. I revel in his scent, fresh like a lakeside breeze, but with a hint of muskiness. His lips continue, soft yet firm, hungry yet patient. I exhale his name and Zephyr eases back.

The burning intensity and desire in his eyes undoes me. His hand grasps mine. "I need to stop," he says breathlessly.

I can hardly breathe, too. "Why?"

"Paige..."

"I've waited long enough," I say.

His grip on my hand tightens, and he peers into me as if he needs further permission. Whatever he sees settles matters. Zephyr leads me into his room. A shiver of pleasure races down my spine as his fingers trace my back.

"I've been waiting a long time to kiss your lips," he says. His voice rumbles with a heated desire that makes me wild. "Properly. Outside of dreams and without some big, devastating event around us. Just you and me. And those lips." His thumb brushes my lower lip.

I hesitate. He's right. We haven't truly had space to ourselves like this since we met to really enjoy one another. This moment feels so much more sacred than that last kiss had been. Our first real kiss outside of dreams had been on the heels of Baron's death. Our second was surrounded by the end of the world—not that he would remember that kiss. His gaze sinks to my lips.

"Do it, then," I say, challenging him to get on with it. I can't stand how slowly he is moving.

Zephyr's lips crash into mine, hungry and ruthless and full of passion. A sound of delight slips up my throat and into his mouth. His desire rolls out like thunderous waves in a storm. There is nothing gentle and slow about this kiss. It's uninhibited, a release of months of pent-up desire. If he is the stormy waters, I am the gale-force winds whipping us into a tempest. His mouth shapes to mine until I can taste him. The kiss transforms me into a mess of longing.

Then the storm shifts. His lips pull back, angling against my own, jerking at a core of acute need within me. My fingers slide under the hem of his shirt, and he groans against my lips as my fingers brush his skin. His fingers tangle in my hair as the other hand tugs at my shirt. I'm burning now. Our bodies press together in desperate need.

Once more, his lips blaze a trail along my jaw and neck. My fingers slide up his shirt, exploring the muscles of his back.

"Zephyr." My voice is a breathless growl.

He pulls back just a moment and our eyes meet. That's the end of all reservation. We dive onto the bed together, giving in to the overwhelming waves of passion and hunger and desire until the storm abates.

53

ZEPHYR

I'M NOT NEARLY AS eager to get moving in the morning as Paige. Last night was the best night of my life. Nothing even comes remotely close. Paige is not the first girl I've been with, but something about the way we connected last night transcended space and time. It fused my soul to hers and shattered every hesitation I've ever harbored about love. I *wanted* to go slowly. I tried. But the moment our lips finally met, I lost all sense of self.

Paige walks purposefully toward the truck as I trail behind her. I wish I could share her determination to see this through, but all I want is to hide away and steal as many moments with her as possible. I want to hoard her all to myself for eternity. Every step takes us closer to our inevitable fates and possible death. I can't lose her. Not again. Not ever. I will either save her or die with her because there is no life for me without her in it.

Paige hauls her backpack into the back of the truck before I've made it ten steps out of the hotel. I'm dragging my feet on purpose as if it can stall the inevitable.

Coercing that promise out of me had been a dirty trick. I won't do it. I should resent her for it, but I don't think I could ever resent her for anything.

"Tired, Zephyr?" she teases as she stands by the driver's doorway of the truck. The smirk on her face makes me chuckle and pick up my pace. She won't let me slow her down, and I shouldn't want to. It only increases the chances I will have to carry through on my promise.

I toss my backpack in the truck with hers and see the other two already seated and waiting in the backseat. I sigh and climb into the passenger seat.

Drake casts a devilish smirk at me as I buckle. How does *he* know?

"You two are loud," Gavin says bluntly.

My face flames. Paige laughs and starts the engine. "Suck it up, bro."

How much did they hear? Regardless, I can't help the embarrassment from coloring my face.

The truck begins the lumbering trek northeast.

Despite what is coming tomorrow morning, the energy in the truck is upbeat. Paige and Drake exchange stories about Gavin that he only half notices as he picks apart whatever is on that tablet. The miles fly past far too quickly, leaving behind a trail of time with Paige that I will never recover.

Eventually, the flat land shifts into gently rolling hills, then forests. I'm terribly aware of how close to the inevitable we have come. Gavin stresses about some kind of calculation, but I can't stop worrying about the million ways I can fail Paige.

What if I overestimated my new ability? What if I can't actually help her funnel her magic for better control? What if her death results from my failure?

Gavin releases a whoop of delight that makes me jump. I shift so I can see him over the seat. "I did it. There's a ninety-eight percent chance that it's correct."

Hope sparks in my chest, and I see it mirrored in his eyes. "You can save her?" I ask.

Gavin licks his lips and nods. "There's about a one-point-nine percent chance it will fail, but yes."

That he isn't a hundred percent sure sends a spike of worry through me. "Why not totally sure?" I ask.

Paige smirks at me. "Scared?"

"Yes."

Gavin eyes me like I've lost my mind. "Science isn't perfect. There's always a slight chance of failure. Trust me, this is about as good as we can hope for."

"Can we go over the details again?" I ask.

Paige glances my way only for a moment as if to tell me it's fine. It isn't.

Gavin launches into an explanation. "Zephyr, your first job when we set up on location is to draw out Paige's Psionic Power and funnel it into a Power stone bracelet that I will give you."

"I thought touching the stones was dangerous," Paige says. "It takes Powers and kills people."

I frown. "That...doesn't sound right."

"It isn't," Gavin admits. "Our understanding of Power stones in Elpis is new and not wholly accurate. I looked at one of the Tribute bracelets they made you girls wear. The bracelets had Power stones in them, yet all of you kept your Powers and survived. Using the proper conduit material, size, and combination is key. The Kingdom cracked the code on that for me."

The Tribute bracelets were designed decades ago to keep the royal family safe from the Tributes should they attempt to use their magic against us. I never stopped to think about how they work. Apparently, Gavin has.

"Those bracelets block magic," I say. "How will I use my magic if I'm wearing one?"

"Because my design is unique." Gavin's confidence startles me, and somehow also relieves me a little. "It shouldn't take me more than a minute to reverse it. Once you have her Psychic Power in the stone, you will give it to me so I can harness the Power to create a Psychic Shield."

"How?" Drake asks.

"I have a few working theories," Gavin says, waving the question off. "But Paige won't be able to focus on protecting people while she hits the reset button."

Drake scrunches his face. "Reset button?"

"Her Power." Without missing a beat, Gavin says, "Paige, I will make a disc that you have to keep on top of until we're done completely. It will protect all of us and give me the ability to quickly and safely use Power stones to store your Powers away."

I examine Paige for a reaction. Her jaw tightens and her focus on the path ahead intensifies. I don't like that look. She's worried about something.

"What will happen to her once her magic is gone?" I ask, not taking my gaze from her. Paige's lips thin, but she doesn't flinch.

"Hopefully nothing," Gavin says, as if her well-being is little more than a passing concern. How can he be so cavalier about his sister's life?

"Hopefully," I grumble. My jaw tenses.

Paige reaches over and takes my hand. Our eyes meet for a moment, and her smile is forced and frail. "I trust my brother just as much as I trust you."

"That's nice. I trusted mine, too," I snap. I'm not really angry at Gavin, but at this entire situation. My reaction is unfair and I know it. I'm deflecting my anxiety at him.

Paige scowls at me and gives a tight shake of her head in warning. I've overstepped.

"Sorry," I mutter.

Gavin's stone-gray eyes shimmer with hurt. I avert my gaze, ashamed of myself, only to find Drake staring daggers at me. Great. A moment of impulse and I've alienated everyone.

Gavin clears his throat and continues, but his confidence is shaken. "Zephyr, you will help Paige focus her Power and control it for a more gradual, controlled emission. It may require you to use your Negation and Absorption at the same time."

I've never tried such a thing before. Is it even possible?

"Your Powers may be linked the moment you pull hers in," Gavin explains, "and there's a chance that, when I remove her Power, it can take yours with it."

No magic? I flex my fingers, wondering what it would be like to live without magic. It's a part of me, like another organ.

"I will do my best to prevent that from happening," Gavin continues, trying to reassure me. He doesn't need to. If losing my magic is what it takes to save Paige, then it isn't a problem. "But your Powers might bind, in which case there's nothing even I can do."

I nod, peering out the side window now. "Do what's necessary to save her."

Paige's reflection examines me. She must know by now that I will fight for her, sacrifice for her. A rueful expression perches on my face. Mom and Baron warned me about this. Love makes us all act like idiots, but at least I understand what it feels like now. Like a light in the darkness, chasing the demons away. Like a hand shielding my heart and soul, binding to it, giving it strength. Love strengthens us.

"As Paige resets the planet with Zephyr's help, I will follow behind with my own Powers to restore it," Gavin continues. "It will take all my focus. Drake, you need to monitor all of us. Make sure nothing seems to go wrong. Stay close to me, just in case."

Drake takes Gavin's hand. "Where else do you think I would go?"

They share a warm smile.

"Once she's done, Zephyr, you need to help me pull out her Powers and funnel them into the Powers stones," Gavin says. "I will pull as much as I can from the mine. Just...don't touch them. I can protect us from death, but not if you touch the stones. After it's done, Zephyr, get her out of there. I will bury that disc so far in the earth no one ever finds it, but I have to do it quickly or the proximity of the Power stones could still kill us."

I nod. "Get her out quick. I can handle that."

"We're here," Paige announces, shifting the truck into park. Sure enough, our guidance system indicates we have reached our destination.

I flinch. Everyone else hops out to set up camp, but I can't make myself move.

Paige opens my door, leaning against it with her brows raised. "Are you planning to sleep in here? Because I suppose I can make it work."

I stare straight ahead as the terror clenches my chest. "I have failed everyone in my life. Mom, Baron, Cypress, and even Dominic. They're dead because of me. What if...?" The words choke off in my throat. I close my eyes and lean my head against the headrest. "I'm terrified I'll fail you, too."

"You won't," Paige says with so much certainty I almost believe her. She climbs in the truck and straddles my lap, cradling my face in her hands. I can't help but meet her determined gaze. My hands slide to her hips. "Zephyr, I know you won't fail because you know what's at stake here. You won't want to fulfill that promise you made to me last night. That alone will motivate you."

I don't want it to come to killing her. She's right about that much. But that doesn't mean I won't fail, anyway. I've attempted nothing like this before. No one has.

"Come on. Get out of the truck." Paige slides out and pulls me along behind her. "It's late, and we are wasting time."

"Time for what?" I ask.

We march together around the truck to where the tent has been set up. How long was I staring out the front window? I jerk to a halt and peer out over the sunken ground. This is the Haven? What is even left of this place? There's nothing here but a crater and fallen trees. *And they were worried about the Kingdom. They should have been more concerned about what would happen when their precious Idols arrived.*

Gavin stands at the edge of the sunken earth, his shoulders hunched and hands buried deep in his pockets. Drake stands beside him, rubbing his back and murmuring something in his ear. Gavin nods stiffly, but neither of them moves. They are cute together, a natural symmetry of all that makes us human.

"Zephyr," Paige hisses, holding the door to the tent open.

More Elpis advancements. The tent is attached to the back of the truck and extends out to create a cramped living space. Paige has already connected two of the sleeping bags to create one large space for both of us.

She pats the bedding as I linger in the doorway.

"I'm not tired," I grumble.

"I know."

"I'm not really...in the mood either." All I can think about is what will happen tomorrow. The tension transforms into me pacing the cramped space.

"Zephyr, I just need you close," Paige says. "I may put on a brave face, but I'm scared, too."

Turning towards her, I spear my fingers through my hair. "Don't tell me that. I liked it better when you weren't."

Paige rises and wraps her arms around my neck. She's shaking. I hate that she's shaking. It only confirms that she really is scared. Her fingers thread into the hair at the nape of my neck. "I need you to keep me distracted."

I chuckle and shake my head. "No. Come on."

Paige swats my shoulder playfully. "Not what I meant. I just want you to hold me."

I hug her close to my body—she molds perfectly against me—and I agree to her terms. That much I can handle.

Paige and I snuggle into the sleeping bags together and whisper until she falls asleep, but I can't sleep. My mind is racing, and my fear has a firm grip on my intestines. It doesn't help that I can feel her magic growing stronger again. The inhibitor is breaking down quickly, just like Gavin predicted. We don't have long.

I JOLT AWAKE BESIDE an inferno. At some point, I must have dozed off, but the heat and magical power rolling off Paige's body makes it impossible to sleep for long. The dream had been glorious. Paige and I were on a beach alone, with nothing but each other and time.

Reality is much harsher.

Sweat creates a sheen on Paige's skin and her body quivers. The magic hums with wild energy. Something is wrong.

The tablet emits a horrible alarm. Gavin is up in seconds, checking the data. He curses under his breath and clicks the tablet off, tossing it aside.

"We're out of time," he says.

But I can already tell. "Where does she need to be?" I ask as I rip open the sleeping bags and hoist her into my arms.

"This way." Gavin darts out of the tent.

Drake grumbles as he wakes, cursing us until he realizes something is wrong.

I race after Gavin, clutching Paige's shivering body as tight to my body as possible. "It'll be okay, Paige. We will fix this."

But terror has taken hold of my insides and won't let go.

GAVIN

THE GROUND SHAKES AROUND us, making trees shake and leaves flutter to the ground two seasons too soon. I don't have time to be delicate as Zephyr charges on my heels with Paige in his arms. Dirt bounces on the ground, then rolls out of the way as I lift a massive, round disc of gray stone from the earth. In a blink, I create a bridge between the edge of the sunken remains of the Haven and the disc I create. A nearby tree cracks, then falls back away from the Haven.

Zephyr doesn't hesitate when he reaches the foot of the bridge, sprinting across to the disc.

Drake rushes up beside me when I skid to a halt on this side of the bridge, watching Zephyr's back. Zephyr lies Paige on the disc, kneeling at her side and smoothing out her hair from her face.

Drake plants his hands on his hips and watches. "How can I help?"

I chew the inside of my cheek and slip a hand into my pocket. "If you have issues, or something looks like it's going wrong, buzz me." I nod at his rope bracelet. "Can you watch our surroundings for me? My focus must remain on the task to prevent failure."

"Yeah. Sure. Is that it?"

I turn to Drake, pulling a Tribute bracelet from my pocket covertly. A sweet girl named River gave it to me quite willingly. There's no other choice. It's the only way to protect him from the Power stones. Without this, he could die. I step closer to Drake and slip the bracelet on his other wrist without his permission. The second I clasp it, Drake hisses and shakes his head.

He grabs the clasp to pull it off. "No. Nope."

I close a hand over his and press urgently against his fingers. "Please, Drake. The Power stones are dangerous. Zephyr, Paige, and I will not be affected the same as you. I've looked at our DNA. I know what we can handle. But I don't know about you. This will inhibit the stones to help protect you."

"And I won't be able to use my Silence to help you," Drake argues, glaring at me. "You can't ask me to stand aside while you three do everything. I'm here. Let me help."

"And you will. With your eyes, not with your Power."

"But Zephyr—"

"I don't know how his Power will react once those stones come into play," I insist. "Not for you. Trust me. Please, I'm begging."

Drake clenches his jaw so tightly it twitches at the edge. His dark eyes glare at me, searching, but he won't find any hesitation or give in to me. To protect him, I must do this.

I kiss his cheek. "If I'm worried about your safety, I can't concentrate. And I can't afford to lose focus. If I do, all of this could fall apart."

Drake glares at the ground at his side. I can sense his frustration and I'm worried he won't listen. When he nods, I sigh in relief.

I turn away from Drake and march over to the edge of the moat. Haven Ministers worked for decades, attempting to perfect what Zephyr should be able to do with ease.

Zephyr scowls as he clasps another Tribute bracelet around his wrist, courtesy of Summer. On the way here, I focused my Power on converting the bracelet, allowing him to use his Powers—possibly even amplify them temporarily—and funnel Paige's Psychic Power into the stones embedded in the gold. Then he will give it to me, and I will use my calculations to infuse the Power into myself so Paige can focus on controlling the rest of her Powers.

Paige stirs awake at Zephyr's feet.

"Give me the stone the second you're done," I call to Zephyr. "Then keep her from exploding until I use her Psychic Power to protect everyone. The two of you will be alone from that point until it's done."

"Understood," Zephyr calls back, kneeling beside Paige.

I want to hug my sister, but we don't have time for sentimentality. The clock is ticking.

54

PAIGE

FIRE. FURY. HEAT. RAGE. Destruction. They burn through me, devour me like a starving monster. Agony tears at my bones. This is the beginning of the end.

"Zephyr," I moan feebly. Sweat clings to my skin. I can barely move.

"I'm right here." His hand clings to me, like ice against my hot skin. "Hold on, Paige. We're almost ready."

"It...it's too late." I fight to open my eyes, to chase away the darkness consuming me.

"No." He growls. His face slowly comes into focus, beautiful, rigid, and determined.

Overhead, the sky fades to a sickly shade of red. An ominous storm brews. The wind kicks up wildly, whipping Zephyr's hair as he crouches over me, smoothing my hair away from my face, his hand remarkably steady, all things considered.

The two of us are on a massive stone disc, surrounded by a deep drop into the earth like a moat. Thunder rumbles across the sky, shaking everything around us. I whimper.

"It's okay," Zephyr says, attempting to reassure me. "We're almost ready."

The wild fire of my Powers rages, thrashing beneath the surface. I grit my teeth to keep it from breaking free, but it spreads across my body. I whimper as it glows with dangerous light. "You promised."

"It isn't time."

"Please." I squeeze my eyes closed. This pain is unbearable. "It hurts. Holding it back hurts so much."

"I know." He leans over and kisses my forehead. "I'm so sorry. It started early and caught us by surprise. Just hang in there a little longer."

Sweat beads on his brow. The muscles in his neck strain. Is he siphoning some of my Power right now? Is it so bad that even with his help, it's agony?

My fingers twitch. Red lightning rips out of the clouds and lights trees around our ring on fire. A moment of torrential rain pours down from the red-gray clouds above, extinguishing the flames. Was that Gavin?

Zephyr takes my arm and helps me to my knees. I don't have the strength to stand on my own feet. Even on my knees, I sag against him. He holds me in his arms, stroking my hair. His breath rustles my hair as he whispers in my ear.

"Paige, I need you to focus, just like we discussed," he murmurs. "Focus on your psychic magic. Put all your energy into that focus."

Were it not for his hold on me, I would flutter away in the wind. I shake my head as everything swims. "I can't."

A storm unleashes around us. The wind howls and kicks at our bodies. I'm a leaf in a storm, clinging to Zephyr like he's the tree keeping me from drifting away.

"Paige." Zephyr pulls back, stroking my face. "You can do this."

I close my eyes, struggle to imagine the sea of stars, but flames consume my vision. They create a box around me, closing tighter. I whimper.

"Breathe," Zephyr whispers in my ear.

Anxiety grips my chest, and I struggle to pull in a breath. The flames close tighter around my body.

"In," he coaches softly. "Out."

We focus on breathing together. Then, I once more imagine myself in a sea of stars.

ZEPHYR

T HE MAGIC HAMMERS INTO me. Weeks of practice acclimating myself to this assault when Paige trained on the island help, but even that flow of magic was nothing compared to what rips around me now. I grit my teeth and fight the tide threatening to pull me under.

I focus everything I have on Paige and her magic. Hundreds, thousands of tendrils of magic surround her body and mind—more and more. Finding one among the chaos is like trying to pull in a man overboard in a storm at sea in the dark.

Here. Paige's voice in my head accompanies one tendril as it pulses and glows brighter than the rest. I hold her close in one arm as I focus on drawing the magic into me, then back out into the bracelet. It bucks, resists, relents, and jerks away. Fire lances through my mind.

Then all the pain and anguish vanish as if I've walked through a door and sealed it away. Silence folds around me. I'm standing in a sea of stars, alone and cold. My body trembles against my will. I reach out and brush my fingers over one star, not fully understanding where I am.

Suddenly, I'm elsewhere. Emil rises from his chair at the door to a massive underground tunnel. His eyes widen as he casts his gaze toward the blood-red sky. "You had better come back, boy," he mutters. Tears burn the back of my eyes when I realize he's talking about me.

I jerk my hand away and touch another. Enid sits on a bed in a green bedroom, sobbing into her hands. Then her head jerks up and her eyes bore into me, widening in alarm. I stumble a step back before realizing she doesn't see me. She's looking out the window at the same blood-red sky.

"Zephyr, hurry." Gavin's voice pulses from another star.

I squeeze my eyes closed and shift focus to the bracelet around my wrist; the stones waiting for use. The gold burns against my skin.

"Zephyr..." Bronwyn's voice breaks my concentration.

I open my eyes in a moment of terror.

Easton stands on a palace balcony, holding Bronwyn close as they both gaze out at the ominous red sky. Tears roll down her cheeks. I can almost taste her worry and fear. I can't fail. Everyone I love is counting on me.

Paige is counting on me.

"Hold tight, Paige," I say, unsure where she is, if she can even hear me.

Then I harness that thread of Psychic magic and pull with all my might. It resists, pulls me close, then slides free. Gasping for breath, I push it into the stones in the bracelet. Once more, the gold burns against my skin. I grit my teeth, pushing all this newfound magic into the hungry green stones. I close my eyes and tighten my fist around the stone in my palm. It burns against my skin as I push all this newfound magic into its hungry green body.

When I open my eyes, Paige is staring at me with wide, tear-filled eyes. I kiss her temple, pushing my Negation into her. The relief is evident on her face. The magic is still there, burning like a fire inside of her, but for the moment she knows relief, like water over a burn. "Stay here. I'll be right back."

She nods.

I sprint across the bridge to where Gavin waits, ripping the bracelet off as I go. The second I reach him, I slap the gold band into his palm. Gavin closes a fist around it. When he opens his hand, the gold is ground into a fine powder. Without hesitation, Gavin slaps the small green stones into a device in his hand, then presses it against his neck and pushes the trigger. He hisses as green light glows in the veins of his neck, climbing up his neck. I watch in horror as the veins in his temples enlarge and turn green, seeping back toward his mind. *What did he just do?*

A massive pulse of magic slams into my back, throwing me off balance. I stumble into Drake who catches me, but his eyes widen as he peers past me at Paige.

"Go. Now," he hisses.

Paige screams.

I spin around as her body slowly lifts from the ground, sending spikes of red magic out in every direction like a ball of angry energy. "Paige..."

Terror rushes through me, and I sprint as fast as my feet can carry me across the bridge.

GAVIN

MY MIND OPENS TO the endless sea of stars. I don't just see all of them; I *feel* them pulsing with energy and life. Time is my enemy. I reach out to the nearest star, connecting it to me, then branch out to the next and the next and the next until I've created a massive network of stars like a celestial mind net. Every living creature on the planet. And there are *so many* more than we suspected!

Then *she* appears beside me. A woman I've only seen a flash of before. Dark hair. Emerald eyes. A dress made of stars. I instantly know who she is from stories Dad told me. Celeste.

"You can't do this alone," Celeste says, reaching her hand out to me.

I slide my hand into hers and see everything about her past, present, and future in a flash. Tears flood my eyes as I understand who this is. Not just Celeste. She's so much more than that. She is the embodiment of space and time. A god, if there ever was one. This truth overwhelms my senses.

Her grip on my hand tightens, grounding me in the task once more. We work together to create a protective psychic shield around each creature, and each community, on the planet. It invigorates me, humming with boundless life, opportunity. I feel everything and see everything.

When the task is done, Celeste places a hand on my cheek and smiles fondly. "You are late. Hurry, Gavin. And remember to balance red and blue in tandem, or all will collapse inward."

I nod, understanding exactly what she means.

Paige cannot do this alone.

Neither can I.

Creation and Desolation must complete this mission together. Just like the Prophet predicted.

PAIGE

THE POWERS TAKE CONTROL, hoisting me off the ground. The rot inside the earth calls to me like a siren. I want it, need it, pull it into me. The heat and death fill me with a sickening yet glorious sensation of power. It slithers around my skin like silk. In an instant, shots of death and rot fire out in all directions. Trees catch fire and turn to ash. Grass shrivels and dies instantaneously.

Then everything around us trembles violently as the red sky spreads outward like a threatening wave, hungry to devour the world. It hurts so much my nerves no longer understand what pain is.

"Paige!" Zephyr stands near me in the storm's eye, reaching for my hand. His hair whips in all directions as the wind kicks up untamed around us.

I stretch, reaching for his hand. The moment he makes contact, his fingers snap around mine, pulling me toward him as if scared that letting go will make me drift away. Zephyr pulls me back to the earth and cocoons me in his arms.

My stomach clenches in agony like something has reached inside of me and is squeezing with all its might. Tears roll down my cheeks. "Please... Make it stop..."

Zephyr's reddened eyes plead with me. "I'm here, Paige. We can do this. Together."

"No." The word is a moan of agony. He will die if he pulls any of this into him. It's too much.

"Done!" Gavin shouts, though his voice is distant, as if shouting from a mountain peak miles away. It echoes in my mind.

Zephyr clings to me, his eyes locked on me. Neither of us dares to look away, as if doing so will create a chasm we will never again cross. He is my tether to life. "Pull in as much as you can, Paige, and let me help you control the release."

The storm above expands. The earth shakes so violently that it creates fissures several feet wide. If Zephyr doesn't stop me, I won't just turn the world barren. I will break it apart completely.

Zephyr brushes my tears away with his thumbs, clinging to my face in a fierce, desperate need. I curl against his chest, grateful to have him here with me, terrified of what comes next. His presence gives me every ounce of remaining strength.

But the Power still rages with wild life, lashing out everywhere. Somewhere in the distance, I hear a thunderous crack, followed by a seemingly endless rumble, as if thousands of stones are falling from the sky.

"I'm right here," he murmurs.

Power breaks the world and I can only cry, unable to harness it.

"It's unstoppable," I moan in despair.

"I can help," he says, holding out his other hand. "Just take my hands."

I peer up at him through my tears. I want him to run as far from me as he can get. But he was right the other night. This is where he was supposed to be. This was always inevitable.

I cling to him desperately. Something shifts. Power pulses like erratic red energy between the two of us, a tug of war just waiting to explode. Zephyr's face pales, but he holds me tight in his grasp. The red light shifts, coiling first around his limbs, then his body. As he pulls my Power into him, he pushes his own out into me. It creates balance, but it's so delicate that the slightest shift could set everything off.

This was always the plan, but it feels doomed to fail. How can the two of us hope to control something so wild and untamed? I pull back a little, worried about what will happen to him if he takes on too much.

"Are you ready?" he asks. Sweat beads on his brow and his muscles draw tighter under my hands.

Another crack. Fire breathes across the sky, roaring like an angry dragon. I'm losing control. "Zephyr, I don't know how to do this."

His hold on me tightens, pulling me against his hard body. "You're resisting my help. Let go."

It's so hard to open myself up to anyone, to let go of my control. Dominic left his mark in more ways than one.

"Paige, please. Let me help."

Zephyr's lips brush against mine, anchoring me to him more solidly. I'm helpless in his arms as the Power rages with frenzied life. He slides a hand up to cup my face. The two of us are caught in the eye of the red storm as it buzzes and zips and burns around us. My Powers thrash, then reach out for him, pouring into him. I can't let him do this. It will kill him. Yet I can't stop him either.

Zephyr deepens the kiss, and my fear slowly dissolves as I lean against him. My Power isn't fading. The two of us, locked in this glorious, passionate kiss, are binding our Powers together. He takes on some of my wild Power, reducing the assault on my senses. I grasp his Negation and coil it around us as if it can protect us from backlash. I cling to him, parting my lips. His tongue brushes past my lips. I breathe in the scent of him—lake water tinged with musky sweat. It's gloriously Zephyr. He kisses me like the world is ending—and maybe it is. He kisses me like he never wants to let go, and I don't want him to. If this is the end, I will die in his arms, in this kiss.

When we come up for air, both of us are transformed, hovering several feet over the ground. Both of us shine red, wrapped in this deadly Power. It pulses visibly in our veins. His usually dark eyes glow. My Powers continue building, but as our lips pull apart and he presses his sweaty forehead to my own, the Powers aren't as wild any longer. The storm above us calms but doesn't disperse.

"I love you," he whispers. His breath rolls across my already heated cheeks.

"I love you," I echo the words back.

"Let's do this together," he says.

I nod stiffly, then close my eyes and focus as Zephyr holds back the tide attempting to carry me away. I don't know how he does it, and I don't dare ask.

55

GAVIN

I CAN SEE EVERYTHING and everyone everywhere all at once. The fabric of the world unfolds before me like lines of code. The sky burns red. Paige and Zephyr have created a red storm sphere around themselves as they hover over the disc in each other's arms. Then the Power pushes outward in flashes of red in every direction.

In the wake of her Power, everything crumbles, resetting to the basic building blocks of the universe in a glorious wave of fury. It's beautiful and devastating. Were it not for the network of protection Celeste and I placed around everyone, Paige would have wiped the planet clean for a full reset.

I send my own Power out on her heels. Ruins of cities vanish in a blink under Paige's Power. I immediately follow, collecting that matter and restoring it to something functional, useful. No more radiation or desolate wastelands.

Mountains fall and new ones rise. Rivers dry, but I create new ones. Continents shift. Forests vanish in a flash and fresh ones spring to life in their wake. Flashes of red and blue dance around one another all across the planet in a delicate balance of cleansing and creating.

The ground beneath me shakes. A thunderous inferno blazes in my ears, challenging my focus. As I work, flashes of the battlefield hammer against me as if I'm there again, alone and overwhelmed. My focus breaks.

DRAKE

HERE AT THE HELM of Creation, my insides writhe in terror. It's horrific and beautiful. The forest around us vanishes in a flash, to be replaced moments later by brand new trees. Every beautiful aspect of change arrives on the heels of desolation. My gut twists as I watch. Tears well in my eyes and I can't be sure if I'm crying at the beauty or sadness of it all.

Paige and Zephyr have vanished in a blazing, bright sphere of red that I can only assume is normal. So far, they seem to have matters under control. A few feet to my left, Gavin's head tilts toward the sky. His arms stretch out around him, moving like an artist painting on an invisible canvas. Except the canvas is the world. How different will it be?

Gavin's body hums with blue energy. His stone-gray eyes glow with the same blue light as his Power. It rolls from his body in wisps and swirls, flying in tandem with flashes of red emitting from the sphere.

I release a shuddering breath, taking in the glory of it all. Who could ever claim to stand at the exact point where the world was remade, watching it happen? I allow myself to absorb this moment. It deserves stories, poems, songs.

When we were taught of the Idols changing the world, saving it, I'm not sure what I envisioned. I'm not sure my mind could have possibly conceived of it. Certainly, it was nothing as glorious as this moment.

The ground beneath my feet cracks. I gasp, stepping toward Gavin, watching as the cracks spread. Thunderous noise follows, though I can't tell what it is or where it comes from.

My gaze darts to Gavin, praying he knows what's happening and has it under control, but the way his face scrunches tells me all I need to know.

Something is wrong.

Gavin flinches as the thunder continues, seeming to come from everywhere. It roars in my ears, deafening me. I tug nervously at the bracelet binding my gifts away.

He warned me that he couldn't afford to lose focus or all of this could fall apart. Yet, Gavin is so sensitive to loud noises. I chew my lip, inching a step closer. His arms droop. Another step. He sinks to his knees.

I rip off the bracelet, throwing it on the ground. Protection be damned. I won't let this fail now. This is my contribution. Keep Creation focused to save the world.

The glorious warmth of my gift rushes back through me. Without a moment of hesitation, I reach out a hand, coiling Silence around Gavin tight enough to keep out the deafening roar even as his hands move toward his ears. Nausea takes root in my stomach, making me dizzy with sickness. I swallow repeatedly and sink to my knees beside Gavin, sucking down breaths to keep from throwing up.

For a split second, Gavin glances at me, at my wrist, and sorrow pours out of him. Then the blue energy whips out of control, away from his body, lashing at the red sphere. Gavin lifts his hands again, and in an instant, he is back to focusing on the task at hand.

But the sphere cracks. A hiss rumbles in my ears like water putting out an enormous fire.

The ground shakes. The red sphere thrashes tendrils of dangerous power. Sweat rolls down Gavin's temples.

Zephyr screams, but I can't make out what he says from inside the sphere.

Green stones shoot up out of the earth, creating a dome around Paige and Zephyr. My stomach instantly roils. I fight to hold my Silence over Gavin, protecting him as the Power stones greedily pull at my gift. Despite my best efforts, I cannot stop the vomit from climbing up my throat as I clutch my stomach and grit my teeth. I've never felt so sick so quickly before. Death is close, clawing at me. But I can't fail Gavin. I can't fail the world.

56

PAIGE

MY POWER RACES AWAY from me, tearing the earth apart as Gavin's Power follows in my wake to repair it. Zephyr holds on, tugging at my Power when it becomes too much, pushing more into me when I grow weak. It's like a dance we share as we carry out our task. His hold is steady, practiced, leading me with ease through this dangerous dance of Power.

The closeness of our Powers coiled around one another is as intimate and deeply connected as our own hearts and bodies were the other night. Every part of me has bonded with him, and him with me. It's an otherworldly experience.

My red Power has cocooned the two of us and expands slowly. Yet I feel no pain or fear. Only bliss. My lips part, eager to tell Zephyr what he means to me, but nothing happens.

"No." Zephyr's terror clenches my heart, yet even though I know something is wrong, I still can't feel fear. His fingers swipe my lips and come away with blood. Yet still I am not scared.

The world is right. Zephyr is with me.

"Paige!" Zephyr catches me as my strength gives out. Our bodies crash down against the disc and he whimpers, worrying over me. "Gavin, hurry!"

Nothing happens.

"Gavin!" Zephyr screams louder than I've ever heard him scream before. Every muscle in his body strains to the limit. The veins in his face and neck are red and visible, as if they are rising to the surface. I don't just see him, I feel him. Every molecule of him, everything that makes him Zephyr. His face has gone pale beneath the red webbing of his veins. He pulls greedily at my Power, sapping it away. The whites of his eyes shift to something redder. He can't hold my Power much longer. I'm not sure if he ever could take it from me the way he wants to.

Though I feel nothing, I sense that I'm losing control. I reach up a trembling hand and stroke his cheek. "Zeph…"

"No." Tears slip down his cheeks and he shakes his head firmly. Grief catches in his throat. "No, it's not time. We aren't there, Paige."

A sad smile graces my lips. "Yes, we are." My voice is oddly calm.

He sniffles, swallowing repeatedly as he gulps down air. "Gavin!"

My Powers spread.

Zephyr screams in denial.

A sphere of green stones springs to life around us, catching my Powers and absorbing most of the blast.

The storm overhead breaks. Red light bursts from my body outward in a shockwave of Power.

ZEPHYR

T HIS MAGIC SUFFOCATES ME. It's like clinging to a tornado by my fingernails. It's consuming Paige from the inside out. Gavin was supposed to have the dome of those stones up around us by now. Then I could redirect this magic and save her. But as she slips from my grasp, terror claws at my insides. I reach more desperately for the magic, pulling in as much as I can, but it's too much. I can't hold it for long.

Where is Gavin's stone sphere? I scream for him, wishing he would get his act together. She's going to die.

No. I won't lose her. I grit my teeth, pulling in everything. I will either save her or die trying.

Tears roll down her temples as blood dribbles from her lips. She's begging me now, but I won't give up. Not ever.

I reach out for more and more to relieve her of the burden. I will let it burn me up before I let it kill her.

When I attempt to push my Negation into her, it backfires. An explosion knocks me back. I have an instant to push everything I'm clinging to into the stones before my back rams into the disc.

The sky turns red as I push myself up on my elbows, and for a second, I think I've failed. Sparks flick against the dome of Power stones, and it devours them like a hungry beast. It's too late. I've failed again, and we will be the last to die caught in the storm's eye. Then flashes of blue consume the red. The storm breaks. A beautiful, pure blue sky shines brightly overhead.

Paige's magic is gone. I no longer feel it pushing against me.

It's over. "We did it." I still don't understand what happened or how, but we prevented the end of the world. "Paige!" I laugh, rolling to pull her close again.

Paige lies on the disc. Terror grips my gut as I crawl toward her.

"Zephyr, get out of there now!" Drake calls down. Even he sounds weak, on the brink of death.

"Paige?" I shake her lamely. "Paige!"

She doesn't stir.

The disc does, though. The stones zip toward the disc like bullets raining around us, embedding in the gray slab.

"Zephyr!" Drake hollers more insistently.

I pull Paige into my arms, stunned and stumbling off the disc across the bridge.

When we reach the other side, I collapse with her in my arms. I'm numb, weeping, and rocking Paige's body.

Drake hesitates and mutters something. Then he seizes my arm. He's shaking and weak. His voice trembles. "Gavin can help her."

How can Gavin help her? She's dead. I failed her, just as I feared. *We were supposed to live or die together.*

I'm helpless, broken, worthless. If I thought I knew grief before, it's nothing compared to what I feel now. Sorrow overwhelms me as a sob rips from my throat.

A hand on my shoulder eases me back. I cry out and cling to Paige, but the fingers press firmly into my shoulder and pull me back insistently. Drake flops onto his back, sucking down deep breaths as he struggles to clasp a bracelet back around his wrist.

I blink through my tears, watching as the blurred face of her brother moves closer. Gavin sinks to his knees and his hand hovers over Paige's chest. He mutters to himself. Then he closes his eyes.

I don't dare say a word as I hold my breath, not daring to hope he can bring her back to life.

PAIGE

T HE SUN RISES OVER the horizon, casting brilliant hues of pink across the sky. Cypress sits on the bench, facing me, angled toward the window on the padded bench in the King's Bar at the top of the palace. I've been here twice before; when I Dreamwalked and overheard a conversation between him and Dominic, and on that disastrous date.

Now, Cypress studies me with those beautiful blue eyes, his face drawn in tight lines. He shakes his head. "Why are you here?"

My gaze flits across the water. Something looks different about it. It takes a moment before I notice the stone bridge that connects the island to the mainland. That didn't exist before. And the mainland seems...closer. Something about this place feels off.

"I tried to save you," I say, hoping to offer some sort of apology for failing him.

Cypress shakes his head, making those dark waves sway. "It wasn't your fault or your job. All is as it was meant to be."

I blink back tears. I wish I could believe him.

"Paige." Cypress leans forward, taking my hand in his. "Zephyr needs you."

My lips part, but I don't know what to say. I don't understand what's happening.

Cypress kisses my hand. "Go to him."

I yelp as I'm jerked from the bar, through the stars, and land on the ground in front of Gavin, Drake...and Zephyr.

Drake releases a hysterical laugh, running his fingers through his hair where he lies on the ground. Gavin's face is pale and streaked with tears, too stunned to know how to respond.

Zephyr's face is streaked with tears. He blinks furiously, and his breath releases in a whoosh. Then he pulls me into his arms, hugging me tight against his chest. His embrace comforts me. Yet something deep in my soul is gone, hollowed out.

"Is it over?" I ask.

Zephyr kisses the top of my head, then presses his cheek against my head. "Yes, Paige. It's over."

I sag with relief against him.

Drake grins at Gavin, pale-faced and unsteady. "What did I tell you?"

"Don't start," Gavin mutters. His worried gaze sweeps over his boyfriend. Drake doesn't look too good. "We need to get you out of here, Drake. The stones are buried, but they've gotten to you. Let's go home."

Epilogue

Gavin

1 Year After Restoration

"ARE YOU SURE ABOUT this, Gavin?" Drake asks.

Drake and I made a pilgrimage to the far south with one purpose in mind.

I nod. "This is for the best. No one person should have this kind of Power."

"But it's all or nothing," he says. "Paige hasn't been herself ever since the disc."

I peer out at the mountainous island I created months ago for this sole purpose. We are far from any other signs of life here. Getting to this location was easy with my Powers. Getting home will be much harder. We are thousands of miles from Elpis, and even farther still from where Paige's Powers were embedded in the disc and buried deep underground in the Power stone mine.

"I know." I push the rowboat into the water. "You coming?"

Drake grins. "Like you would dare to do this without me." He climbs in and the two of us set to work, paddling lazily toward the mountain island. My seasickness is much milder in a small rowboat.

Just as Paige left her Powers in the Haven, I will bury mine here. Councilwoman Howser was right about one thing. These Powers are too dangerous for this world. The farther apart these two forces are, the better the chances that they will never be found. Someone could, hypothetically, find a way to absorb the Powers and start this cycle over again. But it's highly unlikely, based on my calculations, and if it happened, it would be so far in the future. Who knows what the world will be like by then?

Sadly, I can't selectively hold some of my Powers. That's not how it works. Either all of them go, or none. I will be Powerless, just like Dad. That can't be such a bad thing. He's done well for himself. And Paige and Zephyr are recovering from losing their Powers.

After we returned to Elpis, Drake and I spent a few weeks with my parents, Paige, and Zephyr. Drake blossomed as part of the family. It's the first time he's had a family since he was a little boy. When he hugged me one night and thanked me for sharing my family with him, I knew I would never share my family or my life with anyone else. Drake is my everything. We didn't bother with a wedding. The promises we exchanged after the Haven collapsed felt so binding to both of us that we just accepted that was that.

As I predicted, some of the Havenites are integrating into Elpis life. The Council of Representatives was still sorting out some details when we left, but ultimately the choices belong to the individuals. Elpis is now an open city, free for anyone to come and go. Just like the Capital and all its territories.

Some Havenites began exploring the new world and established a new town, New Eden. I visited once but have no interest in going back. I'm happy they have found their perfect place, but there isn't room for me in it. They will never see me as anything but the Idol of Creation. I will never be that again. Not after today.

It takes the better part of the day before we reach the island. The mountain opens for me, and I set it to collapse once we exit after the deed is done. Moving a mountain has become effortless. It should *never* be effortless.

When we reach the center of the mountain, deep in the ground, I close my eyes and push out with my Powers. All around us, green crystals glow with life. Blue ribbons of Power stream outward from my body, wrapping around the crystals where they are absorbed. I continue until there's nothing left.

Tears roll down my cheeks. It feels like some part of me is hollowed out, as if someone has removed a piece of my soul. Drake pulls me into his arms and wipes my tears away. "You okay?"

"I will be." After giving him a peck on the cheek, we turn and leave. I will need him in the years to come. No one can survive Post-Traumatic Powerloss Depression for long alone. But if Zephyr and Paige can do it together, then I can do it with Drake at my side.

Drake helps me to the exit. When we step on the trap, the tunnel collapses from the inside outward, sealing my Powers away for good.

This is as it should be.

Now I can live an ordinary life in Elpis, just like I always wanted.

ZEPHYR

15 MONTHS AFTER RESTORATION

THE WORLD IS NOT what it used to be. Dominic's vision did come to fruition, just not with a tyrant emperor in charge. The earth is making a resurgence as life thrives and humans expand into new locations. We have yet to encounter other territories, but Paige and Gavin were both certain there *are* others out there.

Trade and peace and travel between the Kingdom of Tides, Elpis, and New Eden are plentiful. Our alliance will be critical to prepare us for whoever else might come our way from the world beyond. Hopefully, there won't be any more Dominic's in my lifetime.

Queen Bronwyn rules over the Kingdom. Within days of Easton's return to the Capital, she arrived in Elpis via a gateway—courtesy of Layla—to meet with the Council of Representatives and establish peace. I attended to act as the intermediary since the Council and the Kingdom were both familiar with me. But Bronwyn did all the heavy lifting, and she did so gloriously.

After a few weeks with the Powers family in Elpis, Paige and I returned to the Capital. Bronwyn gave us the keys to a cozy home near the north shore, away from the growing swells of citizens. For now, the two of us spend time together to explore our relationship without danger looming over our shoulders. It's been the best year and a half of my life.

"Paige, we gotta go!" I call from the entryway, fastening my cufflinks in place.

Paige hops down the steps, fighting off a smirk that doesn't quite reach her eyes—it rarely does anymore. My jaw slackens as my gaze slides over her.

"What do you think?" she asks, spinning as she dances closer to me.

A lump climbs up my throat and I swallow it down, taking in the blue and red dress with black crow feathers around her legs. The same dress she wore to the winter ball years ago.

I clear my throat. "I think Elena will have a heart attack."

She waves the comment off. "She never liked me, anyway."

I chuckle at the joke. She doesn't offer many of them these days, and they often feel forced. Losing her magic changed her. On the surface, she's still Paige. But, as her father warned me would happen, Paige falls into darker, distant moments. I haven't had the same problem. My magic is gone, and while there is a piece of me missing, a bigger piece feels like it has fallen into place. Paige has filled the void in my soul that has always been there. Maybe my familiarity with having missing pieces is why I am not affected like she is.

I stroll toward her as she closes the gap and I curse the time for getting in my way. "She never liked me either," I say, sliding my arms around her waist. "We have a little time, right?"

She nudges me back. "No."

I groan in dismay as we leave the cottage.

The carriage ride to the palace is only a few minutes long—everything on this island is close together—and we climb out with the rest of the attendees. Hundreds of eyes track the two of us from all directions. Everyone knows who we are, even if we don't get out much—it's *why* we don't get out much. They quickly connected news of the red and blue sky and the reshaping of the world to us. Not that anyone truly understands what we did or what we sacrificed. Nor do we care to explain.

The palace is decked out more than I've ever seen before. White flower arrangements spill out from every vase the servants could scrounge up. A string quartet plays music in the lobby to welcome guests.

I place my hand on the small of Paige's back and guide her up the stairs to the massive ballroom. Rows upon rows of chairs are connected with white tulle and red flowers along the aisle. We make our way to the front where our seats are waiting.

Enid and Ugene sit near the front as well, given special placement after the new treaties were signed. Drake and Gavin are beside them, looking dapper in their formalwear. Drake grins at me as we say our hellos. Ever since he and Gavin returned from their adventure south, Drake has been pestering me about proposing. It makes me uncomfortable. I love Paige, but I don't enjoy being pressured by others. My cheeks heat.

Ugene greets us warmly, pulling me into a hug I've grown accustomed to—he's a hugger, unlike his wife. Then he slides something into my hand. I close my fist around it and nod.

This is the final piece of acceptance. I meet Enid's gaze, and she gives me a small nod. That little gesture means more than Ugene's hug.

I smile, sliding my arm along the chair behind Paige as I sit. She leans against me. I adore these little moments.

PAIGE

I T ISN'T LONG BEFORE the ceremony begins. Zephyr and I cut our arrival close. If we arrived late, we never would have been forgiven. Easton stressed the importance of arriving on time so firmly I wanted to slap him. But I chalk it up to the stress. He's under a lot of pressure.

A half dozen richly dressed guards march up the aisle with Easton. His suit has a high collar that is clearly causing him discomfort, but even with the eyepatch, he's strikingly handsome. He glances in our direction, and his nerves are all over his face. He takes his place on the dais at the head of the ballroom. Then the quartet strikes up a new song, and Bronwyn enters as Easton anxiously tugs at his sleeves.

Their wedding is beautiful, but not a quick affair. Easton isn't just promising himself to Bronwyn, but to a queen, which apparently requires a whole other set of vows. He won't rule, just as Queen Elena never ruled. But he will still live his life in service to the Kingdom. Since the war ended, Easton has been busy with Bronwyn creating an outreach program that helps the poor and disenfranchised both on the island and beyond. Zephyr and I started working for the program a year ago, and I find I enjoy it. But after how hard Easton worked to become a Specialist, his knack for social work surprised me. I expected him to insist on becoming head of the Royal Guard or something. He seems content to leave the fighting to others these days.

After the ceremony, Zephyr and I follow Elena out to be the first to celebrate the new couple. As I approach, Easton grimaces and tugs at his collar. I hug Bronwyn first, and she asks the same question I know my parents will ask before this day is over.

"How much longer until you two are ready?" Bronwyn asks me.

I flush and clear my throat. "We aren't in a rush."

She raises her eyebrows pointedly at Zephyr. He just shrugs. We are comfortable where we are.

The two of us remain at the banquet as long as etiquette requires, but the questions people ask us about the red sky makes my anxiety kick in. The moment Bronwyn gives us permission, we say our goodbyes to my parents and brother, inviting everyone over the next day for a casual visit, then we return home.

Weddings are an overwhelming affair. All the pomp and circumstance to affirm what two people already know. I don't see the point of a big ceremony. Bronwyn's wedding, I understand. She is the Queen, so the ceremony should reflect her station and bind Easton to the people. But that isn't me.

Zephyr stops at the credenza in the entryway and removes his cufflinks and tie, dropping them on the polished surface. I slip off my heels, rub my sore feet, and grumble about the impractical footwear. Zephyr smirks at me. I love the way the corners of his mouth curl upward.

Some unknown force pulls me toward the back door, as it often does. I step out, gliding toward the sandy beach in our backyard. As I rip off the feathers around my lower legs, I spot Zephyr leaning in the doorway, watching me curiously. I toss the feathers in the air, watching them flutter away, then wade out into the lake.

The water is cool, but not freezing. Summer on the island is beautiful, and the water is usually warm enough to swim. Not that I have the energy to swim tonight. Besides, the sun is already sinking toward the horizon.

Zephyr rolls up the legs of his pants and wades out with me. He has been the one thing that keeps me tethered when I feel adrift. I would be lost without him. When I'm drifting from shore, he is always there to pull me back and make me smile. I love him more now than I did months ago.

I slide my arms around his waist, leaning my head against his shoulder. We watch the sunset in silence, enjoying the beauty of this new world.

Everything changed because of Gavin, Zephyr, and me. The world doesn't even look the same anymore. I should want to explore it, but all I want is this cottage and this beach and this man. I've had enough adventure for a lifetime.

A deep sense of loss settles over me as I think about everyone we lost. Ivy, Nora, January...Cypress. A lump lodges in my throat. It's been so long, yet the loss still feels fresh for both of us. We only bring up his name in sacred moments. The monument Bronwyn created to commemorate Cypress' fight against tyranny is good for the people, but we were there when he died. It felt a lot like he died for nothing.

I quickly wipe away my tears before Zephyr notices them. He gets so worried when I cry. Thankfully, he hasn't taken notice tonight.

"Do you want a wedding?" Zephyr asks, resting his cheek against the top of my head as the colors in the sky deepen.

I snort and roll my eyes. Not that he sees it. "Is that your idea of a proposal? Because it's terrible."

He chuckles, and the sound warms my soul as it rumbles in his chest. "No. I would never dream of giving you anything less than the perfect proposal."

"Good," I say. "Because I may not want a wedding, but I *do* expect a damn good proposal. And I suppose someday it might be nice to make this official."

Zephyr pulls back and peers down at me with so much love I think my heart might explode. He strokes my cheek. "This isn't official enough for you?"

I force a grin up at him. "Nope."

"Hm."

Once more, we fall into a comfortable silence. As the last hues of color threaten to burn away from the horizon, leaving a deep shade of red in its wake before darkness takes hold, he once more kisses my head, then pulls away, holding my hand. I'm about to turn toward the house when he raises a brow at me.

"How about this?" he asks.

My stomach twists into knots when he drops to a knee and pulls a ring from his pocket. "Princess Powers, will you grace me with your hand in marriage, without the gaudy wedding, and make me the happiest lordliness in this new world?"

I gape at the ring in his hand, stunned. "Don't mess with me."

He chuckles nervously. "You're killing me."

"Is that my grandmother's ring?" I ask. How did he get that ring? Dad must have given it to him. Mom only *just* started calling him by his name. For over a year, she simply directed him around without the use of a name. Pronouns and finger-pointing were enough for her. The first time she said his name, I thought we all froze in time. If they gave him that ring, this was planned...and my parents approved.

"Paige? You're making me nervous."

I sink to my knees in the sand. Water laps over our legs. "No big wedding."

"Agreed."

"Just you and me, our families, and this beach."

"Sounds ideal."

I bite my lip, then throw myself at him hard enough to knock us both into the sand. As we kiss, he slides the ring on my finger.

Warmth and love and desire and peace all settle over me. For the first time since the disc, I feel whole.

All my life, I wanted to prove I was worthy, that I was my father's daughter.

But I don't need to *prove* myself worthy.

I always was. A page from his book, rewriting this new world.

———◦◉◦———

The adventure continues in Powers Origins! Get your copy of *Miller* now.

———◦◉◦———

I hope you enjoyed Paige, Gavin, and Zephyr's story. If you did, please consider leaving me a review. I love hearing what people liked about the book.

Acknowledgements

I want to give a shout-out to *everyone* who made it this far. It was a rough ride, but you crossed the finish line! This series pushed outside the confines of the Powers world we all know and love, and the ride was a little bumpier than the original Powers series featuring Ugene. I hope you found the journey rewarding, and that you had moments when you laughed, cried, pumped your fist in excitement, and felt deep emotional connections to each character and each moment.

Gavin, it's okay. You don't have to be a battle-ready fighter like some of the other characters. We still love you. Paige, I really tortured you in this book, but you handled it with so much courage! Zephyr, I'm so glad you were able to find peace with your past and yourself.

As always, a special thanks to my husband. I promise to take a few weeks off to finish all the projects around the house that I've neglected for months. Thanks for continuing to give me the space and time to do what I love. To my kids: First of all, the pool is now open for the summer! Secondly, I know you hate cleaning bathrooms and doing dishes, but your help relieves a big burden on my shoulders. To my daughter... Yes, Easton married a queen. I know you wanted him to die. I tried. Sadly, he found his way to happily ever after. I hope you can forgive me. I failed to live up to my Character Assassin name for you.

This book—hell, this series—wouldn't be where it is without the dedication of my beta readers: Kevin Mackie, TaniaRina Perry, Jared Goldman, Kris Shotts, and Jennifer Garcia. Nor would it have been fit for print without the steady hand of my editor, Maddy, who always has the best suggestions, advice, and praise alike. Thanks for taking multiple passes through this book to make it as clean as we can manage as a team. The support from my fellow dystopian authors in the Dystopian Author League has helped promote this series. You should read their books, too. I promise they're all amazing!

To Cole R. Eubanks, the voice you gave my characters still amazes me, but just as valuable is the encouragement you've given me every step of the way. Thanks for the amazing praise!

POWERS TRILOGY SERIES

A POWERS UNIVERSE SERIES

A SUPERPOWER DYSTOPIAN SCI-FI SERIES
FEATURING DIVERSE CHARACTERS,
FOUND FAMILY, DYNAMIC FRIENDSHIPS,
AND POLITICAL CORRUPTION

WWW.STARRZDAVIES.COM/POWERS-UNIVERSE

About Starr Z. Davies

STARR Z. DAVIES is an award-winning author of over 20 tales that span dystopian realms, epic fantasies, and echoes of forgotten histories. Dubbed the "Character Assassin," she weaves stories where heroes are tested by fire—both emotional and physical.

From her woodland home in northern Wisconsin, she crafts worlds while surrounded by her greatest allies: a supportive husband, two imaginative children, and a curious menagerie of robotic pets. When not conjuring new adventures, she dabbles in home enchantments, swims like a siren, battles through video game quests, and devours books like ancient tomes of power.

If you want to become friends with Starr, dark chocolate, Doctor Who, Parks & Rec, The Office, and the MCU are all fantastic ways into her heart. That or a love for fantasy books by indie authors.

Learn more about Starr and her books.

Keep up with Starr by signing up for her newsletter.

Want to be part of her community? Follow Starr on social media.
facebook.com/szdavies
instagram.com/s.z.davies
threads.com/s.z.davies
tiktok.com/starrzdavies